A Perfect St

Written by Bruce

Authors Note

A series of stories about a man and his family living through war and separation, political upheaval, religious conflict, pain and laughter, good and bad! Wildlife and wild people!

A narrative derived from a mix of true incidents spiced with poetic licence and pure fiction.

The places are real the names of the characters portrayed are fictional. I gratefully thank all the many friends and family who have helped me bring this book to fruition.

© *Bruce Davidson 2012*
First published in Great Britain 2012

The right of Bruce Davidson to be identified as
author of this work has been asserted by him
in accordance with the Copyright, Designs
and Patents Act 1988.

ISBN No   978-0-9574321-0-9

Typeset & Printed in Great Britain by
Rufford Printing Company, Mawdesley, Lancashire L40 3SY

Published by Bruce Davidson
c/o 29 Railway Street
Southport PR8 5BB,

Contents

Book One - Peter

Book Two - Ian

Book Three - Robert

About the Author

Bruce was born in Rhodesia. He spent much of his life defending the erosion of his hard earned privileged lifestyle. The turmoil of those years brought him futility and heartache with changes everywhere! His family, all of whom were farmers in Rhodesia have been dispossessed! Since coming into "exile" in Great Britain, he has had to rethink all the structures which were his lifestyle and change and adapt to a very different outlook. The writing of this story has helped him bring into focus a new sound footing and perspective on life. Bruce is married with two sons and a daughter. He is presently living in Southport with his wife and their two rescue dogs named Wena and Mukiwa - and a wealth of friends!

Book One
Peter

WHATEVER

I was found as a baby in a basket on the steps of the Gatsville Trinity Church in the Eastern Cape. A note left with me by my mother said she could no longer care for me. No one knows my real name, where I was born or my date of birth and there is no record of my nationality, my family or my religion.

The church placed me in their orphanage from where I was adopted when I was four and a half years old.

I remember the day clearly.

The sun shone hot and bright.

I cried when I realised I was leaving the orphanage. The staff cried too.

My new parents took me on the blue train to my new home. Somewhere along the way my new father held me up to look out at the emptiness sliding past our window. I saw waves of dust drifting over a donkey cart waiting alongside the track at 'Buffers Fontein' siding. The man sitting in the cart looked up as the train passed. Our eyes met for an instant.

How the train made dust I am not sure.

XXXXXXX

I struggled to grow up in my new home.

Music helped me. It became my life - not the music of the country people we lived amongst. No! My music grew from so deep in my heart that I was unable to express it to others.

My new father was a farmer - cattle, pigs and crops. People in our district knew him as a man of integrity. He was an elder in the most righteous church in our district.

My new mother was always ready to smile but her eyes were full of sadness.

I went to the local school.

I learnt very little there.

The teachers abandoned me as a 'waster'.

I was happy to be a waster.

Friends were hard to come by at the school. The other children belonged to each other - bonded by their backgrounds - they were all 'country' people of the kind whose fathers drank far too much beer, ate far too much and talked far too loudly. They hated anyone different to themselves, but I think that deep down in their hearts they hated themselves even more. I wonder, "Are there 'such people' in the place where I was born?"

XXXXXXX

WHO?

One hot dry morning a stranger arrived in our town. He was tall and arrogant. The ladies studied him from under their eyelashes. The men glared at him. He was not one of them. Nobody knew who he was or where he came from or what he was doing here. They were all too afraid to ask him and he never said!

Whenever he walked into a room or amongst the towns folk, everyone stopped talking. They fidgeted, looking this way and that. He made them feel that what they had to say was of no account.

He had a large nose beaking out of a grey bearded face. Bushy, black, eyebrows hung over orbs of green fire! I liked the stranger - I felt at ease with him - he was so strong he did not have to pretend so he said and did exactly what he wanted to.

I first met him on Main Street in town. He and a lady were standing together on the far side watching me walk towards the café'. He crossed the street and spoke to me,

"Hi!" He smiled, "Where is your home, boy?"

"Here in town but my father also has a farm." I held his eyes with mine.

"What's your name?"

"I don't know my real name but people call me Edward."

"Will you walk with me and maybe we can work out what your real name is!"

"Sorry I can't! I must buy milk and bread for my new mother."

"Yes, so you must!"

I ran into the cafe and selected a warm seeded brown loaf from the shelf and some bottled milk from the huge fridge. The girl at the counter counted my money and put the bread and milk in a plastic bag.

"Greetings to Ma." She smiled with her eyes.

"Thank you." I replied politely.

Wind blow in from the street and the music inside me started. I danced down the steps to the pavement. It wasn't a real pavement but the people called it a pavement to raise the status of the town.

I was disappointed to find the stranger no longer there.

I marched down the street to the drumbeats in my heart.

Passing the hotel on the way home I saw three little old men perched on stiff backed chairs on the porch.

They shook their heads and wagged their fingers as they watched me swing the plastic bag in time to my swagger.

Why did the stranger say he could work out what my real name is? What does he know? Why does he make me feel good when he makes most people feel bad?

I stopped outside the church. I often stopped there! It reminded me of my story of the basket found on the steps of the Trinity church. So many people went in that door on Sundays, their heads bowed, looking either sad and humble or excited and bursting to tell someone of their latest vision or blessing. They sang songs, they clapped hands to the happy music, they listened to the preacher's preaching and they shared with each other.

Today is Monday. The door of the church is open. The maid cleans the church on Monday because of all the dirt the people bring in on Sunday.

The church is said to be Holy. I think about that. Wasn't outside the church also Holy? Biting my tongue till it hurt I march through the door promising myself to 'not be like' the others when they walked in - so I hold my head up, pull my shoulders back and smile with my eyes. The effort fans emotions deep within me and tears wet my cheeks. In my mind the door to the Holy church becomes the door to my past and to my future.

I march past the pews donated by members of the congregation right on up to the altar. Light flooding in from a stained glass window bathes the altar in brilliant colours. The music deep within me swells until I am sure the people out in the street will hear it. The rhythm beats out words in my mind.

Dropping the plastic bag, I throw my arms up high and dance around the altar.

Only the cleaning maid sees me.

She smiles a lonely smile.

XXXXXXXX

IN THE DUMPS

"Go where no one else goes
and you end up alone!"

I often felt the need to be alone. It grew with the music. Maybe alone I would hear the words to the melodies.

xxxxxxx

Pink mine dumps squat to the east of town. In winter they hide the rising of the sun. People said they are worse than a desert. Lifeless!

Kids were not allowed to go there.

One Saturday, after breakfast, I filled my backpack with biscuits and a bottle of green cool drink. There is a path meandering past the back of our house, it leads towards the sunrise and the dumps. I climbed through the barbed wire garden fence and out onto the path.

I tore my shirt.

My new father's angry face clouded my mind.

Crouching on the other side of the fence I listened. No sound except for my slow breathing and fast heart beats. Looking around I saw the sun rising over the tops of the mine dumps - it burnt my eyes. Keeping my head down I followed the path listening for any trouble that might follow from behind.

The path led across white sands tufted with dry grey grass. Ahead of me the dumps grew up out of the haze.

And then there was no longer any need for a path - I was there!

Rain and wind had eaten at the sides of the dump carving castles with turrets and balconies out of its cliffs.

Mudslides flooding from the lower slopes swam out into the grey flat surrounds. The sun beat at the shadows. It burnt deep into the open spaces of the earth.

I shivered.

Climbing the nearest slope I found no sign of life, not even a lizard! I looked back. Only my footprints were following me. The town and its people disappeared into hazy distances. Above me a cliff shouldered its way out of the earth cutting the sky off from the world.

Alone, I clambered up and over the cliff-edge onto a flat, pink and grey expanse. Waves of loose sand sketched by the wind curved in a harmony of drifts and drives across the flat surfaces of the dumps. Pieces of rusted railway line reared up out of the sand like sentinels in a windy sea.

I walked to the centre of the dumps, stretched my arms out sideways and turned round and round like a ballet dancer. Faster I turned. Circles of footprints gathered after me sliding and then holding as they followed my wild dance over the waves.

Alone – exhausted – a little dizzy, I sat down.

Alone, I sipped the sickly sweet cool drink so artificial in this land of emptiness. I crunched the brown biscuits washing them down as their taste faded.

Alone, I sat for many hours - time lost all its meaning as eternity taking its place became the new reality. In that instant of recognition, my past and my future blended into the 'one-ness' of now!

Maybe there is no past and no future?

"Is everything now?"

Closing my eyes I watched coloured lights swimming in magnificent swirls through my thoughts. The music from deep within me joined with the lights building a crescendo of sound and majestic movements.

The soft humming of many voices sang a new song - unintelligible but full of emotion - bringing unknown yet familiar pictures to my mind.

Someone was calling,

"Peter! Peter!"

Were they calling me?

"Yes?" I cried out, and again "Yes?"

Is 'Peter' my real name?

The sun blistered the back of my neck. The visions vanished and the music died.

Alone, I sat in the intense heat shivering with apprehension. Fear caught me. Clutching my backpack close to my chest, I stood up. A hissing wind blew in over the dumps. Sand and dust spewing before it, blinding me! My heartbeat clashed with the rhythm of fear.

I had never felt so afraid, not even on a bad Sunday at church!

The wind increased.

From the howling depths of its cry a hidden language grew.

Alone, I was thrown headlong onto the sand.

Alone, I crawled before the wind - breathing through my shirt collar clutched over my nose. I lost my backpack. It tumbled with the wind in a crazy set of leaps and bounds and disappeared into the thick dust.

My new father's face clouded my mind.

I crawled on my belly looking for somewhere to hide. The sand stung my ears. My shirt was wrenched over my head as the wild wind song grew in a crescendo of fury and hate.

Ahead of me lay the sanctuary of the edge of the dump where I could hide in the shelter of a slope, or, hidden ahead lay the danger of a vertical drop over which I might be blown in my attempt to escape.

I remembered the stranger. He knew my real name. What would he do? Lying flat on my stomach I thought about that. In my mind I saw the stranger lying next to me. I watched him. He looked at me with those eyes of his. Raising his head he gave me a challenging grin, then standing up, he swung his body round and into the wind. He held his right hand up, palm facing the blast.

He told the wind to stop.

The stranger faded out of my mind.

I allowed myself no choice.

Slitting my eyes I took a deep breath, held it, then leaping up I swung around and facing straight into the furious wind I shouted with all my might!

"Stop!"

My mouth filled with sand
My eyes swam in sand.
The sand stung my face.

I staggered back from the howling fury beating at me. Then, suddenly! With a defeated sigh, the wild wind song strangled on its own last breath and died.

Alone again I stood surrounded by a new pattern of waves in the sand. No footprints to show where I had come from, only my shadow outlined by the sun, pointing to where I should go.

Peace flowed over the dumps.

I became king of all I could see.

Time to go home!

Sliding down a steep slope I began to roll head over heels to the flatness below. Looking up from the bottom I saw the dumps standing above me, proud and vibrating with new colour and new shapes.

My backpack lay at my side.

The people were wrong.

The dumps are alive.

More alive than the people!

XXXXXXX

HOUSE RULES

A family with five kids came to visit us. They were new friends of my new parents.

"Get your toys out for the kids to play with." My new father told me.

I hesitated.

"Move it!" His voice hardened.

"They are my toys." I said.

"You must learn to share!" My new mother said sweetly.

Reluctantly I brought the least valuable of my toys in for the kids to play with.

New father scowled,

"Where is the new tractor I gave you?"

"I don't want them to play with it, they might break it!"

"Get it!" He stormed "You selfish little brat."

I brought it and gave it to them to play with.

They broke the steering wheel and both front wheels.

When they left I buried the tractor in the rubbish bin outside.

Back in the sitting room my new mother told me to clean up the mess made by the visiting kids. Standing in the doorway I said to her,

"Other people buy their slaves, you adopted yours!"

New father, letting out a yell, grabbed me by the shirt collar and dragged me into his office.

He slammed the door behind him.

"Who the hell do you think you are you ungrateful little jerk?"

I stood up straight, like a soldier.

"You make so many rules," I said "and then you break them all yourself!"

"What?"

Trembling a little, I forced myself to carry on and say,

"I think that sometimes you punish me when I am not wrong!"

He frowned.

Taking a chance I continued,

"You gave me that tractor. You did not lend it to me. You made it mine by giving it to me! Then you forget it is mine and force me to give it to some kids who are not even friends of mine to play with! Surely you have no rights over someone else's property! Any way, they broke it! Then they made a mess in the house and you say I must clean it up. I did not invite them here, you did! It's your responsibility not mine!"

I waited for the expected tirade, but for the first time ever, he was listening to what I had to say!

I dared to carry on,

"If I volunteer to help your wife clean up her visitor's mess, that would be a right and proper thing to do, or if she asks me nicely I would be bound to say yes. But is it not unreasonable of her to force me to clean it up?

And you, my new father, have made so many little rules in this house that no one can keep up with them. I am always in danger of a beating for doing something I must not do, or for not doing something I must do."

I waited for the expected tirade.

"Go on." He said.

Surprised by the response, I dared to stammer,

"Why don't you simplify the rules in your house so that everyone knows what it's all about?"

New father sat down in his desk chair,

"What rules do I make and then break myself?"

"Well, if I can't lend your Land Rover to my friends parents without your permission. And If I did and they broke your Land Rover there would be hell to pay. But you can lend my tractor to your friend's children, without my permission, and when I complain about them breaking it I am called selfish."

Looking down at his desk top he said,

"Ok, off you go, let me think about this."

I walked to the town cafe. Sitting down in a corner I put my elbows on the table and my head on my hands. I fought the tears.

Someone sat down opposite me.

I looked up.

It was the stranger. Gently he asked,

"Problems at home?"

"Yes! Too many rules!"

"There is only one acceptable home rule!"

"Oh! And what is that?"

"Everyone in the home is free to do what ever they want to do subject to one condition and that condition is, 'If they want to do it with someone else's property they must have the owner's permission.' Simple!"

He stood up.

I asked,

"Is that all?"

"Think about it!"

"Thank you." I said.

Nodding politely, he turned to leave.

"Wait." I begged him "There is something else I want to ask you."

He sat down at the table with me, and raising an eyebrow, he asked,

"Yes?"

"Sometimes, when you are no where near me you seem to come into my mind almost as if you were really with me and you talk to me! Is it my imagination or what?"

He laughed,

"Tell me!" he asked, "Have you ever spoken on a mobile phone or telephone to someone from far away?"

"Yes."

"And that someone answers you!"

"Yes."

"Have you ever watched television and seen someone from another country talking and moving around?"

"Yes."

"So, if you are happy with people from miles away talking to you on your mobile telephone, or down a wire or across the air on TV, what worries you about me talking to you in a similar way?"

"But nobody else can do that!"

"Oh yes everyone can but only some people do!"

"Who and how?"

"Who? Those who take the trouble to make the connection! How? By developing a form of what most people call extra sensory perception."

He smiled, got up and walked out.

I ran home.

"New father." I said excitedly.

"Yes?"

"I have found an answer to the problem of too many rules."

"Really?"

"Only one rule. I call it boundaries! Everyone has his own private space! What I mean is that each member of the family is free to do whatever they want to do with their own personal and private things inside their own personal private space, but if they do it either with someone else's property or in someone else's private space they must have the owners permission."

"Is that it?"

"Yes."

"What about the noise you make when I am reading or watching television?"

"The noise I make is irritating your ears in your TV room. They, your ears and the TV room are your property, so I can't do that without your permission."

Grunting he asked,

"Messing up the sitting room?"

"The sitting room is communal so I can't mess it up without the agreement of both new mother and you."

"And?"

"And my tractor is mine! Nobody can use it without my permission."

He smiled,

"And your untidy room?"

"Is it not my room that I make untidy?"

"And who pays the maid that cleans it up for you?"

"Well! If we all kept our own space clean she would have nothing to do all day and you would have to fire her."

"That's very cleverly manipulative! Where is your tractor?"

"I threw it away."

"Please fetch it and bring it to my office."

I did.

"Well," he pondered, "I am responsible for the state of this tractor, yes?"

"Yes."

"Okay, if I can't fix it like new I'll get you another one."

"You don't have to fix it like new. I am also guilty! I let you force me into lending it to those children because I was more afraid of a hiding from you than I was of the truth."

He stared at me

"I see!" He said, "Will you help me fix it?"

"Yes, oh yes!"

"You got the wheels?"

"Yes."

The repaired tractor was parked on the mantelpiece of the fireplace as a reminder to all of us of the new 'House Rule'.

XXXXXXX

THESE SHOES ARE MEANT FOR WALKING

I love to lie in a warm bath at night – day-dreaming! The stranger says dreams are important because they help release your inner thoughts.

I stretch out holding my big toe against the hot tap to control the flow of water thereby keeping the bath temperature at maximum pleasure level.

With eyes shut, I close my mind to the world and drift in and out of conscious dreamland.

Tonight, in my bath, a picture of the wooden pulpit in our church swims into my mind. I see myself standing in the pulpit like the preacher does. Two shoeboxes lie on the sloping top before me.

Looking up I see the church is full. Everyone in town is here. They are surprised, as I am neither qualified nor wanted at their pulpit.

At the back of the church, leaning against the wall, stands the stranger.

The pastor is nowhere to be seen. I stare at the two shoeboxes.
Written in red on both shoeboxes is the product name. "Walker's Shoes"

But! On the one box, in small red print, is written 'made in Goldtown' whereas on the other box is written in black, made in Nickeltown'.

Opening the two boxes I take out the shoes. The two pairs look identical. I hold them up and looking out and over the now openly antagonistic congregation I say,

"See! You can't tell the difference."

Picking up both boxes I continue,

"But they are different! Check where they are made. Nickeltown on this box and Goldtown on the other."

I put the shoes and their boxes down on the pulpit facing the congregation.

Taking a pamphlet out of the 'Goldtown' box, I read aloud.

"ONCE IN A LIFETIME OFFER"

"Study the accompanying instructions and apply for your, 'once in a life time prize'. If you are successful in your application, you will receive the following."

1/ A magnificent luxurious home set in a fully developed garden in up-market Goldtown.

2/ An account, opened in your name, at the manufacturer's bank, credited with cash enough to 'last for ever'!

3/ Life citizenship to Goldtown!

Adopting a salesman's 'sales pitch tone' I continue,

"The accompanying pamphlet is written in the language and dialect of Gold Town to this effect –

'The Author will make himself available at an appropriate time and place for the purpose of interpreting and translating this offer to any authorised party. An authorised party is any person who is the recipient of the accompanying application form and who walks in these shoes!

Identification documents matching those entered on the head of the application form must be produced when requested.

Warning

Translations or interpretations or copies of the terms and conditions of this offer by any party, other than the author will lead to a misunderstanding of the contents as written herein and may result in the applicant's failure to meet the requirements as laid down.

Such failure to meet the entry requirements will disqualify you in your application for this "once in a lifetime" opportunity.

"There are no second chances."

Note the entry requirements are listed in the second pamphlet."

Reading the second pamphlet I see there is only one comment, viz. -

"Wear your 'Walker's shoes' when you come for your interview with the manufacturer."

I pick up the shoes and pack them into their respective boxes. Folding the pamphlets, I tuck them into the box holding the shoes made in Goldtown.

Looking around the church I see the stranger walking out of the side-door into the morning sunshine. He turns and smiles at me.

The bath water cools.

Bending my large toe I open the hot tap a little. I yawn, relax and closing my eyes I wait for the next daydream.

I find myself in a spotless white walled room with a marble floor.

Lying on a stainless steel table in front of me are a scalpel, two test tubes, a bottle and a key. An attendant in his white coat is holding out his left hand. He looks familiar.

"Your identity document and your shoes please."

I hand him my papers and remove my 'Walker's shoes. Placing them on the table I watch as the attendant deftly slices a small piece of leather off each shoe. He puts one piece in each test tube and adds a measure of the watery contents of the bottle.

Nothing happens. The attendant smiles, looks up at me, eyes dancing, he says,

"Okay! Put your shoes on. Here is the key. Go through that small door into the next room."

"Am I permitted to ask a question?"

He nods. I ask,

"Is that all? As far as I can see, nothing happened in that test tube!"

He laughs. A throaty, warm, laugh,

"If the shoes are made by Walker's of Goldtown there is no reaction because the shoes are the real thing. If, however, there is a reaction and the pieces of shoe disappear on contact with the water," his face grows serious, "the shoes are not made in Goldtown - they are counterfeit shoes from Nickeltown."

"What happens then?" I ask.

"You fail the test!"

"And what is through that door you showed me?"

"Your new home, your new bank account and your citizenship! Wear the right shoes and bingo!"

The hot tap burning my toe jerks me back to reality.

XXXXXXX

THE NEW BOY

YOU DON'T FIND MUCH RAIN IN A DESERT!
OR IS IT THAT YOU DON'T FIND A DESERT IN MUCH RAIN?

A new boy joined our class. He was even more different to the other school kids than I was.

He was black.

The first black boy in our school!

His parents called him Jim.

One Friday, a few months after he came to our school, I came across him sobbing behind the boy's toilets.

I stared at him. Should I go to him or should I leave him in his private agony? Being a teenager he should be able to cope on his own! But?

If I offered help he could say yes or he could say no!

If I walked away I would never know if he needed me or not.

I decided better to take a chance and know the answer than to do nothing and be guilty of not reaching out to him because of fear.

"Hey you?" I asked, "You need some help?"

Startled, he twisted his face up to look at me. His eyes were red and running wet. Turning away again he sobbed into his clenched fists.

"Okay," I sat down next to him, "what's your problem?"

"Nothing!"

"So you cry for nothing?"

"No! Its nothing you would understand!"

"Try me."

Turning, he thrust his tear washed face into mine, and screamed.

"I said that it's nothing you would understand. You are not black. You cannot understand."

"Okay." I stood up to go.

"Wait!" he cried out to me, "Please wait, will you walk with me back to my home?"

37

"Okay."

He dragged himself up and with head hanging low walked away from the toilets towards the school gate.

Conscious of the stares of other kids, I walked with him.

xxxxxxx

His house was new. No lawn yet. No garden. A very expensive, metallic silver, four wheel drive vehicle was parked at the front door. A woman sat on the porch step. She held a basket on her knees.

Jim hesitated.

"I brought a friend home." He muttered.

The woman searched my face.

"Take him in. There are cool drinks and cakes in the fridge."

He beckoned to me. Following him into a neat sitting room I sat on a very expensive chair. He poured two cool drinks and handed one to me. He didn't offer me a cake from the fridge.

We sipped at our drinks. I waited for his story.

Frowning, he drew a deep breath and blurted out,

"Today I found out what it's like to be black! People say blacks and whites are the same, only different in colour!"

I nodded.

"Well today I learnt the truth! We are not the same! We are totally different!"

He searched for words to explain the glimmer of understanding darting in and out of his mind,

"It is truly devastating!" He moaned.

"What is?"

"Look at me. Don't look at my clothes. Look at me and see me. I am a black kid!"

"Yes."

"My parents and ancestors as far back as you cannot remember are black. Okay?"

"Okay!"

"So you see a black man's kid sitting in this room! Now, forget about him for a while and take a look at the room he sits in. The white man made everything you see in this room! Do you see that?"

"Yes I suppose so."

"The truth is that there is nothing of 'me' in this room, but there is everything of you. You could say, in that sense, the room is not mine!"

"Carry on."

He paused. A lonely sadness crept over the two of us.

"Like I said, here I am, a black kid with black forefathers. But I live as a white child! It seems the main difference between us blacks and you whites is that the whites invented and made nearly everything that has ever been made by man whereas us blacks have invented virtually nothing of all that was made by man."

He sobbed,

"Nothing here is of me or of my family! None of it is of my race! Not even my clothes. Our house is a white man's house, so too are my language, my father's car, my education; every material possession we have is not of my family the black man! No! It is of your family, the white man. Think about it!"

I said nothing.

"I have a list." he continued, "Would I be pedantic if I read some of it out to you? Do you want to hear?"

"If it helps!"

"It does!" He stared at me,

I nodded. "Ok then, just a few of the white man's inventions! Things that we blacks use but never conceived of like democracy - motor cars - guns - airplanes - modern medicine - television - cutlery - modern furniture - concrete structures - tarmac roads - telephones - radios - paper - pens - shoes - electricity - computers - plastic - glass and my list goes on for twenty-one pages. All these things are the creations of the white man. Not one of them is a black man's creation and that is the difference and it is that difference which hurts."

Rubbing his eyes he stared at the floor,

"No wonder blacks are frustrated. We live in a new world that is alien to us - but worse than that and sadly, most of us do not even realise it is alien! We don't see our own predicament."

He finished his drink.

"Damn it all," he cried, "we are not the previously disadvantaged, we are the permanently disadvantaged. The fault lies within us. We are born with it. It is our burden in life."

I thought about his problem.

"Maybe you have forgotten something," I said, "I think you have to see the whole story and not only that part which bothers you at this time."

"And what is the whole story?"

"Well, it's like this. You know the stranger? He told me African people do think differently to Europeans and they do behave and look different to them. But leave odious comparisons out and rather look for what is individually good in both the black and the white and you will find a balance.

May I ask if you believe in God?"

"Yes of course, that's if you mean the white man's God!"

"Whatever! Well, if God made everything then obviously He made both of us. You with me?"

He shrugged, saying,

"Not really, in the white man's religion which we blacks have adopted is the concept that God made man in his own image. If that is so and we are both human then we would not be different to you!"

"Hey! You said it!" I sat up straight "Oh yes, you hit the nail right on the head. The stranger told me that because God made us, and He makes no mistakes, then every man is perfect. You see - every man is a 'one off' perfect example of himself. What I mean is, no one has the same fingerprints or the same genetic heritage as any one else. Everyone is born an individual. So it follows that every man is as he is meant to be. This confirms what you said, man is made in the image of God and God is 'One', an individual, so then is every man also an individual but we do all have common features in that we share a common heritage from within and outside of all creation! But it is our individuality that makes each one of us the same! Each one is a 'one off' perfect individual person. That is of course within the common factor of being human.

There is and always has been and always will be only one of you and one of me. Even identical twins are not totally identical. It is the differences between us which forms the basis for a perfect balance which makes up the whole of creation."

I smiled.

He whispered,

"You said 'balance' what balance?"

"If you look at the whole of creation and not just the part you are locked into and you accept that everything is here for a specific purpose. When you accept that there is nothing lacking in creation - then will you begin to see the purpose in everything instead of seeing only the good or the bad. You will see the truth and the truth is this, not only is the difference between black and white natural but the purpose behind there being such a difference, as I said, is it is that very difference which allows for a natural balance between and within them and it is so for a good reason.

The denial of that truth makes us believe we should be altogether the same and this brings about a wrong perspective leading to the incorrect perceptions that there is an unnatural and frustrating imbalance. When people expect everyone to be equal, like they do in England, they get angry with anyone who is different and they then have to invent crazy laws preventing anyone from stating the obvious. What happened with Hitler and his followers and their perspective of the Jews is a good example of insisting you are right and everyone who is not the same should be put down.

The reason you are upset about what you have discovered is not because you have found out an unpalatable truth, but that you have exposed an unpalatable lie.

The people you trusted - lied to you!

What they told you denied you your own special abilities, your own virtues, your own identity. You were repeatedly told the lie that all men are equal, that all men are the same, whereas knowing they are not equal sets you free to be yourself and them free to accept you as you are and not as they think you should be.

All the fullness of variety cannot exist in one person. No one man can have within himself the total of what all men have.

It is our differences that make it possible for an infinite variety of differing abilities and talents to be manifested and shared out among all men.

Equality destroys mankind by limiting him to the lowest denominator. What I mean is that if men are to be equal then whatever irreversible fault we may find in any one man must become a fault in all men. So if one man is mad, and his madness cannot be cured, then all men will have to be made mad in order to be equal.

Inequality allows people to develop individually in their own way in any and all directions, then, by sharing, by association, and by acceptance, we can all benefit from each other's differences. Ability compliments disability and vice versa. Seeing this opens the way to the truth of the matter. Frustration comes from pretending that you are the same as someone who is different. Do not think of your difference as a lack but rather seek your own abilities and work within their structures and you will be immensely successful and doubly so if you balance your abilities with those of the different people around you.

Take cattle as an example. All cattle are bovine, yet some are dairy cattle and produce twenty litres of milk a day. Others are beef cattle and produce only a couple of litres a day. You cannot educate a beef cow into producing twenty litres like a dairy cow. Similarly the quality and quantity of beef on a dairy cow leaves much to be desired - you cannot feed it into being good beef. They are different. Their differences allow for optimum milk and beef production. Believing they are equal and then treating them as equal would lead to total frustration.

That dog you have in the yard is by nature a guard dog and not a lap dog nor a tracker.

If you can accept that different breeds amongst the same animals have different values and different abilities, surely you can see that people also have differing values and abilities. Races differ in their attributes, as do the individuals within each race. And a very good perspective lies in what someone once said, 'There is as much variation within a breed as there is between breeds!'

You got it?

Don't cry over your natural heritage. Take this as an example, you, as a black African have what is called 'Ubuntu' which is inherent warmth towards other people. You are communal and friendly whilst so-called whites tend to be private and relatively elitist. Tell me, generally speaking, in this country, who is it that most often stops on the road to help someone in trouble, a white man? No most definitely not! It is nearly always a black man.

I ask you, if your car was broken down on a lonely road, would you prefer an unfriendly but highly qualified European motor engineer to pass you by, or would you hope for a friendly, black, bush mechanic to stop and help you?

The quality or nature of a man's ability is of no use to you if he does not share it. The lack of such in a generous person who stops to help you does not destroy his value as a helper. I think I have said enough about how I see it, except to say, I believe you can find your true self by firstly accepting the differences existing between us and then developing your own very special talents. If you persist in denying those differences you will sink deeper into the mire of pain, hate and self- destruction.

"Oh yes! One more thing," I said "you cannot judge a man for falling until you have carried the load he is carrying along the road he is travelling. Nor can you praise him for his success until you have tasted his opportunities. What do you think of that?"

He sat up straight and grinned at me,

"I just thought of something, there is only one thing in which all men are equal – each one is equally different to the rest."

He asked, "Would you care for another cool drink and a large helping of special fridge cake?"

"Thanks. Hey! I have also just realised something, a man and a woman are very, very different! Wow! Share that and you get a huge bonus added to the intrinsic pleasure of male female relationships!"

"Like what?"

"New life! A baby!"

"Yes you are so right! Hey! Do you think it is possible that long ago, in ancient history, like in the days before the pyramids were built in Egypt, we Africans thought and behaved differently to now? What I mean is maybe then we were creative in the scientific fields as well as in the arts! If so, could it be that the communal systems we subsequently became subject to and have lived under for thousands of years restricted our ability to conceive of new ideas? The communal system discourages individualistic behaviour denying the individual the right to own that which he may create resulting in it being a waste of time for him to conceptualise or to invent and create in the scientific fields as there is for him, no possible gain!"

"Man oh man!" I exploded, "What a thought! Yes and that would explain so many historical contradictions from thousands of years ago! It would mean that genetically you are still able but, to put it simply, you have been limited by inheriting the confines of your ancestors."

I put my hand on his shoulder.

"You my friend have just broken those confines. You have set yourself free to be what you really are so - go for it!"

XXXXXXX

MONEY MATTERS

Lalapanzi is a tiny village hidden in the depths of central Africa. It is comprised of a few old fashioned houses, a very small hotel, a fly blown butchery and a little grocery shop all set in a friendly farming community. Business, if any, is very quiet.

The northwest bound railway line passes through but trains only stop for the occasional passenger. The in coming postbag is thrown out onto the deserted platform as the train rushes through. I don't know how they get the out going post bag back onto the train again.

xxxxxxx

New father took our family to Lalapanzi to visit Aunt Irene. He said Aunt Irene could be very difficult. He said she was an eccentric artist living alone with a menagerie of stray cats and scruffy dogs. He said we might not be welcome and told us that when we arrived in the village he would take the precaution of checking in at the hotel.

Parking his Land Rover at the hotel entrance, he heaved himself out and climbed up the veranda steps. Shade from the old corrugated iron roof welcomed him. He disappeared into the gloom of an open door. I clambered out of the hot back of the Land Rover and ran after him.

New father rang an old brass bell on the reception desk.

We waited.

He rang it again.

A tired old man came through from deep inside the hotel. He peered at us.

"Yes? Can I help you?"

"We may have to stay over tonight." new father said, "May I make a provisional booking for one double room and one single?"

"No problem! But I have to ask you for a deposit. We don't have much business these days so I will have to get in a few provisions."

"How much?"

"A hundred notes!"

45

"Okay." New father handed the money over to him saying,

"See you later."

"If you decide to stay, supper is at eight. If not, please let us know so we don't cook too much food!"

xxxxxxx

Aunt Irene's farm nestled between two grey rocky hillocks west of the village. We drove out to it along a twisted bush track. Her house, a rambling Victorian affair lay, as if discarded, in an overgrown garden.

Aunt Irene stood on the porch, legs akimbo, arms crossed, glaring out at her uninvited visitors.

"They suit each other." Muttered my new mother.

"Who?"

"The old house and the old woman!"

"Humph."

New father stopped the engine.

"Lets go." He growled.

Walking up the pathway to the house I saw Aunt Irene turn around and open the front door. A mob of howling dogs poured out.

It reminded me of the song 'who let the dogs out'.

Aunt Irene recognised my new father and screamed at the dogs. They thought she was encouraging them. The racket grew. Wading through the snuffling, barking mob we reached the porch.

Today was a good day. Aunt Irene grinned - we were welcome!

Soon the smell of cooking and the sound of laughter filled the house. We relaxed in her comfortable old chairs. New mother picked at dog and cat hairs sticking to her clothes.

"Oh dear!" She exclaimed, "The hotel!"

New father and I drove back into the village. The sun was setting. The hotel office was closed. The bar was open. Two men were sipping drinks at the counter. Mine host ran a wet rag over the worn teak bar top. A third man sat in a far corner - apart and alone.

"Hey!" Said the tallest man leaning against the bar, "I want to pay

46

off part of my account!"

"About time!" grinned mine host.

"Here you are then." The tall man counted the notes onto the counter.

"You come into some money?" asked our host.

"No, no." Laughed the tall one "Mike here paid his account at the store today, so we celebrate."

Mike grinned,

"That's it!" He pointed a chubby finger at mine host "When you bought all that meat for your guests and paid off most of your account, I had enough to pay my store account with Jim here. So business is flourishing once more in Lalapanzi."

Mike grinned at us,

"You guys thirsty?"

"Sure." New father slid onto a barstool. Smiling at the two men at the counter, he said to them, "This round is on me."

They ordered.

I sat on a lounge chair.

Mine host picked up the money off the counter and put it in the till. He pushed the drinks across the bar saying to us, "Your rooms are ready and supper is waiting to be put on the stove."

"Actually," new father pleaded, "if it is ok with you I would like to cancel the booking as Aunt Irene has asked us to stay over at her place for the next three nights."

"No problem!" said mine host, "I'll refund you your deposit." He beamed at us as he opened the till and counted out the money. "It's truly amazing!" he laughed, "This afternoon we were all short of cash. The village was dead. No business. I owed the butcher. The butcher owed the store. The store owed the bar." Leaning over the counter he grinned at new father and whispered conspiratorially, "Then here comes this visitor who makes a provisional booking. He leaves a deposit. A hundred notes. I use the deposit to pay the butcher and get fresh provisions for the hotel. The butcher takes the hundred notes and pays towards his account at the store. The store man takes the hundred notes and pays his bar bill." Turning to my new father, he says,

"You come in and take back the hundred notes. Just like that! The hundred comes in. The hundred goes out. While it was in we all did business." The tiredness left his face. "And now we can all enjoy a chat around the bar. Business as usual, hey!" Pointing at his two friends he laughed, "That's what money is all about!"

The man sitting alone in the corner raised his head. Familiar, startling eyes set under shaggy eyebrows, studied me.

"Yes!" he said, "That is exactly what money is! No more or less! A number system designed to value items in order to facilitate trade!"

XXXXXXX

THE PIG FARM

I rode my bike out to the farm. Dog ran with me. We went down to the pigsties. The manager was there.

"Come." He said, "I want to show you something most people don't know."

He took me to a new sty under a large fig tree built separately from the others. The walls were painted in bright colours. A sow lay against the farrowing rail with her piglets sleeping in a row against her belly.

The sty was spotlessly clean.

"What can you see that you won't see in the other sties?" The manager asked.

"Clean!"

"You know why?"

"No."

"Pigs are naturally clean."

"But everyone says they're dirty! They call dirty people 'pigs'. All the other sties are dirty and smelly."

"True. But this sty has been built differently. See! There are three open doorways in the back wall and one in the sidewall. The one at the back on the left is a toilet. The centre one is a shower room. The one on the right is the feed room. This big area in front is the living area and the door on the side is a bedroom. The mother pig uses the toilet as a toilet! She showers in the shower room! She eats in the eating room! And when it's too cold or too hot in the living area she sleeps in the side room!"

"How does she shower and use the toilet?"

"She learnt to press the buttons on the shower and the toilet taps. She carries new bedding from that pile over there into her bedroom and throws the old bedding out. I am hoping she will learn to push the old bedding to the gate for us to remove."

"So pigs are not dirty?"

"No, people build sties which pigs find hard to keep clean and the pigs give up trying."

"Oh! I see!"

He left Dog and I watching the clean pig.

A deep voice whispered behind me,

"Hi there!"

Surprised, I turned. The stranger sat on the sidewall of the pigsty.

"Oh hi!" I said, "I didn't know you were here."

He stepped down - came around to me and said,

"Ever thought about pigs?"

"What do you mean?"

"Well, people are funny about pigs, some won't eat them and some won't let them near. The demons in the bible story asked to be 'put into pigs' and when that happened the pigs went crazy and ran off a cliff into the sea. You can use pig's body parts as replacement parts in humans.

Then there are other people who worship pigs and some who treat them as if they were their own kids. They even breast feed them!

Pigs are used to describe peoples habits, you know, behave like a pig. Eat like a pig. Live like a pig. You are a pig and so on."

"I heard in school that cannibals say human flesh looks and tastes just like pork!"

Pointing at the sow he said,

"That's right! No other animal has such close links with man."

"Is there a reason or did it just happen like that?"

"There is a very good reason. You think about it and one day I will show you what it's all about."

"Why one day? Why not tell me now?"

"First you need to experience the initiation of your own understanding growing from within you. Otherwise you won't be open to believe what I say."

The stranger walked around to the back of the pigsty. I waited for him but he did not come back. When I looked for him he had gone.

I rode back home with Dog running alongside.

I thought about the new understanding growing in me. "Pigs? When will I be ready for his story?" I wondered.

XXXXXXX

TO CATCH A THIEF

An intruder paid us a visit last night! Dog heard him walking across the lawn. He left his sleeping mat, padded across to my bed and pushed his cold wet nose into my ear.

He rumbled.

I sat up and listened to the night sounds. Hearing nothing I slipped out of bed and crossed over to the window. Cupping my hands behind my ears to cut out the sounds of Dog's excited breathing I heard the sitting room window being pulled open. Tiptoeing ever so quietly to new father in his bedroom I tapped him on the shoulder. He woke. Seeing my finger held against my lips he nodded at me - climbed quietly out of bed, pulled on a pair of shorts, picked up his first world war Luger 9mm pistol from the bedside drawer and walked quietly out of the bedroom.

I followed him into the sitting room. A shadowy figure was climbing through the window. He had one foot inside and the other foot out side. His shoulder was pressed against the curtain.

New father waited there at the window and as the intruder stepped into the room he greeted him,

"Welcome to our home!"

The man let out a fearful wail and turning back, tore at the tangle of curtains as he tried to get out. New father took hold of a flailing arm and dragged him back into the room.

"Lights!" He barked.

I switched on the lights.

New father grinned at me.

"Good work! Please make us all a cup of coffee."

Turning to the unhappy man, he asked,

"Do you take sugar and milk in your coffee?"

Strangling on his words, the man gasped

"Yes sir."

"Sit!" New father pointed at a chair.

He sat. "And to what do we owe the pleasure of your company?" New father asked him,

"Sorry sir, I was lost!"

"Were you lost before you climbed into the house or after?"

"Sorry sir, I was always lost."

"Do you think I should call the police?" New father asked him.

"Yes sir."

"What were you looking for? Something to steal?"

"Yes sir."

New father chatted to the man and the man, who, enjoying his coffee, relaxed.

The police arrived. New father let them in and asked me to make more coffee. I left for the kitchen as new father explained the problem of our visitor and laid a formal charge of housebreaking with intent against him.

"What do you have to say?" The police corporal asked the intruder.

"Ah my brother, I do not know what this man is talking about! I never broke into his house, no! He met me in the street and asked me if I was cold and hungry. I said yes. He offered me a cup of coffee and brought me into this room. Did you ever see a thief being given coffee after he broke into a house? No my brother, this man is lying and I do not know why!"

The corporal raised his eyebrows.

The constable glared at new father.

New father laughed.

"I'll be damned!" he said, "This thief has great potential as a politician." Eyeing the intruder he continued "A good story but unfortunately it's not the truth.

Tell me, my friend off the street, what kind of a person drinks coffee in another man's house and then lies about his friendly host to the police?"

The thief, gaining confidence, loudly protested his innocence.

New father asked the corporal,

"What is the fine for common assault assuming it is a first offence and no permanent damage is done?"

"Five hundred notes plus or minus depending on the circumstances. Why?"

"The same fine whether the assault is serious or minor?"

"Probably!"

New father walked over to the wall safe, opened it and drew out five large notes. He brought them to the corporal and winking at him as he handed him the money, he said,

"Here is my 'admission of guilt' fine for assault."

"What assault?" Asked the grinning corporal.

"The assault on this intruder."

"You are going to assault him?"

"Yes."

The constable stood up straight and glared at the corporal and new father. The corporal ignored him and asked new father,

"How badly will you assault him?"

"To the full extent implicit in the amount of the fine. In other words, I will thoroughly beat him, But! I will not break any of his bones!"

The intruder's wide eyes darted from police officer to police officer and back again. Stuttering he bleated,

"No! No! Don't let him beat me! What he said is the truth! I broke in through that window. Please sir, don't let him beat me."

The constable returned the five hundred.

"Thank you for the coffee and the entertainment!" He smiled, "Come thief!" Taking the thief by the arm, he led him out to the police van.

"Bye!"

"Bye!"

New father closing the front door said,

"My turn to make coffee."

After new father went back to bed I was too wide-awake to go to sleep so I drew a bath and lowered myself into the hot water. I thought about the intruder and new father. The warm bath soaked through to my mind. I drifted into dreamland where I saw a pathway leading to heaven. A gate dividing Heaven from earth, hung across the path. Seated in the shade of a fig tree at its entrance was a white haired man. I assumed he was the Apostle Peter that some Christians say has the keys to the gate into Heaven. He was reading from books lying open on a large table.

Two men stood facing the table, one wearing a fashionable suit, the other in blue workers overalls.

A long line of people of all colours and creeds, men, women and children waited along the path.

The white haired man looked up at the two men before him.

He spoke to the worker,

"It is recorded here that you stole tools from your employer."

"That is correct sir."

"You were caught?"

"Yes sir."

"What happened?"

"I was beaten. My employer recovered some of his tools from me. He deducted the value of the other tools from my pay. I was dismissed from my job. Sir!"

"Who did all this to you?"

"My employer, sir."

"Your employer is the gentleman standing with you?"

"Yes sir."

"Do you believe it was right and proper for you to be punished?"

"Yes sir."

"Even though you were punished in three different ways for the same offence!"

"Yes sir! I was in the wrong but because he did not report me to the police I have no criminal record."

The white haired man spoke to the man in the suit.

"You caught this man stealing!"

"Yes."

"He says you beat him! You recovered some of the stolen tools and deducted the value of the rest from his pay! Then you fired him!"

"Yes."

The white haired man wrote in his book. When finished he spoke,

"Worker."

"Sir?"

"You have already been more than adequately punished for your crime! You are free to enter the gate, go to the place prepared for you. Go home!"

Tears flooded the workers eyes.

Reaching out to the employer, the worker said,

"I thank you for punishing me, you did not know it, but by punishing me, you set me free! See you later."

The white haired man spoke to the man in the suit.

"You sir took it upon yourself to punish your worker yet you know full well from the many Sundays you attended your church that 'Vengeance is mine, says the Lord.' Is it possible for a just God to punish a man already punished?"

The employer remained silent.

The white haired man continued

"It is impossible for the creator to punish a wrongdoer if he has already been punished, especially in this case where the wrong doer has been punished much more than his crime deserved.

So you denied the Father the opportunity to exact his vengeance on the worker yet that vengeance still has to be enacted for the father said 'vengeance is mine'. You, Mister Employer, have brought upon yourself the vengeance you subverted. I find you to be arrogantly self-righteous for you have arbitrarily assumed the work of God without his express directive and authority. Do you remember the prayer you so often prayed where you categorically stated that your sins are forgiven to the degree that you forgive others who sin against you?"

"I remember."

"By the words of your own mouth you are denied entrance until you accept upon yourself the vengeance you subverted."

xxxxxxx

Five men took the place of the two at the table, a black man with a broken nose, a young white university student, the student's uncle and two black policemen.

The white haired man spoke,

"Do you gentlemen remember the day a car was broken into in Black-River? You were all involved!"

"Yes Sir." They chorused.

"Firstly you," he addressed the man with the broken nose. "I see from this report that you were involved at all times in this incident. Correct?"

"Yes Sir."

"Tell me your story."

"A friend of mine and I were walking down Opportunity Street bent on affirmative action shopping - "

The white haired man interrupted

"What do you mean Opportunity Street and affirmative action shopping'?"

"We, the poor guys were looking for something to steal from the rich guys!"

"I see. Please continue."

"We came across a car parked outside a store. In it were an expensive looking radio and lying on the seat, a purse. There being no people near by we agreed it was worth a try. My friend broke the passenger window and I broke the driver's window. I removed the car radio whilst he grabbed the purse. We thought no one saw us so we walked quietly away but someone shouted behind us. It was this young white man. He saw me carrying the radio. My friend and I turned to run but these two policemen appeared around the corner in front of us. Thrusting the radio into my friend's hand I whispered to him, "Go into this shop and out the back door. I will lead them astray."

He did as I told him.

The police and the young man chased me for two blocks. They caught me.

The young white man said he had seen me with the radio taken from his uncle's car. The police led me back to the car.

Broken glass lay all over. The police asked me,

"What do you have to say?"

I knew it was no use lying.

"I broke the window and stole the radio."

"And the purse?"

"My friend stole the purse."

"Where is the radio?"

"I gave it to my friend when this young man started to chase me."

"Where is your friend?"

"I don't know. He ran away."

"You're lying, you bastard!"

The policemen forced my arms behind my back. They hand cuffed my hands together. They began to beat me. I fell. One of them stood with a boot in my stomach whilst the other kicked me. The pain was serious.

One of the policemen said to the young man,

"Do you want to beat him too? Teach him a lesson?"

The young man beat me - he kicked me – he jumped on my chest. I battled for breath.

The young man's uncle came out of the shop. He asked his nephew what was going on.

The nephew said,

"This bloody thief broke your car's windows and stole the car radio and my purse."

The biggest policeman asked,

"This your car?"

The uncle said,

"Yes."

The policeman kicked me in the crotch. He shouted at me and then he said to my uncle,

"He won't get much of a sentence in court! Far better that you beat the thief yourself!"

The uncle kicked me. He stamped on my face. He broke my nose. I heard the young man say.

'That will teach you to never steal again!'

That is what happened, - sir."

The white haired man spoke to the others,

"Is this the truth of the matter?"

"Yes sir." They answered.

"May I ask you two questions?"

"Yes sir." They chorused

"Which is the greater crime, for a thief to break a car window and steal the radio and then confess to the theft," he paused "or - for two male members of a strong Christian church to beat a defenceless man who is handcuffed and held down on the ground by two 'officers of the law' who had themselves already illegally beaten him?"

They remained silent.

"The beatings" said the white haired man "resulted in a broken nose, fractured ribs, severe damage to his reproductive organs, bruising and cuts all over his body!"

He paused.

The uncle interrupted,

"Do we have to answer?"

"No. The answer is already known, whether you accept it or not."

The thief begged for a hearing,

"Sir," the thief said, "these men, the uncle and his nephew were angry at their worldly property being broken and stolen. I understand their frustration and anger. I forgave them long ago for the beating they gave me.

It turned out that my broken nose added character to my face. As for the two policemen, they inherited a culture allowing for such behaviour. They did not understand the western concept of justice and fair play. Please sir, I had to forgive them too for they really did not know what they were doing.

In mitigation for the crime I committed I must say that I, and my fellow countrymen - the true South Africans, have been oppressed by a white supremacist society for generations. I had been denied my rights to all that was available to the white man in this country. My personality has been deformed by the disadvantages imposed on me. I felt a sense of rightness when stealing from our oppressors."

Bowing his head he said,

"I thank you sir."

The white haired gentleman, leaning back in his chair said to the thief,

"Scripture is still applicable this side of the gate. I see that you have forgiven these men for their behaviour and this is taken into account - as is your confession at the time. Also noted is your refusal to hand your brother over to the authorities and your bad attitude towards the white South Africans."

Turning to the uncle he asked,

"What do you have to say? Do you forgive the thief?"

"No!" the uncle grew tense "I do not. A thief is a thief. As far as I can see the whole judicial system in our country is falling apart. Honest people live behind security fences while criminals roam free. The concept of human rights, which is new to our country, was conceived of thousands of years ago by and in the west. The Magna Charta was written when none of these so called previously disadvantaged people even knew there was such a thing as writing.

The concept of Human rights is a Western and not an African ideology.

No! I do not forgive him - he uses the excuse of supposedly being previously oppressed to take by force from those who work to get what they have. He steals from the very people he so dismally tries to emulate.

It could be argued that his disadvantage pertains to land but he is not disadvantaged in education, medical care, housing, or in any other modern civilised concept for these things were never his in the first place. He gained all of them as gifts from previous white governments, from white 'Do Gooders' and white NGO's. Aid comes from the West to Africa! You never hear of aid being sent by Africa to the West!

No sir! This man has absolutely no justification for his thieving, but I do have justification for beating him.

I concede I beat him excessively and that to beat a man tied up and lying on the ground is totally unacceptable. Yes it is an abominable crime - a far worse sin than stealing a radio.

But in mitigation may I say I was exasperated beyond belief by the concept that those who create should be the servants of those who either cannot, or will not create. I cannot accept that servants should be the masters of their employers or that school children control their teachers or that by law children are no longer disciplined so encouraging them to become un-discipline-able adults!

In the new South Africa you have to stop at a stop street when you are being tested for your drivers licence but once you have your licence you don't lose it if thereafter you do not stop at a stop street.

The chance of bringing law and order back into this country is negated by the fact that more than half of our police force can, and do take bribes - sometimes demand bribes!

I cannot accept that affirmative action in a non-racial society should be limited to benefit one race making up more than ninety nine per cent of the population and denied another race who are only nine per cent. Nor can I accept that a private landowner is forced to let a dismissed worker carry on living on the landowners land because of long service whereas the government can and often does throw you out of your own house and into the street whenever they want to!

No sir, this man can try to cover up his guilt with lies about equality or human rights and disadvantages but the fact remains, he is the product of his own kind, a nation of incompetents riding the bandwagons of misguided liberals.

Again I say, no sir, he is a thief and just as I am a white racist, a product of a particularly obnoxious section of society for which crime I must in due course pay, so he also should be brought to book.

To let him off the hook because he was caught and only as a result of being caught did he admit his mistake and was sorry and forgiving, or even worse that his mistakes are forgiven because of the mistakes we made when we beat him!

I say he did not pay for his mistakes. The beatings he was subjected to were not 'his' payment for theft. No! They were the result of an angry and merciless attack on him by others. He is trying to claim that another man's sin is payment for his own. Many are the sins this thief committed which he has neither repented of nor admitted to. Some of his sins he refuses to see as sins. So is it also with me. The very prayer you mentioned states that when we ask for forgiveness we should also forgive those who sin against us. This is a God given universal law. Has this man forgiven his old colonial masters? No!

God will not break His own laws of Vengeance or His law of forgiveness. So He must forgive or He places Himself at odds with the very law that He promulgated. I forgive God as the potter who made me as I am. He made me for His purpose and He forgives me for being the pot that He knowingly made me to be. The penalty for the sin I commit as a result, is paid for by God through his Son.

Yes I belonged to a Christian church! Yes I think I am on the right track but no more than any other man on earth has thought before me whatever his religion or politics might be!

I have but this to say, 'I am as God made me!' so let His purpose in me be fulfilled.

Do as you will in this matter for neither you, nor I can do anything beyond that which we were created to do. The man is without doubt guilty, but so are we all! He is sorry, but so are we all! Especially when our mistakes are brought out in the open for all to see.

So in this he is no better, nor worse, than I am.

And Peter, I beat him because I was thoroughly fed up with the very nature of his kind who believes it is their right to bite the hand that feeds them. I am fed up with my own kind who compromised principle and gave away my heritage for expediencies sake.

I beat him because I could find no way of beating myself for allowing his kind to dictate to me in matters, which are mine by virtue of my having created them myself.

I beat him because I had subjected myself to the very thing I hated most in the world - that is the lie spoken by those we trust, designed to distort the truth with imitation honey. If I remember correctly you, the disciple initially known as Simon and then later as Peter, denied the Son of God at the most painful time of his life! Yes! And not once but three times despite the fact that you knew the Son personally and through Him and your new name you had come to know the Father! I have not met the Father nor have I met the Son as you have. Yet you! You who denied Him, Lord it over me who knew Him not, yet have I ever denied him? You Peter, have been placed here at this gate with authority to decide if I may go in or stay out! Really sir, you call that justice!" The uncle turned away to stare down the path he had been destined to climb in this world.

The white haired man smiled, adjusted his books and asked the nephew,

"And you? What do you have to say?"

"The thief is right! Not only has he paid for what he did by way of having been beaten, and even more so, by admitting his guilt and by forgiving us for what we did he is totally exonerated. I don't see that the collapse of the legal and justice system in our country gave us the right to take it even further down the road of degeneration by taking the law into our own hands."

"And you two police men?"

"In our ancient customs we have always been subject to the Chief of the tribe or the local Headman regardless as to the rightness or otherwise of their decisions. We have acted in this matter on that basis. You are now in authority. We therefore subject ourselves to that authority and in so doing we accept whatever your judgement may be over us."

The white haired man smiled. He waved the police, the 'thief' and the nephew through the gate. The nephew hesitated. Turning, he held his hand out to his uncle, but the uncle was no longer there. Surprised, he searched for him in the queue of waiting people. He saw him far down the path - he was talking to the Stranger.

Morning sunlight flooded the bathroom.

XXXXXXXXX/

INITIATION

THE SUN COMES UP,
THE SUN GOES DOWN'

We were walking along the banks of a stream in the village park.

The stranger said,

"Kids have to learn self discipline whilst they are still young. You can't teach old dogs new tricks. You can't teach adults self discipline!"

"Is that why the Jews had to spend forty years in the desert before they could go into the Promised Land? First all the older people had to die off because they had been brought up as slaves and were too old to learn the discipline of freedom?"

"Hey! You got it right!"

"Figures," I said, "but what then is the purpose of initiation? Why do we have to go through the dying of the old before we move on to the new? The Christians have to die to themselves and be born again. School kids die to their old school and are then initiated into their new school. The army destroys your old self and forces a new perspective on you. You become legally responsible when you turn sixteen or eighteen or twenty-one. Why?"

"Everything dies to make way for the new. A seed dies, it gets buried in the dark soil, it gets soaked, it swells and cracks open allowing a new plant to grow from inside. If it does not die it cannot grow. When children are brought up their parents take them through the various stages of first dying to their infant ways then dying to their childhood ways and lastly, dying to their teenage ways. The parents are responsible for their children's behaviour until the children have grown up. This is why parents should be held liable and legally and financially responsible for the actions of their children until the children mature. This would make the parents more careful, not only about sparing the rod and spoiling the child, but also about the emotional needs of the 'for ever changing' perspective of children as they learn self-discipline and self-awareness.

What most people do not understand is that when children are old enough to have a baby they are obviously mature enough to look after it. Maturity implies responsibility for their actions. It is during the period in a persons life before they become responsible, up to say twelve years, that they should be taught self discipline and that is taught by both enlightening them and by not sparing the rod!"

"But," I interrupted, "the government is planning on outlawing the beating of kids like they have done in England!"

"Exactly, and the end result will be absolute mayhem. As I said, kids have to be taught self-discipline and the use of the rod guarantees this. To deny it and give teenagers the false cover of being too young to be responsible for their own actions breaks down the natural laws of self-discipline and the result can be seen in England where feral teenagers are now running riot and those who have grown up are into all the despicable things in life!"

"Isn't the government doing it to stop parents being cruel to their kids?"

"That's what they say. But cruel parents will be cruel regardless of the law, especially if the punishment for child molestation is inadequate. The new laws stop only the decent parents and good teachers from bringing kids up properly."

The Stranger left.

I thought, "Yes! I had a problem at school. I could not understand why I had to be the same as all the other kids. My new mother said I was being difficult. I said the school authorities were being difficult.

I was regularly beaten, chastised, reprimanded put in detention and given impositions by the teachers and the headmaster.

I asked New father what to do about all the hiding's I got at school. He said,

"Remember your story about one rule in the house. Most people don't believe in that principle. School teachers are notorious for their insistence that all the kids behave in the same manner and that manner is the one the teachers have worked out to make their job easier and not to make the kids life at school easier."

"But New father, are we at school to make the teachers jobs easier or are we at school to improve ourselves?"

"Obviously to improve yourselves."

"Then if they destroy our 'selves' to make their jobs easier they have failed in their jobs before they even start."

"You have a point, but the need for discipline in a school is obvious."

"Yes of course but," I asked, "would you be happy if I let them change me into a carbon copy of their understanding of what a person should be?"

"No, I suppose not!"

"Can I refuse to change?"

"It will be very tough on you. But there is a huge advantage in putting your own principles to the test and being punished for being different - you will develop fantastic self discipline!"

"Yes! And if I know that you are with me I will be able to take whatever they dish out and, as you say, the self discipline it builds up in me will be phenomenal!"

New father held out his hand.

xxxxxxx

The school prefects did not like my attitude. They took me to the head master.

"Right!" He said, "I have heard of your refusal to follow the rules of this school?"

"Some of them, yes."

"Yes Sir!" interrupted a prefect "You must say, 'Sir' as a sign of respect."

"Yes."

"I said call him Sir!"

"You said I must call him Sir as a sign of respect!"

"You don't respect the headmaster?"

The headmaster interrupted,

"I will teach you to respect me boy, who do you think you are to refuse my authority?"

"I am who I am and that is enough reason for me to not bow down to anyone if I think they are wrong, be they the headmaster or the yard sweeper."

The headmaster exploded.

"You my boy, had better get over your arrogant self righteous importance and very quickly! I give you two weeks grace to change your attitude."

Spittle sprayed out of his mouth.

I waited.

"You understand!" he stormed.

"I hear you Mr Headmaster, but I do not understand. Why must I become what you want me to be? I am happy as I am. I don't want to change you and I don't want you to change me. I do not want to be what other people say I should be. No! Not you or my mother, not the preacher, not the government, not the school, not the army!

You can beat me as much as you like but I assure you it will only serve to strengthen my resolve to be exactly as God made me and that is, 'to be as I Am!'"

"You of all people will be fully reformed!" He shouted, "I will see to that my self!"

"Whatever!" I said.

"Get out of my office."

xxxxxxx

Many months later, our housemaster called me into his study.

"Boy." he said "You have been repeatedly beaten by the prefects, by the headmaster, by the teachers and I have beaten you more than I have ever beaten any other boy in this school. Do you understand that we will carry on beating you until you conform? This school has a reputation to maintain. I say again, we will beat you until you obey the rules."

The housemaster was red in the face.

He exploded.

"Do you understand?"

"Yes."

"Have you anything to say before I thrash you to the limit of my authority?"

"Yes!"

"What?"

"I spoke to the stranger about this and he explained the basic cause of the problem!"

"And?"

"Empowerment of the victim!"

"I beg your pardon?"

"It is easy to beat someone smaller than yourself. It is easy to be nice to very nice people. It is easy to exert authority when a power or force greater than the situation is backing you. What does take guts and principle is to be nice to the unattractive - attack the giant and listen to the victim.

I, being young, small, and in terms of the school authorities, an insignificant part of the whole, am left with no way to make a stand.

Is not the child the reason for the school?

Up to the age of sixteen I am forced by law to attend school. It seems that I am to be brainwashed, not into accepting the cultures and traditions of my heritage as they really are, but as the school sees them to be!

My parents would be remiss if they did not have me educated within the educational system. Imagine the blot on the community's landscape. Society would be horrified.

I am disempowered by the structures that the department of education, the school and society put in place to force me to bend to their perspective of right and wrong.

In truth we are all individuals with individual talents and both good and bad points. We can only become the same if we deny ourselves, and others, the right to be free.

I will not obey your rules until you stop beating me. But! If you do stop beating me, I will obey only those rules, which are necessary for the good and proper running of the school in terms of creating a correct and acceptable atmosphere for education. By that I mean tertiary education! I accept the principle of the penalty fitting the crime! More so, I believe that the penalty should be harsh enough to prevent the crime! It is the definition of the crime that I am arguing. I accept that my freedom and my rights are sacred but that does not give me the right to destroy another's right and freedom nor does it give you the right to destroy mine.

Sir, with all due respect, I have no wish to hurt anyone but I also have no wish to submit myself to patently wrong disciplines which reduce me to the level of 'only a number'."

The housemaster sat down.

He placed the cane on the desktop and rested his chin on his hands.

Feeling a little guilty, I said,

"Sorry sir!"

He looked up,

"No!" He said, "Don't be sorry! If I accept that you are correct in fighting for your right to be an individual, then must I examine my position in this school from the same point of view! Have I lost my own identity by submitting my individuality to the school's perspective of who and what I should be and do?

Am I beating you because you are wrong or because I fit and you do not?"

He sat perfectly still! Then suddenly! He grinned, laughed, stood up, walked around to my side of the desk, held out his hand to me and said,

"Its a deal, I'll organise it with the headmaster tomorrow. From now on I will fight for your right to be what you are within the perspective of morality, integrity and respect for the truth."

"Really sir?"

"Really!"

Tears ran down my cheeks. He smiled,

"Hey!" He spoke ever so softly, "You never cried when you were beaten!"

Taking me by the hand he led me over to his house for tea with his family.   Never again was I beaten at that school.

XXXXXXX

MANONE AND RIBOMINE

My New father never told me fairy stories. He said there are no fairies! Animals don't speak human languages and pigs can't fly. He believed that telling kids about Father Christmas or the tooth mouse was teaching the kids to believe lies and when they grew up and found out all those stories were not true it would subconsciously undermine their trust in their parents and society. He also said that the violence and the exaggerated monsters and filth built into children's games would drive those who participated into becoming degenerated teenagers and adults.

My new mother loved fairy tales! She loved the concept of Easter - Christmas - birthdays and mother's days. New father ignored them. Everyone said he was quirky!

I asked the Stranger about that. He smiled,

"Can you imagine someone who tells you that late one night, as he was sitting out on the steps of his home, he looked up at the sky and saw a Red Coated, bearded old man riding through clouds on a sleigh drawn by reindeers!

The Red-coated man drove his sleigh to the roof of the neighbour's house. Telling his reindeers to 'stay' he picked up a bag full of toys from the back of the sleigh and carried it along the pitch of the snow covered roof to the chimney. Ignoring the fact that the chimney was very small and full of soot, he climbed down into the room below where he left presents in the good children's socks and then putting the presents meant for the bad children back in his bag, he climbed out through and up inside the chimney to the roof.

He stood there, spotlessly clean, no black soot or dirt on him and then with a loud laugh he shouted 'Ho, Ho, Ho!' jumped onto his sleigh, and drove away into the dark midnight sky. You see the picture?"

"Yes."

"Who is quirky?" He asked. "The man who believes that story? Or your father who does not!"

I smiled in understanding. He continued,

"There are two ways to tell a story without denying the truth. The

73

first way is just the way it is with no frills and the second way is by way of illustration."

"What do you mean, illustration?"

"Telling a made up story about the truth. They call such stories parables. This way, difficult ideas can be illustrated in a way the listener can more easily understand."

"Tell me one please."

He found a comfortable spot in soft sand and sitting there with his back against a tree, he told me this story.

"Manone was a young gardener living in a valley called 'Free' in the land of 'Dom'.

One day Manone lay down in the shade of a blooming 'know it all' tree for the sun bore more than a hint of burning. He closed his eyes. He saw nothing. This pleased him for nothing meant a lot more than something - at least it did to Manone. 'Nothing' always left wide open the doorway to an infinite variety of new and unfettered ideas. 'Nothing' left his mind free to accept or reject, to follow or to simply observe. Whereas 'Something' was altogether different! 'Something' always brought on Manone the need to understand, to justify, or worse still, it sometimes led him to have to 'DO' something! But worst of all was to have something on his mind which denied entry of any other more interesting or valuable passing concept.

This day, as he closed his eyes 'nothing' took over and total emptiness filled his deepest senses as majestic peace settled on him, wrapping him in silk.

"Hey! Manone." A voice from great distances called.

Manone grunted.

"Hey Manone! Hey you! Listen to me! I have a question to ask."

Again Manone grunted.

"Manone why do you do nothing all day?"

Manone sat up.

"Hey Manone, Hey?"

Manone muttered as turning his head from side to side he searched for the owner of the voice.

"Hey Manone you better take notice of me. After all, I am the designated Boss around here. If you don't acknowledge me it could lead to you being ostracised."

The voice came from high up in the tree.

It continued.

"I have already spoken to your wife."

"What do you mean 'my wife'?"

"That cloned girl you live with! Remember her? She is your wife!"

"Since when?"

"Since you accepted her when she was given to you! What's more you, as her husband, have the responsibility of caring for her. You know what I mean, things like food, clothing, a home. You can't expect her, as a married woman, to walk around naked! Nor can you, as a married man, walk around naked!"

"But," protested Manone "I was made this way and so was she. I love her, as she is - not covered up. What has she got to hide?"

"Oh boy! What has she got to hide? For that matter what do you both have to hide? Well let's first look at the things you do not have that everyone else does have!

You both don't have navels!

I mean talk is cheap! What do you think the people from the valley have to say about a man and his girl who have no belly buttons! Hey! Hey? And it is no longer behind their hands that they talk."

Manone suppressed a yawn.

"Okay. Okay." he muttered. "What do you want me to do?"

"That's better. First, take up your responsibilities. Start with a list of what you should do and what you should not do, you know, get to know what is right and what is wrong. If necessary, find yourself a teacher to help you understand the difference. Next, you must work! There is no way you can just idle about living off nature! I have spoken to your wife about this and she has already started on her new way. Talk to her and see the difference for yourself."

The voice paused for effect then interrupted as Manone opened his mouth to speak.

"Wait," said the voice "I have not given you authority to speak! There are many other aspects to living in this world that you have to learn. Here is a list for you to study."

A roll of paper dropped out of the tree at Manone's feet.

"Huge benefits will grow out of learning the difference between right and wrong. Things like learning how to manipulate money, like power over lesser beings or better still, power over greater beings! You will also come to understand politics and religion and how you can use these to bring people into subjection by promising and giving them that which is not rightfully theirs such as money which they have not earned! You must weaken them in order to make them easier to rule! But more important! When you come to know all of the differences - you will be perfect!"

"But," protested Manone "I already have everything I want. It is supplied in great abundance all around me - available by simply reaching out my hand! I do not have any needs!"

The voice purred on,

"You do not know what you are missing. You cannot grow if you just lie around eating fruit and then sleeping it off. Listen to your wife! She has tasted something you ought to at least try. I will return from time to time to keep you abreast of developments in this world." The voice grew louder and full of authority "I run the world," it thundered, "you can either help me run it or you can refuse. But remember, refusal makes me your enemy!"

Manone shuddered. Picking up the roll of paper he stood and looking uncertainly around him decided to move across the valley to rest under a quieter tree.

"Ribomine," he shouted, "where are you?"

"Right here beside you Nitwit!" She whispered.

Manone turning to her stopped short. New emotions flooded his body. Ribomine stood inquiringly by his side. Naked!

"You are very desirable," Manone breathed. "I never saw you this way before. But we have to go to the other tree, I have this paper authorising me to know every thing. Run with me."

"No. Wait." She lowered her eyelashes and lent against him, "I see you are naked too! I see you want me! Let us spend a little time together on the banks of the river before we go to the other tree. I have some fruit for you to taste."

Manone, breathing hard, touched her fine golden hair with the tips of his trembling fingers.

"Oh yes! Yes! I want to know you and share your fruit!"

xxxxxxx

Manone rose from the banks of the beautiful river. He picked large leaves from a nearby bush and plaited them into two aprons using stringy grass as thread, one for Ribomine and one for himself.

They dressed each other, covering their nakedness.

"That's better," said Manone "even your tummy is covered! Now I know you and that makes you mine and only I may look at what is mine."

"And you Manone," she answered ever so softly, "are mine only!"

So they took possession of each other, denying access to any other.

Manone held Ribomine's hand as he escorted her along the narrow path leading to the other tree. As they drew near they saw a strange figure standing in the way and grew very afraid. They hid in thick bush at the side of the path.

Manone knew this figure spelt disaster, but in what manner?

"We must be quiet." He whispered.

Light lit the tree before them. Light brighter even than the sun. Guards surrounded the tree.

"What on earth is going on?"

The figure in the path held an awesome flaming sword in one hand and a collection of words in the other. A pile of skins lay at his feet. He dropped the words onto the skins. Taking two steps back the figure adopted an on guard position. From the illuminated tree a soft voice thundered. The owner of the voice pretended to not know where Manone and Ribomine were hiding. It spoke to them but they could not understand the meaning behind the words. Their minds were full of 'something' and in no way could any thing, soft and gentle that thundered, interrupt or dispel their new thoughts. They were locked into a prison of misunderstanding. Yet somehow, at the edge of his consciousness Manone knew that later, much later, the word would be made plain to him by a descendant of his, by another man - just like him. Manone decided he would study the word when that happened. One meaning did get through his mass of newfound knowledge, the tree before him was full of light because the tree was alive. The new knowledge gained by Manone and Ribomine to the effect that they still had a lot to learn, prevented them from passing the guard and reaching the shelter of the living tree of light.

Manone grew excited about this new understanding. He picked up the bundle of skins and the words and retreated.

Ribomine followed at a distance.

Manone sat down at a safe distance to read the words thrown down on the skins. He scowled at Ribomine for now that he had his mind full of something - nothing else could get in. He no longer had a choice! The words were not to his liking!

"It was you who led me into this!" He shouted at Ribomine.

For the first time, feelings of anger flooded his soul and with them a sense of power. It was obvious that from now on, because of her leading him astray, Ribomine must obey him regardless.

She interrupted his thoughts "No Manone! I am made out of you! Any fault I may have comes from you so it is actually you who are the cause of this problem!"

He never heard a word she said for he was fuming as he came to fully understand what was written on the skins as being a decree. He realised he must leave the garden and work all day in the hot sun to get food.

Ribomine spoke to him in a honeyed, manipulative tone.

"Manone, you will have to love me because I am part of you and if you hate me you will in fact be, hating yourself!" She pouted her lips "I will see to it that you love me always. It is my right!"

Irritated by some subtly hidden distortion in what she said he stood up and responded.

"And you must obey me at all times. In fact I will make sure you obey me in all things. As you say, you are made from me so you are mine. Your behaviour and freedom are in my hands!"

Together, no longer by choice, but by force of circumstance, they walked away from the Tree of Light, which was the Tree of Life itself, into an all-enveloping darkness to live as slaves in the house of 'fret' in the land of 'fool'."

xxxxxxx

The Stranger paused.

I asked, "Is that the truth?"

"The story is not the truth but the truth is in the story!"

"Were those real people?"

"The story is about real people but Manone and Ribomine were not their real names."

"Wow! My first fairy tale story about the truth!"

XXXXXXX

BEGGAR IN THE MIRROR

I brush my teeth three times a day.

My New father has false teeth because he didn't brush his teeth three times a day when he was young. Not only does he suffer when he has them in his mouth, but worse, he looks pathetic when he takes them out.

Sometimes when I have to go to his room early in the morning I find him fast asleep on his back with his mouth wide open. His lips fall inside his mouth and they flutter as he breathes.

His teeth snarl at me from the glass jar on his bedside table.

My New mother also sleeps on her back because she has hair curlers behind her ears. She snores louder than he does.

xxxxxxx

I always watch myself in the mirror when I brush my teeth. I like to pull funny faces. Today, for the first time, I noticed something most strange. My face in the wall mirror was back to front. When I put my left hand up the face in the mirror put its right hand up. Startled, I snatched the hand mirror off the bathroom dresser and checked my reflection in it. The same again! I was back to front in that mirror too.

"I wonder which way round other people see me? What if 'back to front' is actually the right way?"

That day I was lost to the teachers at school. Using a small hand mirror I studied the differences between reflected faces of kids in the class and their real faces. While doing this I remembered a biology lesson where they explained that our eyes see everything upside down.

But the mirror did not turn everything upside down - it turned everything back to front! So when I look with my eyes through the mirror I see everything upside down and back to front, or is it that I am upside down and back to front and I see the right way round in the mirror?

At break time the school kids were talking about an old beggar who had arrived in town the day before. Some of the bigger boys had been 'beggar baiting' him. They laughed about it a lot. I tried to see the funny side too but it was beyond me.

That afternoon I wandered around the village looking for the beggar. Dog came with me. We shared a burger. I love Dog. He loves burgers.

I wondered which face I would see in the beggar tramp. Would it be his real face or his back to front face? Would there be a difference other than left and right.

I tried the mirror out on Dog.

"Dog." I drew his attention "Let me see you through the mirror." I studied his face looking for a difference. There was a huge difference! In the mirror his face seemed to speak to me. Looking quickly back and forwards from mirror image to his real face, I saw the two perspectives of his face merge into each other. I had to concentrate so as to see correctly. The two faces melted into one and a third face grew out of the confusion. The third face was serene and complete but it faded as soon as I held my eyes steady on his.

Holding Dog's head in my two hands I tried to focus on the memory of his third face. Everything blurred. Then out of the blur his eyes came alive and I could see his inner self in his eyes. His third face matched his inner self. His third face was his inner self.

I was so thrilled I started crying.

Dog put his tongue out and touched the tip of my nose.

He understood.

I wagged my butt.

He smiled.

Across the street a tall man was buying bananas from a vendor. Turning to look over at me, he beckoned. Dog and I sauntered over.

"Hi." He said.

His face was hidden under his floppy old bush hat. His eyes shone in the shade. Just like my Dog. I tried to make a picture of his face by staring into his eyes. Dog barked. The man laughed.

"Want a banana?"

"Yes please."

"And the bone in my pocket is for Dog!"

Dog slurped his yes please.

"Sit on the step with me?"

"Okay." I said.

"You don't seem to remember me?"

"I do, but you are very different!"

"Maybe you see me through new eyes. Like when you saw your dog a while ago!"

"Yes! Today I see you as the real life stranger, not the stranger of my imagination?"

Tilting his head back he allowed a ray of sunlight to fall on his face highlighting his large nose, bushy eyebrows and scraggly grey beard.

He dropped his head.

I thought to myself 'Is this the beggar the kids were talking about?'

"Yes." He said. "This is the beggar."

We ate our bananas. Dog chewed his bone.

I smiled,

"I have a small problem!" I said,

"What?"

The church my parents go to believe in the Trinity but the church a friend from school goes to says it's a lot of nonsense and another friend says it doesn't matter because there is no God anyway!"

"So? What do you believe?"

"I don't know! Do you know?"

"Well I think they could each one have it wrong depending on what their hidden motives or objectives are!"

"Oh?"

"You need to come to the understanding that every civilisation in history, every nation, every continent, every Religion, Sect, town or village, each group of people down to each family and finally every single member of any or all of these has a different view point in one way or another to and from all the rest.

So, people may be similar and belong to the same group but no one is exactly the same as any one else."

I looked at my hands,

"Yes! Everyone has different fingerprints!"

"And everyone has a different perspective in one way or another!"

"So what about the Trinity?"

"Three in One is a numerical statement so may I suggest you look at the Trinity from the numerical point of view! One and Three are both numbers. But! One has the interesting value of including every number there is whereas three has only one value!"

"What do you mean?"

"The number seven is one number. The number one million two hundred thousand is also one number. So every number is one example of that number!"

"That doesn't help me understand the reason for the different beliefs."

"Well to start of with you need to understand the meaning of BELIEF! When you believe something the implication is that you do not know it is so, you only believe it to be so. In that case the only way to establish the truth of your belief is to put it into practice and the result will confirm it either way and you will then no longer just believe! You will know!"

"Okay," I asked, "If the Trinity is simply a numerical perspective, how do I find out exactly what that means?"

"Hey! I did not say it is only a numerical perspective, I said there is a numerical perspective to it. The essence of the Trinity is Three in One! So may I suggest that when you get home take your calculator and as a first step divide three into one and write down the answer. Second step, divide the answer you get by three again and write that number down. Third step, divide that last number once again by three and write that answer down.

You will find that the results are most enlightening. For example the first step, you have the original number which is one and then three new different numbers for the remaining steps. That is, one divided by three equals .33333333 infinitely recurring. Divide .33333 recurring by 3 and you get .11111 recurring. Divide .11111 recurring and you get .037037 recurring and divide that by 3 and you get .012345679!

Keep the last result separate.

Study your answers and we will talk about it next time we meet and then try to find any hidden answer that may prove which Trinity perspective if any, is right!

And! As I said, always remember that there are thousands of very differing religions believing in many different God's! There are also many not very religious people who believe in a very simple form of God and of course there are those who deny the whole concept of God and make a religion out of believing in evolution and things like the big bang theory. So we have atheists, agnostics, believers and many who don't really care either way."

"So?"

"Each religion forms a base for the members of that religion to exist as a community. Unfortunately there is a lot of intolerance between people of differing beliefs leading to intolerance between different people. The majority of people believe they are right and they are not prepared to even consider anyone else's point of view. This often leads to disputes, separation, torture and war!

An example of how your own perspective can affect you is a leading Bishop in South Africa is reported as having said, "If the Bible preaches separate development or racism, then I reject the Bible." What he intimated was that he was only prepared to believe those parts of the bible which suited his perspective so by saying what he said he contradicts his own and his church's claim to believing and trusting in the bible as the Truth, the Word of God! Most people do the same, they have their own view and they are of course the only ones who are right, or so they believe!""

"Splitting hairs?"

"Sometimes a person misses death by a split hair. The road to your final destination is narrow so a split hairs difference in your understanding at the beginning of your walk could lead to total separation at the end. One degree out where we stand is nothing, but five kilometres off it amounts to quite a few hundred metres. Similarly, if you start your walk separated from your objective but keep your eyes on it you will most likely end your walk on target.

The same with believing in a God!"

"What about if you believe in God and it turns out that there is no such entity as God?"

"Then there is no problem and you end up with an Atheist's perspective. But there could be a problem if there is a God and you are an Atheist, or maybe that problem would be over-ridden at the end by God!

As I suggested earlier, I believe that everyone, as a starting point, develops faith in what they believe and by putting that belief into practise they will prove it either way for them selves!"

"The Pastor also says the Trinity is a mystery that we cannot understand."

"Ah! Yes of course he does and there are two possibilities leading to not understanding - the first is obvious - a man who is still part of the world can't understand because scripture is a mystery to him.

The second is in a way similar - if a certain part of the bible is a mystery to a Christian Minister then the full understanding of that particular part of the scripture has not been revealed to him. So by saying the Trinity is a mystery the Pastor acknowledges the fact that either one of these possibilities has him by the short hairs.

Ask your Pastor which category he falls into. The non-believer who cannot understand the truth because it is hidden from him? Or the believer who cannot understand because the truth is hidden behind his refusal to accept it as such."

"That would make him angry!"

"Of course! So ask him why does it make him angry? You see it could be that the answer to the problem is the same as the answer to the true identity of Jesus Christ. So read scripture as it is and do not twist it to suit your perspective!"

"You say that but you also said that there are many contradictions in the bible!" I smiled and asked "So who do you say Christ is?"

"Me! Well, from my understanding and belief I say He is 'The Christ' written about by numerous people both at the time of his living on earth and after. As such He is reported as having said, 'I do only what I see the Father doing!' so obviously in that case if you came to see Christ you would also see The Father. In other words when you see the Son you see the Father in him for as The Christ He must have come from the Father and therefore he does only what he sees the Father doing. This is why He said, 'If you knew the Father you would have known me.' so in that sense 'The Christ' officially represents the Father!

An interesting point is that if you see Christ in me you will also see The Father in me because He is in the Christ who you see in me. This raises the question 'does what you see in me mean that I am that which you see in me or does it not?' If it does then it suggests that Christ, The Father, The Holy Spirit and I are four in one? Or does it simply mean that God is in each one of us and each one of us is in God, which could lead us to understand the saying that one day God will be seen as being all in all! OR! You haven't actually seen the truth of the matter and are guided by your perspectives into believing!

The advantage is that even though 'the all' of understanding cannot be experienced by any one man or by any one church or any one religion, it can be shared out through the joint and several experiences of all men and all religions. Obviously 'the all' also includes the non-believers with the believers! Then one day, what they call Judgement Day which is said to come when everything has been experienced that has to be experienced, the eyes of all men will be opened and everything there is to know of good and evil or right and wrong will become known to all men as a result of them sharing their joint and several experiences in life.

With the fullness of knowing comes the ability to make an enlightened and therefore correct choice. And! Just like people, the Bible is, as I said, full of contradictions, which allows for all perspectives of the truth to be experienced by different churches and by different groups within a church and by different individuals within each group and by non-believers! This encourages discussion and argument.

Added to this is the natural worldly problem of man seeing as if in a mirror. He sees everything back to front. Every one holds his 'own mirror' at a different angle and at a different distance and in a different position. This makes for infinite variations in the theme ot back to front-ness. It creates endless variations of perspective, which serve to teach us that which we could otherwise never learn.

Obviously the truth is absolute! It is in the way man perceives the truth that error occurs and it is the many different ways that man understands the truth, which brings about differences of understanding and differences of opinion.

Truth stands on its own! But it is hard to learn what the truth is, if there is nothing to compare it with. It is the darkness that creates a need for and an understanding of light. It is the lie that reveals the truth. You can only lie about the truth so you could say that if you look into the reason for a lie you should be able to find the truth.

Obviously it is difficult to look at things objectively if one looks at everything as if through a dark mirror. When a man is set free of this problem, that is when his eyes and his mind are opened, he will see things as they are and not as he thinks they should be. Such a man is said to be 'born out of the world of lies and into the truth' so setting him free to see the whole picture and come to understand the reality of it all.

Talking about opening the mind, I believe it is opened not so much as to let the truth in but to let the lies out. The truth is already in you. The lies of the world you inherit and accumulate prevent you from seeing it. This is why everything in this world is born to die whereas everything going into the next world has to die in order to be born again.

Your personal perspectives must die in order for you to see and live the truth. The curtain in the temple of your mind must be torn to expose the truth and so set you free."

"Wow!" I shouted, "My mirror just shattered!"

"Good!

The Stranger looked hard and long at me then spoke gently,

"Sounds as if you could be on the right road! So do you understand that not only is the Three in One concept as a purely mathematical perspective not understood by many people, it is not even vaguely known to the vast majority."

The Stranger stared at me,

May I ask you something?"

"Like what?"

"Why are you so afraid of your Church and the people in it?"

"I don't know! It just seems wrong to me!"

"Has it got anything to do with you being looked after by a Church orphanage when they found you on the steps?"

"Maybe! My mother abandoned me to the Church and asked them to look after me. Why did she do that? Why give me away? The Church kept me for a few years and then they also gave me away as if I didn't mean anything to them. I loved the people at the orphanage. Why did they throw me away? They preach love. They preach justice. But they didn't practice it with me. So how can I trust them?"

Bursting into tears I sobbed,

"They just gave me away!"

The Stranger held my hand. He said,

"I understand, but maybe they thought you would be better cared for in a proper family like where you are now. Your mother loved you! The orphanage staff loved you and your foster parents love you!"

"So one day my New parents will give me away to another better family just like my mother and the church did, and say they did it because of love!"

"Your mother had a very serious problem and she thought the best she could do for you was to separate you from it."

"Everyone has some kind of a problem! So why did she use hers as an excuse to get rid of me? I hate her! I hate the church and I don't trust my New parents!"

The stranger spoke strongly,

"As you say, everyone has a problem and yours is one of not trusting. If you want to be what you should be you better either get rid of your problem before you use it to justify hurting someone else like you say your mother and the church did to you, or even better, you must learn to understand and accept that all people have problems and set them free from your condemnation. If you don't you will end up being just like your mother and the church! "

I closed my eyes. Was what he said the truth? If I accepted my mother and the church as being influenced by their own specific perspectives and then forgive them would this set them and me free! I asked the stranger "What kind of problem could be so big that it forces a mother to abandon her baby on some steps hoping someone would find it and take care of it? Why didn't she take it to the church and speak to the Pastor?"

"Mothers on their own often have gigantic problems such as money, guilt, despair, psychiatric, physiological, post natal depression and so on. When they find themselves in a desperate state their only way out often seems to be to give up. If they do that, hopefully they leave the baby somewhere safe to be cared for. Thank your mother for that!"

I tried to hide my tears. The Stranger challenged me,

"Come on, let's both dress up as beggars this weekend, disguise our faces but not our eyes and go into town. I'll be and old bent beggar and you can be a filthy street kid. What do you say?"

"What for?"

"Lets do it firstly for fun and then to see how all the town people react - your neighbours - the people in your church - the people who know you! I bet they won't allow themselves to see who you are. They won't want to accept that they know you."

"Could be fun. I won't have to try and be what others want me to be!"

"Look for me on the street tomorrow."

XXXXXXX

TOMORROW

Tomorrow dawned as Saturday. It was one of those still, humid days when it felt hotter than it really was.

I searched for the Stranger.

A bent and weary tramp wearing a red cap accosted me in Main Street. Avoiding him, I turned away.

He reached out a grimy hand,

"Hey boy? What's the matter?"

"Nothing." I spluttered, blushing with shame.

The tramp said,

"I had kids once."

Turning back to face him, I stood my full height and glared at him.

The stranger grinned back at me from under his tramps cap.

"Wow!" I exclaimed, "You look even more different than yesterday. How do you do it?"

Laughing, he said,

"I've got some disgusting clothes for you too! Come and put them on then change your attitude. You are now lost and hungry, no friends, no family. Disowned! You have no money and no hope. You are too old for a boy's home and too young for a pension. Your attitude is wrong for a lowly job, your appearance too decrepit for a top job.

You have put on the outward nature of an untouchable and you are now both despised and pitied by the people you will come into contact with. They will not recognise you because they never really knew you! They only knew the outside of you - they never looked into your soul.

Come! Let's enjoy a day on the town."

Laughing, he took me by the elbow and led me behind the town junk store where I changed. As I put the rotten old clothes on, some too large and some too small, I felt the degradation they imposed on me. I could no longer stand up straight. I could not look anyone in the eye. I was ashamed.

"Do we have to do this?" I pleaded.

"Think about it."

Smearing dirt on my face as I looked in my mirror I exclaimed,

"Oh no! I look absolutely disgusting! Okay! Let's do it!"

xxxxxxx

Four elderly matrons from the local old age home were sitting on their favourite bench on Main Street. They enjoyed spending the day watching the passers by and making comments befitting their observations.

A weary old man and a dirty young boy scuttled out of the restaurant across the road. A cursing waiter pushed them off the pavement. The old man danced from one leg to the other as he looked helplessly around. Seeing the hedge across the other side of the road, he stumbled across to it.

The boy followed.

"Why won't the restaurant let you use their toilet?" He asked the old man.

"We are tramps."

"Don't tramps need to go to the toilet?"

"Yes, but we are dirty! They built their toilets for clean people."

"Where can you go? It's too far to walk to our house or out of town!"

"I am bursting." He muttered

The old tramp broke into a shambling run. Reaching the church he relieved himself against the hedge.

One of the old ladies on the bench, the one dressed in red, prodded her neighbour,

"Quickly!" she begged, "Lend me your phone I want to call the police. That disgusting man needs to be taught some manners."

The lady next to her, dressed in white, pressed her mobile phone into the red ladies hand. She, the lady in white didn't even look at the tramp, after all she was a lady and ladies do not see such things!

The third lady, the one in blue, lent forward the better to watch the old tramp.

The fourth lady, dressed in a rainbow of colours smiled. She beckoned to the boy. He responded.

"Hello boy, can you see what's going on here?"

"What?"

"There are two things in life that you have to do. Do you know what they are?"

The boy shook his head.

"You have to go to the toilet and you have to die. Its amazing how few people know that!"

The boy answered, "I think there is one more thing you have to do!"

She raised her eyebrows.

"There comes a day" he said "when you will be asked to make one decision and you will not be able to avoid making that one decision."

Surprised, the pretty lady frowned,

"And what is that decision and when will it arise?"

"You will be led into the truth and then you will be compelled to decide whether to accept the truth or deny it. If you accept it, if you say 'yes', then the truth will set you free!"

Looking intently at the boy she exclaimed,

"Hey! I know you! Oh yes I do! You I know!"

The boy smiled, joined the tramp and they walked away.

The lady in blue cried out to the lady dressed in bright colours,

"Hey! What's with you? You've got tears in your eyes."

The old tramp nodded at the boy.

"You see," he said, "it's all a matter of perspective. What people see may be the truth but the problem is each one sees it differently. Like the old ladies, each one judges by their differing understanding of right and wrong. It is true that they cannot judge any other way for they have locked themselves into the prison of self righteousness."

The two tramps strolled along the dusty pavement towards Jimmie's butchery. Townspeople on the sidewalks averted their eyes. A few made rude comments. Not one of them recognised the boy or the Stranger for that matter. They could not see beyond their filthy clothes and listless attitudes.

Their closed minds opened the boy's eyes.

Reaching the butchery the old tramp leant against a veranda pillar. He watched the customers as they stepped out from the darkness of the building.

"A house selling bits and pieces of butchered animals." He muttered.

Some of them were pleased with their purchases while others felt a little cheated. Their reaction to the tramps as they saw them slouching in the half shade, varied. The richer people with the larger pieces of dead animals saw them as separate to the building. Not belonging - a disgrace to humanity. Loafers! Trash! Not worth taking any notice of.

The poorer people saw them as a threat to the food they were taking home. There was not enough to share with them.

Our Pastor drove up. Parking the church Mercedes against the kerb he climbed out, clean and upright. Seeing the tramps he nodded and stepping briskly into the shop he let the swing door slam behind him.

The tramps waited.

Eventually the Pastor came out. He had to! He couldn't stay in there all day! Hesitating on the step, he looked up and down the street - no one was watching. Squaring his shoulders he walked stiff necked to his car. Surviving on his Pastor's pay caused friction in his home.

He drove off without looking back.

"What was that all about?"

"Whited sepulchre."

"What?"

"Painted beautiful on the outside to camouflage the inside! Did you see the pain in his eyes?"

"No he hid them."

"I looked!"

"And?"

"Pain!"

The Stranger looked sad,

"One day you must remind me to tell you what I think it's all about."

He stood.

"Let's walk to the Pastor's house. He normally has visitors at this time of day, sometimes elders, sometimes ordinary members of the congregation."

"Okay, but why?"

"Lets see how he treats us in front of his community! Will he hide his problem and treat us differently to satisfy his congregation?"

The Pastor lived in a noble residence behind the church. The view over the valley was magnificent - it made you feel above the world! The tramp and the boy sat on the kerb of the paved drive leading through cool lawns to the house.

A car drove up. It slowed at the entrance. A pair of tinted glasses peered out at us. The car drove in.

A second car stopped at the entrance. Two lovely ladies, one with blue hair, blue eyes and a blue dress greeted us courteously and drove in.

The Church bookkeeper's car was the third and the last to arrive. He was never known to have smiled. His look was angry. Sticking his head out the window he growled,

"What in the hell are you two doing here? This is private property. Pull yourselves together! Now get out of here and make it fast!"

"Oh dear," the tramp purred, "we want to see the Pastor, could you let him know we are here. It is on a matter of church business."

"What church business?"

"Private!"

"I'll be damned. You better be right or I'll personally kick you off this property."

"Yes, we know that."

Spinning the wheels of his car, he accelerated up the drive.

"Wow!" Said the boy, "He looked really upset!"

The bookkeeper entered the house. A moment later, the Pastor came out with the two ladies. They walked down to us. Smiling sweetly he peeked sideways at the ladies with him before turning to the tramps.

"How may I help you gentlemen?"

The old tramp stood up and pulled the boy to his feet. The boy was sure the Pastor would recognise him.

"My young friend and I are in desperate straights," purred the tramp "we have not eaten since last time. We know you are an honourable church with a wealthy congregation and we beg you for something to eat, or, a little money."

"My good man." beamed the Parson "Of course, of course!"

Digging deep into his inside jacket pocket he pulled out a bunch of notes. Counting out two in front of the ladies he turned to us and looking blankly at me, said in his most silky voice,

"Praise the Lord!"

The tramp took the notes and bowed his thanks.

The Pastor nodded and taking the arm of the wealthiest lady he led the way back to his house. He whispered as he went,

"Probably use the money for cheap wine or cannabis!"

The tramps walked back to the main street.

They did not speak.

The old tramp bought cool drinks. They drank them as they sat together at a road sign watching the reactions of passing motorists.

"When" asked the boy "will this exercise be over?"

"There is one man in town we still have to meet."

"Where?"

"Back at the butchery. He always buys his meat this time of the week and at this time of the day."

They walked back to the butchery and waited there for the man to come.

He arrived on an old pedal bike. He was a Coloured man with lots of scraggly red hair. Whistling, he leant his bike against the butchery wall. Nodding at us, he danced up the steps into the butchery. Much laughter erupted inside the shop. The Coloured man was telling tall stories. Finished at last with his business in the butchery, he swung the doors open and bursting out he smiled. He was happy with the cash discount he had been given in return for his humour.

Two steps and he stopped. Looking at the tramps, he sighed. Reaching into his back pocket he drew out some paper money. He held it a moment treasuring the feel of it. He thought of what it could buy for his family. He walked over to the tramps, where, smiling as he handed the money over to the old tramp, he said,

"May God bless you!"

"You too." Said the old tramp.

"But you gave us all your money!" Exclaimed the boy.

"It was mine to give." The Coloured man laughed. Then looking closely at the boy he said,

"Hey, I know you! Your father is the pig farmer!"

"That's right." The tramp answered, "How did you recognise him?"

"His eyes." Said the coloured man.

"Wow!" Exclaimed the boy.

The Coloured waved 'good bye' and rode off.

I looked at the stranger, "He didn't ask for his money back when he recognised me nor did he ask me why I was dressed up as a tramp!"

"No, he gave it to me not you! Come."

The old tramp walked too fast for the boy to ask any more questions. Arriving at the gate to the Coloured's home he pulled a fat wallet out of his pocket. Counting out five thousand notes he stuffed them into the post box. He led the boy away from the little house. They stopped on the corner of the boy's home street. Touching the boy's shoulder the old tramp said,

"You are no longer 'the boy' you are your old self again. As I go may I say to you, never judge a man by his outward appearance. Look into his eyes. They are the windows of the soul. It is in his eyes that you will see the living person inside who carries the worldly burden of his outer self throughout his life here on earth. And you, my boy, live through your own tribulations with gladness in your heart for the burden you must carry is the very special task that has been specifically assigned to you in this world. And remember this! Your burden is individually designed to bring the fruits of certain truths into focus."

Laying his hand on my shoulder he whispered,

"Please don't forget to wash your face and change your clothes!"

They laughed!

XXXXXXX

BIRTHDAY!

It was New mother's birthday.

All her lady friends from the village came to our house bringing with them little bunches of flowers, little presents and little babies. When the babies cried the ladies talked louder and then the babies cried louder. It does not seem to be a good idea bringing little babies to big people's parties.

New mother laughed with her visitors as they ate syrupy 'koek sisters' and drank lots of red bush tea, but her eyes were sad. New father was in trouble. He always forgot New mother's birthday.

Today he went out very early to the farm without wishing her many happy returns!

The party faded. The afternoon passed and it was evening. The last glow of sunset shared the sky with the first glow of a full moon. It seems that people get led this way often, I mean, out of the old light into a new darkness, then back again into a new light. The visitors had all left. I waited on the steps for my New father to come home.

"I must tell him it is his wife's birthday before he goes inside!"

The call of doves settling down for the night reached out to lost souls.

I am not afraid of the dark – but I do love the light.

The knocking sound of New father's old diesel Land Rover brought a scramble of barking dogs from behind the house. The headlights swept away the special evening glow and the engine drowned the singing of the doves.

He was home.

Tired. Irritable. Uncompromising.

"New father?"

He grunted.

"It was New mother's birthday today!"

He swore. Staring at me he muttered,

"Thanks! I forgot."

Shrugging his shoulders he spat on the ground and walked up the steps. Looking back at me he said again,

"Thank you."

I stayed outside watching the shadows cast by the rising moon. The doves went to sleep. A far away jackal howled.

From inside the house came the rumble of controlled voices. Hers had a sort of whine to it, his, a refusal to be guilty.

At last New mother cried out,

"You wouldn't forget my birthday if you loved me!"

New father stormed out of the house. Thrusting his large body into the Land Rover, he slammed the door, crashed the gears and raced off into the night.

He slept at the farm manager's house.

For him it was a dark night.

New mother sobbed all night. She sobbed on the phone to her mother, to her sister and to her best friend. She sobbed in her pillow.

For her it was a dark night.

I knew nobody would miss me if I went for a walk in the moonlight and staying at the house with all that self-pity would dry me up inside. Riding out to the farm to be with my angry New father was not an option.

So I walked Dog out to the dumps.

They stood creamy white in the new moonlight like a living iceberg in a living sea. I decided to spend the night there.

Alone with Dog!

Reaching the highest level of the dumps I lay down on my belly and cradling my chin in my hands I soaked up the warmth of the sand under me and the cool of the night above.

Staring out at the world I thought about the problems of birthdays, about the problems of mothers and fathers, of men and women and kids.

"Of course, I said to the landscape stretched out in front of me, "they are all wrong. She uses his forgetfulness to manipulate him.

He uses her illogical comments to justify his anger at that which he refuses to understand.

What about me?"

The call of a nightjar drifted up to me.

"Please Lord - save my soul." It cried. His mate answered from open ground a long way off,

"Good lord - preserve us!"

Christmas beetles with high-pitched voices argued with frogs with low grumbling voices.

"Sounds like my new parents." I thought, "I may as well have stayed at home! At least I understood their language. Hey! Maybe if I listen I can hear what the crickets and frogs are saying to each other - after all I understood the night jars!"

Listening to all the sounds of the night stilled my senses.

I drifted into a deep sleep.

"Hello!" Someone called out.

I must be dreaming.

"Hello there, can you hear me?"

"Yes" I mumbled, just a little bit irritated. "Who is it? What do you want?"

"I am father Christmas." The voice boomed. "Ho, ho, ho!"

"I don't need you," I said, "I know you are not real, I'm not a little kid any more!"

"Aha" a squeaky voice said "I am the tooth fairy that puts money in your shoes at night in payment for your baby teeth when they fall out."

"Ha! You don't know me," a gurgling voice laughed, "I am the bath plug 'Gogga' that makes sure you don't stay too long in the bath. You can't say I am not real. You hear me gurgling every time you pull the plug out!"

I shouted,

"The noise coming from the plug hole is only the sound of the water draining away!"

A moment of quiet was broken by,

"What about me? I am superman! I can fly. I catch all the bad guys in the world. You want me to put a stop to all these voices?"

"Please," I whined, "you are all nothing. Not one of you is real."

I twisted this way and that in my despair,

"It's all lies." I shouted, "You make people demand special attention for nebulous nothings created by the manipulative minds of control freaks. You make others guilty of things that they should not be guilty of. You don't exist."

"Hey! That was good!" I thought to myself, "I never knew I could use such big words."

The night breeze rustled leaves in the trees below.

Again I spoke out loud,

"All of you! Go away! I used to believe in you. Lies! All lies. New father is right!"

The nightjar called. His mate did not answer.

"Hello there." A new voice murmured!

"This is crazy!" I bellowed, "What can I do to stop all this nonsense? Oh no! Please! No! Whoever you are," I begged, "get lost! I know you are not real. You are someone's insane story. Just go away!"

"Whatever you want," the voice replied ever so quietly, "but I ask you to remember that it was you who told me to go away. By the way, my name is Jesus."

Clouds built up in the east. Lightning flashed through them. They were still too far away for me to hear the thunder, but by morning time, it would surely rain a deluge of tears.

XXXXXXX

THE LION OR THE DOG

The lady was watching me. I knew her. She was the widow living across the street from the Happy Hand Clapper's Church. She had a very large garden and a big house set back over an open lawn. People said she was a very strong Christian.

She beckoned to me,

"Come."

I walked across to her. She smiled, saying,

"I need your help!"

"Me?"

"Yes, I had a dream last night and it involved you and your big dog."

"Oh! How can I help?"

"Have you got time to listen to my story?"

I remembered the Stranger talking about all people having problems.

"Yes."

She led the way to her house, up the steps, through the front doors, through the hall and into her kitchen.

"Please sit while I get you a cool drink."

I sat on the edge of a kitchen chair. She passed me a glass of mango juice and took a seat on the chair opposite me.

I sipped my drink.

She smiled again. She looked worried.

"As I said," she spoke quietly, "I had a dream last night, almost a nightmare! You ready to listen?"

"Yes."

"In the dream I was sitting out on my porch and people were bringing their dogs to me so that I could give the dogs injections to keep them alive.

You brought your big dog. Everybody was afraid of it. I knew you and although I was not afraid I was concerned for all the little ones waiting for their daily injections. You told us to not be frightened of your dog but rather to be afraid of the lion.

I asked you what you meant. You said that your dog was not really very big, just bigger than those belonging to other people. You offered to take me to see something worth worrying about.

Big enough to be afraid of!

You and your dog led me deep into a forest laced by streams. The further into the wood we walked the bigger the trees and the wider the streams. It was very quiet and very beautiful! At the foot of a steep hill you stopped and showed me a strong fence made out of wooden poles set very close together. I could see between the poles but could not walk through. You told me to stay there and watch. You said that when I began to see what was on the other side of the fence I must decide whether to wait for you to come back or to break down the fence and follow you.

You walked through the fence as if it was not there. Your dog stayed with me. All the other peoples little dogs were crowding around yapping and whining. I watched you looking into the scrub and trees around you. There was a lion lying in the shade at the edge of a clearing. When you saw him you walked up to it. The lion stood up, black mane flying, eyes gleaming with a deep burning fire. You put your hand out to the lion. It raised a paw. You stood together like that for a full minute. I was terrified of the lion. I prayed the fence would not fall apart.

You turned to me saying,

"Come!"

The dream ended.

She paused, holding her arms tight around her chest she said,

"I know you can tell me what it is all about because you took me there!"

Tears wet her eyelashes.

"Please."

I sat up straight,

"I know someone who can tell you!"

"Who?"

"The Stranger!"

"No please," she begged, "you tell me."

"Well," I muttered, "I can only say what I think."

"Oh yes, you do that."

"Okay! First, those little dogs the people brought to you! They are the beliefs that people have about themselves, their politics and their God. They are the dogmas of your religion, the dogmas of your own church and your political beliefs. They form the basis of the social contract that people make with themselves and their community. They include both the truth and the lies that people use to avoid painful change.

You need to believe that what your community or church or government teaches is the truth. You want to believe that the teachings that separate you and your church from other churches and from other people are scripturally correct. You think you and your fellow church members are the chosen few who really 'Know that you know that you know!'

To keep these dogmas alive in your heart and mind and in those of the people who brought their dogs to you, you injected their dogs with your acceptance and thereby hid their wrongness. You wanted to belong to your community because you were afraid to be a reject and live alone and of course they wanted you to be with them.

When I brought a bigger dog you were all afraid that it would attack your little dogs and reveal their weaknesses.

The Stranger once told me that people see everything through a dark mirror. That is how we see things in this world - darkly and back to front. Dogs are so full of love that even when we treat them abominably they still love us and come back for more. Think of dogs as 'manifestations' of God's love for us. We hurt God continually, but he is always there for us.

Dog, spelt back to front as in a mirror, is God.

In other words the little dogs you kept alive were other people's little Gods, which they held up to themselves and to others as 'the truth'. Even though my big dog might be closer to the truth than the others, he is still only my perspective of the truth.

In your dream we went together into the trees and water and mountains of God's purpose. The fence was the final barrier between you and the truth. My dog had flaws and could not go through. You saw me as a child in God's eyes so I had no problem with it.

The fence is your own. You erected it! It stands between what you want to believe and the truth. When you saw me on the other side of the fence with the lion and knew I was safe you still had doubts about your own understanding. All the little dogs were at your feet begging you to remember them or they would cease to exist as all misconceptions eventually do! The lion on the other side of the fence represented the real truth.

You must now decide what you want to do when you go back to the world. Will you stay on your side of the fence with the world or will you break the fence down and set yourself free? The truth, which in your case is called 'The Christ' - will bring you trial and tribulation as the world and all the followers of the lie known as the counterfeit Christ attack you for exposing them. Your community will ostracise you and this is what you are most afraid of.

Now must you choose the Lion of God, or little yapping dogs."

We sat quietly at her kitchen table.

Eventually she spoke.

"I think you have answered my question and I thank you." She paused, "By the way, who is this stranger you mentioned?"

"I don't really know. He comes to me when I need direction. He helps me. You might say he is the one who teaches me what I should hold onto and what I should throw away!"

"How does he do that?"

"By leading me into experiencing both sides of the story before I choose. He knows we cannot choose without full experience of all the aspects affecting our choice. It seems he knows what we 'do not know'."

"I would like to meet him."

"You already have."

"Oh?"

"You did not recognise him for what he is and that is why he is still a perfect stranger to you."

XXXXXXX

THE BIG DEAL MANIPULATORS

We were drawing pictures in the sand - with our fingers.

As we concentrated on our drawings the world around us seemed to retreat until our surroundings disappeared and all we could see were the pictures at our feet.

"Why do we have to go to school?" My friend asked.

"Because!"

"That's no answer."

"That's the answer they give us, the ones who make us go to school."

"They say it's to get educated. If you have no education you won't get a decent job."

"My friend says it's for 'them' to get control over us."

"What friend?"

"The Stranger."

"Oh! And who is 'Them' and how do 'Them' get control?"

"Them, is those who claim to know! How, is first they make you fit in and in order to do that you have to conform to their ideas of what is right and wrong. Then you have to perform - you have to do what they tell you to do. You can't pass their exams if you give your own answers! You have to give them the answers they want and those are of course 'their answers!' it doesn't matter if their answer is right or wrong, you won't pass if you don't give them 'their answer.'"

"That's sick!'

"Yes, and then they force you to become a part of their society like they did in the old days when 'them' said the world was flat and 'them' tortured and burnt to death anyone who said it was round."

"Yeah! I heard the other day that some people in the jungle hate us because we bury our parents when they die. They say we all came out of our parents so they honour their parents by taking them back into themselves - when they die they eat them! To them we are barbaric because we dishonour our parents when we bury or burn ours! Who is right, them, or, us?"

"Depends on your perspective. Maybe that's why they send us to school so we never develop our own perspective. That way we will always walk in their shadows and we will always conform and be easy to control."

"I hate school."

"What are you drawing?"

"Freedom."

"How do you draw freedom?"

"By leaving out everything that prevents you from being free!"

"Like?"

"Well you leave out duty, you leave out obligation and the demands of other people. You leave out everything that others expect of you."

"That leaves nothing!"

"No. That leaves you the freedom to do what you want to do."

"Selfish!"

My friend grinned at me,

"Could be," he said, "but doing things in your own best interest is in fact selfish and if your right to be selfish is balanced by the obligation to allow other people the same right, it works!"

"So you are saying it is in your own selfish interest to search for the truth? Then it must be the truth that to do everything in your best interest is in reality just pure selfishness?"

"You got it! It is a fact that to be free you have to do only what you want to do and never do what others demand you do."

"That's real heavy. What about the obligations?"

"Yes! Yes! Obviously there must be a balance for it to work! Morality says you should not take your gain at someone else's pain. Some people do right and some do wrong. Freedom allows for both! Each one bears its own reward or punishment."

"Makes sense. Next question! Where does the desire to do good or to do bad come from?"

"All good questions have a simple answer."

"And that is?"

"Everything is connected to or part of what we call creation and as the sum total of any concept is greater than its parts then must creation also be greater than any of its parts! It follows that if you believe in a Creator God then the personality of that Creator God is either greater than or at least equal to the all of everything and obviously nothing can happen without His sanction! So your question 'where does the desire come from' is answered by the fact that each one of us is preordained to have a desire to either accept or reject! There is a biblical statement which reads, 'and those who were so ordained, believed!'"

We sat silent for a long time.

He broke the silence.

"Can you go against this personality called God? Can you decide to not do whatever He leads you into doing?"

"Yes of course, but you must not be surprised if you fail and then yes again, if you decide to go against something it could be that it is because God put it in your heart to do just that. The stranger told me that each and every person is 'ordained' to be what he is meant to be so predetermining him to be and do exactly what he is meant to and to react exactly as he is meant to react! So relax my friend, you are being you as you were designed to be! You must learn to accept where this fundamental inherent perspective leads you and fight against accepting or bowing down to man's interpretation of what you should or should not be or do!"

"Getting complicated!"

"Okay, if you find that in your heart you want to do something, do it!"

"Otherwise you fail?"

"No you don't fail! The decision to do it is what counts. If a particular religion is the path you have been set on then that is the path you have to take! When you join a Church remember that every Church thinks differently, every member thinks differently and you think differently so the reason why you should join is that you all have a desire to meet with The Christ or the Buddha or the Prophet or whoever. That is what holds you together. The purpose in this is that every perspective, especially your own, has to be proven right or wrong."

"So then," he said, "if you get to God by wanting to, it follows that if you want to do something because it is in your heart to do it and you do it, then you are free. If you do it because you are obliged to, you are not free. Is that it? Is that what you are getting at? Is that the truth?"

"Almost! But you are mixing it all up again. Simply put, a way of seeing who God is could be said to be that God is truth and wanting God is wanting truth and it is that very truth that sets you free."

"You didn't answer my question! Free from what?"

"Free from customs, politics, social mores, religions, free from all the things that are based on man's tradition of following mans interpretation of the rules to get you somewhere that someone else said you ought to get to in order for you to be acceptable and that destroys the essence of selfishness! I say you should do it because of who you are and not because of what others say you should be. Everyone has a mental block to seeing certain things while at the same time everyone also has a split in the curtain of their minds through which they can see their own relevant part of reality.

That split can be opened wider by being your self whereas the split is closed and the mental block strengthened by accepting the impositions of other people!"

We kept silence again.

Then he said,

"Any idea how you overcome the problem of being led by a mixture of your own makeup and other peoples perspectives?"

"Well maybe one way is to be what they call 'born again'! It could be that in being born again you die to all the genetic rubbish that you inherited from your fore fathers, all the lies you have been led to believe in your life and all the wrongs you have done!"

"I think you could be right! Is it possible you can also do it yourself? If you open your understanding and so lose some of the blind spots in your mind by simply coming to accept that they are there, will they fade away?"

"Maybe, but then you have to understand rather than know and so not be like most people who claim to be right because they are deluded into knowing that they are!"

"So you think it is possible to change just by deciding to? What about what you said regarding you being stuck with your inherited genetic or God given nature?"

I leapt to my feet. Kicked sand all over my picture and shouted at the sky.

"Obey your own nature when it leads you to decide and not the rules of your society. It only counts if you are an atheist or follow Jesus or Mahomet or the Buddha because you want to! You can't follow any of them with any real degree of success if you do it because you've been taught that it is a good idea or because it is the religion of your community. Everything you do must come from your innermost natural desire to do it and the same with everything you do not do. Why is it that those who claim they know all about everything do not tell you that? Damn them!"

"No my friend." he pleaded, "That's wrong! If you damn them you are doing just what they do! You are demanding that they do what you expect of them and not what is in their hearts to do. You are trying to control them. Oh yes you are! Out of your desire to be free you deny their freedom. You justify damning them and you put them in chains or go to war against them and sometimes you even torture and crucify them."

He took a deep breath,

"To be truly free you have to allow others to be free. Then you can live free regardless of the circumstances you find yourself in. Yes! You should refuse to walk in the shadows of other people but what is just as important or even more important is that you do not demand they walk in yours!"

"Big words! Easy to say but hard to do!"

"Too true, come on, race you home."

XXXXXXX

EYE WITNESS

The Stranger asked me if I had ever gone hunting.

"Once!" I said.

He looked deep into my eyes,

"Are you free to meet me at the café' tomorrow afternoon to tell me about it?"

"Sure!"

xxxxxxx

The Stranger ordered cool drinks,

"Ok, tell me about the hunting."

"Well it was when I was about fourteen years old. As you know, just about everyone in our village goes hunting except my family.

One day, when my parents were away, I decided to go out to the farm and try. I wanted to find out if I would enjoy hunting.

So I took my new father's old .303 ex army rifle out of the gun cupboard. I cleaned the oil out of the barrel with a rod and checked the breach loading mechanism. The magazine was full of soft nosed bullets. I called Dog and we set off for the farm in the old Land Rover.

There are numerous duiker, impala, small buck and kudu in the hills and bush on the far side of the farm.

I drove as far as we could along a fence road and left the Land Rover under a shady Marula tree. Dog and I crawled through the fence into thick bush. He is well trained - he seemed to know we were doing something needing quiet and stealth and walked obediently at heel.

The bush was starting to dry out as the summer died. The leaves golden red and the grass pale yellow, the ground brown, cracked and dusty. It was hard to see animals of the same colour as they rested in the midday shade.

We climbed the first small hill. Boulders stuck out of it like sore thumbs. Scrub thorn clung to the steep sides. I realised we were making too much noise to surprise any wildlife so we crawled back down into a small valley covered in stunted thorn trees and Mopani bush. I found a place to sit as in an ambush. Dog lay at my side, still but alert!

Mopani flies ruled the air. They settled all over me. I twitched and wriggled but I could not slap at them, as it would warn game of my presence.

We waited.

Scuffling drew my attention. A young male duiker was making its slow way through the tangled undergrowth towards me. Carefully and slowly I raised the rifle to my shoulder. Quietly releasing the safety catch, I drew a deep breath and took aim.

The duiker stopped. It looked in my direction. No more than twenty feet separated us. I could see the hairs on and around his nose. Dog held his breath. I pinpointed a spot in the middle of the duiker's forehead. It took an inquiring step towards me. Something made me wait. The duiker looked puzzled. I found myself looking deep into its innocent eyes. Slowly I let my breath out then drew in another long, slow, deep breath. The duiker was staring at me. It could see me! It lifted its head up - horns short and sharp - nose held down, forehead high. Staring at me! I saw the soul of the duiker in those warm loving eyes.

I removed my finger from the trigger.

Resetting the safety catch I lowered the gun and relaxed.

The duiker, knowing it was safe, gave a soft snort, turned aside and ambled off!

Now I know why New Father does not hunt!"

I looked at the stranger,

"Will I ever be able to shoot an animal?"

"Well," he murmured, "I congratulate you. Most people love to hunt and to kill. They do it for pleasure. I remember an American game hunter saying he had seen this beautiful Koedoe bull standing proud against a backdrop of lovely green bush and he couldn't wait to get it in his sights! Sad! Of course sometimes you may have to shoot an animal for food or safety or to put it out of its misery." He looked into the distance, "Oh well! Enough of that! Would you like to try clay pigeon shooting?"

"Shoot pigeons, I thought you said killing for pleasure is not your scene!"

He laughed,

"No, no! Clay pigeons are not alive, they are made of clay and don't even look like pigeons. Come with me this weekend and I will introduce you to a new sport!"

XXXXXXX

SHOW ME

There was a programme on TV about healing.

I saw the healing of the sick, the lame and the weary! Sometimes even the lazy!

Amongst the healers and those seeking healing were many different kinds of people, many different faiths and many different nationalities. Yet they all either healed or were healed.

There seemed to be one common factor, one constant - in nearly every case it worked! So where did the ability come from?

I looked at my hands. If others could do it! Why not me?

I tried to remember everything I had seen on the programme. It did not seem to matter what they claimed as the source of their power. What did seem to matter was the belief that they could do it. They put their faith into practice. Some only tried to heal the believers belonging to their own religion. Others healed only those who had faith in the healer himself. A few healed regardless.

Our Church Pastor said if you healed people in the power of Christ, it was okay, but if you did it in any other power it was the devils work.

I asked him what about the people before Christ and what about the people now who had never heard of Christ.

He became angry.

"You are being contentious." He said and walked away.

I asked one of the Sunday school teachers

"Which is right? To do something wrong when you believe in the Christ you have been taught about, or to do something right having never heard about Christ."

She looked stern and muttered,

"Why are you always so difficult?"

I asked a visiting Preacher,

"Is it better to help someone in trouble, like heal them, or is it better to not help them?"

"What do you mean boy?" He asked pleasantly.

"I mean, which is more important to help someone regardless of either who they are or who you are, or is it more important to help them only if they fit?"

"I still don't really understand your question boy. Are you trying to trick me?"

"Would trying to trick you in Christ be ok? Would, not tricking you without Christ be wrong?"

"That's enough boy. Be on your way, I have better things to do than argue with an impudent kid."

I tried one more man, the second hand car dealer on Luke Street.

"What is right and what is wrong?"

He laughed,

"The customer is always right!"

He saw I was serious.

"Okay." he answered, "If it is true that everything that was made, was made by God, then obviously nothing happens without God's permission. So everything that seems to be wrong in this world is actually right in the same way as is everything that seems to be right is also right! But maybe I am wrong!"

"What?"

"If I am wrong then I am right! Depends on how you look at it, from the world's point of view or from God's. The truth is everything God made is perfect and therefore right because the concept of God is such that it does not allow for Him to make a mistake.

What I mean is that God, being God, knows exactly what He is doing and therefore He cannot make a mistake! See what I am getting at?"

"Yes."

"Well then, if God made man, it was not a mistake! If He made animals it was not a mistake and so on, agree!"

"Yes."

"Well then, he was right when he made the angel Lucifer who

became the devil! God knew what He was doing and what Lucifer would do! Also when He made Judas Iscariot and Moses and the Pharaoh and Jesus and when He programmed the whole of creation and the generations of man and so on and on and on!

In fact when He made everything!

He is even reported in the Bible to have said that He made both the darkness and the light, both good and evil! There is a saying 'Sufficient unto the day is the evil thereof!' So obviously everything works to His purpose regardless."

"So what you say is that whether you do it in Christ or not, it is neither right nor wrong?"

"No. I say that if you are drawn by God to Christ then you belong to Christ and whatever you do, you must do it in Christ. Likewise, if you are drawn, by God to Muhammed then you belong to Muhammed and so you do everything in Muhammed. The Muslims have a prayer. It goes like this – "Thank you God for making me a Moslem!" You can't argue with that can you? Especially when both religions refer to the same God of the Old Testament!

Finally, it is God who keeps most people's eyes, ears, and hearts closed or open to those things, which He so wishes to be fulfilled for His purpose! We have no say! It is God who opens or closes them when He wants to, not us!"

He looked closely at me.

"You know what!" he said, "If I admit I am wrong I have a good chance of learning what is right but if I insist that I am right I have very little chance of learning anything."

"Yes, you are so right!" I said.

He laughed,

"Brilliant! You gave the right answer!"

But I still did not have the answer I needed, even though the car sales man who was known as the biggest crook in town gave me the best answers so far. Maybe crooks have to think like that to balance their crookedness!

Oh well, maybe religious people also have to think differently to justify their religiosity!

I think that as long as you give credit to the source of the power in which you heal, whatever your understanding of that source may be, God, Christ, Mahomet, the spirit world or even if you believe it is your own 'inner self', your search for the truth can begin to bear fruit.

And healing?

I must try. Why not? If I don't try, I will never know.

XXXXXXX

THE DAY I TRIED!

I accompanied my mother when she went to see the eye specialist.

We sat together in the waiting room. It was crowded with people of all descriptions.

A man of about forty years of age was sitting three places from us. He was unbelievably thin. He was crying. The tears ran down his cheeks. He wiped them off with a damp handkerchief. He sat all huddled up and sad.

I thought about the healing programme. Feeling his pain, I decided that I had to try. Knowing nothing about how to do it, I quietly and without letting him or anyone else know what I was doing, offered him my energy. I certainly had plenty of that. My doctor said I had so much energy it burnt me up and made me tired. So I sat quietly thinking from the front of my head and from my heart - thinking the thought that he could take as much energy from me as he needed.

We sat there - my New Mother oblivious to what I was trying to do. A minute went by. Suddenly the man sat up straight, wiped his eyes and looked around the room. Slowly, he stood. He was so thin he had no buttocks. Then, again slowly and very carefully, he walked around the room.

He smiled, held his head up and began to walk faster.

There was a large poster on a wall. He stopped at it and leaning forward he read it - mouthing every word. Then he walked over to a large glass cabinet and stared at the ornaments inside. He stood there, enraptured.

Back again he walked to the poster where he read it a second time.

Turning, he looked around the room. A huge glowing cloud of soft golden light built up around him.

The sister called out his name.

He strode over to her grinning from ear to ear. Startled she led him into the surgery.

She shut the door.

A few moments later I heard loud, happy laughter.

Wow!

It works!

XXXXXXX

THE RING AND I

Sometimes your parents don't know as much about you as they would have you believe. I was tall, thin and a bit gawky. My New Father was large, strong and agile. He played all the hard sports except for tennis, squash and boxing. His name was written in gold on all the boards at the senior school. The youngest head boy ever! The youngest captain of rugby and cricket! Top of the class in his schoolwork! I could never hope to compete so I decided to take up the sports he never took part in like tennis, squash and boxing and the subjects he had no feeling for like art and acting!   I spoke to the Stranger about it. "Well!" He smiled, "I may be able to help you a little!"

"How?"

"Lets take boxing first – I have a few theories of my own. The first is based on the fact that your body is about three quarter's water!"

I grunted,

"Yes they told us that in biology class."

"You ever made a splash in water or made stones skip across water?"

"Yes. Why?"

"Well let's take the splash first. Imagine a bucket full of water. What way would you be better able to make a large splash in the water? Jabbing your finger into it or smacking it with the flat of your hand?"

"Smacking it with your open hand!"

"Yes! And how would you make a stone skip across the water?"

"By throwing it almost parallel to the water."

"Ok, so if the body is seventy six percent water then you would best hit it at ninety degrees with the flat of your hand. If you hit at an angle the force would bounce off the body, like the stone on the water. But straight on, all of the force would go deep into the body! So, if you hit straight on with the flat of your hand, you would deliver a jarring impact deep into the body!"

"Makes sense!"

"Next!" he said, "How do you make a whip crack?"

"Well, an ox whip has a wooden handle and attached to it is a long lash made out of hide with a short thin string like piece at the end. You swing the handle up and back, behind yourself, in an arc dragging the lash and string behind you and then as the handle gets to the end of its backward swing you throw it forward to the front pointing it at the place you want the whip to crack. The lash snakes out in front of you in the direction of your swing and then just as the string gets to the end of its length, you snap the handle back and the string at the end goes into a wild whip lash and cracks loudly. Like the sound of a gunshot! Is that right?"

"Not bad. So the jerk back at the end of the movement accentuates the speed and energy of the string as it flows to the end of its length and it explodes with a force far greater than that with which you threw it out."

"Yes!"

"So the secret of how to use a whip is a combination of the way you start to throw and then the sudden pull back at the end of the throw!"

"Yes!"

"Well then, imagine your body as the handle of the whip, your arm as the lash and your hand as the thin end of the lash. Start your move with your right side of your body pulled back and your arm bent with the fist close to your chest. Twist your body forward and throw your fist out at the target like you would do with a whip. As the fist reaches its target snap it and your body back. The shock effect is magnified just like with the whip lash and strikes with a far greater smack than the conventional way of hitting.

But I suggest that if you need to hit someone outside of the boxing ring, keep your hand open and slap him using the same whiplash movement or hit him straight on with the butt of your palm and not your closed fist. This way you can have tremendous effect without causing permanent damage to the one you hit and remember to keep your body moving so as to be able to initiate another hit without hesitation.

Now you repeat what I said so I can see if you got the idea right."

"I must hit as if I am striking with a whip. So I start by moving my left foot towards the target. Then as my left foot comes to rest, I lean forward slightly with my left shoulder. I follow this movement with my right hip and leg and my right shoulder and I fling my right arm and fist out towards the target. I let the flow of the punch take direction and momentum from that first step forward. As my fist reaches the target strike point, I jerk my fist and arm and my right shoulder back. At the same time I use my hips and legs to exaggerate the return of the punch so that the snapping back of my hand develops a tremendous whip lash force just as it reaches its target. In other words, a snap reversal of the movement of your body into your hand and you will make a lightning flash hit with an immense amount of kinetic force more than trebled as a result of the swing back.

So! If you hit like you crack a whip, the power you create at the fist end will be many times greater than that of a direct punch and you will automatically bring your body back into position for the next hit!

Wow!" I grew excited,

"I must practice that!"

"Do so! Use a punch bag made out of a big flour bag filled with wet sand. When you have learnt to hit correctly the bag will burst. And remember, boxers are taught to follow through with their punches! That also works but not as well. If you move fast both on your feet and with whip like punches, no conventional boxer will ever get the best of you."

xxxxxxx

The day came when the punch bag burst!

I applied to join the school boxing team.

The instructor was sceptical.

"What makes you think you could ever feature as a boxer?" He asked.

"Try me!" I said.

"Well, maybe, but why?"

"I am tall for my weight and so I have a longer reach than my opponent. I move much faster than heavy guys. I have fantastic stamina. I love music. It will work!"

125

He laughed,

"What on earth has music to do with boxing?"

"I will develop a rhythm that confounds my opponent and my long reach combined with that rhythm will make me a winner!"

"And what rhythm could that be?"

"You will see!"

"Maybe!"

I started my training.

Three months later the school boxing championships were on. My new parents did not come! They were busy with something or other. One round in the ring and my opponent was running scared. Every time he threw a punch at me, I was out of his way and my follow up punch got him off balance because he could not reach me with his short arms. Every time he ducked I came in with an upper cut. I danced around him throwing fast and furious whiplash strikes till he cowered in a corner. The tears ran down his face. I could not bring myself to hit him anymore. I put my hand out to him. He cringed and sobbed out a desperate plea. I stepped back and turned away. The bell rang. The bout was awarded to me. The crowd clapped. It was the first time ever that a crowd approved of me. I saw the Stranger in the front row. He nodded his head and smiled.

That night New Father asked me how the boxing had gone.

"Not too bad." I said.

He did not enquire further. He looked a bit unhappy. Probably thought I had made a fool of myself. The next day he heard from other parents that I had done very well.

Surprisingly well.

New father was devastated. He had missed the match. He bought me a proper punch bag, set it up in a veranda doorway and held my hand tight when I said thanks. There was a lonely tear in his eye.

I took up tennis. My answer to competition was to fight to win without worrying who won in the end. I hit hard and fast. I served with the same whiplash movement I had learnt from the Stranger. I won.

I took up squash. What a wonderful energetic and individualistic game it is. I loved it. A whole new world opened to me.

And best of all - New father changed a lot in the way he shared with me.

XXXXXXX

THE STRAY DOG

I wake up startled! Almost drowned by the drumming of rain on the roof I hear something? I listen.

Far away the rumble of a heavy truck. Its exhaust brake's echo the rhythm of changing gears. Near by a fruity snore - sleeping family unaware of the world around them! Safe in their unknowing?

It is a cold, wet, dark night.

I track down my memory, listening for recent reactions. Yes, a soft sad sound.

Weeping? Whimpering? Begging?

Quietly I creep out of bed, drape a towel around my waist and shoe-less I move from dark window to dark window, listening.

At the front door I hear it again.

Desperate.

Dog twists his head and raises his ears.

I take him into the bedroom and shut the door.

Back in the sitting room I kneel at the gap between door and post, I hear a sniff.

Dangerous? No!

A curious urge fills me. Reaching for the keys I unlock the door and quietly, slowly, I open it. In the faint glow of night I see a thin, wet, emaciated dog lying on the steps.

Careful not to frighten it I place my hand on its head, gently enough for the dog to not over react to the touch, firm enough to give him hope.

My eyes burn with emotion, my stomach tightens. I stroke his head. The dog sigh's a long drawn out sigh.

Reaching across him with my free hand I take hold of the skin around his neck.

I murmur "Hello dog." His eyes open and startled he struggles to get upright but is too weak. Realising his disadvantage he collapses against my knee. I half carry, half drag the dog into the kitchen.

Although emaciated, he is a big dog and very heavy. Shutting the door with my foot, I reach for the light switch. I turn the heater on then sitting down next to him I stroke his head. My hand touches something sharp behind his ear - the frayed end of a wire snare. I bend the snare end straight and slip it out of its loop. The dog cringes from the pain but, keeping his eye on me, lies still.

Congealed blood and torn skin hold the loosened snare in his fur. I cut the hair with bathroom scissors and remove the wire.

Hundreds of ticks suck at his emaciated body. I feed the dog, warm his body, pull as many of the ticks off as I can find and give him a small mattress to sleep on.

His eyes, full of gratitude, follow me around the room. The tip of his tail twitches back and forth sending out signals of love. The truth of what many people say about dogs understanding people and knowing what you are thinking suddenly becomes very clear to me. I hope I learn to understand dogs and so get to know what they are thinking!

Covering him with a blanket, I sprawl out in a chair drawn up next to him and with my hand on his head I fall asleep.

I wake early in the morning long before any of the others come into the room. Looking at the dog I see his one eye open, staring at me. His eye pours out a torrent of love.

I lean across and gently stroke him. His body stiffens. His eye loses its personality. He dies.

XXXXXXX

GIVE ME LOVE

"Give me love." There is a song says that.

What is love? A song!

Or maybe its flat-topped trees carpeting a crimson horizon or cattle being herded home raising dust clouds into a purple sunset.

Or, a small boy bouncing stones across still water.

xxxxxxx.

Our neighbours have a beautiful garden. We often share a quiet evening on their lawn sipping 'sun-downers' together. This evening the soulful thrumming of a guitar harmonises with the gentle crooning of a young man. The girl sitting at his feet looking sideways at him swings her hair out in an arc of yellow gold.

They share a secret smile.

Young love.

The boy's parents touch fingers and remember. Old friends. New friends. Times together. Times apart. Soul mates.

Mature love.

Two cats mingle purrs and kisses and become one.

The stretched out Great Dane raises a lazy eye brow.

What is love? It seems to make men do both great and small things. Do both good and bad. I walked out and away from their house listening to the sound of the guitar as it faded into the night sounds.

A cow calls its calf. Dogs bark. Darkness encroaches and the road loses its colour becoming a strip of lighter darkness. I look to one side of the shapes forming out of the night. An old man who was a spitfire pilot in the second world-war taught me how to see in the dark. He said that in the day you look straight at an object but at night you look slightly to one side and you can see the object better.

It seems your eyes are everything! They are windows into and out of your very being. The windows of your soul! Just like the Stranger's eyes!

He knows the meaning of love.

xxxxxxx

I walked far into the night.

I suppose when you have love you do not walk alone. I have seen love, seen the sharing, the togetherness, but not often! Mostly it seems there is no sharing, only taking. People say they have a right to be loved and cared for.

They demand love. They don't give it.

Too expensive!

Only dogs can afford to give unconditional love. They have everything to gain and nothing to lose! Do I have anything to lose?

I stopped walking at the cross roads and leant against the stop sign listening to the night and watching the half moon slip behind tall gum trees.

A gentle snoring prodded my senses. It came from bushes on the other side of the main road. I listened - probably some bum - a beggar - a 'drop-out'.

"Be careful of strangers!" my New Mother had warned me, "You could lose your life. You can't trust anyone that you don't know and even some that you do know! It is no longer safe to walk alone at night."

The snoring faltered. A cough and then movement!

I thought about my question 'what is love?'

The man coughed again. At least it sounded like a man - could it be a woman?

Ok, I had nothing to lose, or did I?

There is a song called, 'A stranger's just a friend you do not know!'

I walked over. A red 'Volks Wagen' beach buggy was parked behind some bushes. The snoring came from the open window.

"Hey," I called "you okay?"

The snoring stopped. The man in the front seat pulled his hat away from his eyes, raising his head he said,

"Hi there!"

He smiled.

Startled, I stepped back.

He stretched.

"Nice to see you!" He said, "You going to sit with me for a while."

I hesitated then sat on a large stone a little to one side. Not too close, not too far!

The man laughed.

"You know me?" I asked.

"Yes." He said.

We sat silent for a while.

"Who are you?" I asked.

The man leant forward and taking off his hat turned to face me. A large chiselled nose reflected a glimmer of moonlight.

The Stranger sat there before me - not as I remembered him - for now he looked tired. Worn out - alone!

"What happened?" I asked.

Softly he replied,

"Not only is it the son of man who has no where to lay his head, sometimes his friend also! The place I usually stay at is no longer open to me!"

I thought about that.

"That may be so," I agreed "but the friend of the friend of the son of man does have a place. Come home with me. You can sleep in my room. There is an en-suite bath room and food in the fridge." Leaning towards him I said 'come'."

"Hold on," he said, "let me unlock the passenger door for you."

On the way back to my home I asked,

"How do you always know where I am? How do you know what I am thinking?"

"The ability to know is latent in all of us. Some of us are blessed by having that ability brought to the surface. I told you a little about it when you asked me how we could speak to each other even when separated by distance. Some call it a 'discerning spirit' others call it intuition or Meta Physics. "It is the ability to see and to reach out beyond yourself!"

"Oh! May I ask you a personal question?"

"Go ahead."

"You said you had a family?"

"Yes but I lost my family a long time ago."

"You miss them?"

"Very much! I did find my children but too late, they have been blessed with wonderful new families. I love them too much to destroy what they now have so I limit my contact with them."

"And your wife?"

"She disappeared shortly after giving birth to the last baby."

"Sorry!"

"Yes!"

We arrived at the house. I ran a bath for him. He took a clean set of clothing out of his suitcase. I brought some supper - set it on the bedside table - wished him good night and went to sleep with Dog on the couch in the sitting room.

The morning dawned full of promise. More birds than usual! More sunlight! More hope! I stood at the window and raising my arms above my head I stretched to the ceiling.

The kettle boiled and I made tea for my new parents, for myself and for the stranger.

He was not in my room.

The bed had been remade with clean linen from the cupboard. A note lay on the pillow. I read it.

"Now we both know what love is! Thank you!"

I shut my eyes, tight.

"Yes!" I whispered, "Now I know what love is."

XXXXXXX

COUSINS

My New Mother's older sister is married to my New Father's elder brother. They live at their safari camp in another country far to the north of us called Caprivi. They also have an adopted son. He is about five years older than I am.

I asked my new mother why she and her sister had both adopted children. Why did they not have children of their own? She sat me on the couch and holding my hands in hers she explained.

"My sister and I had a brother. He died when he was still a teenager. He was born with a serious problem. His blood could not clot. He was a 'bleeder'. He went out with his dog one day and a stray dog attacked his dog. My brother fought off the other dog. He was badly bitten. He bled to death.

The condition he had is called haemophilia. It is passed on from generation to generation through the mother to the male children. My sister and I both decided we should not risk having children. Our husbands agreed. So my sister adopted Ian from an orphanage when he was six years old. He was so traumatised when he was put into the orphanage that he could not remember anything of his life up till then. They live far from civilisation and schools and because of Ian's problem and because he is so precious to them, they have educated him through home schooling.

Ian is a very special boy living a very unusual life."

"Will I ever meet him?"

"Oh yes, they're coming down to spend a week with us over Christmas."

xxxxxxx

It is Christmas and my uncle and his family are here. My uncle has black hair and looks angry - even when he laughs! When he talks to people he waves his right hand at them with his fingers stuck out like a bunch of hairy bananas. His wife loves him very much. She laughs a lot when he is around. She knows how soft he is inside his hard outside.

Ian is tall and very strong. He talks little but smiles much. I am fifteen years old and he is twenty. When he is with me he acts as if we are the same age.

On the last day of their holiday with us Ian and I went into town together. He was checking out the girls.

"No girls where I live!" He said.

"No neighbours?" I asked.

"Nearest with a family are a hundred and twenty kilometres away and they don't visit us. They don't like my father!"

People were gathering around the entrance to our church.

"What's going on there?" asked Ian.

"Dunno! Let's go see."

We sauntered up to the group, hands in our pockets smiles on our faces.

"Looks like a party, maybe we get to eat some cake if we join them." Ian joked.

Set under the trees, were circles of chairs facing a large table. On the far side of the chairs other tables sagged under tea, coffee and plates of eats.

"Wow!" exclaimed Ian.

Ian and I chose two chairs nearest the food table. We listened to visiting speakers from another town. The pastor stood up when their speeches and question time were over.

"On behalf of us all, I thank our visitors for coming so far today to talk and share their experiences with us." He smiled,

"Refreshments are on the tables, let us eat and meet and enjoy! Thank you."

Ian and I grinned at each other as we scrambled for the nearest table with cakes on it. People around us were laughing and talking about the meeting. Ian joined in. I listened.

Walking back home later that afternoon Ian said,

"It's amazing how different people are!"

"What do you mean?"

"Well if you take all the different cultures in the world and all the different people within each culture, the divergence of understanding is so great that you begin to wonder if we all live on the same planet. I was told that there are over two thousand different Christian churches. I mean different denominations and each one has its own different idea of what is the truth.

It seems that no one understands, let alone accepts, that there is not one single man alive who has any where near all the answers to what it is actually all about, yet everyone you speak to acts like he knows it all and he is not only 'so right' but he is also prepared to fight for his rightness! Yes fight! Sometimes to the extent of being prepared to kill others who dare to have a different opinion!"

Why can't they see that the amount of brainpower and experience needed to see even a small part of the whole picture is not available to anyone! If only they did see it, we could maybe have some real peace!"

I kept quiet. He spoke again, very quietly as if to himself,

"The people who we met today believe they are Christians!" He looked at me, "There are those in Christ who must be part of a church community and those in Christ who are outside of church communities and then there are those not of Christ, also both in and out of church communities!"

I decided it would be wiser to say nothing.

XXXXXXX

IT DEPENDS WHO DID IT!

I told Ian the story about what happened when I was a six-year old kid attending primary school.

xxxxxxx

I had a friend who loved to play with fire. He collected scraps of this and that which he compounded into ingredients for his fireballs. Some of them produced truly magnificent displays of colour and sound.

One day during tea break at school he and I made a hill out of sand and stone for our dinky cars to drive over.

My friend said.

"Lets make a volcano."

"How?"

"Dig a hole in the top of this hill and put a tin in it. Fill the tin with paraffin and old engine oil and squibs and little bits of wood chips and put a match to it."

We collected what we needed over the next two days.

At playtime on the third day he called the kids at school to come and watch our show.

When all was ready my friend told everyone to stand back. He struck a match and threw it into the tin.

The match flared and went out.

We poured paraffin over a cloth, wrapped it into a small ball, lit it and when it was burning well he dropped it into the tin.

A whisper of black smoke spiralled up.

Suddenly flames erupted from the volcano. We scattered as bits and pieces of burning cloth flew up to be carried away by the wind. A squib exploded and drops of burning oil and red wood chips spewed out.

Just like a real volcano.

Above the squeals of delight an anxious voice shouted as a teacher ran into the playground.

She was furious.

We ran for our lives.

My friend's father was angry.

"If you carry on playing with fire you will surely get burnt." He warned.

xxxxxxx

School closed over the public holidays.

On one such holiday I visited my friend. His father left us at home while he went to town to attend to some business.

"Now don't you play with fire," he warned, "or you will burn yourselves and remember, my office is out of bounds! You may not touch anything in it. If you disobey me you will surely regret it."

His father left. His office door was open. My friend darted into the office and brought out an old candle and some powder which he retrieved from one of the cupboards. Setting the candle on a saucer on the carpet in the living room he lit it and using a teaspoon he poured a pinch of the powder onto the flame.

A shower of coloured sparks flew up. Gleefully he poured more on.

"Your dad said not to play with fire!"

"Just one more time." He begged.

"He said not to go into the office."

"I know what is right and wrong in this house! I know what I am doing!"

"I am going home," I shouted, "I don't want to stay with you if you play with fire."

I left in a hurry, slamming the front door behind me.

At home I told my New Mother

"New mother," I said, "my friend is playing with fire and he is going to burn himself. His father told him not to go into the office but he went in and got powder for the fire. Please come quickly and help me stop him?"

"Let me finish the baking." She said.

Impatiently I waited.

Five minutes later we heard a siren wail. New mother looked out the window.

"Oh my God!" She cried.

We rushed out into the street. Heavy black smoke billowed up into the sky from the direction of my friend's house.

We ran.

The fire engine was showering the roof and windows of his house with water.

An ambulance screeched to a stop.

I never saw my friend again.

The police apprehended his father.

xxxxxxx

His father's case was brought to court. Nearly all the town's folk attended the hearing.

I had to be there also because I had been with him at the time and although I was far too young to testify, I was the only witness.

The father was ordered to swear on the bible. Standing in the witness box, he placed his hand on the Bible and said in a strong, clear voice.

"I swear to tell the truth, the whole truth and nothing but the truth!" he paused then added "In so far as I know it, so help me God!""

As I understood it, my friend's father was charged with culpable homicide or negligence leading to his son's death in that he left his young son alone in a locked house where all the makings necessary for playing with fire were readily available in the office, which he had left open.

He did this knowing of the problem his son had and what the consequences might be.

The prosecutor finished laying the charge.

"How does the defendant plead?" boomed the Judge.

The father, holding his head erect, squared his shoulders and said,

"The house was not locked your honour, I left the front door open, other than that, I plead guilty as charged!"

A murmur of surprise filled the courtroom.

The Judge hesitated, pursed his lips and holding his hands together, as if in prayer said,

"I observe no sign of remorse in the accused. The door was found closed and locked. I am therefore inclined to set the maximum penalty provided."

Again he paused, then, turning to the accused he asked,

"Do you have anything to say in mitigation?"

"Yes, your honour."

"Go ahead."

"Your honour, the proceedings today started with the court asking me to swear on the Bible provided by the court for that purpose." Pointing at the Bible lying on the desk he continued, "I see it is a King James Version."

The Judge nodded.

The father continued.

"Your honour! May I refer the court to one of the first stories in the bible, to be precise, chapters two and three of Genesis. I am sure you are well aware of the content of those two chapters, the bible being the basis on which the truth is evaluated by this court."

He paused.

"Please continue." Ordered the Judge.

"It tells the story of a Father who left His son in the home provided for him by the Father - the Garden of Eden. It tells of how the Father warned his son and the son's companion to the effect that they must not eat the fruit of a certain tree in the garden. If they disobeyed, the penalty would be that on the day they did eat of it they would surely die!

The Father then left the garden, presumably to attend to His business in heaven.

Thus they, the son and his lady friend, remained in the sanctuary of the garden - alone! Please note that the Father left the tree that He had planted in the garden, the one He had warned His son about, open and easily accessible to His son.

Further more, in this case, a talking snake was provided in the tree to tempt the son and His son's companion into the eating of the fruit of the tree.

So not only did the Father leave the two alone, He also set them up knowing they would be enticed into disobeying His commandment which as you know, they did!

We live with the consequences of this story even to this day.

My plea is this, if the court condemns the actions of the Father in the very Bible, which this court chose as a basis for truth to be sworn to then I accept the courts condemnation of my-self. If the court believes the Father in Genesis is guilty of culpable homicide and negligence and should be punished, then the court should do likewise to me and I will accept the courts punishment of my self.

But if the court does not find the Father in Genesis guilty, then I also cannot accept this court finding me guilty.

I do accept I am responsible for my actions, but I say that any wrong that I may have committed is negated by this court in that the court places its dependence of right and wrong on the Bible and God cannot be wrong or He would not be God. Because of this, your answer must be that, just as the Father in Genesis is neither wrong nor guilty, then nor am I!

I repeat. You cannot therefore in all honesty judge me contrary to the precedent so accepted by yourselves unless of course you decide to deny the truth of the matter and crucify me on the cross of your own misconceptions."

The father sat down.

Emotions broke me! I ran up to the judge and I reached out to take his hand. Sobbing, I cried out to him.

The officer of the court took me by the arm to lead me away.

The Judge waved him aside.

"What is it my boy?" He asked.

The courtroom fell silent.

"No, no, you got it wrong!" I sobbed, "When I slammed the front door shut, it locked by itself! It was my fault he could not get out! My friend's father left the door open. My friend loved his father! He loved him 'cause he let my friend learn, with guidance, by his own mistakes. My friend said his father loved him more than the whole world. Please Sir," I begged him, "his father did not kill him, he killed himself. He knew he would be burnt if he played with fire. You brought the wrong person to trial!"

Turning to my friend's father I blurted out,

"My friend said you gave him freedom. He said you were the 'best' dad ever. He said he loved you very, very much!"

The father bowed his head and wept.

xxxxxxx

The Judge sat silent for a full minute. Then, looking up at the father he said, very quietly,

"What you say is true, God makes no mistakes. He carries the full responsibility of all creation on His shoulders. His law to the effect that 'the penalty of sin is death!' cannot be subverted and He, God the father, being righteous, would not break that law.

In the bible you quoted from is the statement made by God 'I made both good and I made evil' therefore the payment for good and evil rests with God! He paid the prescribed penalty for evil through the death of His one and only begotten Son. Therefore God cannot be found guilty! But! He can be found responsible and He honours His responsibility to the fullest.

So, by your own declaration, must you accept your responsibility in this matter and with it the outcome!

Your admission of guilt is accepted.

Your plea has been heard and understood. The matter of the locked door has been resolved.

Sentence will be passed when court is reconvened tomorrow."

xxxxxxx

I remember leaving the courthouse in tears. I broke away from my new family and ran down the street.

I did not understand the judge. Why lay the pain of guilt on the bleeding stripes of loss. Why drag a man through hell when he has just come back from there.

I stopped in the shade of a pavement Jacaranda tree. The town council was destroying all the Jacaranda trees. They said they were an alien species. Were we, as colonials in Africa also alien to this land? Must we also be cut down?

"Hi." The Stranger stood at my side. "You look sad?"

"Why must the father pay?" I blurted out.

"It is always the father who must pay." He answered.

"But!" I shouted, "His son did not know that what he was doing would lead to all this."

"Exactly, but the father did know what he was doing. He gave his son the direction and freedom to do what the son would do. He gave him the open office. He knew the likely result. That is why he warned his son. It is the father who is responsible especially as the father had not adequately taught his son self discipline!"

"So now," I cried out "he must pay three times. He loses his son, he loses his good name then on top of all that he pays the penalty."

"Yes! Take it as a lesson about this country and the people who built it out of their inherent competency. Their ancestry is rooted in creative endeavour and they are what their parents were. They are responsible for what they create. But, after all this they, in fear of outside pressures, gave it away to people who by virtue of who they are and where they come from do not understand what they have been given and so will not be able to manage it because it is totally foreign to them!"

"You mean that if our country burns, if it collapses into anarchy like those to the north of us, it is the fault of those who built it then handed it over and not the fault of those who kill it?"

"Exactly."

"But the new government is educated! It is not like all the countries to the north."

"Understanding and education are two very different aspects. Knowledge does not imply understanding. You must accept that if these people were able to understand or desire the so called perspective of western civilisation and technology they would have long ago built up a politically strong, productive and highly technologically developed society themselves which our forefathers would never have been able to colonise!"

"So the responsibility for the collapse of Zimbabwe and South Africa into anarchy lies with the old regime and not the new?"

"That's right and think about this, Mugabe will never give in regardless of how wrong we think he may be or how far down the road to anarchy and destruction he appears to lead Zimbabwe whereas Ian Smith wilted like a wet lettuce leaf despite him having said that 'never in a thousand years' would he give in. He sent his own people to the bush war to fight and many to die but when the threat came too close to him for his own comfort, he gave in. Yes! He gave in to the British despite the fact that he led a country which was known as the breadbasket of Africa into warfare, corruption and collapse! It was not Rhodesia that submitted to the British imposition of sanctions and the British crazy perspective of democracy it was Smith and his cohorts. And because of this the members of the old Rhodesian regime will not only lose their sons and daughters, their homes and all they created here, but more important, they have given up on their integrity and will eventually be required to pay the final penalty."

"And the African people will suffer terribly!"

"Exactly! The British will never admit liability for the present chaos in Zimbabwe. But it was Britain who forced the country into its present predicament. Britain put in place, by force, the mechanisms which led to Mugabe gaining power and I bet that Britain will never acknowledge it or take responsibility for the result of their actions."

"True! Is it the same in Afghanistan and Iraq and Israel and many other helpless countries!"

"Yes! That's what it is all about!"

"By the way, you said they will have to pay the final penalty, just what is the final penalty?"

"What is the truth?"

"So that is why you say the father of my friend has to pay the penalty!"

XXXXXXX

YOU MUST WRITE

"You must write." A voice inside me said.

I was daydreaming and the words took me by surprise.

I had been thinking how little I knew about girls. When they do not say what they mean - you are supposed to guess what they mean. If you guess wrong, you are stupid. If you guess right, you are crazy!

Again the voice interrupted my thoughts.

"Write down what I tell you. Write what was before, what is now and what is to come!"

I looked around. There was no one there.

xxxxxxx

My English teacher said I would be a writer.

My art teacher said I would be an artist.

My new father said I would be a farmer.

My head master said I would be a nothing. I think he was right!

How can a nothing write something?

I sat down with a pencil and paper and decided to write a true story about a friend. I failed. The story was cold. Dead!

I tried again. I made up a story, fiction, about a friend I did not have. I failed. You could feel the lie in the story.

I left writing for a while.

xxxxxxx

There is a computer in our study. My new father said I could use it. It had two programmes on it, Microsoft word and the Bible. No games. No Internet. I enjoyed looking up the biblical verses used by our preacher in his sermons and I would search before and after the referred to verse to get its true meaning. Too often I found he seemed to have taken the meaning of the verse out of context – maybe to make it fit his own perception.

Do we all do that?

Today I sat before the computer. I had nothing to search for in the bible so I set up 'Microsoft word'.

What should I write about?

I remembered what the voice told me.

"Write what I tell you to write."

"Okay," I said, "I don't know who you are but I remember what you told me! Anyway, tell me again. Now! I am listening!"

The voice in my head said, "Only if you are nothing will you be able to write what I want you to write."

"Ok," I answered, "I accept I am nothing!"

So I punched an arbitrary letter onto the screen. It was the letter "I".

xxxxxxx

My New Father was shouting my name. He had been shouting for some time. Anger grew in his voice. Taking my eyes off the computer for a moment I looked around in amazement. The darkness of the room told me I had been sitting there for many hours.

Before me the computer vibrated with words. I saved the work and rushed out to look for New Father who had stormed outside in his search for me. We met on the back lawn. The light of his torch blinded me as he whispered,

"Where in the hell have you been?"

Shielding my eyes I whispered back,

"Writing."

"Oh!"

We walked back to the house together. Silent!

I have never seen his anger die so quickly.

In the kitchen he asked,

"Tea or coffee?"

"Coffee, please."

"You said 'writing'?"

"Yes."

148

"Excellent."

"Thank you."

"When you are ready, when it is finished, may I read it?"

"Yes"

"What are you writing?"

"I don't know!"

"Excellent!"

He smiled. The first real smile I ever saw him direct at me.

My eyes burnt.

Placing his hand on my shoulder, he said,

"Go for it!"

We drank our coffee in silence.

XXXXXXX

LIONS AND LAMBS

My new father's friends from America are on holiday in Africa. They spent three weeks with us. The week before they left new father took us all to the Kruger National Game Park. On our last evening at the park we were sitting around the camp table, our faces softened by candle light as the African night held us captive. The distant strumming of a guitar accompanied by soft singing synchronised with the rumbles of night predators - an orchestra of African sounds led by the haunting duet of the singer and a lonely nightjar.

The trip had been every tourist's daydream of Africa - hot and dusty, hard and brown. Memories of screaming elephant cavorting in green pools set about by giant riverine trees and of hippo performing as only hippo do! A camouflaged kudu standing proud in the grey barked scrub. A majestic fish eagle and then today, at sunset, a lion kill!

I became aware of the penetrating eyes of our friend's teenage daughter. I raised an eyebrow. She looked away. Her eyes were wet, her lips trembling as she stared into the night.

"Claire?" I asked.

"Yes?" She answered, quietly.

"What is it?"

Turning again to me she breathed a question,

"You saw it?"

"Yes." I answered, gently.

"What?" Her father asked.

"The buck."

"What buck my girl?"

"And the lion."

"Tell us." He whispered.

Eyes closed in tears. Fists clenched under the table. Head down. She whispered to me,

"My parents didn't see. They were too busy with themselves to see."

She hesitated, afraid of her emotions. Then, feeling her way round the words she looked up at her father saying,

"But I saw! While you watched the lions - I saw. You said they were proud kings of the beasts. Strong! Efficient! Yes! You watched as the females stalked that impala. You watched as the male lion sat there in his own glory - waiting for his due. You watched as the cubs learnt from their parents. You were excited and took photographs of them against the sunset. The action! The power! The short chase! The quick death! It took only one minuet for the impala to die. That's all, and I, oh yes, I was watching too! But I was not looking for thrills to justify the expense of coming to Africa.

I saw that you had the same look in your eyes as was in the eyes of the killer lioness. I saw you and mum nudging each other, whispering.

"This is real. This is nature in the raw. Man oh man what a sight. We are truly blessed to be a part of this."

I never knew what you meant when we arrived here and you said to me,

'Now my dear you will see for yourself the magnificence of Africa.' No, you never told me about your expectations or about your lusts and so I was free to see the truth of what happened. I don't think you really want to hear what I saw but you asked so I will tell you."

She paused, looked around the table, drew a hand across her eyes, then fastening a pain filled stare on me, she said,

"You said nothing!" She frowned, "Did you really see?"

"Yes!" I looked into her heart.

She wavered, then spoke on, eyes locked in mine,

"I saw the impala's eyes. She was pulling away from the lioness, but not to get away, no! She was looking back over her shoulder. Her eyes showed not fear but despair. She cried out, not in agony but in love. She struggled - not to get away. No. She struggled to look back. I followed her eyes back to a low bush at the edge of her vision. Through the moans, the roars and your animated voices I saw what it was that she was fastening her whole being on. A fawn! Her baby huddled under the bush with head stretched out towards its mother - echoing the pain of impending loss.

The mother seeing her fawn abandoned to hunger and exposure - seeing the waiting scavengers - imagining them chewing at her babies small living body - imagining its desperate aloneness, shuddered at the harsh unfeeling reality of death as the final answer to all things born into this world. She turned to look at you father! Yes you! While you manoeuvred for a better view I saw the mother cry out to you for help! Only you could save her baby, only you could save her! But please, her baby. In an agony of despair she again looked back at the fawn. It whimpered at the message in its mother's eyes. It tried to overcome its own fear sending a hopeless plea back as it watched its mother give everything of life to this last memory of her doomed baby. Lowering its head onto dead leaves the fawn cried for something that could never be. And you, my father, gushed out your appreciation of the spectacle of a lion living at the pain of a lesser animal. And you my mother! Awed by your husbands distorted perceptions of life, empty of any of your own, smiled your sweet smile and looking sideways at my friends new father, you soaked up the 'khaki fever' of macho men in Africa while the stench of hopelessness spilt as blood into that dust bowl of a living death. That is what I saw!"

The man with the guitar began to sing.

> There are many ways to live
> And many ways to die
> Many ways to tell the truth
> And many ways to lie
> Many ways to work
> And many ways to play
> Many ways to curse
> And many ways to pray
> The secret is to listen
> To the answer in the rain
> Remember in your quiet times
> That always is it the pain
> Which makes the hunter laugh
> And makes the lover cry
> That makes the gentle weep
> And makes the sadist high

A hippo sobbed deep in its belly.

XXXXXXX

INFINITY

Late winter. Early summer.

First thunderclouds challenge dry horizons.

Humid air sucks life from arid valleys. I sit with feet dangling over the edge of the cliff face watching distant shapes twist and turn, fade and grow as the heat haze tortures them.

Ballerinas dancing with nature!

The dumps are always different. I let the difference filter through my thoughts and wait for new understandings to grow.

Today, the hot damp air, heavy on the dry ground, is solid. It presses me down into the earth, beats at my face, pulls at my clothes drawing sweat as it fills me with its energy then sucking me dry again with its need.

Eyes barely open I search the ground way below me.

It seems I am sitting at the edge of the deepest precipice in the world and the world loses focus in my mind.

I imagine the Stranger resting at my side. He looks out over the distance to a place beyond the giant clouds.

"What do you see?" I ask.

"Distance!" he answers, "No matter how far you look in any direction you cannot see the beginning or the end of time or distance or space. This seems to confirm my perspective that infinity has no beginning or end but it also allows for the understanding that infinity for you and I is dependent on where we are and what we are! So it is that 'infinity' is in reality for us simply 'here and now.'"

"You saying that infinity of space, distance and time begins and ends with who, what and where I am?"

"Something like that, yes! And it is you that infinitely shares infinity!"

We share a moment of infinite silence.

He speaks again.

xxxxxxxx

FIRST GIRL FRIEND

You see love in some people's eyes!

In others you see only emptiness!

I fell in love.

She was beautiful.

Love grew inside me demanding recognition from the object of my love. Love drank all my energy, it gnawed at my soul.

I came alive only when my loved one took notice of me.

I died in her absence. I cried at night. Anger filled me when another boy caught her attention.

I hated her admirers.

She owed me!

xxxxxxx

I sat alone on the park bench. Waiting! What was keeping her? Why was she late?

Tension built up inside me. Wild thoughts chased through my mind tangling my emotions. Love seemed to be more pain than pleasure.

Stars crowded the dark sky.

Shadows filled the depths around me.

I felt the Stranger near.

I closed my eyes.

Distant music flowed in and out of my space.

"You alone?" he asked.

"You know I'm alone! Sorry! That was a bit too abrupt! Yes, I am alone. I'm waiting for her!"

"And?"

"She's late!"

"Why?"

"How can I know?"

"She not dancing to your drum beat?"

"What?"

"Do you dance to her drum beat?"

"What?"

"You behave as if she owes you. You impose your will on her because you love her! Must she live under your shadow? If you did not love her would she still owe you? It seems your love places obligations on her and she has to perform simply because you love her. Do you believe your emotions justify your right to control her?"

We sat together, sharing shooting stars.

I thought about what he said.

"What about you?" He asked, "What if a girl loves you? Would you have to suffer the same restrictions and demands from her as you impose on your girl? What if two girls loved you but you loved a third. Which one of you would have the right to control which other one? Would you be allowed to choose?"

"I would choose."

"If you have the right to choose then surely you must allow the one you love to have the right to choose as well?"

The night wind cooled the hot air.

The Stranger resting his head against a tree trunk shut his eyes as if in sleep. He murmured,

"I know of a man who found a diamond buried in soft soil in a beautiful green pasture. Sheep grazed the succulent grass. He dug up the diamond and took it to his home. To him the diamond was the most beautiful thing he had ever seen. He polished it, set it in gold and placed it in a frame on the middle of his desk.

He made it to be 'his' diamond.

One day, afraid that some one would steal his diamond, he hired a security firm to secure his premises. He locked the diamond in his office safe, which was guarded day and night. In no time at all he came to realise that having the diamond without being able to share it was very sad.

So he had a duplicate made, a counterfeit copy. He shared this with everyone around him showing it off at parties and in articles in the press. He even had an author write 'the story' of the diamond and allowed photographs of the duplicate diamond to be included in the author's book."

The Stranger chewed at the soft stem of a blade of grass.

"Then one day, money began to lose its value. They call it inflation. Everything the man had was valued in monetary terms. He decided to have an accurate and up to date re-evaluation done on all his properties and assets.

Especially his diamond!

The insurers found the original diamond had lost all of its value and the counterfeit diamond was now worth more than the original.

The man suffered a heart attack and died."

"What are you trying to tell me?"

"The diamond belonged in its field. The field of grass and trees! Sheep lived there. The field was a kingdom. The diamond was its king. The sheep were the King's subjects. The land gave the diamond its value and the diamond gave the land its value. If you separate them, take one part away and make it support your fantasies, you lose sight of its true value and you will end up losing both the diamond and the field, both the King and the Kingdom.

If you ever find a diamond of great value don't take it away from its rightful place, rather buy into the whole field and own the diamond by becoming part of the field - part of the Kingdom.

When you do find a girl to love, love her where you find her. Love her for what she is. Enjoy the love you have for her. Place no impositions on her. You should set her free in your love and let her follow you because of her own desire to do so. Never expect her to follow you because of your perceived rights over her."

The sound of running footsteps blew in with the wind.

Breathless, the girl halted at my feet - suddenly wary.

I laughed in pure delight.

No questions as to why she was late.

No demands thrusting out at her.

Standing up I reached out and placing my hands on her shoulders I whispered,

"You are so beautiful I would happily wait for you for ever!"

Glowing in her newfound freedom, she kissed me.

XXXXXXX

The Stranger says freedom is living in the realm of true love.

Truly, I love freedom.

XXXXXXX

WITHOUT ME
THERE IS NO BEACH

I am like a drop in the ocean. It is the infinite nature of the ocean that gives meaning to the drop that I am.

Without the ocean the drop that I am would evaporate as in a waterless desert and I would disappear as if I never was.

If I wish to survive I must from time to time immerse myself in the ocean so that when I surface I will find myself rejuvenated, washed, filtered, purified and filled once more with the perfection that is available only in that dimension which by its very nature is able to bring to naught the insignificant clutter of negatives eating into my soul. Those dusty fears and hates that I gather into me whilst living in the merciless drought that is the world!

Of course there is another aspect. I remember what the Stranger once said to me, 'If I did not exist, then neither would the ocean exist! Nor for that matter would anything exist, not even God!'

At least that is for me they wouldn't! So then, what am I? Everything?

Hey that's it! At last I am beginning to understand! Why didn't someone tell me?

"Being 'I AM' means that I must tell my mind what to think and not let my mind tell me! I must tell my brain how to work and not be subject to it! I must tell my body what to do and not the other way around.

I don't belong to my body or my mind or my brain! No! They all belong to me!

That's what it's all about!

XXXXXXX

YES AND NO

I heard about numerology. The numbers of your date of birth and the numerical value of the name you were first given describes your character. Add up the value of the vowels in your name and you get your special purpose in life. When I tried to do it I found an insurmountable problem. No one knew what day I was born on or what the first name I was given was or what my family name was or where I was born!

I had no beginning and no family.

Does that mean that I am not subject to numerology? Am I free to be whatever I want to be or am I just unaware of my true identity?

"Anyway," I thought, "at least the Stranger knows who I am even if he won't tell me. But, how is it that numbers make a difference? He used numbers to explain the concept of three in one. Do numbers really dictate your value? Can you change your numbers and so change your code and your self? A number has three values, first as it is, second as minus, third as plus. A minus two is totally different to a plus two, which is different again to an ordinary two. What are metaphysics or sidekicks or psychics? Do the numbers of numerology take into account minus and plus, negative or positive? What about the 'Golden Mean' or the 'Davinci Code'? The code shows that numbers are the bases of all nature. 1.618 is the length of ac to ab and is the same ratio of ab to bc. What?

I know people and all of nature fit the code but are the numbers either minus or plus or are they a mixture of plus and minus. Does a mixture create internal conflict or is a number always inclusive of its variable polarity

As for me, if I have no numbers how can I come to know myself or know who I am?"

Maybe a visit to the dumps would help me reach some new understanding.

XXXXXXX

TO THE DUMPS

The dumps were quiet. The still air bred a bitter winter cold. No bird song. No movement. I sat at the cliff edge hugging my knees to my chest.

Drifting back in memory to the first time I climbed the dumps I let my imagination wander.

The Stranger walked into my mind. I saw him standing at the edge of my dream world. I watched him take a small object from his pocket. He held it out over the emptiness at the cliff edge. He dropped it. Leaning forward to get a better view, he stared down at it. Then seemingly satisfied he stood up and without a backward glance strode off into the emptiness surrounding me.

Intrigued, I wandered over to where he had dropped the object. Looking over the edge, as he had done, I saw some three metres down a section of rusted railway line jutting out from the cliff face. Attached to it was a magnet. Was it the object the stranger dropped or had it been there all the time? I think he might have dropped it because it looked new and clean as it gleamed in the weak sunlight.

I sat where he had stood.

The music hidden in the surrounding stillness echoed the quiet in me. I stared down at the magnet. The answer stared back at me. Magnets have both positive and negative polarity. In magnets the opposites attract, negative attracts positive and the same polarities repel. Funny that! What is it in the piece of old metal railway line that is attractive to either the positive or the negative of a magnet?

A picture grew in my mind. I saw the world of nature as physical, like a magnet, where opposites attract but likes repel! Then I imagined the spiritual world! It is totally different! Opposites repel, and likes attract. Good attracts good and bad attracts' bad. So what is it that attracts both negative and positive, both the good and the bad in the world! Is there a way of having all without the need to attract or repel?

Well, let's start with the spiritual world. Ok so it is based in morality whereas the physical world, because of its contradiction, has no morality. Mud does not know right from wrong but personality does! But you can't say that the world has no polarity because there is a north and a south pole!

"Oh well I can't figure it out! Anyway, what is morality?" I wondered.

Behind me the Stranger answered.

"Morality is based in the freedom to make an enlightened choice and that enlightenment can only come to be when you know all the options and the possible results related to the subject of your choice.

No normal person in this world knows all the answers so no one can make a morally acceptable choice.

The spirit, which is eternal and therefore all knowing, is based in morality, whereas the flesh which is temporal and material has no concept of moral perspectives."

"Then how can spirit and matter exist together? What is it that attracts both of them and holds them together like the iron attracts both sides of the magnet? Is it that the joining of the spirit and the physical produces a likeness to a magnet with one side positive and one side negative and it is that which holds it together?"

"Ah! Maybe that was the problem with creation. How to make the lion lie down with the lamb!

The answer as to what is morality lies in man, for man was made of both the earth and the spirit but as you have just found out, the two are incompatible. Just as you need a catalyst to mix oil and water so do you need a catalyst to mix earth and spirit! The soul was created as a catalyst for this purpose and has been given the task of bringing about, through experience, a shared moral nature in spiritual/physical man."

"Why didn't God simply make the lion and the lamb lie down together in the first place? Why all the pain of learning the hard way? I mean, couldn't man have been told or programmed to know right from wrong when he was created?"

"No, that would not allow him to make a free choice after experiencing the facts for himself. That is what morality is all about - freedom of choice. For the lion and the lamb to have no real choice in the matter would be immoral. So man was made free to choose to love or not love! Without the freedom to choose, man's love for God would have to be imposed on him and would then be of no real value. The problem with man in this world as he is now is that man does not and cannot know all of everything! As a result it is impossible for him to make an informed and therefore correct choice! Do you understand? In this world man is neither unfettered nor is he all knowing, so he cannot see the whole picture. As I said, it is the task of the soul to learn the difference between good and evil so that it can eventually share experiences with other souls and make an enlightened choice!"

"And numerology?"

"Numerology confirms the overall plan set up at the beginning of creation. The plan that establishes on a daily or yearly or generation basis the nature of all things pertinent to this or that moment, to that day or time and to those particular sets of circumstance. This is how and why everything works together for the purpose of the Creator. Numerology works in everything, like the da Vinci code or the Bible code and similar codes in so called 'ordinary' books, as in the seasons, the time, the ageing process, understanding, knowledge, you name it - there is a numerical value underlying and influencing everything."

"Okay," I said, "that's why they call it "generations!"

"Yes! So numerology, you could say, is instrumental in preparing for and supplying the guidelines for each second, each day, for each generation and each person, and thus for all creation! Numerology makes them fit together. It enables the exposing and experiencing in full of all the perspectives of what is right and what is wrong, of good and evil. This exposure will eventually bring about the climate where a truly free and enlightened choice between good and evil can be made by all of creation.

At the so called day of judgment no stone will have been left unturned, no question left unanswered leaving no possibility of any awkward questions such as 'but what if?'"

"I hear you." I said, "May I ask if my understanding that the spiritual, because of its ability to bond positive with positive, is stronger than the world which bonds positive with negative?"

"Correct."

"Does this mean that eventually the world will be so weakened by its perpetual conflict within itself that it will just burn up and die and that the 'spiritual' strengthened by its morality will grow and live?"

"Yes."

"When the present world dies, will the new world also be physical but totally subject to 'morality' through the work done by the soul in the spirit?"

"Yes."

"And will all the presently 'blind souls' eventually be given the opportunity of understanding so that they can reject the wrong and choose the right because they have jointly and severally experienced the fullness of both?"

"That's right."

"And all of creation will come together having voluntarily rejected evil because of experience and a real understanding of God will show Him to be all in all? Is that the overall plan?"

"Amen. Your understanding is almost complete!"

With the equations now exposed and the fullness of understanding opening my mind, my walk back to the village was full of surprises.

Every step I took in the material world reflected the world's subjection to my newfound positive spiritual attitude.

The cold winter sun clothed me in light as it bowed out in a brilliant sunset of acceptance.

Now I knew that wherever I set my foot, that place was my home.

I ran the last distance to the house of my New Mother and my New Father.

Alarmed by my excited footsteps they rushed to the door. Tears streamed down their faces as they saw, at last, in my eyes, my acceptance of them as my own family.

For the first time, I stepped over the welcome mat into my 'own' home.

From that day on, I kept the Stranger's face constantly in my mind and the proof of overcoming the world by positive spirituality was thereafter constantly and amazingly demonstrated to me time and time again.

XXXXXXX

A STRANGE EVENING

Mother invited the Stranger to dinner.

We sat out on the veranda, sipping sundowners. The western sky was a brilliant mixture of orange, red and purple. Mosquitoes started whining around us as the frogs set up their nightly chorus.

"Well," said father to the stranger, "we have never been properly introduced! We don't even know your name or for that matter we don't know anything about you. Everyone in town calls you 'The Stranger'!"

"Sorry!" The stranger apologised, "My fault! Actually I have been here in your home before! I slept here one night but I left early in the morning before you woke. Anyway, my name is Robert, I am a Rhodesian and I come from a family of farmers."

Father smiled,

"That was easy!" He leaned across and shook Robert's hand.

"Good to meet you!"

Robert laughed,

"And good to meet you guys too!"

"Tell us a bit about yourself. The whole village whispers that you are so secretive, as to who and what you are and that you come and go and then come again with no apparent purpose so you must have some connection with the intelligence services!"

Robert laughed,

"Intelligence services? Anything but that!"

"Well you would never admit to it or you would blow your cover!"

"Too true!"

All laugh. Father asks,

"Well then, tell us about yourself."

"Okay. Where shall I begin, as a child, or as an adult?"

"Wherever!"

"That could take a long time!"

"All right start wherever and don't worry about the time because we will tell you when we've had enough!"

"I think it would be better to just tell you those parts of my life that led me to be what I have become. I think one of the most interesting things that happened to me as a young man was the time my mother and step father asked me to build a new home for them on their new farm. The experience of building that house led me on to search for remains of past civilisations in central Africa.

My mother wanted to live on a small hill, what we call a kopjie. She enjoyed the eastern view over the farm towards the distant mountains.

The hill she wanted the house to be built on was rounded at the top so we had to level it out. When we started digging we found that there was a huge rock area about the middle of where the house would be. I had to dynamite the top of the rock.

When the rubble from the blasting was dug away we found a crevice within the rock that on clearing led down into a large cave. It was full of ash! There was also a lot of ash and evidence of smelting strewn all over both on and around the hill!

At the far end of the cave were two graves.

The labourers were too scared to work anywhere near the graves. Their superstitions got the better of them. So I dug up the graves with the intention of reburying the corpses at the bottom of the hill.

The first corpse appeared to have been a very tall person. He had copper and elephant hair bracelets around his wrists and ankles and a magnificent gold ring with a huge emerald on one finger.

The second skeleton also had bracelets but it was that of a short man.

I kept the skulls and the leg femurs and tibia from both skeletons. And of course, the ring! The rest we buried in a new grave at the foot of the hill. The workers went back to work.

A few weeks later I took the bones I had kept aside to the Bulawayo Museum and asked them to identify them and estimate the date of death. My mother left the ring at a Jewellers shop to have it valued.

Doctor Bond from the museum later wrote to me saying that the very tall man was a Caucasian and the short man was a Mongolian cross Negro. He wrote that their estimated time of death at that time was over six hundred years ago.

My mother told me she collected the ring from the jewellers and brought it home but I never saw it again and nobody would tell me its value or what really happened to it.

What was interesting to me was that there were Europeans and Mongolians in Rhodesia over six hundred years ago! That would be long before the Mashona people ever arrived in Zimbabwe!"

"That suggests that it was the Mashona who colonised the country after the Europeans arrived and not the other way around as the politicians say!"

"Exactly!" Robert frowned, "If I remember correctly the Rhodesian authorities, long before independence, invited a lady from overseas to come and try and settle the argument as to who built the Zimbabwe ruins and who farmed the extensive irrigation schemes in the eastern districts. Due to the ransacking of the ruins by many treasure hunters she found no trace of any artefacts within the main ruins which could prove either way as to who built them. Being a little more switched on than previous investigators she hired a small plane and flew over the ruins and the surrounding countryside to look for any untouched sites. On a hill some distance from the main ruins she spotted a structure that appeared to have not been ransacked. Back on the ground she took her team up to the small ruin and uncovered a lot of substantial evidence confirming that the original occupants of that particular site had been African - most likely Kalanga people.

Her findings were accepted! It was agreed and made official to the effect that the ruins had been built by Africans!

What no one ever questioned was why the Africans who built the complex - now known as the Zimbabwe ruins and those who developed the irrigation schemes in the eastern districts and developed mines and built paved roads through the eastern mountains suddenly changed to subsistence farming and living in mud huts. The second point they missed out on is that obviously the creators of the Zimbabwe ruins lived in the main super structures and their workers lived in small quarters up in the hills. You might say the workers lived in compounds or locations. That is why she found African artefacts there! The people who occupied the small ruins in the surrounding hills were the labourers not the creators!

The story of the Caucasoid and the Mongolian corpses has been conveniently ignored!"

"You mentioned smelting!" Father asked, "What mineral?"

"We never went to the trouble of establishing what they were mining but the ash in the cave and around the hill amounted to many cubic meters so it must have been in a reasonable quantity. We also found nozzles from the old bellows.

At the foot of the hill in a flat granite area were large holes or craters gouged out of the rock possibly where the ore was ground into powder. On another hill about three miles south of the house site we found a stone platform built facing the rising sun. There is a cave full of sand and seashells on a hill to the east. Ten miles from the house site to the northeast were what appeared to be underground storage rooms. Near them were numerous small perfectly round holes like dishes carved into a flat granite rock. The authorities said they were ore grinding sites.

But more important, the surrounding countryside was all sand stone country so what on earth could they have been mining?

Nobody could give us an answer!"

"Strange." Father muttered, "Very strange!"

"And then there is also the story of the ruins on my father's farm a hundred miles north."

"What about them?"

"Again nobody could give me an answer to some of the things I came across in those ruins!"

"Have another drink?"

"Thank you."

"Tell us about these other ruins." Mother begged.

"After supper!" Said father, "Would you prefer to eat out here or inside?"

"In the dining room would be fine thanks."

Supper was a fantastic spread. We were too busy enjoying it to speak much.

After supper father suggested we had coffee in front of the fire in the sitting room.

Robert seemed a little agitated.

"You okay?" Asked mother.

"Yes, sorry! Memories you know!"

We enjoyed the glow of the fire and the hot Irish coffee.

"You were saying?" Prompted mother.

"Oh yes." Robert grinned, "You sure I am not talking too much?"

"Yes, you definitely are!" Laughed father, "But it is very interesting! Please don't stop. You were about to tell us the story of the other ruins on your fathers farm."

"Yes! They were big! Covered about five hundred acres if you included the tower, the main ruins, the village and the cattle kraals! At least I assumed they were cattle kraals, they could have been a slave camp. Anyway the ruins had been investigated by the relevant authorities and excavations carried out at two points to establish the meaning of what appeared to be ventilation shafts. The reported findings were of a typically bureaucratic nature."

"What do you mean by that?" Asked father.

"Well it is normal for the bureaucracy of any country or for that matter any organisation to have preconceived ideas about most things and they manipulate everything to fit these conceptions. In this case it was generally politically accepted that the Zimbabwe ruins were built by the Monomatapa regime. Whites were definitely not part of that regime. They said the ruins had religious significance and they described the air vents as drainage systems. Now in all fairness why would a raised area of small loose rocks need to be drained? It would drain naturally!

I invited an expert to come to the ruins with me. He was a man connected to the Salisbury University who was conversant with the history and architecture of the ruins in Zimbabwe from the vast irrigation systems of the east to the main ruins in the south and right down to the small gold and silver mines scattered all over the country.

I showed him two walls outside the main ruin that appeared to have had sections of their outer stone work stripped off and two sections of the main ruins walls where entrances to the ruins had been neatly filled in. The rocks used to gap fill the entrances were smaller than the stones in the main walls and guess what? Those smaller stones were the same size as those remaining on the outer walls!

I showed him the position of the so called drainage shafts in that they were opposite sections of the outer wall that had alter like structures built against the outside of the wall also with small stones from the stripped walls. I suggested that the quantity of stone used to conceal the entrances seemed to be the same as that removed from the covering of the stripped walls.

Guess what?"

"What?"

"He said 'Rubbish!' and left!"

"So what happened then?"

I spent time at the ruins, alone! I studied the way the old entrances had been sealed. I studied the stripped walls and the vents in the flooring on top of the ruins. I studied what they called the grain storage bins made of stone that lay fifty meters away from the main ruins. I decided that from my perspective one of two things had happened."

He paused,

"Any chance of more coffee, all this talking has made my throat dry!"

Mother collected our cups and went to the kitchen.

"So what were the two things?" I asked.

"Well, either the original occupants of the ruins had warning of an approaching inhospitable force so they quickly buried their gold and silver in or around the main building using stone from outside walls to cover up. It certainly looks like they had to leave in a hurry before they could complete their work as they left some gold ingots lying on the ground inside the ruins, which were found by an early British pioneer. Or, another story all together."

"Go on, this is getting exciting!"

"When Lobengula the king of the Matabele was running away from the British forces, the guards with him who controlled the slaves carrying his treasure were told to go and hide the treasure somewhere safe. That safe place and the hidden treasure in it have never been found!

It is possible they ran south to the ruins I am talking about and buried the treasure there because they knew no one would touch it in fear of the ancestral spirits resident in the ruins. The guards then killed off the slave carriers and left.

The same reason probably applied relating to the removal of and use of stone cladding to cover the burial sites - there was no time to do it any other way.

"Wow!"

"How come you could see the story of the stone wall cladding when the expert from Salisbury couldn't?" I asked.

"When I was a teenager I used to walk all over the farm enjoying nature. One morning, as I sat on a neat pile of rocks on the south side of the ruins near a part where the outer wall had been broken down - the early morning sun shone directly at the inner wall through the gap in the outer wall. I noticed that there was a section of the inner wall, like a large doorway closed up with different sized stones. The places where the smaller stones met the larger stones were neat and vertical. I climbed up onto the inner wall and saw that the original wall of large stones curved neatly in on two sides forming a passage-way. The smaller stones had been built in so very carefully that you would not notice it if you did not look at that section of wall from the vantage point where I had sat that day!"

"And nobody else could see what you could see?"

"Well let's just say they weren't prepared to see it - so they didn't! Just like the story of who built the Zimbabwe ruins.

Anyway, back to the version where the original occupiers of the ruin buried their gold and silver when they had to leave in a hurry! And what I told you about the two corpses at my mother's farm. I connected these two stories. But! Again! Nobody wanted to believe me!"

"So?"

"So, nothing! Except that this is special coffee!"

Father said, "From what you say it would be worth going to the ruins to investigate."

"Yes, but it could be dangerous!"

"Why?"

The local people in the ruins area being Matabele are terrorised by the Mugabe forces. So I think that the best way to do it would be to combine a very fast manoeuvre with gifts of food and money to the locals - get in and out before anyone has time to report and induce a reaction from Mugabe supporters and then you would have to find a way to move maybe many tons of gold and silver ingots across and out of the country and where to and what would you do with it?"

Father asked,

"Would you be willing for us to join forces with you and go for it?"

"Yes!"

"Ok, let's work on it and see what we can come up with."

I felt a thrill run up my spine,

"I am coming with you!" I whispered.

"Oh yes, most definitely!" Said Robert, "Anyway, let's work it all out. But please, don't talk to anyone about it. You don't want to end up being shot or worse still, being tortured and starved to death in a Zimbabwe jail."

"What would we need in the way of equipment?"

"A metal detector, that can read at least twelve feet underground and an auger to clean out the air vents. Hand tools to dig fast and accurately. Also some food for the locals who help us! I reckon we would have to go in first and check with the metal detector to find exactly where we have to dig. Pay the locals and give them some acceptable story as to who and why, we are there. Subtly get them on our side and then when we know what and where, we can get the excavation tools together, go in again and dig. We need a large helicopter to come in at night and load the loot and if necessary us too and get out of there fast! The digging and moving must be over and done within one night! Also, and very important, we need to plan where we are going to take ourselves and the gold to!"

"Right!" Said father, "Let's get on with it."

Robert interrupted,

"I have to go to Namibia in a couple of weeks. If I get a chance on the way, I will check out my mother's house with a metal detector, it may also be worth having a go at tracing and digging for any buried treasure there. I don't expect to be in Namibia for long, say a few days, but meantime I will be around here for you to contact. I will be staying at the hotel outside town."

Mother spoke,

"When you're in Namibia you could look up my sister and brother in law. I will let them know you are coming. In fact he might be just the right sort of guy to have along with us when we do the ruins."

"Sounds good! Where can I find them or contact them?"

"They have a camp on the Kwando River in the Caprivi. Contact is best by radio, the post takes too long."

"The Kwando River? Do they have a son called Ian?"

"Yes! Do you know them?"

"I certainly do. Spent a couple of months with them a few years ago!"

Mother was thrilled,

"What a coincidence!" She said softly.

"And!" He added, "I met Ian again in Namibia - on his walk about! He helped me check out old ruins in the desert and also along the coast. I have a good idea as to where he is at this time! In fact I was planning to go back to that area soon. I know he would love to join us so I'll call him. I have his mobile phone number."

Father laughed,

"What a coincidence!"

XXXXXXX

IAN'S FAMILY ARRIVE

Robert stopped in at Somewhere Camp while he was in Namibia to tell my uncle and aunt about our planned trip to the ruins. He then travelled on down the coast into South Africa to look for Ian.

As a result of his visit the Namibian family have come down to us to finalise plans.

It is 'dinner time'.

My uncle smiles a sad smile,

"It has been a long time since Ian left on his walk about. We all miss him!"

Father raises his glass,

"To Ian, where ever he may be, God bless him!"

A knock on the door!

Father opens it.

It is Ian! He stands framed by the door posts, back pack in hand, tall, lean, suntanned and hard.

He walks in.

We sit stunned!

Ian's face is serene. His lips sketch a distant smile. His eyes laugh at us.

"Hi Mom. Hi Dad. Hi you all!"

Ian's father leaps to his feet bursts into tears and runs around the table to him.

"Oh my God," he sobs "Oh my God."

Ian drops his backpack - hugging his father, he says,

"I have been on a fantastic trip where the most important thing I learnt is how much I love you Dad."

He laughs and grinning as he turns to his mother he whispers, "And you Mum!"

She weeps! Ian walks around the table to her where taking her hand, he bends down and gently kisses it. Looking round he sees no vacant chair so he sits on the sideboard, grinning at everybody.

Mother goes to the kitchen for another plate of food.

Everybody talks at once.

"When did you get back?"

"You look so fit!"

"I can't believe you just walked in after all these years!"

"Did you go home first? How did you know we were here?"

"Let him eat."

"Get Ian a chair."

He eats slowly and little as looking around the table he says,

"I walked almost all the way from Somewhere Camp westwards through the bush and desert to the sea then down the coast to the Western Cape where Robert picked me up and brought me here. You remember him?" He looked at his father. His father nodded. "Well I joined him on some of his expeditions. He found me again two days ago and brought me here. He said he knew all of you and will be coming here again the day after tomorrow. He has some business to attend to.

He told me about you all wanting to go with him to some ruins in Zimbabwe!"

Mother got excited,

"Wonder why he didn't come in?"

"I think he was too tired. But isn't that amazing! He knows all of us but never told me until today! He certainly is different!"

So was Ian! Very different to all the people I had ever met or even heard of. He walked around as if he owned everything he saw.

Later on, in the afternoon, I took him to the dumps.

We sat at my favourite spot.

"Will you tell me about your 'walk about?' I asked him.

XXXXXXX

BOOK 2

"IAN"

IAN'S STORY

"I left home the day after my twenty first birthday. Why did I leave? Well, as you know I have a memory loss of the first years of my life and being an orphan my parents were afraid to let me grow up in my own way in case the problem got worse. My father decided I was his responsibility beyond the normal father and son relationship. I believed him, after all I am his son, or should I say I am his adopted son.

My parents kept me at the camp and put me onto a home school course. I grew up in isolation and never learnt how to get on with children of my own age because there weren't any at the camp. I became frustrated and started to blame my parents for limiting me by taking too much care of me. I felt I had to get out and meet the real world. So with their understanding, but also with their pain, I left home on a walk about.

It has taken me a long time to come to realise that it wasn't my father who was wrong! I was me that was wrong! I submitted myself to the excessive authority he exercised over me, but because he is so caring and loving, I allowed him to do so!

When I left for my walk about I thought I was running away from him but in reality I was running away from myself.

Leaving home was easy. Packing a backpack with dried fruit, dried meat, my passport, antibiotics, snake bite serum and pain killers I said goodbye and literally took off into the sunset. I walked west through the Caprivi bush towards Namibia. There were very few people that way! I wanted to avoid people for a while.

Living off nature turned out to be relatively easy. Water was not a problem at first even though it was sometimes suspect, but food was often a problem. I talked myself into not needing food every day, after all lions don't eat every day and they still have enough energy to catch their prey even a week after their last meal.

It worked.

Watching nature taught me what was edible and what was not.

I ate what baboons ate. I watched birds and ate what they ate. At first my mind rejected the insects and grubs but hunger soon resolved that problem.

A few weeks after leaving home I came across a remote Lozwe village. The huts were built of poles and reeds and thatched with palm leaves from a nearby seasonal swamp.

Loneliness led me into the village. Some of the villagers had worked on the gold mines in South Africa so language was not a problem. We chatted and laughed together in the mine language called 'Funigalo'. They were surprised to see me so far from civilisation but they were too polite to ask me where I came from or why I was there.

On my second day at the village I was invited to join them in a traditional ceremony to be held that night.

Late that afternoon the men gathered around a huge fire in the centre of the village whilst the women sang and danced outside the circle. Their wailing, their chanting and the stamping of their feet reflected the primal rhythm of the leaping flames in the fire.

Realising I was out of sync with the beliefs of the village I decided to move on.

I left the next morning and walked westward for many days.

Other than one small airplane zigzagging across the desert I saw no sign of people. Not even Bushmen.

Then came a time when the water ran out. It was too far to walk back to the last water hole and I had no idea where the next one would be so I climbed a barren rocky outcrop where, from its highest point, I looked out in all directions hoping to see maybe a bit of green or signs of human habitation or a road?

I saw nothing.

Moving round the outcrop I found a cool place under a slanting rock and spent the hot part of that day resting in its shade. Sunset forced on me the decision on which direction to take. I decided to carry on westwards as I believed the chance of crossing a north bound road or track was greater that way.

I walked for the whole night.

Early morning brought fine dew on the ground. I ran my tongue over damp stones.

There was no shade for miles around so I took my ragged clothes off and stretched them carefully between two large rocks and curled up in the tiny square of shade.

Late that afternoon, when the heat began to dissipate, I put my clothes on again. My dry tongue and screaming body fought with my mind. My mind won and I staggered towards the west again - slowly and carefully breathing in time to my steps.

Walking during the cool of night helped.

Early morning showed me a small hillock catching the first rays of sunlight. I staggered across rough ground to it and climbing to the top I selected a spot on the highest point and set up my shelter of clothes.

I doubted I could walk again that night so I built a small cairn of stones and placed a piece of torn coloured shirt and some newly broken white quartz stones, as a signal, on the highest point of the rock!

Painfully I dragged my exhausted body into my little shelter.

The sun beat unmercifully on the ground around me.

Being dehydrated dried up my sweat.

I began to hallucinate.

The unmistakeable sound of a spluttering Volkswagen exhaust brought me to my senses. I heard the beating of drums and soft music. The Volkswagen noise died but the music continued.

A hand touched my forehead. It pushed my head back. Water trickled into my parched mouth.

A man bent over me.

Picking me up, he carried me in his arms, like a baby, to the car.

The man drove to his camp where, with his help, I crawled out of the Volkswagen into the luxuriant shade of a large tent. He indicated a camp bed on which I gratefully lay down.

The man mixed some white stuff into a glass of water and offering it to me suggested,

"Drink it slowly."

I did.

Recovery was fast.

Swinging my legs off the bed to sit up I realised I was still without clothes.

He smiled and throwing a pair of too large shorts and a belt at me, said,

"Put them on."

Turning to the camp cooker he set about preparing a meal.

He was tall, wiry and very strong. His eyes were brilliant. His shaggy beard and long hair hid his face. He had little to say.

When the food was ready he set it on the camp table and sat on the only chair indicating I sit on a cushion he had placed on a large 'cool' box.

We ate together.

Strong herbal tea completed the meal.

"Well?" He asked.

"Thank you! How did you find me?"

"Your beacon!"

Offering more tea he smiled.

We sat quietly, studying each other.

My faculties came back. I started remembering more than the last few days.

I asked,

"Don't I know you?"

"Yes Ian, you do! I visited your camp a few years ago when we both had short hair and short beards. Now you look like a thin scraggly shrub! No matter! I will cut your hair and beard for you - after you've rested."

"Oh yes! Now I remember. You had a red beach buggy! Why yes! That's it outside and your name is Robert. My father said you were a strange man!" I laughed, "But he meant it in a nice way - something about you being more aware than other people. What are you doing out here in the desert?"

"Collecting."

"What?"

"Lanthanide."

"What is that?"

"It is a derivative of Gedanide which is a non earth element. This place here where we are now is named after an Israeli town called Gedanide. The sons of Shelah lived at Gedanide. They were the King's potters. They made clay pots using Lanthanide."

"What will you use Lanthanide for?"

"The same as the potters!"

I waited for more.

"As I said it is a non earth element. I can best explain what I do with it by saying I use it to help mould a spiritual character into living pots. You could say it is like 'spiritual putty' in my hands!"

"I don't really understand." I said.

He smiled but kept quiet.

"How did you know I would be in this area?" I asked.

"I was waiting for you!"

"How come?"

"You needed help."

"How did you know?"

"The same way you knew you had to put your shirt up as a little beacon at that particular point? Anyway, it's getting late, what do you say to bed time?"

"I say 'good night and thank you!'"

Next morning found me rested, hair cut and much stronger.

Robert made breakfast. We sat at table as on the previous night, he on the chair and I on the cool box.

"I want to show you something." He said, "There are some ruins of an old temple in the desert. They look almost the same but much smaller than the original temple of the Israelites in the desert. But first let me give you something to read which I wrote last night. It is related to the origin of the ruins!"

Taking the note from him, I read,

"So many are the lies so few the truths
It is no surprise we falter!
Although it is clearly written in the book,
We seem to hear only a wilderness of words,
Interminable myths, Man's imagination gone wild!
If we are to save a generation
Full of compelling delusion
From final damnation
We must show that mere speculation
About the abomination lodging in the temple of your mind
hidden since the beginning of creation
Till the final revolution,
Can no longer suffice!
That abomination must now be brought to light,
For it is the adversary
Who uses a mirror as his witness!
And through this simple distortion
Exercises his claim.

XXXXXXX

THE TEMPLE

After breakfast Robert drove deep into the desert. He parked the beach buggy at the edge of a protected area. I felt I had been here before.

Deja vu?

We walked across rough ground to some ancient stone ruins. It looked as if it could be the Temple he was talking about. When we got to the first crumbled wall, Robert stopped and gently told me to go in through the gateway. On my own!

My spine tingled as standing at the entrance I recalled a vivid dream I had long ago. It was about this very place.

In the dream the area was extremely hot and dry, vast and barren. A crumbling wall circled a weathered and very old building in the middle of a deserted sanctuary. Inside the dusty yard and near the main entrance stood an altar full of hot coals. At the far side there was a stand with what looked like a birdbath on top and a rim forming a basin at the bottom. Both were filled with water.

In the dream a guide approached me.

He led me to the burning altar. He asked me to throw into the fire all knowledge of the sins I had committed in my life. The fire burnt them all. A gentle wind blew the disgusting stench away.

The guide led me on to the water stand where, on instruction, I washed my hands in the top bath and my feet in the bottom basin. I was then led through the far door of the courtyard into the windowless building.

The guide and I waited inside in the musty darkness. To our left a candle flared up and then another until seven candles burnt together on a gold candlestick holder. I saw in front of us another smaller altar and behind this a door way with a heavy curtain hanging across it. The guide led me to the right of the room to a table covered with a white cloth and laden with small flat bread cakes. As we stood at the table a crowd of people gathered on the other side where a lady in a Nun's habit handed out pieces of the bread. She told us that we were all to be ground into fine white flour, sifted, washed with water, cleansed by fire and brought together into one family.

After the ceremony everyone lost their worldly identity and as the Nun ate the last piece of bread she was freed from her Nun's robes. We were led across to the seven candles giving light to the room. The guide told us that each candle had a specific value or purpose. He then led me away from the candles to the small altar at the far doorway.

Behind the altar I saw 'an infinity of people' gathered together. Amongst them were groups of skinheads, motorbike enthusiasts, priests, businessmen, tramps and politicians. I saw people of every imaginable colour, creed, religion or persuasion who had accepted the bread from the table in the light from the candles. They were singing happy songs of respect, honour and worth-ship.

Slowly the singing lessened and the people faded away. The guide led me through the curtain covering the door behind the small altar into a room where in the dark I could barely make out the shape of a covered table made like a ship with objects placed on and in it.

High above the table an infinite, magnificent power radiated from and into infinity and eternity. A minute trickle of this power flowed down to the table. That small trickle fuelled the whole of creation. I fell to the floor and the dream faded.

Here I was again, so many years after the dream.

xxxxxxx

Laughing happily at Robert, I strode eagerly through the open door into the familiar courtyard. But reality was vastly different to the dream. The place was a ruin, overgrown, crumbling, taken so far back into nature that the signs of its original purpose and its human involvement were almost entirely obliterated.

Robert walked in from behind and stood with me. He smiled.

"Come," he said, "I want to show you something!"

Making his way through all the weeds and thorn shrubs to the remains of the doorway leading into the inner sanctuary Robert took his long knife from his belt and cut through the creepers blocking the way and stepped inside. Bees buzzed in consternation. Flies and lizards shot back and forth. Robert took his torch out and shone it into the little room.

I looked over his shoulder. The remains of the small altar stood as it had in my dream. Robert walked over to it and reaching under it scratched away the dirt and pulled out a cylindrical tube. It was covered in grime and dust.

He looked around - grunted and walked out the door. I followed.

"What is it?" I asked.

"A scroll like the ones found in the Dead Sea."

"How did you know it would be here?"

"I heard about it when I was in Zambia."

"And now?"

"On to the next place. But first let's take a few photographs. Can you put this scroll in the box in the boot of the car while I set up the camera? Thanks!"

XXXXXX

BACK TO NOW AT THE DUMPS

Ian relaxed for a moment as he reflected on his journey.

"Hey!" I asked Ian, "Did Robert ever tell you about the ruins in Zimbabwe?"

"Yes!"

"Well we have been planning an expedition to them! Your father is coming with us! We were meant to go a little while ago but all sorts of things got in the way. Maybe at last we can do it now and you're coming too, aren't you?"

"Yes of course! Robert has already asked me! That's why he came to get me and that is why I came back with him!"

"Oh! Anyway! Sorry I interrupted your story. Please carry on."

"Well, after the visit to the ruins I spent a few weeks with Robert helping him collect his 'non earth element'.

When he had enough we loaded it into a large trunk in his trailer and made our way to the coast where we spent many days exploring and talking. He showed me some of the things that had been hidden deep in my mind.

Then one day, as we sat together at a small fresh water spring between the dunes and the sea, he said,

"Time up! I want to get this scroll deciphered by a friend in Cape Town."

We packed his gear into the beach buggy.

"See you at the next place!" He said and drove away.

Funny! Robert never told me his full name! All he said was what my name meant, 'the one who was loved because he had learnt humility.'

I walked southwards down the coast into gale force winds and a sea of liquid ice.

My diet changed to crabs and mussels. I learnt to catch fish without a rod and line. I found birds eggs in the cliffs.

I lived!

With no one to talk with I learnt to talk with myself. I listened to my body. I argued with my mind. I listened to nature.

I found my spirit.

Leaving behind all the bigoted traditions of men I was set free from what seemed to be man's biggest problem, his denial of his real identity in order to be what other people demanded he should be.

I changed.

One day, as I lay on the sand enjoying the warm caress of the sun I heard the distant growl of a motorcar. It came from up the north beach. I ran to a dune where crouching behind scraggly brush at its crest I watched a land cruiser drive along the wet line on the beach left by retreating waves. There were two men in the vehicle. They stopped across the beach from where I lay. Unpacking, they set up camp then took their fishing tackle off the vehicle's roof rack and walked beers in one hand and tackle in the other, to the surf. I slid down the back slope of the dune to get away from the fishermen and made my way further south until quite a few kilometres separated us.

Having spent a long time on what I came to look upon as "my stretch" and then having to leave it created in me an urge to wander. The fishermen were to the north so I went south and sometimes a little inland away from the sea into the arid semi desert country which stretched eastwards to cold, blue, mountains. But mostly I wandered along the coast sleeping wherever night found me. I carried precious drinking water in a shoulder bag and in two water bottles tied to my belt. My perspective of life was changing. I heard sounds not heard before. I felt new emotions grow out of those long ago locked deep within me by the world of men.

Instead of talking at nature and trying to control it I began to listen to it and nature, surprised to find a human prepared to listen, responded magnificently. The wind sang to me, the waves laughed with me. Insects clustered round me for company. Water birds walked the beaches with me and dolphins followed me down the coast.

I had many friends.

The beach seemed to stretch forever. I counted the number of full moons since leaving my father and learnt to miss him. I came to love him as never before.

I also came to love myself.

xxxxxxx

The coast led in a curve southwards to civilisation, to people, to noise, arrogance, self righteousness, anger and hate, but also occasionally, here and there, to love and caring!

The time came for me to find new clothes to wear. I had to conform to the civilised worlds perceptions of decent behaviour. I would have to learn again to speak to people who don't listen and to listen to people who have nothing to say.

I would have to find a way through all of them to the other side - the other side of what? The other side of tomorrow where today waits!

I found clothes at the rubbish dump outside the first town I came to. Not too bad either, worn but not torn. I washed them under a tap near the dumps and after drying them on a bush I put them on and walked barefoot into town. Not many people noticed me. I was surprised because I noticed all of them. Their bodies talked to me. Sad people. People lost in their race against time. People hurting in their not knowing!

Leaving town with food I scavenged from behind a grocery store I looked for a sheltered place among the rocks on the beach. A 'South Easter' wind was blowing up a storm.

The bread I ate cramped my stomach and I learnt again the feeling of constipation.

XXXXXXX

THE LIFT

Cold morning mist clung to a lonely stretch of road. I flagged a car down. The driver looked nervous. He talked non-stop. He drove too fast. His car stank of nicotine and stale beer. He jerked the steering wheel from side to side. My head swam. Motion sickness. I was no longer sure if I should be grateful for the lift.

We had travelled about two hundred and sixty miles when we came across a car parked at the side of the road. A woman in jeans was waving for us to stop. A small hillock of jumbled rocks lay close to the other side of the car.

The driver drove past.

"Aren't you going to stop?" I cried.

"Bugger her." He swore, "Probably a set up for a high-jacking."

"You are just going to leave her there? We should at least check."

"No ways! I don't want to get hurt! You can trust no one these days!"

"What if she's genuine?"

"Doubt it. What's she doing all by herself on this lonely stretch of road?"

"Please stop." I begged.

"No ways!" he shouted, "If you want to help you can get out."

Slamming on brakes, he slewed the car around and across the road.

He swore again as he shouted at me,

"Now see what you've done! Get out."

I got out.

Without waiting for me to collect my bag from the back seat he spun the wheels on the gravel verge and drove off.

I walked back to the broken down car.

The woman was a girl. She looked wary.

"Don't worry!" I reassured her "Maybe I can help or at least stay with you till someone stops who can."

"Thank you. I've been here for hours. Nobody stops. Nobody even looks. The world's gone crazy. People I know from our district passed me!"

"What's the problem with the car?"

"Simple. Flat wheel! No pump and no jack."

"You got a spare?"

She walked round to the open boot. The spare wheel lay there. Picking it up, I bounced it on the ground. It was full of air.

"Right so far" I smiled "let's collect some rocks."

We built a sloping ramp under the car - in front of the flat wheel.

I asked her to start the car and drive slowly forward until the flat wheel rested on top of the improvised ramp.

I waved her to stop.

Together we built another pile of rocks between the wheels and up to the chassis. She reversed the car a few inches back off the first ramp till the chassis met the second pile of rocks. I dug away the ramp rocks from under the flat wheel. The wheel hung free of the ground. Replacing it with the spare wheel I wedged a stone in front and under it. She drove the car forward up the stone a few inches so taking the weight off the chassis. We removed the jack rocks and she reversed the car off the ones under the wheel.

"So simple," she laughed, "I would never have thought of that! Well now we can be on our way. Thank you oh so much!" She burst into tears.

"Hey" I said, "we made it, no need to cry."

Hunching her shoulders, she wiped her eyes with a grimy hand and smiled.

She was rather good looking.

"Lets go!" She said.

Only trouble was she was going back the way I had come.

xxxxxxx

The girl drove me to her home in a village about thirty kilometres off the main road. We arrived there late in the afternoon, unpacked the car and I took it down to the local garage to have the puncture fixed and buy a car jack.

Back at her cottage again I found her bathed, hair brushed, lip stick on and preparing a meal for us.

"You have been so helpful!" She smiled "Have a bath! Supper will be on the table in a moment. I put some of my brother's clean clothes out for you," she pointed "in the spare room. You can sleep there tonight."

We shared a quiet meal.

She poured coffee and we moved out to relax on the veranda.

"Why did you stop?" She asked.

"You needed help."

"But people don't stop these days, it's too dangerous! So why did you?"

"If I did not stop and you were beaten up and raped I would be guilty. If I do stop and it's a trap and I get beaten up or shot, then you are guilty. Not me! So! No problem."

"That's most unusual. Where are you from? How did you come to keep such an old fashioned perspective in these days of greed, immorality and selfishness?"

"I grew up in the bush. There is no place for weakness there. And you?" I asked, "Where are you from?"

"I?" She looked sad. "I am alone! My family don't want to understand me. This house is mine. I write and do Homeopathy and Reiki healing for a living. I am into walking - swimming in the sea - dancing - music - art - nature. I have five brothers - only one of them visits and not very often. Those are his clothes you are wearing."

She poured more coffee. A half moon slipped over the horizon. Reaching out she took my hand in hers. Holding it to her face she murmured.

"Thank you for helping me. You've made me feel everything is worth while."

Gently kissing my knuckles, she replaced my hand on my lap.

We went back into the cottage.

xxxxxxx

Early morning sunshine flooded my room. Birds whistled me awake. The girl stood at the foot of my bed holding two cups of tea. Our eyes met and understanding grew. Placing the cups on the bedside table she sat down on the bed. Her blond hair tousled from sleep. Her gown silky and hugging her body! Her eyes, misty!

Ever so slowly, she bent over and touched my lips with hers. Soft warm and very, very, special!

The tea grew cold.

xxxxxxx

I walked into the village to the cafeteria and asked if any one knew the man with the Mercedes.

"Yep, he lives in Gatvill but he also has a business here."

"I got a lift with him yesterday! I left my bag in his car. Any chance you know when he will be back?"

"He's already back, drove in half an hour ago. You can find him at the hardware shop on the corner. He owns it."

I walked to the corner. The Mercedes was parked outside the store. My bag lay on the back seat. The car was locked. I asked a counter hand where I could find the man. He pointed to an open door.

I knocked on the door and walked in. He was bent over a desk. Looking up he smiled,

"Hi there, so sorry about yesterday," he said "I've got your bag in the car." Waving his hand at an office chair he said "Have some tea with me."

"Thanks." I sat.

"What was the story with the woman?"

"Flat tyre! We got it fixed. She lives here in this village. Maybe you know her, the writer, artist and Reiki healer!"

"Oh hell. Will I ever get it right?"

Tea arrived with biscuits.

"Why were you afraid to stop?" I asked.

"I used to stop and help people but somehow over the years my attitude has changed. This new South Africa is affecting me in a strange way. I swear, I drink, I blame everyone else for everything I think is wrong and now I use the excuse that I am afraid of being hurt as a reason to not do what I should do."

Shaking his head he said,

"You know what I thought of after I dropped you?"

"No."

"The last time I went to church the pastor preached the story of the good Samaritan. What the hell has gone wrong with me? It takes a bushy hitch hiker from the desert to bring it home to me."

"Someone once said to me that Jesus Christ's message to the Jews at the crucifixion was `No matter how much you hurt me, even if you kill me, I will not let you touch my soul!' and then he forgave them for killing his body because he understood that had they known what they were doing they would never have done it and the whole purpose would have been lost! I think we no longer understand that it is better to die as a honourable man than to live as a coward. Better to do right and die for it than to do wrong to save your own life."

He nodded.

I said, "My father told me that in the old days, when the South African Afrikaner people stood as individuals believing in the seven virtues, they built little empires stretching from the Cape all the way to Kenya. But when they stood together as one under the Nationalist Party their strong spirit was subdued by the mindlessness of unbridled democratic politics and they began to blame everyone else for any pain they felt.

The old Afrikaner died and a new, self righteous – arrogant - bully Boer was born."

"Yah, yah!" He said "Probably right - and now?"

"Well the truly sad part is that generally speaking the majority of white South Africans not only agreed to give their country away, they also gave their children's inheritance and future away and destroyed the long term security of their parents. They subjected everybody to a certain bitter future. The natural reaction to denying the truth is to slip deeper into the lie. Swapping integrity for immorality has led us deeper and deeper into degenerative thought and actions. We are now sick right down into our hearts and it shows in our immoral behaviour. We have to learn how go back to being individuals belonging to a culture built on integrity and a high moral code. The white South African will have to learn all over again to live a life worth living by adopting a new attitude or maybe re-adopting an old attitude. Forget our anger at the British or the locals. Remember it was us and our fellow South Africans who gave our heritage away - nobody took it from us!"

Angrily he said,

"Yes! And subconsciously we all know we gave up knowing it was wrong to do so. We know we chose expediency above morality and with it the result, our fast deteriorating moral perspective!

Yes you are right, South Africa is rotting and the very people who claimed their independence from us, are now suffering far more than when we ruled! The sad thing is that our country is degenerating into mindless mayhem!"

He looked desperate. I spoke,

"Stand up! It does not matter if no one stands with you! You are a practising Christian so you know that when Christ died on the cross no one stood with Him but because of his attitude his purpose has lived on as it never could have done had he given in to fear like Ian Smith or Botha!"

"It's so easy to say but hard to do."

"It is so with everything that is worthwhile."

xxxxxxx

I stood at the dinning room table with my packed bag at my feet.

"Why must you go?" She cried, "We have so much in common, so much to share."

"I belong outside your life."

"I'll follow you wherever you go!"

"Where I go you cannot come. I am also torn apart by this decision to leave."

"The whole town loves you! Everyone has changed since you came! What about them?"

"And I love the whole town! But what must be must be! I am leaving tomorrow!"

XXXXXXX

BROKEN BEACH BUGGY

Early next morning, before she woke, I put a bunch of yellow roses on her bedside table, picked up my bag from the floor in the dining room and left the cottage. I caught a lift in a black taxi. Actually the taxi was red - it was the occupants who were black. The driver talked at the top of his voice. The radio blared out huge drumbeats. The taxi smelt of dead cigarettes and stale beer. The driver jerked the steering wheel back and forwards. He drove far too fast. My head swam.

Ahead of us a beach buggy stood at the side of the road with its rear bonnet up. Coincidence again? The taxi screeched to a stop behind the beach buggy. The driver stuck his head out the window and shouted at the man bent over its engine.

"You ok, you need help?"

Grateful for the opportunity, I clambered out of the taxi making sure I dragged my bag with me.

"Don't worry," I shouted to the taxi driver, "I know beach buggies! I will help him."

The taxi roared off in a cloud of smelly black smoke. I turned to the owner of the beach buggy. It was Robert! Together we isolated and repaired a faulty cable. I put my bag on the back seat alongside a pile of groceries. He drove to a turn off to the west where a dirt road led away through small hills and down to the sea.

"I have a camp down there." He nodded southwards. "Why don't you stay with me? You can help me with the digging!"

"What you digging for this time, more non earth elements?"

We laughed.

"No, I'm digging for artefacts."

We drove on to a wayside cafe where we sat talking over a cup of tea.

xxxxxxx

Robert's camp lay partially hidden by a cluster of rocky outcrops.

A huge dog, barking and wagging its tail, ran out to greet us.

"Home." Robert smiled. "I've been up the road for two days. Nero, my dog, stayed behind to look after the camp."

Nero is a huge Bullmastiff cross Saint Bernard! He rushed up to meet us. He licked the Stranger's hands. He licked the bags and the wheels and the car. His tail wagged his body into a frenzy!

"Is he a new dog?"

"Yes! I found him a long way out of civilization. He had been abandoned. He has become a fantastic companion! I love him!"

We unpacked. Robert made tea on his gas burner.

"I am pleased to see you!" He said, "I need a little help with a most unusual find. Tomorrow we work! Today you tell me about your trip down the coast from where I left you and then I will tell you about another place I dug into when I was young!"

xxxxxxx

We talked and talked.

We ate. The dog kept his big brown eyes glued to Robert.

Wiping his lips with a serviette, Robert said,

"Not much time for any long stories now. Suffice it to say that I once found two corpses in graves in Rhodesia. One was a European and the other a Mongolian African cross. They had been buried about six hundred years ago. When we have time one day I will tell you about it all and about some other strange ruins I also investigated."

We set off at sunrise the next day.

Close to the camp was a rock and gravel hillock thrusting up out of the sand like a large pimple. The other hillocks surrounding it were very different. They had slabs of sedimentary rock jutting out at an angle from their sides. Sand was backed up against them on their eastern sides.

Robert had started to dig on the northern side of the rock and gravel hillock. He had tunnelled horizontally for about seven metres into the mound. A vertical flat-sided stone slab blocked his progress. The slab was squared off at the top and sides. We dug around it finding it to be about one metre wide by about one and a half metres high. It was wedged into a wall made up of a dry porridge of gravel and clay.

Robert inserted long steel rods with flat ends like tyre levers into the crack at the side of the rock. We hammered them in deeper with an iron mallet. Satisfied, he grinned at me. It was hot in the little tunnel. Sweat streamed off us. Together we put sideways pressure on the levers and prised the flat stone away from its bed.

Slowly, with much grunting from us, the rock was manoeuvred out of the way and lowered onto the floor of the passage.

A small square hole lay exposed in the gravel-clay wall. Small yes! But big enough for us to climb through!

Robert looked pleased, even a little excited.

"Pass the lamp." He said.

He pushed the lamp into the dark hole. It lit up a level tunnel running another five metres deeper into the mound to where the end was blocked by another flat stone.

Checking first for snakes or any other problems, Robert crawled along the passage. He reached the end and pushed against the slab. It moved. He could not turn around in the small passage. He muttered in the closeness and pushed again. The slab opened. He crawled through. I followed. We stood up inside a domed room and Robert shone the light round and up and all over the room.

At the far end was an oblong rock bench. On it stood a hand-sized statue of a pig. Behind the pig, on a tray, was a neat pile of white, round, ceramic tiles. The floor was clean. The arched ceiling was smooth but unevenly dotted with pebbles - some very small - some the size of a boy's fist. Most were dull but a few were white or coloured either brown or black. One near the top was green.

There was nothing else in the room.

We walked around inspecting the domed roof. It swept down to the floor on all sides. The pebbled areas were separated from the floor to the roof by triangles of blank areas, wide at the bottom and coming to a point together at the top like the petals of a flower.

The pig was beautifully made. It seemed to be a copy of a cross between a warthog and a domestic Landrace pig.

He picked it up.

"Heavy," he mused "either lead or gold."

Passing the pig to me he sat on the rock bench and shone the torch around the ceiling.

"Interesting!" He muttered.

I studied the pig in the changing light.

"Why a pig?" I asked.

Robert grunted.

I kept quiet.

"Okay!" He said at last, pointing "That's us up there! Our world! You see that green rock? The nearest white one to it is our sun. The small black stone close to our world is our moon." He grunted again, "Okay. There's the milky-way - Jupiter - Venus - Mars. Okay! Okay!" He laughed. "We have done it! We found it." Without saying any more he picked up the ceramic tiles, walked back to the hole in the wall, asked me to bring the lamp and the pig and bent over to crawl out.

"Wait!" I shouted, "What are these?"

He turned round, shone his light at where I was pointing on the wall near the floor.

"What?"

"Some more green stones!"

"You kidding!"

"No. Look there are seven here next to each other, see! Right here!"

I stepped closer to the wall, crouched down and shone my torch at the stones. The green stones were grouped around one large white stone. There were lots of small black stones dotted around them. Robert crouched down next to me.

"Well I'll be damned! Looks like these are a whole lot of worlds around one giant sun! Hey look! See there amongst the black stones? See! There's a silver coloured stone. Not round like the others but like an elongated square! Now what on earth is that?"

"A huge space ship!" I laughed.

"Why not? It certainly could be and if so it suggests these green worlds could be occupied! Maybe they're telling us that there is intelligent life way out there beyond our comprehension!"

We took photographs of all the sections of the walls to study on the computer. We found two more separate green stones at the bottom of the far wall, each with its own sun and moon."

"Come, let's go." smiled Robert.

I followed him out with the lamp and the pig.

xxxxxxx

That evening we sat on deck chairs at Robert's camp sipping a delicious white wine. He was blissful.

"Tomorrow we take more photo's of the interior of the roof and take one more careful look then we can close up and make it all look as it was before. I will take you back to the road and you can carry on with your travels, or, if you want, you can come with me and help me for a living. I will pay you! You interested?" raising his eyebrows he looked at me, "What do you say?"

"Sounds good, but why close it up. There may be more to find."

"We found all we need to find." He adopted a conspiratorial air. "You any idea what it is that we found?"

"A hole in the ground with a picture of the skies on its roof, a table and a gold pig, some discs! No I have no idea what we found."

"Remember the temple ruins in the desert? Well that was stage four. This is stage one. We have to find two more stages to complete the story."

I tried to look as if I understood. He laughed happily.

"Dream about it tonight!" He said, "Then let me know tomorrow if you are coming with me or travelling on alone."

xxxxxxx

The morning sun lit a heavy sea.

"Well?" He asked, "Did you dream?"

"Yes, but it was weird. All about pigs and space ships and strange looking people. About scientists and doctors."

"Don't forget your dreams. Rehearse them. Have you decided whether you want to come with me?"

"I'd love to join you. There is so much you know that I want to learn."

"Okay so be it. But for now I will leave you down the road at the next village so that you can carry on with your trip until I am ready to start the next stage. Here, take this mobile phone and sun operated charger. We can keep in contact so that you can let me know where you are when I want to come and get you. Is that okay with you?"

I nodded,

"Thanks!"

"Ok then! I plan to be off to the Cape tomorrow. By the way, you do have travel documents with you don't you?"

"Yes."

"Okay, time for bed! See you in the morning."

"Night!"

XXXXXXX

ANOTHER POINT OF VIEW

I couldn't sleep that night. Eventually I got up, put warm clothes on and walked down to the beach. Sad to have to part with Robert but I think that maybe he is right - for now I must carry on alone! Spray bursting off weathered rocks caught at the grey mist, dragging it down into a boiling sea. I crouched at the edge of the largest rock tasting the salt from centuries of weathering as the early sun, fighting its way out of far hills to the east, spilt wet light across kelp strewn white sand. An eternity of waves thrashing at the shore - etching their signatures on the rocks, dragging the land into the sea!

Robert, also sharing with creation, walked towards me.

Looking once more into the distances before turning to him I said,

"Hello. You're up early!"

"Hi," he answered. "Yes I am. Are you saying goodbye to this place?"

"Yes! Actually I spent most of the night walking along the beach."

"Did you! Well I spent the night in the luxury of a tented apartment." He laughed.

The tide crept over our rock. Spray wet us. Robert smiled a sad smile,

"Come to my apartment for breakfast."

xxxxxxx

After breakfast, we packed up and left. Robert drove as far as the mountains where we stopped for the night at the foot of a magnificent cliff. We talked late. He drew pictures in my mind, pictures of music, words, wind, water, valleys, people!

We said our goodnights.

I drifted off to sleep.

I dreamt Robert took me up the mountain to stand at the edge of a precipice. The world fell away before us in a vertical drop to depths beyond our vision. Behind us, on the slopes of a green valley, nestled a sleepy village.

In the dream I heard Robert speaking.

"We've shared many things!"

"Yes," I said, "and yet I still don't know your full name or who you really are!"

"True." He agreed, "But then although you may know your name, you don't know who you really are!"

"That is so!"

"So I probably know you better than you know yourself."

"How come?"

"Because I see the part of you that you are hiding and from it I know how to get the right answer!"

"Answer to what?"

"To anything or to everything about you. It also helps when looking for the right answer to first ask the right question."

"The world" I said "is full of unanswered questions, full of questions never asked. So how does that bring you to know who I am when I don't know who you are let alone who I might be!"

"Well, that means you haven't asked the right question yet!"

"Okay! Okay! I pass. But I do have another question, what are we doing standing on the edge of this precipice?"

Turning his startling eyes on me he asked,

"Do you trust me?"

"Yes." I looked him in the eye, "Yes I do trust you!"

"Why?"

"You have never let me down!"

"Even when what you experienced was out of the ordinary, like the temple? Crazy stuff - at least by normal people's understanding!"

"Depends what you mean by normal people!"

"Would you agree that living on the edge is not acceptable to so-called 'normal' people?"

"Generally speaking, yes."

"Would you agree that stepping off the edge is not acceptable to anybody, it is so obviously a crazy thing to do!"

Laughing, I said,

"Stepping off the edge of this precipice into nothing would be a crazy thing to do by anybody's reckoning."

"Too true, stepping off into 'nothing' would be a silly thing to do but stepping off into an eternity of truth and love would be a silly thing not to do."

"Yes, but you would be hard pressed to get somebody to step off this precipice, even for a maybe promise of love and the truth."

"Unless they had faith in you!"

"Faith?" I laughed.

"Yes, faith! Never heard of faith? Faith is stepping off the edge into the unknown because someone you trust and have faith in asks you to. If you do it and it works! You will come to know the reality of what was previously unknown to you."

"Okay," I said "putting your faith to the test successfully gives you more faith for the next step you take into the next unknown! Is that it?"

"Yes!"

"But if it fails you will either die or be permanently damaged and that would destroy your faith!"

"Yes! But you, my friend, have been set free by the truth you found in your recent experiences and as a result you are better equipped to accept, without reservation, what I'm now asking you to do!"

Without waiting for my comment he stepped off the edge of the precipice saying,

"Follow me!"

"Hey!" I screamed at him "You crazy or something, you can't do that!"

I woke up shaking. I listened to the night sounds and realising it was a dream I relaxed, rolled over and drifted off into dreamland again.

The picture of the cliff face refocused.

I watched Robert walk on out into the emptiness, leaving me alone with my fear. Looking back at the village behind me I saw the red roof of a house. I saw school playing fields lying partially hidden by giant gum trees. I saw cows as they lay chewing the cud on green pastures. Birds sang. This was my world. I loved it.

Only moments ago I was happy in my world but now my very being cried out "Don't lose him!" While my mind said "Don't lose your world!"

Robert walked on out into space leaving behind clear-cut footprints suspended in the clean blue tinted air.

"Hey you." I screamed. "Hey, wait a minute."

Ignoring my shouting, he walked on.

Turning again to the scene behind me I agonized over my predicament. Tears of pain wet my face. What about my life, my hopes, my friends?

"No! No! No!" I screamed at the fast receding figure. The valley at my feet echoed my plea. From the village drifted the hungry sound of music laced with happy memories - the tinkling of laughter - the aroma of a mother's cooking. In despair I answered the truth of it all.

"Yes!" And I stepped out, oh so very carefully, onto the first footprint.

It held.

I slid my other foot out and over to the next footprint.

I wobbled.

I felt myself falling.

The pack on my back holding my identity documents, my passport, my money, and my raincoat, swung out dragging me off balance. Snatching at the third footprint with one hand I tore at the backpack shoulder straps with the other. The pack and its contents fell away. Free from my burden I hauled myself up and spread my shaking body out over the next three footprints.

Below me clouds floated over bottomless depths. In front, the distant figure of Robert walked on. Struggling to my feet I stepped cautiously from footprint to footprint. As I gained confidence I noticed a tendency for Roberts foot prints to move to meet my searching feet. This encouraged me to stride out. I dared to glance up at the now distant figure silhouetted against the sunset. To my surprise and vast relief I saw him seated at his last footprint.

He was building a small fire.

I ran along the pathway of footprints. Reaching the fire, I sat down on a cushion of air, and relaxed.

Looking up he asked,

"Not so hard hey?"

The tension drained out of me and I laughed. Stretching my hands out to the flames I dared to admit,

"Not so hard but I do have the same problem. For the life of me I still don't know your full name. Everyone calls you a stranger!"

"You said it," he responded "for the life of you it might be an excellent idea for you to learn who I am. I dare say you may be in serious need of that understanding sooner or later. Give me your hand."

I stretched my hand out but seeing it was dirty and his was clean, I jerked it back again. He smiled and said,

"Look at my hand not at yours!"

Reaching out again he took my hand in his. When he let go I saw that my hand was now clean.

We laughed.

"Now, we are one with each other and as I lead you on you will become, as your friends back there would say, 'a chip off the old block'."

Where he was leading me I had no idea and I dared not ask.

xxxxxxx

The light of morning flowed over me.

I woke from my dream.

Robert was gone! I saw his footprints in the sand stretching away towards the morning star. Leaping up I ran after him and on catching up I said,

"What was that all about?"

"What?" He asked.

"You walking on air!"

"You must have been dreaming!" He laughed. "Go back into your dream!"

"This is crazy!" I shouted, "Why won't you tell me?"

Robert looking off into the distance, said,

"There are many different organisations in this world and many different orders - each one having its own purpose in the overall plan. For example there is the order of The Knights Templar or the order of the Bilderbergers. Then of course there are the orders which you could say belong to different groups like that of Lucifer or Satan and churches and religions which are again grouped into different orders."

While he spoke, mountains took shape in front of us as the sun melted the distance away. I became so involved with myself and these new thoughts that I lost sight of Robert! I sat down on the soft grass. Stillness pervaded the place, yet in my inner being I heard music.

Resting back, my head on my arms, I watched fluffy clouds drift through the branches above.

It was right to be alone in this place.

Drifting off to sleep again I found myself back with Robert at the fire in the sky, he was speaking,

"In the world you should say 'yes' to whatever is your understanding of creation, yes to your purpose and finally you say yes to your connection with what most people call the most High God who is beyond the confines of the world's and of the heavens, the one who is beyond, within and before eternity and infinity and beyond our understanding.

Then, in every situation that you find yourself, let yourself be guided by your own spirit into the knowledge and wisdom you need. Guided by the total of the 'all spirit' who will be your advisor, your counsellor, your mentor and your director through its natural connection to your 'I am' within you. Remember, your 'I am' is the way the truth and the life.

Then as you accept the leading of the spirit, look out for those sent to help you on your way as did the Greeks who came to help Christ before his crucifixion. Finally, once you have said yes, choose, not in the matter of material or worldly choices, for as was explained to you, in reality you have no choice there. Choose in the abstract."

"What do you mean abstract?"

"Choose to look inside and wait for the answers to come to you. Choose to live by principle and not by compromise. Choose not to give in but to hang on when everything seems to be against you. Choose happiness in the face of all adversity! Choose to uplift rather than to destroy. Choose action rather than prevarication. Choose to accept your concept of your God and his offer to you rather than to be forever demanding his attention. Choose to die for your fellow man rather than to abandon him in order to live for your self.

Choose to forgive."

He paused then spoke very quietly and slowly,

"Choose life!"

"You mentioned an offer?"

"You have been offered the opportunity to work with what is known by the world as the 'the disciples' but from outside the confines of religion. It is almost as if you do not belong anywhere in this world because you do not remember who you are or who your parents were nor what your real name is or your religion. So by default you come from outside convention and I believe that you are protected by the armour that such a situation provides for you.

So accept it and fight the good fight. Many people these days hate religions and politics and mostly for a good reason but you have been brought up as a Christian so find out exactly who or what The Christ is or is not to you and use that understanding as you do your work. See with what we call the eyes of Christ. Listen with His ears and love with His love. Then your work and the understanding and knowledge not known to this generation will be given to you as and when you need it. And Ian! You must write it down! Speak it! Sing it! Paint it! Live it!"

The dream faded and I slept.

xxxxxxx

The sun woke me. I walked back to Robert at the tent. We did not speak about my dream. He cooked breakfast over a campfire. I looked up at him,

"May I ask you something?"

"Of course."

"Am I wrong when I say 'being born in sin' is like being thrown into deep water as a baby, the water demands that you learn how to swim to survive, as does the sin demand you learn righteousness for the same reason?"

"Could be, and?"

"Lies create the need to search for the truth?"

"Yes!"

"Every lie is about the truth! So every lie has the truth as a starting point."

"Go on."

"Darkness creates the need for light. There is no need for light if there is no darkness."

"Good thinking so far, anything else?"

"Yes, most people try to be both what society demands of them and to be what they wish to be, so they fall between two stools.

They look for recognition from society and satisfaction from themselves and the two do not always compliment each other so they end up failing in both."

"That is so. Both ways are wrong. The way you go depends on your purpose in life."

"Oh!"

"Someone has to be Judas Iscariot otherwise Christ would not have been crucified in the manner that he was nor could Judas's actions be judged, nor his choice to either repent or remain in the world be possible. Someone has to be you for your life to bear the fruit it is designed to bear and be judged both in the good and the bad depending on the Creator who made everything for His purpose of bringing all of creation to the place where everyone can make an enlightened choice."

"Oh, and just who and what is the Creator?"

"We give the name 'God' to explain that part of everything that we have absolutely no idea about. No one seems to really know where we all came from - if anywhere! If the creation had to be created then why does the Creator not also need to be created? If the world had a beginning then what was before the world? Did whatever that was also have a beginning? If God made the world and all of creation, what was He busy doing for the unimaginable time that existed before He made it?

Whether there is a God or there is not! Whatever He is or whatever He isn't we may never come to know! But at the same time it is also possible that we may, one day, come to know! God could be a power leading aliens from another world, or, a power beyond all of our imagination, beyond everything! Then of course, He may not exist at all except in our imaginations! Some religions say that we ourselves are either individual manifestations of God or that we are a part of the totality of the 'All Life' called God, and some even go so far as to say that 'I am God!'

Even Christ said that greater is He within you than anything outside! He also said the Kingdom of Heaven is within you!

We don't know! And that is why we call Him God! That is why there are so many different versions of God and so many different religions and so many different sects within each religion and so many differing perspectives within the people of each sect!

To believe in God is an admission of 'maybe'! Belief and knowing are two vastly different understandings. The word belief implies doubt! Whereas knowing implies it is so!"

"Yes, I believe you may be right. Sad though!"

Robert left me at a small town near the coast. For the first time on this walk about I felt lonely.

XXXXXXX

BOOK THREE

ROBERT

ROBERT

People are gathering on the Victoria Falls Hotel verandah for tea. The bridge spanning the gorge on the Zambezi River, which can be seen from the hotel, is crowded with bungee jumpers. Behind them a diesel locomotive hauls rail trucks, loaded with Zambian copper, over the bridge.

I choose a table near the terrace and sit facing the falls. My mind wanders into the past, the present and what of the future?

An old man walks up to my table - a bottle of coke in each hand.

He interrupts my thoughts,

"Hello Robert. Would you care for a coke?"

Surprised, I look up,

"Why yes, thank you!"

He pulls out a chair, sits down and smiles."

Taking the proffered coke, I grin,

"You here on holiday?"

"No. I'm here to see you!"

"Oh!" Surprised.

"Yes. We certainly do have a lot to talk about. Such as your camps! Your plans to leave Africa! Your family! Your search for the history of man in Central Africa! In fact, your life story!"

"It seems you know a lot about me."

"True, I do!"

I turn to look again at the Victoria Falls, at 'THE SMOKE THAT THUNDERS'. Speaking very softly I say,

"It's lovely sitting here in the late afternoon watching the sun sink though the spray. Beautiful!"

The old man leaning back in his chair nods, he asks,

"May I spend a week or two with you?"

I turn to look at him,

"What? Who are you and why do you want to spend time with me?"

"My name is Redro! Most people call me Red. I have been sent to you."

"What do you mean - sent? Who sent you and what for?"

"Maybe it would be easier for me to say that I have been authorised to bring certain understandings to you which are pertinent to your interest in archaeology - the origin of man and the various political and religious orders that influence the state of the world."

"Humph."

"I have not come to fool you!"

"Really?" I mutter, "Ok, so be it. But I am leaving for South Africa today so if you want to spend time with me you better be ready to travel!"

Red nods, I ask,

"Where's your kit?"

xxxxxxx

We left the Victoria Falls in my old beach buggy, taking the road which leads west to the border post into Botswana.

"You not going via Bulawayo?" Red asked,

"No ways, there's no fuel in Zimbabwe at the moment and a whole heap of trouble. No! We go to South Africa through Botswana! Longer but a lot safer and easier."

"You have a camp in South Africa, in the Soutspansberg Mountains near the town of Louis Trichardt!"

"Yes, but not for long!"

"Why?"

"Local political pressure, land claims, electricity failures, increased criminal activity and a general breakdown of law and order. Reason enough?"

"How come such mayhem?"

"They are trying to mix oil with water without using a catalyst!"

"What?"

"If the Africans wanted our kind of civilisation they would have developed it for themselves long before Africa was colonised."

"That's certainly a different way of looking at it!"

"Whatever!" I turn to look at Red, "There is not one African country that when it got it's so called freedom hasn't moved away from the west's concept of civilisation back towards the African concept. The problems arise during the transition from western concepts back to African are - "

Red interrupted,

"Explain what you mean by that."

"As the rule of law according to the west changes back to the African way there is an intermediary stage where there is mindless contradiction. An example of the result of this is that during the transition period, which is right now, when a report is made by an unknown man to the police in Musina to the effect that you have beaten him, the police arrest you and put you in jail. The fact that you never beat him, you never knew him nor have you ever set eyes on the complainant means nothing, you get to stay in jail until you pay a bribe to get out and while you are there you are raped. This would not happen during either the pre-colonial African civilisation systems nor would it happen under the present western civilisations."

"And just what is the difference between the two that is the cause of the problem?"

"Well my perspective of western civilisation is that it is, or was, based in concepts such as private enterprise, the right to own what you create, a certain type of morality and the rights of the individual. Old Africa has a completely different perspective based in community ownership of land and in traditional moralities. The King or the Chief is right regardless! All that goes with these concepts I see as not civilised! That is in terms of western understanding although I am sure that Africa sees its own ways as civilised by their understanding."

"So then, what is your understanding of genuine civilisation?"

"You want to talk politics so 'here goes!' My understanding is that good government is based on the principle that the most capable should rule and the law should be designed to represent the individual which ensures that as every person is an individual, then everyone is included and covered whereas government elected by and for the majority, by its very nature, excludes a very important section of the population known as 'the minority'.

I say that it is far better to be well governed by those who know how than badly governed by those who haven't a clue and as it is only a small minority who really do know what it is all about then it is better to be well ruled by that minority than badly ruled by an unenlightened majority.

Civilised governments role or duties should be firstly, protection of the individual, secondly the maintenance of law and order, then protection of property rights and finally a monetary system based on money being limited to being a method of valuing for the purpose of trading and no more than that!

What a man earns or what he creates belongs to him and that principle should be upheld and protected by government. This encourages creative energy and protects the resultant product of that energy. It also develops an order that moves forward and not backwards.

The bulk of taxes are paid by the entrenpeurs, the manufacturers, private enterprise etc. The tax paid by the workers is derived from payments made by the entreprneurs"

"Tell me more about money. What you said leaves me a little confused!"

"Well, civilised governments should maintain the value of the purchasing power of money. This is done by relating the amount of money in circulation to the amount of product produced within the country. Explicit in the amount and value of money within the country is the understanding that a loaf of bread, that is the product, gives the value to money and not the other way around. To charge interest on something that in its self has no value will push the cost of relative valuable things up thereby deflating the value or purpose of money! As an example, if you borrow money to buy a house worth a hundred thousand pounds and pay interest on the loan over the next twenty years making a total payment including the interest to the amount of, lets say, a hundred and twenty thousand pounds! It means that as the house is still the same value at the end as it was in the beginning, you have devalued the money used to buy the house by twenty per cent. This leads to inflation and eventually depression.

Then there is the maintenance of standards. This implies that the people and the government uphold the ethics of honour, integrity and virtue. Lastly it is government's duty to effectively discipline those of the adult members of the community who are not naturally moral or self disciplined and thus keep the morality of the nation in hand especially in the matter of preventing the encroachment of the filth of the world on its own community and within it's own affairs. What I mean by 'adult' is the understanding that when children are mature enough to have babies then obviously they are then, by nature, mature enough to care for and take responsibility for those babies! Up until that age the child can be considered as not mature and this is the time or period in which parents, teachers and government departments are duty bound to teach the child self discipline! The biblical saying, 'spare the rod and spoil the child' is relevant." It is too late to teach someone self-discipline after they mature."

"Interesting! So what is the filth of the world?"

"There are two kinds of filth, one is natural like mud or cow dung. The other, the unnatural filth of the world is when man takes something inherently beautiful and uses it in a filthy way. He debases it, defiles it or abuses it. Take the word for making love as an example. The act of sex is the highest compliment a man and a woman can pay each other and as such it is very, very, special! It is an act of love, of procreation, of togetherness, of caring, of family, of commitment. In a civilised, moral society the act of lovemaking is kept both decent and private. But the world today in all it's deviousness demands in the false name of freedom of expression the right to debase and desecrate what is beautiful, so the act of love is turned into a four letter swear word - the "f..." word, and the act is further degraded by making it public and by making pornography legal. When the mindless swearing, cruelty and porn on some of the television programme's and on the streets is acceptable but jokingly saying 'Golly Wog' or 'Paki' or whistling at a pretty girl is not! Then you have to agree it is totally crazy! Especially when it is still ok to say Yankee or Brit!"

Red spoke.

"Sorry it ooomo I oct off a time bomb there. What do you say about tribalism?"

"Well, I say, to me tribalism is an acceptable 'ism' but it does not fit too well with the western concept of civilisation. It is obviously valued by the majority of Africans and their perspective should be recognised and accepted as such by us. People of different origin or culture should be accepted as such as long as they abide by the law of the land.

I do have a problem in the fact that in the tribal system the individual is not recognised. People must conform to the group. They must look after the head of the tribe or the village and whatever the head says is acceptable regardless of whether he is right or wrong. In my concept of a civilised community it is the other way around! The head of the community must look after and guide the community.

 Secondly western civilisation is based on a different understanding of the difference between right and wrong! I see it as objective rather than subjective! Thus if a tribal government bases its governance on the principle that the tribe must support the chief or king simply because he is chief and that his government is for the protection of himself and his government which results in the ordinary individual being of little consequence! That is the African perspective! This is contrary to western civilised systems. Our friend, president Robert Mugabe and his supporters in Zimbabwe are perfect examples of racist tribalism and a total lack of understanding of what money really is and of the nature of production and the western ethical values which lead to both individual and national wealth and prosperity."

Red commented,

"One of the radio announcers in South Africa said about Zimbabwe, and I will try to quote him accurately! He said, "It is criminal that a country with such vast natural wealth and twenty odd million people available to harvest that wealth should suffer poverty. What do you make of that?"

I thought it over.

"Okay, if you put a good manager in charge of a failing business he will pull it round and make it prosperous! But if you put a bad manager in charge of a prosperous business he will drag it to the insolvency court. Agree?"

"Yes."

"Then if Zimbabwe has tremendous natural wealth and an abundance of people to harness and harvest it, yet it is falling deeper and deeper into massive poverty then obviously management must be extremely bad!"

"Isn't it a legacy of apartheid that is the underlying cause?"

I laughed,

"The old so called apartheid which built Zimbabwe into the bread basket of Africa has been replaced with the new black 'it's-all-mine apartheid!' The majority political system has enriched the new 'minority' leaders of Zimbabwe at the cost of the people, both entrepreneurs and workers who built the fantastic country that it once was. Hey, I'm tired of all this political stuff so I am off to bed! Good night and sleep well!"

We slept in the car at the Pontdrift border post.

XXXXXXX

ROBERT'S CAMP

The sun rose in the new 'democratic' South Africa.

Robert and Red woke, took a short walk outside to stretch their legs and then set off on the east bound road to the border town of Musina where they bought groceries and drove on down the south bound road to Robert's camp in the Soutspansberg Mountains.

The camp nestled under giant trees below a small waterfall on the south western end of a long narrow valley.

Robert parked his vehicle behind the thatched, pole and mud plastered main building. They carried the provisions in, placing them on the kitchen table, they set the kettle on to boil and sat down to chat.

"Well Red, now that we are here you can tell me what it is you want from me."

"Yes, but first I would like you to tell me why you are leaving Africa. I know you went on and on yesterday about the new political set up here, but you were born here! You are a third generation African. Your bones are made from the soil of Africa. You have loved it, cared for it, fought for it. Man is supposed to originate from Africa. So it is more than doubly your home! Why leave it now? Remember your grandfather! He rode a horse through southern Africa in the days when there were no roads, no towns, just wild bush and scattered mud hut villages. He slept in lion country with mosquitoes, malaria, tick bite fever and savage attacks from and by locals. He had no idea what lay ahead of him or what was following him or how or even if he would ever get back! Yet he went on! And you! You want to give up!"

"What you say is true, but for me it is really quite simple! As I said yesterday, the African people that is the black ones, fought for their way of life, for their country, for their independence. Simply put, they did not wish to live under the White African's control nor under the influence of Europe and its version of civilisation. They fought for the freedom to be what they are and that is 'African'.

They did not fight for democracy.

Democracy is to them a system imposed on them by Britain which they had to accept in return for being given the basic freedoms they fought for. There was a further benefit in accepting democracy - a guaranteed flow of aid into the country a lot of which could be diverted into the political leader's pockets. In any case they recognise that democracy is simply another way to bring the people of a country to their knees and weaken them so that they cannot fight back! It makes them easier to rule, just like communism or socialism or any other so called liberalism."

"How do they bring the people to their knees?"

"By destroying both the initiative of people to create for themselves and the need for them to be responsible for their own actions. By introducing a benefit system, which by force, robs those who work for a living and gives to those who don't and last, but certainly not least, by bringing in crazy rules where you are not responsible for your own actions!"

"Explain that last statement please."

"A nanny state where health and safety regulations destroy a man's strength and responsibility!"

"Maybe you can explain in more detail!"

"Yes, well! A nanny state turns adults into helpless demanding kids who refuse to help anyone else who needs help because it is the responsibility of the state to help. In any case if you do help someone they will probably use it as an excuse to sue you. You often see TV footage of yobs beating up a little old man for fun and the people around just ignore it! They walk on by! Absolutely disgusting!

Young unmarried girls get benefits when they irresponsibly fall pregnant.

These perspectives when put into practice build up a weak, dependent and immoral nation which is easy to rule and can be lead by the nose in whatever direction the rulers may choose. The powers that be can then lie and cheat with impunity. If you promulgate laws which set the criminal free and condemn the victim, you do this as much for the offender as you do it for the man in Parliament.

You get the picture?

The entrepreneurs who create the wealth of the country, the farmers who produce the food, the manufacturers who produce the goods and the personnel who run the services are in the minority and are accused of being rich at the expense of the poor. But it is these very entrepreneurs who, by taking risks and investing their own money and lives in their businesses, produce the wealth a large part of which is taxed and redistributed to the poor by way of benefits and free services.

In Zimbabwe the productive people have been robbed of their farms, businesses, factories and their dignity. The country is dying! The wise who had foreign citizenship took themselves, their money and their expertise out of the country before it was too late. This is aggravating the situation and is leading to the eventual total collapse of everything.

The world agrees with Mugabe when he blames the old colonial countries like Britain for Zimbabwe's present predicament while forgetting that it was Mugabe, with the worlds leading and backing, who in just a few years, destroyed the second richest nation in southern and central Africa.

Going back to the Africans fight for independence, it is the same reason that they fought which drives me to leave. I do not wish to subject myself to their way. I am not part of the millions of years that bred them into being what they are.

I will go to where my 'own kind' are in control of who and what they are. Back to where I have thousands of years of my ancestry dictating the ways of my country instead of the pathetic four generations of the Europeans in Africa. Four generations, which have collapsed under the power of money, liberalism, expediency and the fear of physical harm."

"You say you are not racist?"

"Most definitely not! I have many fantastic African friends!

I love Africa and I love the African people.

I like to relate the present problem with Africa in this way. If you take a horse and use it as a horse you get satisfaction. If you take a donkey and use it as a donkey you still get satisfaction. But! When you cross breed a horse with a donkey you get a mule and guess what? The mule may work harder because of hybrid vigour but it is infertile.

When you cross the pure African way with the pure European way you also get infertility! The inherent perfection of both races is lost in the mix and is thereby made infertile.

The majority of the new South African politicians, black, white and coloured, respect neither the true African way nor the true Western way but only their own glory and the power they get from democracy. Their understanding cannot bear fruit! It is infertile.

Take a look at poor old Mugabe. He was put there by so called 'GREAT' Britain. Britain imposed him on Rhodesia in the name of a mind-boggling misconception of morality. Britain is famous for imposing its perspectives on other people, for taking sides with the rebels of other countries which always leads that country into crazy degradation! Watch Mugabe on television. He was wears European clothes, speaks a European language, he is driven around by a man dressed as a European chauffeur in a European car. He lives in his European designed and built home and lords it over a European concept of Parliament. Even his education, both school and university was gained from the English! Do you get the picture?

Then the African side hidden under all that camouflage emerges in the dark of night and he shows his true nature such as he can own land in Europe but Europeans can't own land in Zimbabwe. He teaches young boys and girls to torture, to maim and kill for him!"

"Can't the two ways be mixed and the best of both be brought to the fore in Government?"

Robert laughed,

"Not really but they can exist side by side and even be compatible but the ignorant West calls this separate development and colours it with the slogan "racist!" Oil and water do not mix without a catalyst. From the first colonised or independent African state to the last, and that covers quite a few hundred years, the only workable catalyst that has ever been found is representative government combined with separate development and strict discipline. Unfortunately the truth of the matter and how to do it will never be accepted! Certainly not while it is purposefully hidden behind the present distorted concepts of morality, human rights and democracy!

I remember when the first black president of South Africa gave honour, money and support to the then worldwide condemned Presidents of Haiti and Zimbabwe. I also remember when, at the ten years of African democracy festival in South Africa, our friend Robert and his wife were the only ones to be honoured with a standing ovation by the crowd. Yes it was and still is so. Robert Mugabe is cheered as a hero by Africa because he is taking old Rhodesia as new Zimbabwe back to the old African way. The way ahead for South Africa is as clear as giant black writing on a white wall. South Africa will go the same way as Zimbabwe! Modern Africa is for the Africans and the African way. Let it go back or forward to where it should be, to where it was. And so be it! I am not staying for the carnage! I want out of here!

Why do I want to live overseas? Because it is inherent in the people there to understand what their fathers made and therefore they naturally want to stick to the rules.

I am one of those people!"

Red nodded, he spoke with compassion,

"I hear you! But I think you will find that the old Great Britain is no more and that the form of democracy practised there is destroying that once great civilisation. I doubt that Britain will last much longer. It is already on its way to collapsing into financial ruin leading to total anarchy. You look surprised! Well let me ask you, if eighty percent of the cars in a British car park are of a foreign make, then obviously the money to buy those cars went out of the country. Similarly over eighty percent of goods in most super markets and stores are foreign imports. Foreigners own most of the large corporations and business's in Britain! The majority of the manual labourers are foreign because the British are not prepared to work on farms and in factories. Those workers send their profits back to their home countries. Many large companies have moved their manufacturing industries and factories or offices and telephone answering services to India or China. In the UK the hard-pressed taxpayer is forced through taxation to financially support the benefit system, which in turn finances the non-working population and the young mothers of illegitimate children and foreigners who go to Britain because they know they will be well paid to not work!

In England so called human rights are guaranteed to the criminal at the expense of the innocent. When a man takes away someone else's rights you would expect him to automatically lose his own rights. But in England this is not so. In fact it seems the criminal not only goes to court with his own rights guaranteed, but! He goes reinforced by the rights he stole from his innocent victim!

You and I believe that the punishment should be so severe that it prevents the crime! Giving a rapist, a torturer and murderer ten years in a posh prison does not make either him or the next potential murderer think twice about what he is going to do.

The financial system is run on the crazy understanding that money has a value in its self and they trade on it leading irrevocably to financial disaster! If Britain doesn't change the monetary system I certainly don't give their economy much longer than two thousand and fifteen before it collapses into total disarray. For that matter, the worlds economy!

You want me to carry on?"

"Why not, you are all steamed up!"

"Okay. In nanny Britain, if someone gets bitten on the leg by a dog. The dog is put down. Killed. Yet when someone is beaten to death by some yobs the yobs are not put down! No, they are pardoned or given a short break in an institution filled with their own kind and fitted out with television, a gym, good food and you name it!

Yobs believe that the punishment due to an old gentleman for asking a yob to "Please don't swear in front of my wife," is death by beating and kicking. Yet those same yobs are encouraged to believe that the punishment for killing that old gentleman is at most a light sentence in an upmarket institution with his friends!

And more! When yobs are kicking an old woman to death on the street no one, listen to me, 'no one' stops to help her because it is none of their business or they are afraid of legal claims against them! People don't stop to help when they see a man lying across the road! They just drive on by! They say it is government's job to sort it out! Not theirs! Ok! Occasionally someone does interfere but often he gets taken to court for helping. Totally crazy! The other day a car knocked a cyclist down and the following cars simply drove over his legs! Again, no one stopped to help.

A country fast falling into the depths of degradation! Oh yes I mentioned health and safety, so what about it? It used to be that if a visiting man falls over a chair in your sitting room it is his own fault for not looking where he is going, after all it is your own sitting room so you are entitled to put your chairs wherever you like! In

Nanny Britain the owner of the house is guilty! Yes he is! Check it out and see. Health and safety laws have taken away the guts and strength of the people and replaced them with indifference and mind boggling monetary claims against innocent people.

And the rule of law! Don't laugh! I dare to repeat what I said earlier! In Nanny Britain he who instigates a crime and by so doing takes away the human rights of his victim goes to court not only with his own human rights still intact but is also reinforced by the rights he took away from the victim. In nearly every case where a man defends his home or his family or himself against an attacker, he, the victim is jailed and the attacker goes free!"

Robert interrupted,

"Yes I hear you, but at least in Britain when they realise how far down the road to anarchy they have been led they do have the guts and intelligence to restructure the law and return to the old understanding that an English man's home is his castle and not a yobs playground and rewrite the laws to re-establish his real basic rights so that he can react to a criminal intruder in whatever way is necessary to protect his home, his family and himself, even to the extent of shooting the intruder if necessary!"

"Maybe! But when? Hopefully not before it is too late! Let's change the subject with this observation! In Britain the denying of the rod is not only spoiling the children it is also spoiling the country. Do you remember the author Doctor Spock who initiated the concept of not spanking children? He said spanking ruined a child's personality! He was believed because he was considered an expert on the subject and so the laws were changed in America, in Britain and now all over the western world. Did you know that doctor Spock's own son eventually committed suicide! The majority of Britain's children are figuratively going the same way and as a result the whole country is also moving on to committing suicide!

You know that in the U.K. there is a National Health system? Well think about this, when a doctor attends to a patient who is responsible for paying him then the doctor is obviously directly responsible to the patient. But! If the patient is not paying because the government is paying on his behalf, then the doctor is responsible to the government and not the patient. The result is obvious, the patient becomes a number and other than ten minutes of the doctor's time the doctor is not obliged to him in any way. It's not hard to see what this will lead to!

The benefit system destroys the moral nature of people when it encourages those who are neither the very old nor the totally disabled to claim and receive financial support. Like people who have children just to get a free home and their living costs paid by the government or simply refuse to work and demand and receive financial support. There are families who have not worked for two or three generations and they live off the hard working taxpayer!

Britain has taken their liberality too far!"

He smiled,

"And another thing, May I dare to say it? Who the hell are Britain and America to interfere in other countries just because they feel like it but they get very angry when other countries try to interfere with them! You know what I mean?"

"Yes!"

Red spoke gently,

"Before you get too excited! The U.K. is not what you seem to be expecting it to be! Let me explain one especially crazy problem you will certainly get bogged down with when you arrive there! There are many people of British decent whose parents were born in British Colonies who do not qualify as British Citizens! Yet Foreigners, who are not descended from British stock, do qualify and in fact often have more rights in Britain than someone who has a British name and who is descended from a British family going back many generations but was born and brought up outside the UK in a British colony!

Hard to believe but true!

I know your father was born here and that he volunteered to fight for Britain in the last world war and that his Grandmother's family, registered in British Heraldry, goes back forty eight generations! His Grandfathers family tree goes back all the way to the time of William The Conqueror!

But you my friend will most likely not even be accepted as British and deported!"

Red sat quietly, then said,

"Oh well I suppose there is nothing we can do about it!

So! Are you prepared to tell me your story? That is, from the time you were abducted when you lived in the Gokwe area in what was then Southern Rhodesia until now."

XXXXXXX

ROBERT'S STORY

I used to work for the Agricultural Department of the Ministry of Internal Affairs in Rhodesia. We were tasked with teaching modern agriculture to the local Africans who lived in the protected areas known as Tribal Trust Lands. We were supplied with a house to live in and operate from in the civil service village of Gokwe, but I preferred the wilderness and so I built a camp for myself and my family on the Mtanke River about forty kilometres from the village.

The terrorist war was almost over. Ian Smith was about to give in. The Lancaster House agreement was on the table.

The meeting on the Victoria Falls Bridge had born fruit.

xxxxxxx

I had always wanted to explore the junction of the Mtanke and the Umniati rivers some fifteen kilometres east of my camp and decided that the time was now right to do so. Amos, the Internal Affairs messenger seconded to my camp said he would guide me along the very old track to the junction. He was excited about the trip but he said he wanted to let his family know he would be away over the weekend and so took three days off to visit them.

The day of our planned excursion was at hand. Jean, my wife, was eight months pregnant and felt she could not cope with the anticipated roughness of the trip so she stayed at the camp. My son Ian, Amos and I, drove off with two tents and sufficient provisions for a couple of days.

We arrived at the river junction having negotiated some extremely rough country.

"Well?" I asked Ian,

He flashed me a brilliant five year old's smile.

"Wow!"

We sat quietly in the Land Rover absorbing the breathless beauty of unspoilt nature. The tang of the African bush rode the hot air. Giant Toak and Jakkalsbessie trees danced in the heat haze Winter sunlight teased the fallen leaves that painted the rough earth a warm orange.

"Dad?"

"Yes!"

"Can I go down to the river?"

"Yes, but first we check for crocs."

Sliding off his seat Ian swung out onto soft sand. He wriggled his toes. Grinning at me, he ran, stubby legged down the bank onto a wide stretch of white sandy beach.

A lone man in torn clothes was watching us from the river. He shaded his eyes. Suddenly he shouted and dropping his fishing stick, scrambled over the rocks to us. It was the beggar who regularly pestered Jean at the camp. He was a very friendly chap but so insistent that he often brought her close to tears of desperation when only another gift of food or money or clothes would bring his pleading to a halt.

They said he was brain damaged! I said he was a brilliant actor!

"Mambo!" He shouted, "I am honoured to have you come to see me! I have fish for you and some bush oranges. I say welcome!"

Ian ran to him,

"Moses my friend what are you doing here?"

"I live here, up on that ridge."

Amos, the messenger interrupted,

"I will first collect firewood and then come back to help you put up the camp."

He seemed nervous. I frowned. Maybe he was afraid of the beggar. Maybe he believed the apparent mild madness of Moses was something to do with witchcraft. I waved him on and unloaded the Land Rover.

Moses and Ian started playing in the sand.

A quiet descended over the river.

Suddenly the birds stopped singing.

I looked up. Four armed terrorists or, as some called them, 'freedom fighters' depending on which end of the barrel you are looking at, faced me. Two others walked towards my son and the beggar.

My firearm was in the Land Rover, out of reach. I played it cool.

"Morning gentlemen," I said, "Can I help you?"

"Lie down on your stomach." The leader shouted, "With your arms stretched out."

Ian and Moses looked up, startled! Moses gave a yell of fear and ran like a crazy rabbit. The terrorists ignored him. One of them walked across to Ian and grabbing him by the hair dragged him to the Land Rover. Ian's white face and frightened eyes stared at me. He kept quiet.

Amos stepped out from the bush. He came up to the leader.

"You see," he said to the leader "I promised you and I delivered!"

"Ha!" Said the leader.

I was still standing.

One of the four walked towards me, raising the butt of his rifle he prepared to hit me on the head.

"Wait." Shouted the leader. "We have a long way to go. Tie his arms behind his back." Turning, he spoke to me "You make one wrong move and I cut your son's balls off. You got that?"

I looked at Ian. He squared his shoulders. He remembered my saying, never give in to force, rather die in honour than live as a coward. I nodded at the leader. Ian relaxed. I felt a deep fury building up inside me but I had to remain calm. For me to be hurt or die was one thing, for me to cause Ian unnecessary pain was another! They tied my hands together behind my back then tied Ian's left wrist to my right arm. The terrorists took what they wanted from the Land Rover then set it alight. Laughing with glee at the flames and the roaring they began to shake their heads and stamp their feet in a mad dance.

We were led away. Amos, the messenger, was given my rifle. He was told to guard us as we walked. He was happy.

xxxxxxx

BACK AT THE CAMP

Jean relaxed on the lawn in front of our camp. The Mtanke River flowed quietly along its ancient bed of sand. The dogs barked. Jean frowned. All she wanted today was peace and quiet.

"Missus, Missus," an exhausted but familiar voice shouted.

"Missus! Come quickly!"

Jean stood up - furious! "That bloody beggar!" She cursed, "Damn him." She shouted, "Go away! Hamba! Or I will set the dogs on you. Just go away, Voetsak!"

"Missus." Moses called from the gate "The master has problem!"

"Moses! Damn it!" Jean screamed in desperation, "I don't want to hear another word from you. I am setting the dogs free. Go away."

"Oh missus." Moses wailed as he backed off. "Oh missus, please listen to me, please."

Jean went into the thatched camp sitting room and came out with the shotgun. Moses wailed and sprinted into the surrounding thick bush.

He ran up the escarpment.

He ran the forty kilometres to Gokwe village.

Cars passed him. He waved desperately for them to stop. Nobody offered him a lift. He ran into the Gokwe Police Camp, collapsed on the floor and in jerky spittle coated words babbled out his story.

The police called Jean on the radio. They told her what had happened. She collapsed. They sent a PATU (police anti terrorist unit) and a tracker unit out. One vehicle stopped over at the camp to take care of Jean and escort her back to Gokwe.

The second vehicle, with Moses as guide, followed our tracks down to the Umniati River. They found my burnt out Land Rover. A helicopter joined them. Together the trackers and the PATU stick followed us at the run. When the group on the ground got tired they changed with the group in the helicopter.

Our tracks disappeared at the Chirisa Ngoma gorge.

The units made camp there. The helicopter flew back to base.

They never found any further sign of the terrorists or Ian and I and the follow up was called off.

xxxxxxx

The terrorists took us north and then west into the Chirisa game area. On the seventh night, as we sat huddled up in the cold, Ian managed to get the rope around his wrist loose. He did not have the strength to untie me. I was fettered to the root of a large fig tree. The terrorists were all asleep. Loud snoring covered my low whispering. I spoke quietly,

"Ian! You see the outline of the escarpment?" I pointed my chin in a southerly direction. "On that high point is an Internal Affairs camp. We have been there before, you remember?"

He nodded. His eyes were desperate but he said nothing.

"There's a road up the escarpment to the camp and another from there on to Gokwe. There is water at the camp but it's a long way to water after that. If you can't find something to carry water in you must stay at the camp. If you do find something to carry water you can either follow the road or stay at the camp and wait for the patrol which passes every two or three days. They will help you home. Be very careful of lions and elephants. Remember what I taught you about how to see if they are safe to walk past and how to talk to them and listen to their responses? Walk slowly!

Give the snakes time to slide out of your way. Walk on open ground so you can see the puff adders that can't move quickly. Don't frighten anything you see, wait till it relaxes and then walk away at an angle. Remember everything I have told you but most of all remember that I love you!"

Ian stared at me. A lonely tear ran down his cheek.

"I love you too Dad. If you say I must do this, I will!"

"Where these guys are taking us will be far worse than what you are now going to do. Give my love to Mum."

Ian stood up. Strong in mind, yes! But only five years old and both physically and emotionally exhausted.

He nodded at me, put his hand on my head and turning away he tiptoed out of sight and out of hearing.

I sobbed until in desperation sleep overtook me.

In the morning they beat me. They carved their names on my back. I learnt that no matter what they did to my body they could not touch my soul! But they! They were locked into a world of fear and desperation.

Suddenly they stopped torturing me.

The Leader shouted at me,

"Why are you not feeling any pain?" He swore, "Why aren't you pleading for mercy?"

I forced a smile! Searching my aching body for strength I answered him,

"I see that you are doing what you are doing because you are desperate!" He frowned at me, I mumbled on "Your desperation is caused by a problem you have inherited. It is you, my friend, that should be crying, not me!"

"Why you call me your friend?" He screamed, his eyes bulging, his lips quivering.

"Well if we were to meet here at any other time and under different circumstances it would be as friends and we would go fishing together! So 'my friend' you understand that under all this politics and hatred you and I are just friends who haven't been properly introduced."

The leader broke down and wept. His troop looked wary and kept their distance.

"My friend," the leader cried to me, "If I untie you will you promise to not run away?"

"No!"

"I am beginning to understand!" he laughed, "So you will remain tied! Don't worry! We will not follow your son. I hope he gets home and is not eaten by lions."

They took me to Zambia.

XXXXXXX

THE NIGHTMARE

I was released a month after the end of the liberation war and made my way back to Gokwe. My family were no longer there. The police told me the story about Ian and his attempt to make his way to the rest camp on the escarpment. Apparently after leaving me he walked only a very short distance from where the terrorists were holding me. He climbed a tree and hid in the high branches where he planned to wait for them to leave in the morning so that he could make for the escarpment in daylight. He heard and watched them torturing me.

Ian climbed down the tree after the terrorists left. He never found the road. He never found the camp. A poacher came across Ian at a water hole - emaciated but alive! The poacher took him home, fed and washed him.

The poacher left Ian in the care of his wife and walked to the District Commissioner's office in Gokwe to report his find and Ian's story.

When the Patu unit arrived to collect Ian they found him unconscious. He recovered in hospital but the trauma had not only wiped his memory clear of all that had happened to him, he also didn't know who he was or where he came from. He did not know his mother.

Jean blamed herself. She became seriously depressed.

If only she had listened to the beggar.

Jean and Ian waited in Gokwe for news of me but when after three months there was still no report of my whereabouts or my condition, she was advised to return to her home in South Africa. The "Terrorist Victim Relief Fund" in Rhodesia paid her expenses. The department paid her my outstanding salary but not my pension.

XXXXXXXX

ZAMBIA

While I was held in Zambia the leader of the terrorist group and I became firm friends but no matter how hard he tried, he was unable to talk his superiors into setting me free. We shared many evenings together at a camp outside the town of Livingstone where I was held. He brought some of his friends to meet me.

We all learnt to laugh together.

One day a Sangoma (Witch Doctor) came with him who could read your mind and your future. He talked to me about the power of thought and showed me the lie in the story of so called positive thinking. He explained that it was the acceptance of both the positive and the negative in relation to the subject at hand that led you into the truth and then the truth would lead you into working out how to draw what you wanted to you

We discussed African history. He confirmed that several hundred years earlier, before the Mashona people arrived from further north there had been a civilisation based in Zimbabwe which developed and operated large farms, irrigation schemes, residential centres and an extensive and viable mining industry.

"Oh yes!" He murmured, "And it was run by Europeans! The Shona, when they came down from the north disrupted and brought that civilisation down into total ruin!"

The Sangoma taught me the theories of remote viewing, mental telepathy, mind over matter and lastly, how to overcome my programmed mind and release my inherent intelligence.

He helped me practice and develop my own perspectives within these abilities.

I was released from Zambia one month after the signing of the Lancaster House agreement. The local authorities dumped me on the Zambian side of the Victoria Falls Bridge. I had no passport or identification papers so when I saw baboons riding on train trucks to get back and forth over the gorge, I also jumped a train and together with the baboons, crossed into Rhodesia. Being in no fit state to argue with the authorities, I remained hidden in the empty rail wagon until it was shunted into a siding at the Victoria Falls railway station. That night I abandoned the sanctuary of the wagon and made my way to an old friend's house in the suburbs. A week later he took me to Gokwe where I learnt about Ian and Jean's story.

I collected the rest of my pay and benefits from the Internal Affairs office, gave all the furniture and stuff from our home to friends and followed Jean to South Africa where her family told me she had taken Edward to a special home for children with psychological problems. She had her baby and went into post-natal depression. The combination of guilt, despair and depression broke her spirit.

She disappeared with the baby.

Despite enlisting help in their search, they never found or heard of her or the baby ever again!

xxxxxxx

I looked for Jean. I employed a tracing agent! Put adverts in almost every newspaper and magazine in the country.

Nothing.

I went to the special institute Ian had been placed in. They told me he had been adopted.

I tried to find our baby. I checked the local hospitals, the clinics and the midwives for any leads.

A few years later I was talking to a tramp I gave a lift to. He told me he had seen a woman leave a basket on the steps of one of the churches in a Karoo town at about the same time Jean probably had her baby.

I drove to the small town where I spoke to the Pastor of the church. He looked surprised. He said,

"What an amazing coincidence you coming at this time! Yes it happened exactly as you were told! Yes! It was on a Sunday after evening service that we heard the baby crying at the front door! We never saw the mother. The baby was only a couple of weeks old. We took it in and notified the authorities. It was placed in our church orphanage. The baby grew into a little boy. The authorities accepted that he would probably never get together with his missing mother or family so the home eventually put him up for adoption and his new parents took him away just a few days ago. I have the name and address of the new parents. Amazing that you came today! They left town for their home this very morning! They went north by train because their car was giving trouble and they sold it to a local garage."

I scrambled into my Land Rover, filled it with fuel and chased after the train.

Land Rovers are not designed for speed. It started to overheat - a few kilometres before 'Buffels Fontein' siding, the engine seized. I hired a donkey cart from a local on the side of the road and trotted the rest of the way to the siding where a young man told me the train had not yet passed.

"But here it comes now! Listen you can hear the diesel engine."

I waited alongside the track. The train rode into and through the siding. A man and a woman were at one of the carriage windows. The man was holding a young boy up to look out of the window. Our eyes met. I knew the boy was mine.

The train rattled past. I sat in the donkey cart and laughed partly in relief and partly in despair.

The parents looked so happy, the child too!

I rode the donkey cart back to my car. Thieves had stolen the wheels, the battery, my tools and my clothing! Every movable thing that had any value was gone.

Bitter disappointment mixed with boiling anger racked my already emotional state! I took the donkey cart back to its owner, thanked him and paid for its use.

Cursing my stupidity, I walked away from my past life.

XXXXXXX

THE CHANGE

"Have you ever been in the Karoo on a cold wet day with no jacket and no blankets?"

Red shook his head.

"Well I tell you it's no joke! After abandoning the Land Rover I walked west into the fast approaching night. Heavy clouds and a strong wind built up from the South East. I sheltered behind a fence where torn Karroo bush had been blown up against it offering a little protection. About thirty sheep were collected together on the other side of the fence. It started to hail. Golf ball sized hailstones. I climbed through the fence and ran to the sheep. They were huddled up, heads down and centred. Heavy woolly fleeces protecting them from the cold and the hailstones. Crawling under them for protection I lay there, absorbing their warmth and thanking them and God.

It rained all night.

In the morning the sheep broke up their huddle and started grazing. The farmer arrived. He helped me into his truck. He took off his coat and put it around my shoulders. He opened a thermos and poured me a cup of hot Rooibos tea.

He never said one word.

The farmer drove me back to his home, helped me into the kitchen and handed me over to his wife.

I developed pneumonia. His wife nursed me. She gave me injections and fed me. I recovered but for a long time I was too weak to walk. The farmer and his wife led me back to sanity and health. I grew to love them.

I worked on the farm for three years. Building fences, mending fences, shearing sheep, dosing sheep, loving sheep for they had saved me from a most undignified death.

I bought a V.W. beach Buggy and a trailer. I painted them red. I raised the suspension, fitted it out for rough country, said goodbye to my farmer friend and his magnificent wife and drove away.

My old bank account had been frozen - I had not used it for too long. It took time but eventually they paid me out.

Cashing in my pension and cancelling my medical aid, I set myself free and adopted a new perspective and a new personality. I travelled all over southern Africa developing my new identity.

Sitting at my campfire in the far north one still and lonely night I decided to look again for my youngest son. I did not want to disrupt his life, I wanted only to see him, maybe talk to him as a stranger. I packed my bits and pieces and left for the Karoo early next morning. I followed the railway from the siding where I had seen him, looking for a village or town where he might be.

XXXXXXX

MY YOUNGER SON

The first village I came to nestled between small hills to the west and old mine dumps to the east. For the most part the buildings were old colonial style with two modern blocks spoiling the overall character.

I booked into a bed and breakfast cottage, parked the vehicle behind a high wall in the back garden and settled in. The lady of the house told me about the town, I led her into any revelations she might have about an adopted child.

"Yes!" she said, "The pig farmer adopted a boy about three years ago,"

My heart beat wildly, "Funny that," she continued, "Her sister also adopted a boy a few years before. He was about six years old at the time. Shame, he couldn't remember who he was or where he came from!"

I almost shouted,

"What did he look like?"

Surprised at my reaction, she looked into my eyes and seeing only pain there, she whispered,

"Are you alright? Let me get you some more coffee."

"No please, tell me what the older boy looked like."

"Strong. Quiet. Black hair, big nose and large green eyes! Maybe he is just a little arrogant? Yes! Actually he looked like a younger you! Oh no!" She sobbed, "Can it be?"

"Please," I whispered, "please go on. If the boys are mine I beg you to not tell anyone. I want to see how they have settled with their new parents. If all is well with them it would be a crime to destroy their lives and their new parent's lives."

"Wait a minute, what do you mean by 'them'?"

"The pig farmer's son and the older boy are both my children. I lost them when the terrorists abducted me and took me to Zambia. My wife disappeared. The children were eventually adopted."

"Oh you poor man!" She sobbed. "Ok, I won't tell anyone. Oh my

God, what a mess."

We drank our coffee. She looked sideways at me,

"What are you going to do now?"

"I want to see them. I want to meet them but not let them know who I am. Maybe I can become a friend and share a little with them. I was working on a project about life and it took me all over Southern Africa! So if I restart the work I can drop in for a week or two from time to time. I will stay with you if that's alright?"

"Of course - be a pleasure."

"Where do they live?"

"The pig farmer and his wife have a house in town. I'll show you. The older boy is with his new parents in the Caprivi. They have a safari business there."

"Will you show me the house today?"

"Sure."

We walked across town to the pig farmer's house. On the way back we passed a café'.

"There he is!" she pointed at a young boy walking down the street, swinging a basket in his hand. "That's the boy."

"Wait here," I begged her "I want to get close enough to see him well."

The boy strode along the dirt pavement to the cafe. Yes! The same boy I had seen looking out of the train window. Yes, I could see he could be my son.

"Hi." I said. He looked at me. His green eyes, bright! "Where is your home boy?" I asked.

"The pig farm but we live in town!" He said.

"Do you know your real name?" I asked.

"No!"

"Come walk with me and I will try to help you find your real name." Hang on I thought, not so fast, don't make a mistake!

The boy gave me a hard look,

"I must buy milk and bread for my mother." He said.

"Yes." I agreed.

He ran into the café'

I walked back to the lady from the Guest House. She took my hand.

"Your boy?"

"Yes. It's the second time that I have seen him!"

She led me home. I stumbled along with her, consumed by both joy and pain.

She comforted me. We grew very close.

I always stayed with her when I came to see how my son was doing. I never told him who I was. On one such visit the lady asked me,

"Why don't you go to the Caprivi and see if the elder boy is also yours?"

"Yes, I must."

"May I come with you?"

"Wow!" I smiled "That would be a real pleasure!"

XXXXXXX

SOMEWHERE LIES AN ISLAND

When I say the Caprivi is flat, I mean really flat. It used to be part of an immense desert with white sand dunes some few hundred feet high. Then the seasons changed and when the heavy rains came the Eastern Caprivi was washed flat and filled up with water. It became an inland sea.

The next major change took place when a giant earthquake shook the area and a rift at the South Eastern end opened up and let all the water out over what is now the Victoria Falls. The new river is called the Zambezi.

The eastern Caprivi drained out to become a place of swamps and rivers with huge areas of grassland dotted with small outcrops of flat-topped trees. The western Caprivi remained as sand dunes and woodlands.

The Caprivi is a truly magnificent place. I felt an affinity with it. My great grandfather was one of the first Europeans to visit the Caprivi. He stayed for a while with David Livingstone at his camp on the Linyanti River.

The lady and I drove up through Botswana to Katima Mulilo where we spent the night at the Zambezi lodge. We celebrated our first evening on the Zambezi River sipping sundowners on the floating bar.

Chatting to some of the locals we learnt the location of the camp of Ian's foster parents.

We set out early next morning for the Kwando River. I was excited.

We marvelled at the beauty of an early sunrise in the Caprivi.

Turning south and travelling along the western banks of the Kwando River we came upon a sign - a curved piece of log with 'Somewhere' carved on it. I was sweating. A black man dressed in a green army type uniform rowed a canoe across the river. Stepping carefully out of the canoe he pulled it a little out of the water and facing us, asked,

"Can I help you?"

XXXXXXX

SOMEWHERE CAMP

The camp is set amongst tall trees fringing the western bank of Buphili Island. Lawns surrounding thatched chalets flow down sloping banks into the crystal waters of the Kwando River. The chalets, shaped and moulded into their natural surroundings evoke a sense of intimacy with creation. Harmony pervades the island lending peace to an otherwise threatened environment. Lion and elephant animate the dark hours with roars and screams punctuated by the eerie calls of wild dog and hyena. Swamp mosquitoes whine and dine to an orchestra of frogs.

Comes the morning and light lifts bird song through mist-shrouded branches as grunting hippo laugh the darkness of night away. The sudden twittering of a bright-eyed squirrel compliments the chattering of startled monkeys.

Tsetse flies lie in ambush.

People are sitting at an outdoor breakfast table. Their voices drift across the silent river. The aroma of French fried onions tangles with the hazy wood smoke rising from the camp fire as a blackened kettle rocks rhythmically with its boiling.

"What day is it?" A girl asks.

"Tuesday. I think!"

Laughter.

"Okay!" Tilting her head, "What month is it?"

"You got me there! I think it must be October because it is so hot and dry!"

More laughter.

"Tell me." A man spoke. German accent! "How long have you been living in this piece of paradise?"

"Ever since we found it and that," replies a low pitched, Colonial English voice, "is about ten years."

"How did you find this place?" The German asked.

"It's a long story."

"We've got time. Tell us!"

The man in the green uniform rows us across the river and escorts us to the table. The tall angry looking man with the colonial accent stands,

"Hi!" he says, "Can I help you?"

"Well actually, yes!" I reply, "We were looking for Somewhere and now we've found it!"

The Colonial grins,

"And so?"

"Can we stay?"

"Sure" speaking to the uniformed man he says, "Albert, get their stuff and put it in the chalet next to Ian's." To us he says "Join us at the table. Have you had breakfast?"

I nod.

"Ok!" the man says, "Make your-selves at home. By the way the ablutions are in that hut over there." He points. Waving at us to relax he sits down, turning to the German he smiles,

"Sorry, you were saying?"

"I asked you to tell us how you came to get this place."

"But first," interrupts the girl "how did it get the name 'Somewhere'?"

"Well, originally it was 'somewhere' to make a camp and later 'somewhere' to build a home. As time moved on a new perspective evolved and with it the understanding that it was somewhere to run our business, have friends and family to stay and even a spiritual understanding that just as Christ had nowhere to lay his head, we could offer this camp as 'Somewhere' that his disciples would be welcome to lay their heads."

"You religious?" Asks the German.

"No! I wouldn't say that except that I do try to follow the truth."

"What church do you belong to?" Asks the girl.

"No church! No religion, just an acceptance of the fact that everything seems to point to there being a Creator and from that point of view the story of Christ makes sense!"

"Coffee nearly ready." A young man calls out from the kitchen.

Speaking to the German he asks, "How do you like it Fritz? Typically German! Strong, black, no sugar?"

"That's right, thanks Ian, Ja, that is except for my wife. She likes three sugar."

I sit tense, waiting for Ian to come out of the kitchen.

The lady holds my hand under the table. She smiles at me.

"Well? And your story?" Asks the German.

"It was four German tourists who first led us here." Sipping his coffee, the colonial continues. "My son Ian and I were living at Victoria falls. We were painting. You might say we were trying to be artists." He smiled, "Mainly wild life pictures.

Four German tourists asked us to take them to Katima Mulilo in the Caprivi and having never seen this part of central Africa we agreed. We found to our surprise that the area is magnificent, beautiful and very different to Zimbabwe.

As a result of that visit we came back a year later planning on starting a safari business here. The local government administration at the time were very helpful, they granted us ninety-nine year leases on a property in town and another property near here and also one in the swamps.

We started operating safaris. In those days the Caprivi had no real tourism as such and we were the first non hunting safari operators here."

Ian comes out of the sitting room carrying a tray set with cups of steaming coffee. He grins at everyone.

I let out a long slow breath. The lady looks at me. I nod. She squeezes my hand.

The German sucked at his coffee. Swallowing with noisy gulps and much heavy breathing he says,

"You were going to tell us about this place?"

"Ah yes! Somewhere!" The colonial smiled, "It all started when a letter arrived from friends in New Zealand asking us to take them on a safari down the Kwando. At that time, having sold our old camps, we had no place to accommodate them anywhere on the river, so we had to find 'somewhere' to establish a base. I set off early one Sunday with a canoe tied onto the roof carrier bars of my wife's Land Rover and drove westward from Katima Mulilo along the Trans-Caprivi highway and then south down the western bank of the Kwando River until I found a place to stop for tea. Across the river was this island. It had a large lake in its centre. From the southern end of the lake a winding channel led through clumps of reeds and papyrus to the main river. Two enormous crocodiles and a family of hippo claimed sanctuary on a beach of white sand on the far side of the lake. The surrounding reed and grasslands were home to grazing Lechwe and shy Sitatunga. The higher ground supported giant ant-heaps covered by evergreen trees where bush buck, duiker, leopard, wart hog and an infinite variety of birds found shelter.

The island was part of a vast wilderness area.

We applied to the local chief and he accepted us as members of the tribe granting us 'Tribal Ownership' of the island and a piece of land adjoining it on the east bank."

"You must have many an exciting story to tell about your life here?" The girl spoke eagerly.

"Too true! After supper each night, if you wish, Ian and I will tell you some of them."

"Oh please!" she enthused. "A night around the camp fire with stories and during the day - the real thing!" She looked at Ian.

Ian smiled!

And so began, 'A series of camp fire stories!'

XXXXXXX

A SERIES OF CAMP FIRE STORIES

I enjoyed Ian without letting him know who I was. He seemed happy in his new home. His new parents adored him.

One morning, as we sat around the fire whilst waiting for breakfast, I held my hands out to the warmth and rather sheepishly said,

"Most people are not very interested in other people's dreams but the one I had last night was so strange I feel I would like to tell you about it! Do you mind?"

"Go for it."

"If it gets boring just tell me to shut up!" They all laughed. "Well in my dream I saw this giant tree, I mean huge! It reached high above the clouds and covered a vast area. Tangled roots thrusting deep into the earth sucked at the dark heart of the world. Bent and broken branches entangling each other searched for light in a wilderness of shadows. Last night's rain drops slid off brittle leaves to explode on the hard dry ground below.

Surrounding this giant tree and clawing at the coolth of its cast shadows stretched an endless wasteland, barren, thorn-filled and harsh. Fingers of blazing white sand pointed outwards to far mountains blurred by heat haze and the smoke of exhausted fires.

Under the tree, at the edge of the shadows, still and silent, sat a large baboon - alone! He stared out into the vast distance before him. He was waiting for those few clear minutes between dawn and the rise of the day's heat haze when for a moment he would be able to see almost as far as eternity. In that instant of clarity he was able to catch a glimpse of the top branches of another far away tree.

Today, as the morning sunlight streamed past him reaching deep into the tree where it searched out secret places amongst the dark branches he heard his family screech out,

"Wake up! Get up!" They shouted at each other, "Get to work. Get ready. Don't forget this! Don't think about that!"

The shouting, the barking and screaming of his fellow baboons filled the tree overriding all other sound including the music of the early morning. No word could be clearly heard. Confusion reigned.

"Hey you!" shouted a magnificent fellow seated in the crook of a spacious curved branch. Eliciting no response, he pointed his gold ringed finger in the direction of the lone baboon on the ground and barked, "What you doing down there on the ground? You know it is not right to sit on the ground?"

Glaring down at the baboon, he screamed,

"Hey you! Health and Safety regulations say it is dangerous and not allowed for you to sit on the ground especially at the edge of the tree!

Hey you! You are never going to make it in the big wide world if you just sit and take no notice of us. We got here by obeying the rules. Hey you, why don't you answer?"

Another baboon higher up in the tree than the first shouted,

"Leave him alone, he is one of those independent, lone ranger types. He thinks he knows something we don't know. He's not one of us!"

Baboon droppings splattered off the bottom branches onto the blotched ground below. The lower echelons of baboons ducked at the sound of each and every stomach rumble from above.

In that part of the tree set aside for sanctuaries, not quite at the top, perched an assembly of dignified, smiling, empty eyed baboons. They formed a tight circle around their elevated leader. The group lent their attention to his grave words.

"You see!" he murmured, running his manicured fingers through balding silver grey hair, "The public must never hear of this, aha! Ahem! Ah yes! This scandal! They would never understand our preaching and teaching them about what they can and cannot do if they find out that one of our top preachers," he paused for effect, "behaved improperly towards a young choir boy."

"True, true." The others agreed.

"You really must take yourselves in hand!" He warned the preachers "Or we will all be led to ridicule through your wrong doing. You know what this man did is supposed to be wrong! You all know the law of the difference between right and wrong!"

Glaring at everyone he spoke out strongly,

"Ok? Meeting adjourned!"

Nodding and bowing, the group - avoiding eye contact, dispersed to go about their individual pious tasks.

The clamour in the tree grew as the day grew. Each and every baboon shouting out his understanding of their own rights and the wrongs of every other baboon and the rights and wrongs of their different societies! Of their friends, of their families and of their religions!

"You hear what the happy dancers on branch seventy seven times seven are saying? It's blasphemy. Everything they say is wrong! You can't trust them at all."

"What about that new age guru?" Shouted another "I know you are his friend, so who are you to talk about the happy dancers. Hey?"

"The end of this tree is nigh!" Boomed a theatrical voice from the deep shadows, "You can see by the signs! The end of the tree is coming. Learn quickly what is right and wrong for tomorrow you die!"

The baboons shouted, they screamed, they argued about everything under the sun. The elected leaders promulgated new laws. They proposed new moral codes. They expounded on basic baboon rights and condemned the lesser monkeys who ran errands for the top baboons.

Pointing at the nearest monkey a young baboon said,

"Rubbish! They are pure unadulterated rubbish! Wonder what the Maker thought He was doing when He made monkeys?"

A fierce current of hot air shook the tree forcing even the strongest baboons to hang tightly to their branches. Terrified they might be dislodged and carried away by the blast, they whimpered and whined. The wind howled a long sad, grieving howl. Wafting down from the branches it touched the baboon on the ground.

"Hey you," a chorus of barks and grunts fell on him from the millions in the tree.

"Who you think you are? Hey? Hey you! Can't you hear us?"

The lone baboon covered his ears.

"Hey you," shouted the crowd "can't you see you are wrong?"

The baboon covered his eyes.

"Damn you!" They shouted, "Have you nothing to say?"

The baboon covered his mouth and staring intently into the distance searched for a glimpse of the other tree. Above him the troops turned on each other pointing out their differences and condemning each other for their lack of understanding. The clamour was worse today than ever before. The lone baboon cried in his heart. Refusing to look at the other baboons or at the tree above him he lay down in the dust at the edge of the shade and hid his face from his brothers and sisters.

Morning of the next day found our lonely baboon crawling desperately away from his family tree and out through nettles and thorns towards the fading vision of the tree on the far horizon. He refused to look back.

He refused to acknowledge right from wrong. He kept his heart mind and soul on the unknown tree half hidden at the impossibly far horizon and drove his weakening body on and on.

The day sunlight burnt him. The past night's cold air froze him. The new day's dry air scorched his parched throat. The thorns cut him. He found his clothes too restricting and shed them. He forgot his name. He forgot his mother. He forgot his identity. He remembered only the tree in front.

Night returned. He slept huddled up and shivering.

Midday of the second day and the exhausted baboon fell headlong into a swarm of angry ants. He lay there too weak to move. From afar off he heard his forgotten family yelling,

"Come back you idiot!"

"All is forgiven."

"We will listen to you."

"Maybe you are right."

But the worst of all they shouted at him was,

"You don't love us!"

Sobbing the baboon cried out.

"No! No! No!"

Raising his head and looking in the direction of the sought after distant tree he closed his mind to the shouts behind him. A gentle breeze blew over the land filling his mind with majestic music. Deep within, he heard a voice,

"Get up." It said, "This is the way."

And then quietly,

"Follow!"

Knees shaking, he stood. The world spun around him. He cried out.

"Yes. Yes. Oh yes!"

The exhausted baboon staggered on. The tree he sought grew clearer and closer. Brilliant colours of green and gold, filled with light and laughter, filtered through its leaves. He drew strength from it and started to run.

He fell. Forcing himself up again, he ran on, laughing wildly as a strange new song burst out of his burnt lips. He doubled his efforts. Tripping and falling time and time again but with ever increasing excitement he staggered up each time until sprinting the last few steps he flung himself headlong into the welcoming shade of the new tree. He lay there for a moment gasping in the sudden quietness. As his eyes adjusted to the different light he saw in front of him a group of beautiful beings stretching their arms out to him. Warm and loving! He saw with delight their freedom from the regulations of the tree he had run away from. He saw in them a reflection of himself and realised his true identity. He was one of them. He was no longer a baboon. Raising his head he whispered one word.

"Yes!"

XXXXXXX

BIRDS OF A FEATHER

On our third night at the camp Ian's step father David, whom we had nicknamed 'the colonial' started telling us his stories. I listened intently because the stories helped me build an image of how my son had grown up. We were all relaxing around the campfire when he said,

"So many stories to tell and the one I want to tell now is probably my favourite because from beginning to end, it wasn't planned. It just happened.

Ian and I met Mr. Don Juan Bird in the village of Katima Mulilo. Let me give you an idea as to what Mr Bird looked like and you will be able to see his nature.

Don is red!

Everything about him is red! Bushy red eyebrows! Cropped red hair rooted around a granite red face set on a short thick red neck with a large red chin thrusting out at the world.

His purpose in life - discipline!

His favourite comment,

"Rank has privilege!"

But his aggression is undermined by a fine sense of humour and if he liked you, a lovely warm smile!

Don and his family were new to Katima.

We saw them for the first time as they trooped out of his front gate onto the pavement of the main street. Don was guarding the entrance to 'his' home as 'his' family marched out to 'his' car.

Ian said,

"Will you look at that!"

"Wow!" I smiled, "You wouldn't want to tangle with him!"

"Could be interesting!"

"Looks like a regimental sergeant major directing his troops! Let's stop and see."

I parked our car a safe distance from Don and we walked over to his family. Holding our hands out in greeting I said,

"Hi. You new here?"

They hesitated, looking to Don for direction.

"Good morning." Grunted Don, "Yes, we are new here. The name is Bird, Don Juan Bird from Zimbabwe."

He introduced his family,

"My wife Deb, my son Herald and my daughters Liz and Soul."

The family smiled.

Very politely I responded,

"Pleased to meet you, this is my son Ian and I am David. We've been here a few years. We are also from Rhodesia!"

Don grunted. I said,

"We live in the corner house opposite the Community Hall. If you need anything please feel free to look us up."

"Thank you." Said Don.

xxxxxxx

We got to know the Bird family well and I was right! He had been a Regimental Sergeant Major in the Rhodesian Army.

During dinner at his place one evening he told us he was going to see a local headman to negotiate the purchase of an old three-ton truck he had seen lying behind the Headman's house.

I suggested,

"We have come to know the Caprivians both at Court and at home. They are sticklers for custom! If you want to get the truck I suggest you observe the local customs when you meet the owner and you are more then half way there. If you like we can help!"

Don nodded,

"Thanks!" He said.

I continued,

"Okay then. Remember how strict you are about hat's off in your house and how to sit and when to talk?"

He nodded, I continued,

274

"Then purely out of good manners it might be an excellent idea for you to respect the Headman's ways in his court! So when you're ready to go - call me and I'll take you through all the procedures."

"Hey!" Grunted Don "I really appreciate that. Thanks old chap!"

xxxxxxx

On the appointed day Don and I set off for the headman's village and his court. Exchanging tall stories on the way we tested each other's humour as we searched for common interests and experiences. I found I really enjoyed his sense of humour.

We arrived at the court to find it had closed early. Don drove round to the Headman's house. He was in his office with some Senior Ndunas. The Court Messenger met us and asked us to wait on the veranda.

I whispered to Don,

"When the messenger beckons to us we must both go down on one knee, together! Bow our heads together and clap our hands loudly, three times, together! Just follow me, okay?"

Don frowned but nodded.

"After clapping hands, we stand up, keep our heads bowed, walk together slowly to the door where we stop, go down on one knee and once again clap hands three times. You with me?"

"Well? Yes!"

"Okay, then you must watch me! After clapping hands at the door, we crawl in through the doorway in front of us. Keep your eyes lowered all the time. Once inside you must on no account look up or around at anyone in the office. Remember that this place is even more of a sanctuary than the court and normally only the highest members of the local community are allowed in. They have honoured us to by giving us a hearing now!"

Don nodded,

"If you say so!"

"Please," I begged him, "forget for just a moment that you are a Regimental Sergeant Major! A Commander of Companies in an army where no one dares move without your permission. Ok?"

Don glared at me.

Holding up my hand, I emphasised,

"When we are through the door keep your face towards the floor, clap your hands again, three times, then go down and crawl on your belly into the centre of the room - like a leopard crawl in the army! Usually we have to kick our shoes off as we crawl in but I am sure the headman won't be upset if you don't. Just remember to not look anywhere but at the floor in front of you. The Nduna's will be talking and laughing, take no notice of them.

You must wait in the middle of the room lying on your belly until the court interpreter tells you to get up. When he does, you must sit up but keep your eyes on the floor in front of you. You got it?"

Before Don had time to answer, the court messenger called us.

Don and I went down on our knees and clapped hands.

"Excellent," I murmured, "now up and to the door."

We went down again at the door, clapped hands three times, Don stayed on his hands and knees then crawled through the door and lay flat on his belly, face down.

The Court Room was suddenly silent. The Nduna's stared at this red faced white man lying on the floor.

Don tried to kick off his hoes, changed his mind and belly crawled to the centre of the room.

The Nduna's started whispering and giggling.

Don lay down in the middle of the office, face to the floor and dead still, waiting for the order to move or whatever.

One old Nduna, holding his hand over his mouth, spluttered then gave way to uncontrolled laughter. Soon the whole room was laughing.

I walked to a chair, winked at the Nduna's as I held my finger to my lips. The laughing subsided.

Squinting sideways, Don searched for guidance from me but finding no one at his side he raised his head a little and seeing my feet, he looked up to see me sitting in a chair. His face turned purple.

I rushed over to him, laid my hand on his head and spoke to the headman,

"Your Honour," I said, "Mr Bird has a very special request to ask of the most Honourable Chief."

"Speak!" Said the interpreter.

"I believe Mr Bird would be pleased to first greet the most Honourable Headman."

The Headman nodded, eyes bright with the tears of controlled laughter,

I patted Don on his head saying,

"Greet the Headman!"

Don, keeping his eyes on the floor said in a stiff voice,

"Muswihilli, I greet you Honourable Headman."

"I greet you Red Man." the Headman replied, turning to me he asked, "How long is he going to lie on the floor?"

Don went rigid.

"May he rise?" I asked the Headman.

"Certainly!"

"Get up Mr Bird and sit in the chair next to mine." I commanded.

Don, purple faced, rose and head bowed, followed me to his chair where with truly magnificent dignity, he sat down.

Waving aside the Court Interpreter the Headman addressed Don,

"Red man, I am truly delighted to have you here! You are obviously a very important person yet you have honoured both me and this court by observing a very ancient custom of ours as required of an outsider and we are all deeply impressed.

How may we help you sir?"

Answering on Don's behalf, I said,

"Mr. Bird wants to buy the very old and battered truck lying behind your house!"

Sitting up straight in his magnificent, hand carved mahogany chair, the Headman spluttered,

"Madala, how can you say that my beautiful truck is old and battered?"

Hanging my head in shame I answered him.

"Your Honour - do you not remember you yourself told me that your truck was 'buggered'? But I, Your Honour, believed you were being polite and had exaggerated the condition of the truck. In my humble opinion the truck is not buggered but only old and battered! I speak, your honour, with due respect for your opinion in this matter. Sir!"

Don grunted. The smiling Nduna's watched him as he battled with the situation.

The Headman, turning to me changed the subject,

"And who is this 'Mukuwa' this Red Man?"

"He is," I answered, "a friend of mine from Zimbabwe. He was the greatest commander in the greatest army in central Africa. His name is 'Bird'"

"Bird! Is he a pilot?"

"Sometimes he flies a little high your honour, but not a real pilot, no!"

Don glared at me from under his bristling eyebrows.

The Nduna's giggled.

The Headman, smiling, said,

"Then we have no option but to give the gentleman what ever he asks for - both now and in the future. Such a man I have never seen or even heard of before and I have lived many years!"

Smiling at the Nduna's he continued,

"It takes a very big man to humble himself before strangers in order to politely observe the traditions of a foreign Court!"

The assembled Ndunas stood and clapped.

Grinning at me the Headman asked,

"When will he pick up his head?"

Amid huge laughter Don looked up at the Headman who, holding out his hand to Don, said,

"Welcome to the land of the Ba-subia. Come my new friend, let us depart to my house and partake of some real English tea!"

Don stood up, the natural colour returning to his face - he turned to me,

"You!" He threatened, "I will attend to later."

We all burst into happy laughter.

XXXXXXX

THE BUSH TRUCK

A few nights later David told us his story about the bush truck.

'We have a four by four ex army Bedford five ton truck. It is kept at Vubu camp, which is about forty kilometres down stream from Somewhere Island.

It was once a dignified old lady painted bush green and well cared for. Then one-day disaster struck! The department of Nature Conservation decided to burn half of the Mudumu Game Park. The youngster in charge, not knowing what he was doing, started the fire at midday. The heat generated by the combination of fire and sun forced the fire out of control. Driven to a fury by a strong east wind it charged across the dry bush burning all in it's path till it leapt the oxbow lake at Vubu, jumped the Kwando river and blasted it's way deep into Botswana.

The road running between Vubu camp and the advancing fire is not wide enough to stop it and the fire leapt across and attacked our storerooms, the workshops and the tool shed. Drums of fuel exploded drenching surrounding trees and the cab of the Bedford with flaming diesel. The suffocating stench of burning fuel and rubber mixed with the hot billowing smoke barred any attempt to beat it out.

Standing there after the fire amongst the blackened ruins that night, we took stock of the damage. Fortunately only the cab, the electrics and the left front tyre of the Bedford had been destroyed. The brake pipes to the wheel of the burnt tyre were twisted and cut. We could see where flames had licked at the fuel tank.

Listing to one side, her cab burnt, no brakes, no windscreen, the doors welded shut, no instruments, no seats and the steering wheel distorted and rough to the touch, the truck stared at us through her now burnt out and sightless eyes.

We changed the wheel. Removed the doors, connected wires from the battery to starter and control panel, Homemade switches were put in to enable us to start or stop the engine.

With two boxes as seats and a pair of welding gloves as protection for the driver's hands, we were ready.

Ian connected the ignition wires and touched the starter wire to the live cable. The old lady shuddered to life."

"Where is it now? I asked.

"Still at Vubu camp, but we plan to load it with some teak poles to bring here to Somewhere, maybe you would like to help Ian bring it over?"

"Definitely!"

xxxxxxx

A few weeks later David took Ian and I to the old Vubu camp. We loaded the Bedford with heavy teak poles that Albert and his work gang had cut and debarked. David waved goodbye and taking the gang with him, left for Somewhere Island.

I climbed into the cab, settled myself on a cushion on the passenger box seat, and said,

"Let's go!"

Ian muttered from the driver's box,

"Dad can't be serious about this! What about the police road block at the Kwando Bridge?"

"Oh yes." I grunted, "Oh well, I think he knows that we will do our best to get through! So what will be will be!"

"But I know they won't let this truck through! Sure as nuts they will take it off the road. The fine will be horrendous! Taking a chance may make life more interesting but this is just plain crazy!"

"True! But there is no other way to get this load to Somewhere Camp. So! As I said, what will be will be!"

"Okay!" Ian tried his flinty eyed stare on me "Be it on Dad's head!"

Albert clambered onto the back and perched himself on a large log.

Ian drove.

The truck glided gracefully along the bush road. We knew that with no brakes and a heavy load we could not travel at speed. Even so it would take some expert gear changes to bring it to a stop.

Hot October wind blasted through the missing windscreen blowing

282

insects, grass seeds and itchy stuff down our shirtfronts. Ian drove with eyes half closed. The throb of the engine made me drowsy. I hung onto the prayer rail above the door way. Thick thorn bush crowded sections of the road. Elephant foot prints left holes in the dry mud. Tsetse flies blew in and out of the cab, we slapped at them under the dashboard. Dust blew up through the open doorways.

Ian coughed.

Pointing to a dark shape on the road ahead, I asked,

"What's that?"

"Dunno!"

Ian changed down to a lower gear. The truck slowed.

A woman lay sprawled across the right hand side of the road. Ian, now totally alert, changed gears down again, and again.

Albert wailed from the back of the truck.

The roar of the engine woke the woman.

She sat up. She looked up. She saw a monster storming down on her. A fiery, smoking, empty eyed beast with two very white faces shouting out of its open mouth and a screaming black face gesticulating from the top of its head!

She screamed.

Ten metres to go!

Ian swerved to the left of the road into the thorn bush.

Branches lashed the cab.

Scrambling to her feet, the woman threw her hands out to ward off the attack. The Bedford mudguard struck her outstretched hand a gentle blow - enough to send her in a slow spin into the bush on the other side of the road where she was caught and held by the thorny branches. Sucking in great gasps of dust and exhaust fumes she saw through the blur of logs and noise, her son in law, Albert, riding on the back of the monster.

She fainted.

Stalling the truck, Ian leapt out and ran back to the woman. I crawled over the driver's box seat to join him. Untangling her from the branches we set her down alongside the road. She lay, mouth wide open, unharmed but reeking of Mahangu beer.

Albert groaned from the back of the truck. She would never forgive him for this.

When the woman regained some of her senses she refused our offer of a lift to her village.

xxxxxxx

The dirt track we were on joins a northbound gravel road about twenty kilometres from Vubu camp. We stopped at the junction to buy cool drinks from a mud hut store boasting a new paraffin fridge. The rather large lady Store Keeper carefully and slowly banged the cool drinks down on the counter, one at a time, as she methodically counted them.

I ducked out from under the low roof holding a well-used plastic bag with the tins of cool drink in it. Ian was on the ground trying to out stare a skinny chicken.

Grinning up at me he said,

"You reckon Dad knows what he is doing asking us to take this load to Somewhere so you can have the pleasure of driving through the road block!"

He climbed into the passenger side of the truck.

Throwing a cool drink up to Albert and passing another to Ian I put the rest of them between the box seats. Ian handed me the gloves. I put them on and adjusting the loose cushion on the box I took over the driving.

We turned west onto the main tar road leading to western Caprivi. The bush country changed to swamp lands. Ahead of us the red and white boom of a roadblock stretched across the tarmac. The dull green of an army tent lay partially hidden under a giant acacia tree. Making the most of gear change noises I slowed the truck and with loud blasts of air from the servo system I simulated a braking action bringing the Bedford to an elegant stop at the boom.

"Neat!" Said Ian, "This is it!"

Music thumped from the tent. Hot air smells rose from the engine.

Movement! A man peered out of the shadows. His eyebrows shot up as he saw the door-less burnt cab of the truck. Disappearing hastily into the tent, he reappeared clutching an official looking book.

Squinting through the glare reflecting off the calcrete yard he stalked the truck.

His eyes noted the cab, the doors and the burnt paintwork. Albert greeted him from his perch. Looking up, the man frowned. Albert was his brother in law.

We waited in the cab.

The officer, stopped in front of the truck and with furrowed forehead and pursed lips he looked up and down the road and then back at the truck.

I leant out of the open door,

"Good morning." I greeted him. "Muswehili. Today is very hot! Yes?"

"Yes." He said.

"You new here?" Ian asked him, "I haven't seen you before."

"What?" He asked.

"Are you new here?"

"No, I am from Katima Mulilo."

Holding the book against his chest, he squinted up at me,

"This your vehicle?"

"No it belongs to Ian!"

"I suggest you dismount."

"What?" I asked.

"You will be pleased to debus your vehicle."

"Yes." I said.

Swinging my legs out of the cab I dropped to the ground asking,

"You like it here?"

"What?" He asked.

"Are you enjoying the local climate and the clean swamp air?"

He smiled, eyes gleaming he said,

"Yes!" He picked his nose. "I want to check the vehicle."

"Certainly." I said, "What do you want to inspect?"

"Where is the vehicle licence?"

"On the windscreen."

Moving his head to one side he looked up to see Ian grinning at him through the open space where the windscreen used to be.

"Hello! Muswihili!" Said Ian.

"Yes." Said the officer. "Where is the licence?"

"On the windscreen." I answered.

"There is no windscreen." He said through clenched teeth.

"Oh yes there is," I laughed, "It is made of glass that's why you can't see it!"

The officer stepped up closer to truck and pushed his hand through the opening where the windscreen should be. Ian reached forward and grasping his hand he said."

"Nice to meet you, my name is Ian."

Shaking off Ian's hand the officer turned on me,

"There is no windscreen!" He shouted.

I looked at him, startled!

"What?"

"There is no windscreen!" He sounded peeved.

"There is no windscreen!" I repeated.

Joining him in front of the truck, I thrust my hand through the window and bellowed,

"Where is the windscreen?" Looking up at Ian I said, "Someone has stolen your windscreen!" Flinging my hands up in despair I turned to the officer, "You must help me." I pleaded.

"What?" He asked.

"I am reporting the theft of the windscreen to you. You are our witnesses. You showed me the theft!"

"No, no!" he shouted.

"Yes, yes, you discovered the theft!"

"No, no, no! Report it to the charge office in Katima Mulilo."

Pressing my palms together, I bowed,

"Yes of course! Yes you are right. Yes! Thank you for your advice."

He stared at Ian.

Ian smiled.

I waited with palms pressed together, humble! The truck engine purred.

"Ha!" Blurted out the officer, "You have no number plate."

I looked down at my body,

"True!" I agreed, "Must I have a number plate?"

He glared at me.

"Not you! The truck has no number plate!"

"What?"

"There is no number plate on your truck!" He said slowly and clearly.

"Of course not, you are correct."

"Ha! Where is the number plate?"

Looking around conspiratorially I bent forward and whispered,

"My friend, this is a bush truck! Bush trucks do not have number plates!"

He stared at the book in his hand. He looked up at Ian. Turning on me he said oh so softly,

"Ha! No lights."

"Yes!"

"Why? Why are there no lights?"

"Because it is a bush truck."

"Yes I know it is a bush truck, but where are the lights?"

"Bush trucks don't have lights!"

"What?" He said incredulously.

"That's right." I said, "You see, at night the lights on a car point only to the front."

"Ha!"

"So you can't see what is on the sides. It is too dark!"

"Ha!"

"If an elephant is standing on the side of a bush road you would not be able to see him. You agree?"

"Ha!"

"So if you can't see what is on the sides of a bush road you could have a very serious accident, especially if it is with an angry elephant. You know how big they are!"

"Ha!"

"So, of course, bush trucks don't have lights. Too dangerous!"

He stared at his book.

"Haai!" He muttered.

"Haai!" I agreed.

We walked together to the driver's side of the truck.

"Aha!" He smiled across at Ian "No doors!"

"No doors?" Asked Ian.

Standing straight again the officer said,

"No doors!"

"So?" Asked Ian,

"Why?"

Ian smiled sweetly,

"Bush trucks don't have doors!"

"Huh!"

"Well consider this, if a bush truck had doors and if you were driving in the bush and if you had to go to the toilet urgently and if you stopped between two trees, which often happens in the bush, you know what I mean! You would not be able to open the doors because of the trees and that would lead to a disaster. That is why bush trucks don't have doors!"

The officer turned again to me, fixed his eyes on mine and opened his mouth to speak. I smiled. He closed his mouth and grunted. Then he smiled. Ian smiled. Albert smiled.

The trucks servo system let out a blast of air.

"Haai!" He said.

We walked round to Ian's side of the truck. Together we stared at Ian's box seat. Together we stared at the wires hanging under the dashboard. Together we looked across at the rough steering wheel. I held up my hands - together we looked at the welding gloves I wore.

"Haai!" He sighed.

"Haai!" Ian sighed.

"Haai!" I agreed.

Taking a pencil out of his top pocket he announced,

"This truck is not road worthy! Even the seats are not bolted to the floor!"

"Wait!" I begged him "Remember that this truck is a bush truck! The seats are not bolted to the floor so that you can take them out to sit on when you stop to have tea in the bush."

He repeated slowly,

"I said this truck is not road worthy!"

"Of course not, you are so right! It is not road worthy because it is a bush truck! It is a bush worthy truck. Look at the brand new, off road, heavy duty and very expensive tires. No one would put new, heavy duty, bush track truck tires on a road truck!"

Staring unseeingly out over the flood plains the officer sighed. He turned slowly to face me and asked,

"And just what is a bush truck doing on a tar road? Hey!"

"May I ask you how far it is to the nearest town?"

"Yes! Katima is eighty miles from here, why?"

"Well if it is so far away we must be way out in the middle of the bush!"

He glared at me. Scratched his head. Smiled. Laughed. Winked and bowing gracefully said,

"Sir! I have to admit I like your sense of humour! Where are you going with this load of poles?"

"We are turning off the main road just after the bridge," I pointed ahead at the river, "and then a few miles down river to the camp so we won't be on the public road for more than another hundred yards!"

"In that case, sir! You will not be a threat to anyone so," he arched his eyebrows and smiling said, "you may proceed!"

"Thank you most kindly, Sir!" I said.

Ian passed down cold drinks to us, and one up to Albert. The officer and I leant against the side of the bush truck. We drank our cool drinks. We smiled a lot and parted good friends.

Driving on from the road block Ian said,

"God is so good!"

"Haai!" I agreed.

We turned south off the main road and took the track to Somewhere. The soft white sand dragged at the wheels. Heat built up. Wildlife watched from the sanctuary of dense bush. Ian hummed to himself.

Arriving at the river at Somewhere Island we off-loaded the logs, parked the truck and rowed a canoe across to the camp. David was away in Katima Mulilo.

The island lay, as always, drenched in magical beauty. Little waves on the river flirted with stray sunbeams as carmine Bee Eaters swooped over the water. The camp lay on the far bank in the cool shade of towering trees.

After supper that night we relaxed by the fire in comfy bush chairs. Ian sipped a liqueur. The truck stood in the moonlight on the far bank, ready for the return trip. Elephant rumbled - branches broke

- distant lion roars - hippo grunts - a bat flew in.

Ian murmured into his glass,

"And tomorrow?"

"What?"

"The road block!"

"Haai!"

"Come on Robert, stop being obtuse."

"What does obtuse mean?"

"What are we going to do about the truck and the road block tomorrow? By then our friend will be the laughing stock of the police force. What story are you planning to tell them?"

"It's your turn to drive tomorrow. It's your turn to do the talking. Let it flow. Sufficient unto the day is the evil thereof!"

"This time they will take the truck off the road!" Muttered Ian.

The next day dawned. Slanting shafts of silver sunlight sliced through the early morning mist silhouetting the grey shapes of elephant as they drifted across the flood plain.

The smell of coffee brewing!

We ate our breakfast in silence.

We left camp early.

Ian drove. Yesterdays tyre tracks had been obliterated by buffalo during the night. Impala leapt across the road. Warthogs high tailed it through the vlei.

Too soon we were back on the main road and pulling up at the police barrier.

Resting his head on the steering wheel, Ian waited. A man came out of the tent. Not our friend from yesterday. This was a large efficient looking, purposeful man! Seeing the truck, he smiled in anticipation and marched up to us. As he reached the boom there came a shout from the tent.

"Hey whena, mira!"

Our friend of yesterday rushed out. Grabbing the large man by the shoulders he pulled him to a stop in front of the truck.

"Don't make a fool of yourself!" He whispered theatrically, "This is not a road truck, this is a bush truck!"

Turning to Ian he smiled,

"Hello my friend."

Dragging the bewildered man away from the truck, he swung the boom open and waved us through. The large policeman stared in disbelief as his prize, the bush truck, accelerated through the open boom to freedom.

XXXXXXX

THE LOGIC FREE ZONE

One night I asked David to explain his comment about living in Africa, he having once described it as living in the 'The Logic Free Zone'."

He laughed,

"Well, what I am going to tell you is hard to believe but it certainly is true and it explains why we call this part of Africa 'The Logic Free Zone!' A few years ago as we were sitting out in front of our home on the Zambezi in Katima Mulilo watching the sun set over the river, the blast of a hooter at the front gate interrupted our mood. I stomped around the park home as barking dogs scrambled to intercept the intruder.

A sad eyed man sat hunched over the steering wheel of his car. He indicated that he was waiting for me.

Declining my invitation to come in, he nervously said,

"Sorry to interrupt but it is my job!"

"What is your job?"

"Somebody has to be the Sheriff!"

"Are you the Sheriff?"

"Yes!"

"You want to see me about something? Can I help?"

"Yes," he sighed, "I have a warrant from the High Court of South Africa! It has been given status by the High Court in Windhoek. It's a warrant for arrest and imprisonment!"

"That's rough, who is it against?"

"You!"

"What?"

"Yes your old friend in Johannesburg is the plaintiff."

"What old friend? What for? Why was I not given the opportunity to defend?"

"Your ex business partner! It's for money you owe him."

"My ex partner? You mean James? I don't owe him - in fact it is he who owes me. Anyway, how much?"

"Twenty thousand Rand!"

"Gaol without the opportunity to defend for a measly twenty thousand Rand?"

He took another deep breath,

"He has powerful connections."

I looked back at the park home, at my family,

"When?"

"Now!"

"Now! Hang on a bit. Today is Friday! Tomorrow the courts are shut for the weekend and there is no way to get out of gaol. I know this is your job but surely you can wait till Monday so I can get legal advice and so on?"

"Okay, I tell you what, if you go to your Kwando river camp I'll come out to see you on Tuesday. That will give you time to get things in motion. So sorry about this, but as I said, it is my job!"

"Thanks, you're a star."

Blushing, he drove away.

Back at the park home I told my wife that our Joburg friend said he had lent us twenty thousand Rand and wanted it back or me in gaol. She was dumbfounded.

"That's crazy, he never lent you any money. He owes us for running his business while he has been away. Anyway if we did owe him, why not simply deduct it from what he owes us?"

"He must have his reasons, can you check the books and bank statements - maybe we can find out what it's all about."

"Well in February last year he sent twenty thousand to our bank account. His local account had been closed! We used it at his request to pay his rentals and a few other costs.

Maybe that is what he is talking about. I have the records so there's no problem accounting for it. So what now?"

"The Sheriff gave me till Tuesday to try and sort it out. I was going to go to the camp but I think I'll stay here. Let's check with Jim."

She smiled. She always smiled, especially when in a crises!

I telephoned Jim, our lawyer in Windhoek. He agreed to try to stop the court order on Monday and arrange for a hearing.

Tuesday came and I went early to the Sheriff's office. He was uneasy. He said he needed instructions from the other Party's lawyers or from the Court before he could comply with what my lawyer said.

"Until I get an order from the court I have to take you in. Maybe the Member in charge of police can help. Let's go to your house to see what your wife has found. Then phone your lawyer again and then back to the police to see what they say."

We checked the accounts, Faxed the information to our lawyer, had tea then went to the Member in charge.

"No ways!" exploded the Member in charge, "This is a civil case, not a criminal one. The jail here is for criminals. Only in very special circumstances will we lock up a man guilty of a civil offence. I'll get Windhoek to check it out.

Can you come back again on Wednesday?"

"That lets me off the hook!" Smiled the sheriff.

Back at the house we waited for the report from our lawyer.

Ian was much younger then and close to tears. He had a thing about doing everything the right way.

My lawyer phoned. He said the Windhoek High Court and the plaintiffs lawyers insisted I pay or be imprisoned. A date was to be set for a hearing some eighteen months later. My lawyer confirmed that I would still have to go to gaol but that he would get me out within a few days.

A crestfallen sheriff collected me on Thursday.

A sense of inevitability settled on us as I parted from my family.

The Jailor was a short stout Mafwe man from the same district as our Vubu camp. He glared at the Sheriff,

"Never!" he exploded "We all know the Madala. I will not put him in this stinking jail for criminals when he is only involved in a civil action. Never! Take him to the Magistrate and let him sort it out."

Laughing, the sheriff led me to the Magistrates Court,

"You are the hardest man to put in jail that I have ever come across." He chuckled.

Court was in session. The Sheriff beckoned to the Chief Prosecutor who then signalled the Magistrate and came to the door. The sheriff handed the Warrant over to the Chief Prosecutor. He greeted me warmly, read the warrant and took it to the Mmagistrate who read it and then wrote across it, signed it and handed it back to the sheriff.

The Sheriff brought it to us. He laughed out loud,

"You read it!" He said to me.

Across the warrant was written in large red letters – 'under no circumstances put the Madala in jail! Put him under house arrest, negotiate an acceptable security and hold it together with his passport. Report back to Windhoek High Court.'

We went back to my family. Had tea and relaxed. The Sheriff telephoned the plaintiff's lawyers in Windhoek and explained the matter. They accepted.

I handed my passport and my wife's Land Rover over to the Sheriff.

Friday, one week later, a letter from the High Court arrived addressed to me. Expecting notification of acceptance of the arrangements made so far, I opened it.

I had been arbitrarily appointed by the High Court to be the Sheriff of The Caprivi. No explanation was given! No guarantees or deposits asked for, simply, "You have been appointed..."

"Surely," I laughed, "the Courts here do whatever they please!"

I called my lawyer.

"Well," he joked, "I have to admit that living in Africa has its moments!"

"If I am the new Sheriff," I asked him, "may I collect my passport and the Land Rover from the old Sheriff?"

Jim literally purred his reply,

"But of course old chap, indeed you are required to do so." He laughed.

xxxxxxx

The old Sheriff couldn't believe what I told him. He phoned his Windhoek office.

"Oh yes," they said, "we were about to inform you that your request to be relieved of your post has been agreed to and your services will no longer be required. A letter to this effect is in the post."

The old Sheriff was actually rather pleased. The work was tedious and sometimes painful.

I recovered the Land Rover and the passport.

Monday found me telling the story to my doctor friend. He was a master of intrigue. He suggested I call my lawyer again, I did,

"Hi." I said, "The Land Rover belongs to my wife, can the Sheriff hold it without her permission? We are married out of community of property?"

"No!"

"Must I give it back to her?"

"Yes."

"May I borrow it from her?"

"Yes."

"Can I use it?"

"Yes."

"One more thing, may I, the defendant, travel outside the country if the Sheriff holds my passport and accompanies me?"

"Yes. Go for it!" He laughed, "Just so long as the Sheriff accompanies you and takes full responsibility for your safe return."

"Thanks!"

And so it came to pass that I spent the following year and a half consigned to gaol but not in gaol, restricted to the Caprivi but travelling wherever I wished in and out of the Caprivi and Namibia with myself as Sheriff in charge of me holding my own passport as security and driving the Land Rover which was also held as security.

Detained but free! The full might of the law lying both on and with me!

Friday evening eighteen months later!

 I was at the park home trying to work out our finances. The court case was set down for the following Tuesday. The court costs alone were in the region of seven thousand Rand per day. The attorney and the counsel costs would be huge. The trip down to Windhoek and back was over three thousand kilometres.

As usual we were not flush with money.

Our friend in Joburg still believed we had cheated him of the money even after explaining to him how it had been spent at his request and on his instructions and authority on his account.

My lawyer offered a settlement where my Joburg friend would pay his own costs, I would pay mine and we would all call it a day.

My Joburg friend refused. He wanted me in gaol.

I sat on my veranda. What to do? We would certainly win the case. But! How to stop all the nonsense and the pain and the cost?

Andy, a friend in Katima, came over for tea. We talked a great deal, laughed a lot. Shared special thoughts.

Suddenly I had an idea,

"Hey, I've got it!"

"You got what? Where? Why?"

"You know what I'm going to do when I go to court next week?" He shrugged,

"No, tell me!"

"Well," I said, "I'm going to say, 'but that man, the claimant, is not the man who sent us the money. Oh no!"

"What do you mean?"

"Well last time he was here he left his briefcase behind. He phoned from South Africa and asked for details on some form or other in the case. We opened it, inside were four passports and four identification documents each with the same face, same signatures but different names!"

"So?" Asked Andy.

"Well I am just going to point at James and say, 'this man is not James Maloney! He is Harry James!' I will turn to the judge and explain, 'Your Honour, I have details of this man's passport here with me! His name is not the James Maloney that laid the charge against me! No, the man here in court is Harold James!' and I will hand the paper I hold in my hand to the court."

"So how would it help in your case?"

"You must be joking, what would the authorities do if they found out he had five different passports and identification documents and different names but the same signature and same photograph on each? They would lose interest in me and he would be in an awful amount of trouble.

I also have the documents for the import and local registration of one of his cars, again in a different name to the one he uses here, but the same signature. A handwriting expert could verify the situation. Imagine,

'Your honour, the man who is in the court is not the man who is claiming the money'!"

"Ok. I get it."

He left.

Saturday morning - I sat staring out at the river. A bible lay on the tea table. I picked it up. It fell open at Daniel's prayer. I read it. It calmed me. So I put my name in the place of Daniel's and read it again. In short this is what I read.

"Father. I am confused of face. Only you know all. I trust in you. For your sake Father and for your honour put my enemies to rout. For your own glory make right what is wrong. I pray you, please do it and do it right now. Thank you."

Laying the Bible on the table, I relaxed, head against the back of the chair, eyes closed.

The phone rang.

I ignored it. I wanted peace.

It persisted.

Reluctantly I picked up the handset.

"Hello."

"Hi." It was our lawyer, Jim. I felt like telling him, 'Some other time please, not now!' He felt my mood.

"David!" I heard the smile in his voice, "The plaintiff's lawyers have just phoned, they made an offer to settle out of court, do you want to hear it?"

"Yes, why not?"

"They will pay their costs and you pay yours and you both call it a day!"

"I don't believe it!"

"You had better, by the way my costs are a two day visit with a friend of mine to your camp next month. Ok?"

What could I say? I asked him,

"Have you ever heard of Daniel's prayer?"

"No! Why? Do you want me to pass it on to the other lawyers?"

We laughed. I said,

"I wonder what connection my Katima friend has with James?"

He said,

"I don't think you would be surprised! Oh and just out of interest I found out the answer to your other question yesterday, it was the peace corps people who initiated the saying 'Africa is a Logic Free Zone.' I think they may have a point!"

XXXXXXX

A ROAD BLOCK
WITH A DIFFERENCE

We were all sitting around the campfire one evening after a day out on the river when I asked David,

"Did you have any problems here when the South Africans handed over to the new Swapo Government?"

"No! Well not many!" He replied, "There were a few demonstrations, things like marches through town and a couple of road blocks."

"Were you ever personally affected?" I asked.

"I suppose so! Once when I was travelling back here from Katima I came across one of the roadblocks. It was on a Sunday, about midday. The tarmac was wet from rain the night before. Far down the road I saw a large group of people. They had dragged trees across the road. Stopping a little way before the roadblock I got out and locked the four-wheel drive wheel hubs on in case I had to take to the bush. Driving towards the group I noted it was made up of the usual adult misfits and a group of teenage school children led by a recently enlightened political activist. Anger surged through me as I thought of the many innocent people hurt by mindless mobs in the name of some short lived political ideal. A gang at a roadblock the week before had beaten up our local Veterinary Surgeon for no reason at all.

I stopped the car next to the politician but kept the engine running, my foot on the clutch and the gear engaged.

An aggressive, partly uniformed man stepped past the politician to the Land Rover's door. Pointing his AK47 rifle at my head he shouted,

"Get out!"

Excitement rippled through the crowd.

Slowly, deliberately, I slipped the gear lever into neutral and stepped out of the car but remained within the arc of the open door.

"Good afternoon." I greeted him. "Can I help you?"

He looked in the back of the Land Rover,

"Where are you from?"

"Katima Mulilo."

"Why have you got army tents in your truck?"

"They aren't army tents they're green safari tents!"

"You are wearing an army uniform?"

"No, this is a safari uniform."

"You are a South African spy!"

I said nothing.

"You are a white racist pig!"

The crowd grew impatient. I said nothing. His eyes flamed with hate.

I looked out over the crowd. It didn't seem too hostile!

"What are you doing in Namibia?" He demanded.

I smiled at him.

I said nothing.

"You cannot talk!" He sneered. "Answer me you white Boer!"

"Yes." I said.

"Yes what?" He shouted.

"Yes Sir!" I smiled my sweetest smile.

"You are a pig!" He screamed.

"Yes Sir." I smiled sadly.

Someone in the crowd sniggered.

An older man in a green Unita army jacket pushed himself through the crowd. He looked friendly.

"Hello - Muswehilli." I greeted him.

"Ha!" He exclaimed, "You speak Mafwe?"

"No." I admitted "Only how to greet you and say thank you."

The man with the gun interrupted,

"Where are you going to Boer?"

"I am a Scot not a Boer and I am going to my camp on the Kwando River."

"You are a white man not a black man! How can you say 'your camp' on the river? You stole the land!"

"I may be white and you may be black but I have a certificate from the Paramount Chief which says I am a Caprivian and a member of the Mafwe Tribe and that I own land through the Chief's Court. Are you a Mafwe?"

He looked away. He was an Ovambo from many kilometres away.

Someone in the crowd shouted,

"Let him go, we know this Mukuwa."

The man in the Unita jacket touched the shoulder of the man with the AK.

"Yes!" he said, "This Makuwa is known to the elders of the tribe."

I stared at the man with the gun,

"You speak with an Ovambo accent!"

"Yes." He grunted.

"So," I said "you do not pay tax to the local chief! You are a stranger here!"

"No!" He answered defensively, "I am a returnee from the liberation struggle."

"But you are not a Mafwe!"

The crowd grew still.

"No."

"May I ask you some questions?"

He looked sour.

The Unita man, his eyes twinkling, said,

"Certainly."

"Thank you," I turned my attention to the man with the gun.

"Well young man," I asked him, "did you make that gun?"

"No, it is from Russia."

"With love?"

"What?"

"Never mind, I do like your uniform, did you make it?"

"No."

"Did you make the glasses you are wearing or your boots? What about the education you have had, did you make that?"

"No." He shouted, "You know that it is all from the white man!"

"Ok! Who made this tar road, that telephone line over there, this Land Rover, the tents in the back?"

He looked very upset.

"May I ask you, man with the gun, where on earth did you get the gall to stop me on my road, in my car, with my gun, and who are you to demand from me my democracy my medicine, my parliamentary system, my schools, my radio, my money, my everything? Hey! Just who in the hell do you think you are?"

He stared wildly at the crowd around him.

"I say it again - you accuse me in my language, you speak about the human rights that originate from my family. I ask you, you who made nothing! How dare you?"

He looked uncomfortable.

"Hey!" I pleaded, "I understand your problems! Will you please try and understand mine!"

He looked into my eyes. He managed a weak smile.

Laughing, I offered,

"Okay. Don't worry! Please relax – I must tell you that you do make some things and you really do make them well! At least two that I know of."

The crowd grew very quiet. The politician asked,

"What two things?"

"Firstly you make trouble!"

The crowd cheered and clapped.

The man with a gun looked down at his feet.

"Oh yes you do, and you do it very well! Look at this roadblock. What a lot of trouble you make for all the drivers who use the road!" More laughter, "And getting all these people together, you don't even have beer to encourage them! You must have a very strong personality! Yes? I congratulate you sir!"

The crowd clapped hands, laughed and started dancing.

The man with the gun who called himself 'the returnee' looking a little mollified smiled and asked,

"And what is the second thing we make?"

"Babies!"

"Ha," the Unita politician agreed, "many!"

"But!" I said, frowning with mock concentration and holding onto the steering wheel with one hand, ready to leap into the car, slam the door and bolt for it, "You don't make babies very well!"

Surprise and indignation!

"What do you mean? How can we not make babies well?" Shouted the man with the gun.

The politician stood back, smiled at the crowd, shrugged his shoulders and shook his head.

"Well?" Demanded the gunman.

"You," I said "have been making babies for six thousand years but in all that time you have not yet made one white one! If you had done so, maybe just one, he could have invented all these things for yourselves as part of your culture and you would have then had everything you ever wanted without having to fight for it!"

The crowd sighed.

"But more important than tar roads and guns is the fact that the painful desperation you now have at the bottom of your heart would never have been!"

A deathly hush fell over the crowd.

Reaching out my free hand, I took the gun man's hand, and shaking it I said,

"Goodbye to you and to all your friends here. Have a very special day!"

One man laughed. Then two and the crowd burst out laughing, clapping hands and cheering.

"Old man," the politician cried, "go on your way, you will be in need of our prayers and we will pray for you! We are also in need of your prayers, so please pray for us!"

The gunman, tears in his eyes, put his gun on the ground, bent his knees and said,

"God Bless you Madala!"

I drove slowly through the parting crowd.

XXXXXXX

THE SHAPE OF THINGS

Ian and I were walking back to Somewhere Camp late one afternoon. Suddenly he stopped, holding up his hand he laughed.

"What?" I asked.

"We're cut off from the camp by buffalo."

Through the dense bush ahead I saw them as crazy black shapes seen through a jig saw of branches and tall grass.

"Lots!" I muttered.

"Yes!"

"They are between us and the bend in the river where we left the canoe."

Walking from the cover of one tree to the next we were able to estimate there to be over a hundred animals.

Waiting in thick scrub, I asked,

"Any idea how we get to the canoe?"

Ian looked up and down the river.

"We can't chase them away," he muttered, "they are at last learning to accept us and not be afraid and then secondly, it just needs one bull to take exception and we would be done for. We can't shoot because that would frighten the whole herd. I suppose we could wait here until they move on."

"Is that a good idea?" I asked, "We could end up spending the night here and David is expecting us back."

"So what do you suggest?" He grinned at me.

"I think that if we go down on all fours and stick our bums in the air we will be able to crawl right through that herd to the river and grab the canoe and go home."

"You crazy?"

"Look at it this way, if we go on all fours we will be small and wo won't look like humans. Also, it seems to me that all dangerous animals have big shoulders and small backsides. Safe animals have small shoulders and big backsides. So, on our hands and knees and with our bums high in the air, they will see us as small and safe."

"Have you by any chance noticed," Ian asked quietly "those buffalo have large shoulders and small backsides?"

"Yes." I agreed, "So you see I'm right, they are dangerous. So are hyena - lion - wild pig elephant and man. Okay!"

"You are crazy!"

"Maybe but I am going to try. You coming?"

Ian smiled,

"Why not!" Hanging the rifle on its sling over his shoulders he crouched down on all fours and crawled out of the shade.

I followed.

We made our way towards the buffalo.

"If they look aggressive," I spoke low and quietly, "lift your backside up as high as you can and put your head down."

"Oh sure," Ian grunted "and yawn and scratch behind my ear with my left back foot!"

Seeing us, the nearest buffalo stiffened. She raised her head to glare down her nose at us. She stamped and snorted to attract the attention of the herd. In a moment some forty buffalo were snorting and side stepping and glaring down their noses at us. The wind being in our favour they were unable to identify our unusual shapes by smell.

"Oh dear, oh dear." Whispered Ian.

"Don't whisper!" I growled at him "Talk low and quiet."

"Anybody else would be screaming by now!" He retorted.

Two cows dropped their heads, thrust out their noses and stalked towards us.

"Just stand up and they will run away!" Smiled Ian.

"No ways!" I watched him struggle to control his laughter.

"Keep moving as if you're at peace with them." I muttered.

Keeping our quivering bums higher than our heads and our eyes on the buffalo, we crept awkwardly across open ground. Thorns dug into our hands and knees. The cows turned and trotted off a few paces then they whirled around again to stare at us as we struggled on towards the river. The other animals relaxed as we passed them except for two, which decided to follow us. A little further on and the others, which could now smell us, joined them until fifty odd animals were snorting and stamping as they stalked after us. When we reached the bank of the river the closest buffalo stretched out her neck and approaching cautiously, sniffed at our raised behinds. The canoe was drawn up on the riverbank a few paces in front of us. In that one frozen moment the wind changed direction blowing over us and into the rest of the herd. The lead bull, scenting humans close by, blew a thunderclap of air from both ends, whirled and charged back into the startled herd.

Alarmed we pressed our noses into the earth and holding our breaths - we raised our backsides even higher.

Peeping sideways at the buffalo Ian saw them milling around, excited and expectant. We froze until they began to move in for another closer inspection. Deciding caution as the better part of valour we charged down the bank to our canoe and clambering in paddled furiously to the middle of the stream where in comparative safety we looked back to see the astonished herd of buffalo strung out along the bank, staring at us.

That night we shared our new understanding of the shape of things with Ian's father and some American clients.

XXXXXXX

THE WILD CARD CROC

David had gone to Katima Mulilo for the day.

Ian was in the camp workshop repairing an outboard motor.

I sat painting at a table in the shade of a large sausage tree.

The lady sat with me - reading.

The island slept in the stillness of midday.

Across the river lay a partially submerged crocodile, Somewhere Camp reflected in its cold eyes. It lay, as was its custom, waiting for the inevitable mistake that could lead to a meal.

Two men were working on the barge used to ferry heavy building material and equipment across the river. A long cable anchored the barge to a stake, fifty metres up stream. The barge swayed lazily with the current. It floated deeper at the side where the men were chipping old paint off the rusted metal.

The cable dipping into the water a few metres upstream from the barge created an agitated whirl which momentarily caught floating leaves and debris.

Albert, the camp foreman ambled down the bank to check on the work. Pausing at the edge of the water he rolled a cigarette.

A hush fell over the camp. It was almost lunchtime. Digging in his inner pocket for a box of matches Albert glanced up at the workers.

The water near the cable erupted. A blast of spray and wet sound struck Albert as the huge croc torpedoed out of the river. With a terrified yell Albert crumpled in a dead faint. The two workers on the barge leapt backwards, legs and arms flailing as they lost balance amid the loose tools on the floor of the barge.

The croc never saw the cable. It caught in its wide-open mouth, stretched, and the croc, stopped by the cable, somersaulted tail over-head to fall upside down on the bank alongside Albert. The cable snapped out of its mouth and shot back into position. The barge rocked on the water.

Ian heard the screams and ran for his shotgun. We charged down towards the barge where, rushing around a clump of trees bordering the landing, we stumbled to a stop. Sprawled on the floor at the far end of the barge the two petrified workers hung onto each other. Half in the water and half on the bank lay the unconscious body of Albert with the upside down crocodile lying head to tail at his side.

Baboons shouted their glee from trees on the far bank.

Grasping Albert by the ankles Ian and I dragged him up the bank and away from the croc. Ian ran back to the rivers edge and pushed a canoe out to the two men at the far end of the barge. In their fear, they jumped into the canoe, capsizing it. Bug eyed, they abandoned the sinking canoe and arms flailing at the water they swam across to the far bank. The croc collecting its confused thoughts rolled over and dragged itself away from the barge and slid back into the river.

XXXXXXX

TO CATCH A CROC!

The lady and I walked across the island to the hippo pool. We sat on the bank under a huge Marula tree. The quiet and peace lifted our spirits.

"Tell me Robert," she asked, "you seem to really enjoy listening to David's stories! Am I right when I say it's to get an insight as to how Ian grew up here?"

"Yes! And you also have to admit the stories are really interesting and enlightening! They give us a very clear picture of how people have to adjust in order to live out here in this far away corner of the bush country of Africa!"

"And what do you think of it all?"

"Well! If you bring the whole picture into the perspective of the fact that when Ian came here he was suffering from a total loss of memory of his life before he was placed in the psychiatric home and the trauma of not knowing why he had been abandoned by his parents, I think that this place, this island and these people are the best possible thing that could have happened to him. It has helped him develop an acceptable state of mind! Does that make sense to you?"

"Yes!" Reaching out she touched me on my shoulder, "See that croc lying there in the shallows? He has been watching us!"

"Waiting!"

"Look at his eyes!"

Eventually the croc gave up and sinking beneath the surface it disappeared.

"David said that Ian catches young crocodiles to show the tourists!"

"Yes, apparently he is good at it and totally unafraid!"

"I wonder where he gets his lack of fear from, you or David?"

I turned to look at her. She smiled,

"Well?"

"Simple answer! Both of us!"

When David got back to Somewhere Island we told him the story of Alfred and the croc. I asked him,

"Albert told me that Ian catches young crocs from the boat! Will you tell me about it?"

"Yes." He said. He sat down on a camp chair near the open fire. "But maybe it would help you to understand the fullness of our perspective of croc catching if I first told you about a young man called Ralph and his crocodile! I think you will come to appreciate that living with African wild life is much more than most people understand! Catching crocs is only a very small part of the whole picture! It is the 'ins and outs' of the whole story that has led Ian into developing the catching of crocs into an art in the same way that he has come to terms with sharing with lions and snakes, or buffalo and elephant. In fact, with the 'all' of African nature!"

"Tell!" I said.

"We used to operate from Sitwe Camp about seven kilometres down river from here, it was the first camp we had on the Kwando.

One of our regular clients was a Safari Company which took guided tours from Windhoek to Harare. They catered for German visitors.

Ralph was the driver-come-tour-guide of one of the five ton four wheel drive trucks they used. He was a clean cut, immaculate and upright young man. His English needed a lot of help. On his third official trip to us he brought a group of eight young German girls.

Ralph, in his tight fitting khaki clothes should have been in a euphoric state of bliss being escort to those lovely young ladies but fate had ordained that not one of them had as yet shown any interest in him. He was desperate and as it were, wagging his tail like a lovesick puppy.

We settled the group into their bush chalets and invited them to the warm campfire for an early supper.

Ian was away in Katima at the time. Matthew was learning to be a 'Tour Guide' and shared the work of catering for the Germans.

During supper Ralph told the story of Ian catching crocs on previous trips. A slim, tall and gentle girl asked if we could possibly take them on a croc catch outing. I explained that Ian was away. She lowered her eyes - gave me a brilliant smile and raised her eyebrows.

"Ok! You got me!" I laughed and called Matthew over, "Matthew, would you be prepared to catch a small croc tonight like Ian does? Ralph can help with the light?"

"No problem!"

"Hey Ralph!" I shouted, "I am talking to you!"

He smiled but continued to look hopefully at the young ladies seated around the camp fire!

I explained to sad Ralph and Matthew how we would go about it.

"While the boat is moving, Matthew will hold the light and use it to pick out the red eyes of crocs. When we do come across a croc I will bring the boat close to see if it is small enough to catch. If it's too big we will hang in there so that everyone can watch it. If it is small enough to catch and bring into the boat to have a good look at, we will do just that! Ok.

Now Ralph! You must sit on the prow with your feet in the boat and watch how Matthew works the light because it is very easy to lose the croc if the light is not handled correctly. If we do decide to catch a croc, Matthew will hand the light over to you and then you must beam it steadily into the crocs eyes. Keep the light in line with me at the boats controls and the croc otherwise I might lose sight of the reflection in its eyes.

Matthew has often been with Ian and I and he knows how, when and where to catch a croc.

Now you ladies will be in the boat with me behind the roll bar. You must keep still while the croc is caught and brought into the boat and then keep at least a metre away from it. It can move very fast and if it does bite you, remember that it exerts many times its own body weight in pressure and holds on for a long time. Extremely painful and the teeth are full of germs from rotten meat! You got it?"

"Ya, ya!" Chorused the girls.

"Hey Ralph!" I murmured, "Have you been listening or watching the girls?"

The girls laughed.

xxxxxxx

Matthew brought the boat round to the front of the camp. Ralph gallantly helped each one in, holding their hands maybe a second longer than necessary. I pointed out the medical aid box and showed everyone how to put on and adjust the life jackets! Ralph was very pleased to help the girls into their jackets.

Matthew called Ralph into the front of the boat and showed him how to use the spot light. Ralph tried to listen but his main interest was still elsewhere.

We rode upstream for a few kilometres but there were no crocs small enough to catch so we turned round and quietly drifted back with the current. Matthew shone the light on the banks picking out wild life. Lechwe, Reedbuck and the rare Sitatunga.

We passed the side stream entrance to the camp and drifted on towards Paradise Island. In a bend in the river at Paradise Island lay a small to medium sized croc. I swung the boat around and used the engine to keep it from drifting down stream. The croc was about two metres from us. It swam towards the bank, found shallow water and lay in the water on the sand. It was too big to catch, especially with a boat full of people!

Matthew beamed the light on the croc. The girls, crowding me at the roll bar were fascinated.

Suddenly, and without warning, Ralph leapt into the shallow water and grabbing the croc by its belly with both hands he swung around and tried to lift it into the boat. The croc did not like the idea and showed it by snapping its powerful jaws onto Ralph's left arm. They hung onto each other.

Accelerating the engine I rammed the boat up onto the sand bank, where, grabbing the spot light from Mathew I handed it to the nearest girl, vaulted over the roll bar into the prow of the boat shouting at Matthew to help me drag Ralph back into the boat. Together we jumped off the prow into the water. Mathew took hold of the croc by the throat - I grabbed Ralph by his free arm and together we lifted and heaved Ralph and the croc on board.

The girls backed away from the roll bar - their weight moving to the rear lifted the front of the boat up and it slid off the sand bank into the main stream. Matthew and I floundered in the water but managed to hang on to the prow. He helped me over into the boat.

The girl dropped the light. It went out. I pulled Matthew in. We fell about in the dark. We stood on Ralph. We stood on the croc.

I clambered over the roll bar, searched for the light, found it and switched it on. The boat drifted backwards down stream. A hippo grunted.

The tall gentle girl took the steering wheel. I shone the light on Ralph. The croc still held on. Turning the light down stream I saw we were drifting into tall reeds. I handed the light to the gentle girl, took over the steering wheel and accelerated back up stream where I rammed the boat back onto the sand bank.

I asked the gentle girl to keep her friends up at the roll bar so that their weight would hold the prow down on the sand. She nodded.

Turning again to Matthew and Ralph I saw that the croc still had hold of Ralph's arm and Ralph still held the croc by its stomach. Matthew held it by the neck.

"Has any one got any matches?" I asked.

No answer.

"Has anyone got a cigarette lighter?"

"Yah," from a dark haired girl, "vat dju vant dit faw? Vat dju goink to do? Hey! R dju goink to burn da krok?"

"Give me the lighter!"

She refused.

"Angelica," I begged the gentle girl, "Take the lighter from her and give it to me!"

She hushed the dark girl and taking the lighter from her, handed it to me.

"Please keep the spot light on the croc." I asked her and climbed over the roll bar.

"Ralph - Matthew! When the croc lets go of Ralph, you heave it quickly out into the water. Ok?"

I flicked the lighter on and held it to the croc's nostril. Immediately it let go of Ralph's arm. Matthew, still holding it by the neck, kept the head and jaws away from Ralph. I grabbed it by the tail behind its back legs and together we threw the croc over board.

Ralph sat down in the prow and cradled his damaged arm. I took control of the boat and set off at speed up stream.

Back at camp we sat Ralph at a table and told him to hold his damaged arm out. The crock's teeth had punctured deep holes into his muscle but because of the pressure when the croc held him - there was hardly any blood.

The girls crowded round. Angelica - the gentle girl - held Ralph's arm. I opened a bottle of whisky.

"This is going to hurt!" I told him.

Angelica stroked his hand and offered him a comforting smile. Ralph's eyes shone.

I poured the whisky over the holes in his flesh. He stiffened but keeping Angelica in his focus he let out a long tight sigh!

"Maybe ve giff heem to drunk also! Hey?" Angelica asked, "He ver brave, yah!"

We smiled at each other.

She looked at Ralph, a twinkle in her eye as handing the bottle to Ralph she asked,

"En vat ver ju doink mit dee krok? Hey?"

Ralph looked sheepish. He sipped a little whisky and spluttered,

"I not hearink proper to David ven he tol us da katchink of da krok. I see no vun katch da krok! I tink, 'maybe dit iss I to katch dit!' So dis I do. But da krok he nein unerstandt and he bitted me. Angelika, ju ar ver beautiful! I tank ju so veri too mutch!"

Angelica, laying a hand on his forehead, whispered,

"Don yu vorry, I lookink arfta ju."

xxxxxxx

David grinned and looking at me said,

"That story illustrates just how much more there is to meeting up with wildlife in the context of making contact with it than most people understand. Ian has developed the art to it's full!"

"Thank you David! Yes! He has grown into a fantastic son!"

"And we love him dearly!"

I leant back in my chair,

"Any other stories you would like to tell?"

The lady smiled. David answered,

"Well, there are many! We have a lot of Germans visiting Somewhere Island. We found them all to be friendly and most interesting. I remember two from Berlin, both very special people. He was a Judge and she a Prosecutor. They came for a week. There was one other German in the party, a red haired Bavarian.

On the first night the Bavarian asked,

"Hey David! Vat time ve getting up in da mawning?"

"When you wake up," Ian interrupted, David laughed saying,

"He is right, you can't get up before that!"

The lady prosecutor smiled. The Bavarian persisted,

"Ya, but vat time is da brakefirst?"

"When it's cooked!" Said Ian.

"Agh man, den vat time ve goink on se game dryfing?"

"Soon as we are ready!"

The Bavarian pursed his lips,

"Ju play mit me?"

"No! Never!"

The Prosecutor laughed. Early next morning, just as it began to get light, I was woken by a shout.

"Hey ju Mista David! Vake up and den ju kan be gettink up like me!"

At breakfast he said to the other two germans,

"I tink ve must leaf our vatches mit David. He can be putting them in da safe place. Dey useless out here in de Afrika bushes!"

XXXXXXX

THE TALE OF THE CHIEF'S TAIL

David relaxed in his deck chair. He said,

"You have to be careful what you say to these local Caprivians. Ian and I have learnt the hard way!" He smiled at me. "A few years ago, during the safari 'off season' – that's when the rain and heat keeps tourists away, we were enjoying a late breakfast at Somewhere Else camp. The dogs warned us someone was coming.

It was the local Nduna's court messenger. Greeting us with a huge grin, he delivered a written summons to attend court that very day.

"What for?" I asked.

"Ha! Big trouble!"

"What big trouble?"

"Deform-at-tye-on!"

"You mean deformation?"

"Encha - das it!"

"Who? What? When?"

"Come," he grinned, "too much peepols waiting! I take you in your car."

xxxxxxx

An unusually large crowd sat on the ground in front of the court tree. The senior Nduna perched on his wobbly chair. The prosecutor sat on the root of a leadwood tree. The Sub-Ndunas sat cross-legged on the ground to the left of the chief. I sat on the defendant's mat. The Seniour Nduna waved an imperious hand.

'Silence.'

The prosecutor stood up. You could feel the excitement building up in the crowd.

He clapped his hands.

"Honourable Nduna, we salute you." The Senior Nduna nodded. The prosecutor, looking at a sheet of paper in his hand solemnly declared,

"I lay this charge against the Madala David from 'Someplace' I speak in English because the Madala has not yet learnt to speak our Mafwe language!"

The crowd sighed. He continued,

"It has been reported to this honourable court that you, Madala David, referred to the very honourable senior Nduna as a baboon without a tail!" Pausing, he looked around the crowd. They responded by holding their hands in front of their mouths in absolute dismay. "This court," he continued, "has decided to punish the Madala in the traditional way!" The crowd sighed in anticipation. "First we will beat the Madala with a Sjambok!" The crowd groaned out a long 'Aaah!' "Then we will lock the Madala in the hanging jail for three days with no food!" He glared at me "And you will pay the court ten goats or one ox as a fine!"

The crowd clapped gleefully. I would be the first European to be punished by this court in this way. I looked at the jail, a corrugated iron box hanging from four poles. Boiling hot during the day and freezing at night.

Shifting his behind on the uncomfortable chair, the senior Nduna glared at me. He nodded to the messenger. The messenger said,

"Madala David, you have a chance to speak."

I bowed my head and clapped my hands three times,

"Honourable Nduna," I said respectfully. The crowd became still as they tried to listen to my soft words. I was about to continue when pandemonium broke out amongst the sub Nduna's seated on the large tree roots to the left of the Senior Nduna.

"Snake!" They cried out "Bring a stick! Kill the snake. Kill it! Kill it!"

A frightened, small, multicoloured snake darted in and out amongst the scrambling Ndunas.

I leapt up before any one could bring a stick and herded the snake away from the court area into the surrounding bush. Returning to the defendant's mat in front of the now very quiet crowd, I bowed, clapped my hands again and sat down.

"Thank you Madala." Muttered the worried Senior Nduna. "We have seen your gracious risk of life to defend this court. Do you have any thing to say about the charge?"

"Yes honourable Nduna, I do!"

He nodded.

"Your honour I have but one question to ask of the prosecutor and the people."

The senior Nduna nodded,

"Proceed."

"Well," I coughed, "this is most embarrassing - all these people who are your children, from the Ndunas down to the youngest member, know you to be an honourable, decent, and above all, a modest man!"

The crowd sighed.

"I believe it is quite safe for me to say that the most honourable Nduna would never take his clothes off in public!"

I turned to look at the prosecutor for verification; he turned very dark with embarrassment,

"Definitely not!" He spluttered.

The assembly sighed.

"Then it stands to reason that I could never have seen the honourable Nduna without his pants on!" I held my hands up to the prosecutor asking,

"Correct?"

"Yes." he muttered, "Correct! You have said a very true word."

"So!" I bowed in total submission to the senior Nduna, "If I have not seen the honourable Nduna without his pants on, it would be impossible for me to know if he has a tail or if he does not have a tail!"

The crowd held its breath.

"Therefore, I submit, your Honour, that the informant in this matter, has misled the court and he or she should be dealt with in the strongest manner possible. To suggest the Senior Nduna walks around naked is to ridicule the Nduna in a very bad way! And then to put the blame for making such a statement on me, a good friend of the Honourable Nduna, is absolutely disgusting."

I looked at the crowd. They held their breath.

"Finally may I say this, did the man who reported this ridiculous matter to the court realise that as a result the Nduna would have to take his pants off in public to show whether he has a tail or not! If he does not do this, we will all be forever wondering!

So, your honour, I suggest you transfer the punishment you offered me to the rumour monger, he who set you up into such a foul situation."

I bowed, clapped my hands, hung my head and waited.

Silence.

I looked around. The prosecutor was gazing off into the distance, the crowd were whispering. A worried look had settled over the Senior Nduna's face. Remembering that the prosecutor was the leader of the strongest local church, I said,

"Amen! So be it!" And I sat down.

The Senior Nnduna cleared his throat. A distant expression spread over his face,

"This court is dismissed!" He grunted.

The court messenger gave a whoop of joy and running over to me. He took my hand and pumping it vigorously shouted,

"Surely it is true, you would never ever say such a thing!" He winked! "You owe the Senior Nduna and those of us who are your friends a round of cokes at the store!"

"Yes!" I agreed and turning to the crowd I smiled, "I do hereby invite the honourable Nduna and our friends to join me at the store."

As we walked across to the store the court messenger whispered to me,

"Hey Madala, what about the baboon part?"

"Be quiet!" I whispered back.

We laughed.

XXXXXX

IN COURT A SECOND TIME

We sat around the campfire on a beautiful winter's night. Ian served us Irish coffee.

David laughed,

"Talking about stories and the local tribal court I will always remember this one!

Albert approached us one day with that special conspiratorial look that Caprivians adopt when they have something of importance to tell you.

"Muswihili madala." He said.

"Muswihili Albert.

"Madala, there is some big trouble in the land."

"Yes?"

"But I am afraid to tell you Madala!"

"Then do not tell me Albert."

Disappointment darkened his eyes,

"But Madala, it is very important!"

"Then tell me Albert."

"Oh Madala, we all know that you are a good man, but sometimes my Madala, you are not such a good man!"

"You mean I have been bad?"

"I do not say so! Never would I say so! But the people! Oh the people, they are talking. They say that you do nothing for them! That you have taken their land and you are making millions of monies and you give the people none of it. They wish to chase you from the land."

"And?"

"The messenger gave me a letter to call you to court on Thursday, but first I want to tell you that there are many here who are intelligent! They know you are a good man. It is the others who are jealous! They look for a bribe from you to stop their accusations."

"What does the Nduna say?"

"He knows you and your family and what you do for the community but he has to allow this case to come to court!"

"Albert I thank you for this information and I thank you for your loyalty."

"Madala? Does this mean you will not punish me for stealing the petrol from the blue boat?"

Raising my eyebrows I asked,

"What petrol?"

"Oh no! You know nothing of the petrol? That damned Bushman, he said you did know!"

"Albert my friend!"

"Yes my boss!"

"Please thank Ben the Bushman for making you tell me of this serious matter of the theft of petrol. This time I will not punish you. Okay!"

Albert bowed and with eyes twitching, he left,

"Bloody Bayea Bushman!" He muttered.

I decided that a quick visit to the Paramount Chief's court might be of help to my case on Thursday.

The following day, Wednesday, Ian and I travelled to the Paramount Chief's offices at Linyanti. There we paid our annual tax, our business tax and collected receipts. We also collected copies of various other documents and information relating to certain high ranking members of our Senior Nduna's community.

Thursday morning found Ian and I sitting on the mat at the court.

The usual crowd of observers were in an expectant and happy mood.

The local church Pastor was selected as prosecutor. He had a long list of the alleged defaults committed by me. From the look on his face this was serious business.

"The first matter," he boomed "is the matter of not allowing the children of the honourable Nduna to walk across the Buhili Island where the Madala has his camp.

The second matter is the question of authority. Who authorised the Madala and his family to set up a business on Buhili Island and to live there and to change the name to Somewhere Island?

The third matter is the matter of rental. Why does the Madala not pay rental to this court?

Then there is the fourth matter of not allowing the children of the Nduna to eat at the camp table or join with the tourists on his vehicle."

The list was long, mischievous and tedious.

Finally, with a sigh of great sadness, the prosecutor sat down.

"Well?" Asked the senior Nduna, "You cannot have a good answer to all these accusations!"

"Honourable Nduna! Firstly may I say that the prosecutor does not know me very well! He has never been in my house, in my car or with me on any of my business trips. I am not a member of his Church. It is thus obvious that all the accusations he read out are based on hearsay. Other people told him these stories."

Bowing to the Senior Nduna, I continued,

"You, Your Honour, and the prosecutor, know of another man who was once falsely accused and convicted on hearsay evidence and you know that as a result that man was executed. Of all the people here the prosecutor should know better than to use unsubstantiated evidence in court because his church is based on that very man who was so executed."

A low moan escaped from the crowd.

"There is the question of the right to live and work here. You will agree that this court may not evict anyone who is a member of the tribe. Correct? Ok then. Let us start at the beginning."

The Senior Nduna nodded.

"Thank you. The families of men who have land rights inherit such rights from generation to generation, yes?"

"Yes."

"Secondly. Do you collect land rent from members of the tribe?"

"No."

"Thirdly do any of your community members pay business tax here or do they pay it at Linyanti?"

"At Linyanti."

I took out the papers from the Linyanti court and was about to make my case when a large brown cobra slithered across the courtyard. It stopped in front of the Senior Nduna. Crazy! A similar thing happened here last time but then it was only a small grass snake!

Realising the danger it was in the snake turned towards the safe area under and behind the chief's chair. The Senior Nduna, hiding his fear, lifted his feet off the ground. The snake darted under the chair. I got up - told the crowd to be quiet and ushered the snake away from the courtyard. The snake turned as it reached the security of surrounding bush, raised its head and stared me out. I slit my eyes in case it spat at me and held still. The snake, seeing that I was not a threat moved quietly into the thickness of the bush.

The crowd let out a long exaggerated sigh.

Back on the mat I picked up the papers I had dropped and addressed the sub chief,

"Honourable Nduna please do not worry! There will be no more snakes today!" With a long, drawn out sigh, I continued, "I have four papers from Linyanti office. The first is a copy of my own and my family's membership of the tribe. The second, receipts of payments made by my family and I for tribal tax and for business tax.

The third, copies of our Land Rights all registered by and at the office of the Paramount Chief with photographs of the ceremony at 'Somewhere' camp attended by the chief when he officially gave us the land.

The fourth is a list the Paramount Chief asked me to hand to you with the names of members of your community on it who have not paid the amounts due by them for tribal taxes and business taxes.

You have been requested to facilitate in the collecting of these outstanding amounts.

It may interest you to know, Honourable Nduna, that the first name to appear on this list of debtors is also the worst offender. He is this gentleman," I pointed, "The Pastor who is your court prosecutor!"

He has let your honourable court slide into disgrace!"

The crowd moaned.

"But most important today, is the fact that because I am a fully paid up member of the tribe, which these papers prove, neither you, nor your court nor any member of your community has the right to evict me or any member of my family, nor have they the right to interfere in any of my business activities or in my private life!"

A wail from the crowd was followed by happy hand clapping!

Leaning forward as I prepared to stand I said,

"As this case is now over, may I invite you, most Honourable Nduna and your Prosecutor and the Court Messenger to a share a coke with me at the store!"

Loud laughter and much hand clapping and a shout,

"Hey Madala, we are now all of us, your friends!"

xxxxxxx

Saturday evening, three days after the court case, we heard from Albert that a local Sangoma (witch doctor) was holding a meeting to establish the guilt or otherwise of a teenage girl accused by her uncle of laying a curse on him.

If the meeting found the girl guilty she would meet her end in some horrible way.

We prayed for her release.

Distant drums throbbed until the early hours of Sunday.

Albert returned from the meeting at midday on Sunday. I asked him the result. He said the girl had been found not guilty. Excitedly he told us,

"It was excellent my Madala, the Senior Nduna was there. I heard him speak to the Sangoma before the meeting started. I heard him ask the Sangoma,

"Have you heard about the story of the snakes at the council?"

"Yes!"

"Have you heard about the son of the Madala and the black mamba at Somewhere Else?"

"Yes."

329

"Do you have any advice for me in this matter?"

"Yes."

"What is the amount due for the advice?"

"This time, no charge! It is a serious matter of concern to both of us!"

"Well," asked the Nduna, "If snakes obey a certain man and his family is it not a good idea to be careful how we treat such a man? Would it be wise to challenge that certain man in any way?"

The Sangoma pursed his lips and whispered to the Senior Nduna. I stood close to listen. This is what the Sangoma said.

"As you say, any man who has higher authority than snakes is not a man to argue with. It would be very unwise to upset such a certain man in any way whatsoever!"

"Thank you most wise and knowledge-able Sangoma. Thank you!"

xxxxxxx

"Madala," Albert said, "I believe there will be no more trouble for us."

He clapped his hands and went in search of Ben the Bushman to pass on the good news.

xxxxxxx

THE BLACK MAMBA

"So tell me," I asked Ian "what's the story about you and the snake? The black mamba?"

"You know the outside toilet at the 'Somewhere Else' Camp?"

I nodded "Yes it's under that dead Leadwood tree about thirty metres from the camp tents."

"Well last year as I was leaving the toilet I was attracted by the chattering of a wild squirrel perched in a nearby Mangwe tree. I answered it with my version of a twittering sound whilst flicking my fingers in imitation of the squirrels jerky tail movements. The squirrel responded, chattering as it jumped from branch to branch coming closer to me at each move.

I raised my 'flickering finger' hand and holding it close to the gnarled trunk of the Leadwood tree and I started chattering like a happy squirrel as I watched its antics. Suddenly, for no apparent reason, it shrieked and jumping high onto one of the top branches of the tree it shouted at me in increasing agitation.

I was dumbfounded! I doubled my efforts to encourage the squirrel back down the tree but it went berserk and leaping and shouting at me, it crossed from the Mangwe tree to the dead Leadwood where it hung upside down from a high branch and screamed at me.

I carried on twitching my fingers and calling.

In desperation the squirrel jumped onto a lower and closer branch. As my eyes followed it I became aware that the squirrel was looking not at me, but at my flickering hand! Turning my head I saw a two metre long black mamba wrapped around the trunk of the dead tree. Its head was no more than six inches from my twitching fingers.

Taking care to not excite the snake, I carried on calling to the squirrel and, still twitching my fingers, I slowly moved my hand away from the snake's head.

Above me the squirrel, believing I wasn't moving fast enough, let out a final warning scream and threw itself down the trunk of the tree at the snake. The now alarmed snake raised its head to counter the attack. The squirrel sidestepped and darting past the snake's head it shot back up the Leadwood tree with the snake in hot pursuit. The squirrel scrambled into a hole in the tree and out the other side where it leapt across to the Mangwe tree only to turn back again and swear profusely at the very silly human who had brought both of us so close to death.

The mamba followed the squirrel into the hole in the tree where it lost interest and disappeared down the inside of the hollow trunk.

"Amazing!" Exclaimed a listening tourist "How little do we know or understand!"

Ian agreed, he turned again to me,

"By the way," he said "tomorrow I am taking these tourists out on a day trip, do you two want to come?"

"Too true we do! I take it that you are the guide?"

"Yes. First we will canoe from here down to the hippo pool, not too early! We don't want to meet a late night daddy hippo in mid-stream. Then we will canoe on to the oxbow lake where a short walk to the sand dunes will bring us to where Matthew and the Land Rover will meet us and bring us back to Somewhere."

"And the canoes?"

"Mathew will tie them together and row them back to camp!"

XXXXXX

A TOUR GUIDE
WITH A DIFFERENCE

The next day, after an English breakfast of bacon and eggs on toast, Ian led us all down to the river. We listened to his instructions on how to handle a canoe and what signs he would use to guide us.

"As I said," he emphasised "listen to everything around you and do not impose your own perceptions on what you see. The wildlife will speak to you through body language and in their-own language.

If I shout – 'OUT' - you must paddle furiously to the nearest firm ground and get out, don't ask why, just do it. Okay?" He looked around the group, "If a hippo does attack a canoe and it sinks, the occupants must throw off their life jackets, dive under water and swim under water to the nearest bank! Hippos usually don't attack under water. You got it?" We all nodded. "Ok, let's go!"

We drifted down stream through lilies floating in crystal water, past birds, bees, spiders and dragonflies. The grunt and chortle of hippo echoed through the reeds as they settled down to sunbathe on the banks of their personal pools. Beaching the canoes on a bend in the river we walked across a stretch of swampland approaching the main hippo pool from behind scrubby bushes. The pod of hippo lay on the far bank except for one Red-eared bull which remained in the water. Ian sat us down on a bank about thirty metres across from the hippo. He cupped his hands over his mouth and low in his throat called a drawn out deep and mournful cry.

"Hello Hippo!" And again "Hello Hippo!"

The pod came to attention pointing their ears toward us. The bull in the water grunted. Ian answered him from deep in his throat. The bull hippo heaved himself out of the deep water and roaring open mouthed, he charged the group of hippo on the bank - scattering them! Then, whirling back through the waves into the deep water he screamed at us and turning upside down, waggled his legs in the air.

We sat mesmerised.

He flipped himself upright again and erupting from the water charged open mouthed towards us stopping only two metres from our bank.

"Hello Hippo." Grunted Ian.

"Hello! Hello." Answered the hippo and charging back into the pool, tail wagging furiously, he sank beneath the water.

"My friend Albert." Explained Ian, "He often races our boat and loves to tease and play with the dogs at Somewhere. He tried to make friends with me for many months but I was too busy being afraid of him until one day I listened to what he had to say and responded. Now we love each other. We call him Albert after our man at the camp, they both grunt when they speak."

xxxxxxx

Returning from a game drive that evening we came across a distressed bull elephant running wild towards us across open grassland. He was racing away from the smell of local fishermen camped on a nearby island. He must have come in from Angola where elephant are constantly butchered, wounded and harassed by Unita soldiers. Ian cut the Land Rover engine and we all held still. The old bull thundered to a stop. He could hear us in front of him, he could smell the fishermen behind him but because of his poor eyesight he could not see us clearly.

The elephant stood holding his trunk high trying to catch our scent. His terror grew.

Suddenly, screaming in fright, he tossed his head up, lowered his trunk, pulled back his ears and prepared to charge us. Ian leant sideways out of the vehicle and rumbled at the back of his throat a lilting six note sound of love and care.

The bull, throwing his ears forward and out, swung his head towards the sound. Ian called again - so softly we could hardly hear. The great bull dropped its head, flapped its ears, heaved a sigh of relief and walked calmly past the back of our truck.

We drove back to camp in silence.

That night I asked Ian to explain his uncanny understanding of nature especially the wild life.

"If you stop and listen instead of always imposing yourself on others there is a small chance you may learn to see what is right there in front of you and then maybe, if you care, you will learn to become receptive enough to hear the things you cannot see."

334

"Such as what things that you cannot see?" I asked.

He laughed,

"Well! You can't see God!"

XXXXXXXX

TWO MEN FROM KATU

David drove in from Katima. He looked a little disgruntled.

"Ian" he barked "Two South Africans from 'Katu' want to go Tiger fishing on the Zambezi. Unfortunately, without thinking, I agreed to help out. They found two more tourists to go with them this morning. I want you to take them! Get Matthew to drive the second boat."

I interrupted,

"Could I take the second boat? I have fished for Tiger along the Zambezi in Zimbabwe many times!"

David grunted,

"Why not?"

Ian and I left for Katima early next morning.

We launched the boats onto the Zambezi River at the workshop camp. The lady spent the day with David's wife. Ian and I rode down-stream to meet and collect the four fishermen at the Zambezi Lodge floating bar.

He took the two men from Katu. I took the other two.

"Where is Katu?" Asked Ian.

"Next to Kat-one." They laughed.

We drifted down stream towards Hippo Island, the two boats alongside each other.

"What's that?" Asked one of the men from Katu.

A policeman was waving from the southern bank. He shouted and beckoned to us to come over. We steered our boats towards him and reaching the bank Ian pushed the nose of his boat up on the shore.

"We need your help." Pleaded the policeman. "A croc has taken a young boy."

Two more policemen arrived followed by a group of wailing women. "Can we use your boats to look for the croc and the body?" One policeman asked.

"Okay," said Ian "you get in my boat and the other two policemen get in Robert's boat."

Ian roared off following the directions of the policeman. I followed. We searched down stream but finding no sign they asked us to cross the border into Zambian waters.

We did that and drifted down stream.

A shout exploded from the Zambian bank followed by a group of angry Zambian soldiers. They ran out of the reeds onto a sandbank.

"Wait." The policeman in Ian's boat stood up. "We're looking for a crocodile which caught a young boy!" The boat swayed, the policeman staggered "Have you seen anything?"

The soldiers stood with their firearms held at the ready. A sergeant joined them, he bellowed,

"You are in Zambian territory. We should shoot you. No we have not seen the croc or the boy. Get back to your side fast or we will take the necessary action. Have you forgotten our friends in Angola are at war with South Africa?"

The policeman saluted,

"Thank you, thank you! See you one day when peace comes!" He waved.

We revved the outboards and raced back to Namibian waters.

No sign of the croc. No sign of the boy. We dropped the policemen at Hippo Lodge and trawled down stream for tiger fish. The four fishermen started drinking beer. We declined their offer to join them. They were a little shattered by the croc incident and the Zambian army.

About fourteen kilometres down stream, having had no bites, Ian suggested we try one of the side channels where some deep holes in the river usually produced tiger fish.

The men wound in their lines and we raced down to the side channel where Ian cut the throttle on his boat. Turning to the two men from Katu as he let the boat drift to a slow trawl, he said,

"Okay, lets try from here."

Before they could answer, the boat heaved up on one side, a hippo snapped its jaws over and under the prow. It let go then opened it's huge mouth to bite again. Ian revved the motors and the boat shot away from the angry hippo. I followed Ian. He raced on for about three hundred metres then we beached our boats on a sand-spit. His boat was filling with water. We dragged it higher up onto the bank.

I looked at him. He smiled at me.

I looked at the fishermen - the two from Katu were shattered. One of the men in my boat was close to tears.

"And now?" I asked Ian.

He checked his boat.

"Lucky!" He said "Only two holes in the bottom. The top holes don't matter." He turned to one of the Katu fishermen asking, "You were eating toffee?"

The fisherman nodded.

"You had a big bag - is some left?"

"Yes, lots."

"Can I have it?"

"Sure!" He passed the bag to Ian. It was nearly full.

Ian handed six toffees to each one of us and asked us to chew them soft.

"We can plug the holes with toffee mixed with grass." He said. "So long as the boat is on the plane the toffee won't get wet and melt. If we have to slow down and the boat drops back into the water, the toffee blocking the holes should keep the water out so long as we don't keep it under water for too long!"

I collected short, tough, river-grass.

We mixed the chewed toffee with chopped grass and plugged the holes. Pushing the boat back into the water we saw it floated, empty, with the holes well above the water line. Even with two men in it the holes were still clear, with three, the water covered the holes.

The heaviest Katu man swapped with the lightest man in my boat and we set off again.

Trawling up what is known as the 'Skelem' channel we caught a few small Tiger Fish. The toffee-come-grass plugs worked well.

I was dozy from the sun and the slow trawling. Eventually the guys in my boat managed to sort out a way for them to not tangle their lines and began to enjoy each other. We stopped on another sand bank for lunch. The beer began to run freely again. The fishermen relaxed.

"Can we try for bream after lunch?" asked one.

"No problem." said Ian. "We'll go upstream to where there are lots of reeds and quiet pools and catch bream there."

We set off for the pools and stopped at a good spot for bream. The afternoon wore on. The sunlight from above and that reflected off the water bathed me in warmth. The boat engines were idling to keep us from drifting with the current. I fought against falling asleep. The lady back at camp drifted into my mind, a very special person!

I thought of my wife Jean. I missed her terribly.

Through the haze of memories, Ian shouted,

"Watch it!"

Without checking I thrust the throttle hard forward. The boat leapt out of the water. The man from Katu who had joined us lost his balance. He started to fall backwards. His foot caught under the swivel chair. Toppling upside down he fell head first into the water. His jammed foot kept his leg in the boat. He hung onto his rod. The hook on his line caught on a submerged rock. I stalled the outboard motor. We drifted around and down stream. The spluttering man from Katu let the reel spin out but still hung onto his rod. Clambering to the back of the boat I took hold of his free arm. The line in his spool ran out, he hung on not wanting to lose the rod. His head was pulled under the water. I grabbed his collar and his belt and heaved him back into the boat. The line snapped.

Coughing and spitting he shouted,

"I still have the rod!"

It was time to go home. We sailed up the Zambezi in the late afternoon. A red sunset reflected in the wide river.

Ian slowed near some rapids. He told me there was a rock barrier below the water, which stretched across the river. At the northern end of the barrier is a break where water rushes through. To avoid damaging the boats or the motors we took up position at the down stream entrance to the gap and lined the boats up with the radio tower in Katima and a large tree on the upstream southern bank. Then, taking care to not be pushed out of line by the strong current, we drove the boats through the break and continued towards the tower, which meant we travelled across the river at an angle so avoiding damage from the submerged rocks.

I went ahead of Ian through the submerged rock area and slowed the boat at the other end to wait for him. We watched Ian churn through the gap. He was about one hundred metres out of danger and accelerated. The bow came up, the back went down and the boat shot forward. Suddenly the boat dipped down in front, the engine sound changed. The boat started losing ground to the strong current. He drove the boat across to the far bank where he pulled it up on sand. I waited to see what was wrong.

The men with Ian sat huddled in the boat. They were once again in Zambian territory.

Ian waded into the shallow water at the back of the boat. He lifted the left hand motor. The propeller was shattered.

He climbed back into the boat and collected a spare prop and tools from the prow box. He asked the Katu guy to help. They climbed out into the water at the back of the boat where they took off the broken prop and replaced it with the new one. The other man kept his eyes on the Zambian bank, praying out loud.

Ian lowered the repaired motor, pushed the boat back into deep water and they jumped in.

Starting the motors, he guided the boat back into the channel and waved to me to say all was okay.

A shout from the Zambian bank and an angry soldier ran out of the reeds. Ian accelerated and raced his boat across to me. We lost no time in getting back to Katima Mulilo.

Ian docked his boat at the jetty at the Zambezi Lodge. I pulled up alongside. We escorted the four men and their fish up the gangplank to their chalets.

We told them we would join them at seven that evening for a drink at the bar.

Ian said to me,

"They had a rough time and they look really exhausted. I haven't the gall to ask them for payment."

We took the boats back to the plot, had a wash and clean up and drove back to the lodge.

Seven-o-clock we walked into the bar. The place was alive with talk and much laughter. The men from Katu were telling their fishing story and what a fishing story it was. For once they didn't have to exaggerate.

"Hey." One of them beckoned to us "What a day you gave us. Have a drink man. No one will ever believe us when we get home. What's on the menu for tomorrow? Hey what a day man!"

XXXXXX

THE BUSINESS MAN

Our last evening at Somewhere Island!

"We are sad to go," I said "we've learnt so much here. It's good to learn and to share!"

I looked closely at David, "I have a very special friend back in South Africa who is always laughing, always helping or sharing with any one in need but when it came to business he had no feelings at all! He said 'not only is all fair in love and war but also in business!' In a way you are just like him, tough on the outside but gentle on the inside, except that you are a man of integrity!

Can I tell you a typical story about him?"

"Go for it!"

"Well one day a manufacturing company in my friend's home town went into liquidation and was put up for sale. My friend wanted to buy it but the price asked for was more than he could afford. He went to the Liquidator's office at four o'clock the day before the sale. The Liquidator was about to close shop and go home. My friend made an offer of twenty cents in the dollar for the insolvent business.

The liquidator was not amused,

"You must be crazy! The business is worth a damned side more than that. Make it eighty cents and we may be able to come to an agreement, or, better still, come to the sale tomorrow and bid with the rest of them."

"As you will," said my friend, "but I will leave this written offer with you just in case you change your mind and decide to sign it. By the way there is also a bank guaranteed cheque for the full amount I offered, dated today, in the attached envelope. You will see that my offer expires at midnight tonight."

The Liquidator laughed. He placed the envelope on his desk and ushered him out of the office saying,

"Nice try but no! See you at the sale."

That night, one hour after midnight, my friend arrived at the factory, cut the security bolts with a bolt cutter, opened the doors, loaded the equipment, the vehicles, the machinery and all the materials plus the office desks, office equipment and the furniture into four thirty ton trucks.

He stripped the place bare and took everything out to his farm.

xxxxxxx

Saturday dawned and people started arriving at the factory for the sale. They gaped at the open doors.

The Liquidator and Auctioneer arrived.

"Oh my God!" He shouted, "What the hell goes on?"

A worker told him the place had been looted.

The Liquidator swore,

"Hang on everybody, I'm going back to the office but I'll be back in a jiffy." He drove off like a maniac.

My friend arrived. He joined the waiting crowd.

A little later the Liquidator returned. He leapt out of his car, a bundle of papers in his hand.

"Hey" he shouted to my friend "I've got your offer here. It is signed and sealed. The factory and all the movables are yours. I had the cheque deposited by my office. Congratulations!"

"Let me see where you signed."

My friend took the papers from the Liquidator, checked the signatures and noted that the date of the sale agreement was still as he had written it - Friday! Yesterday! The day before the sale!

"Excellent!" Beamed my friend, "Now I can move all my stuff back."

"What do you mean 'all your stuff' – what stuff?" Whispered the Liquidator.

"I mean the stuff which I bought together with the business at your office yesterday! You know, all the loose stuff in the factory! I was afraid vandals might take the opportunity to strip the place of everything knowing there was inadequate security last night. Now that I have the legal confirmation of yesterday's sale I can take up legal occupation! I will make the place safe by setting up a security system and then move everything back again."

"But! Do you mean to say! What the hell!"

"No buts! You have given me my copy of the papers we signed yesterday so the factory and contents became mine at twelve o'clock last night! You say you have already deposited my cheque! What I now do with the business is my affair. And a very good day to you Sir!"

Turning to Ian I said,

"What I learnt from this story is that my friend believed he was not criminal because it was a straight business deal. Rather, he argued that the Liquidator was the dishonest one! You see it was the liquidator who pretended he had signed the day before.

Even though I told my friend that the Liquidator's forgery did not make his own actions right and pointed out the fact that my friend had lost his integrity, it did teach me that everyone has his own perspective of right and wrong. Learning this has helped me check out on my own beliefs and try to correct them when I find that what once seemed right to me is in reality, wrong!"

Albert, the hippo, grunted!

"You named the hippo after Albert!" I said. "I was talking to Albert, I mean Albert the man the other day. He had some 'way out' story about his father and how he died! Is it true?"

XXXXXXX

ALBERT'S STORY

Albert had spoken to me with deep emotion,

"My father was killed by the Police!" He coughed, "Some men came over the Zambian border to our village. They were looking for food and women. They said they were freedom fighters from Angola. They warned us that they would kill all our family if any one told the Namibian authorities that they had been to us.

A few weeks later a South African patrol came to our village. They demanded we tell them who the people were who had come from Zambia. We told them everything we knew except we did not know why they came to our village. The patrol leader did not believe us! He said we belonged to and supported the freedom fighters. My father repeated his claim that he did not know! He told them the freedom fighters had raped some of the women. The police said he was hiding information.

They beat my father and some of the younger men. They said my father was a son of Satan. This is not true as my father belongs to the Full Gospel Church. They said he lied, that all blacks were liars. They said, "Black people were not made by God!"

My father answered, "Everything that was made was made by God, even the Police."

The police said they would teach everyone a lesson so that next time we would tell them the truth.

They pulled a sheet of corrugated iron off the roof of one of the huts. They broke six large bricks from the wall. They made a fire, set the bricks around it and placed the sheet of iron on top.

The police tied my father's hands and feet together. They rolled him onto the hot corrugated iron. They dragged my mother to the fire and held her there to watch.

My father never made a sound! He lay there with his eyes wide open, cooking! He watched my mother - honouring and loving her.

As he died he whispered to her,

"Forgive them for they do not know the truth."

The police laughed as they drove away in their Sarmel army truck."

I asked David,

"Do you know about this story?"

"Yes I heard about it but I never knew it was Albert's father. He never told us."

I asked David,

"If Albert's story is true surely it would have come to the notice of the authorities and they would have investigated?"

"In what we would call a normal society yes! But Southern Africa has its own perspective of normality and just because we do not agree with it does not mean that we are right or that they are wrong. Sometimes we have to accept other people's codes of behaviour if we want to live amongst them! You know the old saying 'when in Rome do as the Romans do' and if you cannot, then get out!"

David looking sad muttered,

"Yes Albert's story is true, but no more true than the mindless cruelty of the so called freedom fighters towards not only their perceived enemies, but also against their own people."

We sat quietly for a while.

"David?"

"Yes?"

"There are many Black African's who hate the White Africans for what they did! Similarly there are many White Africans who hate the Black Africans! It is so very sad that the haters on both sides don't understand that although both sides have committed atrocities against each other and even though both sides claim to have reason to justify their acts, the vast majority of both the Black and White Africans have very special natures and have both love and respect for each other. When I left my farm in Zimbabwe our African neighbours and the farm worker's cried! As did my family and I!

That is what I choose to remember!"

"Yes you are right! How can we reach out to the hurt ones and help them overcome their memories and their hate?"

"Maybe you can't!"

XXXXXXX

GOODBYE SOMEWHERE

Time to leave!

The lady and I took a farewell walk around the island. At the northern end she stopped and stood quiet and still under a Pod Mahogany tree. I waited by her side.

She turned to face me, her eyes wet.

"You look sad?" I asked.

"Yes I am sad. Ian is a wonderful son!"

"Yes. I have two wonderful sons! But why are you sad!"

"When we get back to South Africa we," she held her breath, "no not we, you!" She paused again. Looking away, she lowered her head, "You must go your own way and I must go back to my Bed And Breakfast business!"

"What do you mean?"

"Robert you are very special but the truth is that you have never forgotten your wife. You still love her. You always will!"

I closed my eyes. Would the pain of living never end?

"Yes!" I whispered in agony "Yes, it is the right and proper thing to do!"

We embraced for the last time.

XXXXXXX

BACK AT ROBERT'S CAMP

When I arrived back home at my camp in the mountains I found Red still there. He looked relaxed and happy!

We were enjoying a cup of coffee and telling each other tall stories as we sat under the large wild fig tree overlooking the valley in front of my camp.

Red put his cup down at his feet and spoke,

"Well Robert old chap, all I can say is that you seem to have had a fantastic life and I am sure there's a whole stack of fascinating stories you still have to tell!"

"Maybe, but that's more than enough for now! Come!"

I went back inside and made lunch. Red relaxed in his chair in the sitting room. The big dog snored. An owl hooted.

"Ready." I called.

We ate in silence.

Red finished first.

"Thanks. Delicious! Now tell me about your project."

I frowned,

"Most people think I am crazy. Maybe you don't really want to hear!"

"Oh yes I do. After all, that is one of the reasons I came to see you!"

Relaxing in my chair with stretched out legs I started my story.

"It's really quite simple. It's about the missing link."

"You mean between the apes and man."

"Yes! But actually I am researching both that and information related to the story of the ruins in central Africa. Firstly it seems that the missing link in both cases is not known, not understood or not acknowledged by any one. What I mean regarding man is I think everyone is barking up the wrong tree. It is not a question of man evolving from the apes or the apes evolving from man - the fact of the gorilla's DNA being almost identical to man's does not necessarily mean that the gorilla came from man or that man came from the gorilla! No Red, it is both more complicated and more simple than that! I believe the missing link is neither the ape nor the gorilla nor man!" Feeling a little embarrassed I laughingly said, "Oh well. Might as well tell you - I am of the opinion that the primates and man do come from a common ancestor but not from a so called similar species such as the ape as propounded by scientists - no! I think we are all descendants of another animal altogether, which on the surface looks and seems to be totally different to us but is in reality almost exactly the same! It has the same internal organs, the same skin and cartilage types, almost the same sexual organ functions, the same hair and teeth and so on - almost exactly like man except for an extra artery leading off from near the heart and a modification of the hands, the feet, the nipples and the body shape."

I paused,

"When I say man I am sure you already know that Caucasoid man has differing DNA to other racial types such as Indian and African man. Take the case of the Negroes who not only have different colour to Caucasians but also have different ligaments in their knees, different pelvic bones, different throat muscles and different structures on the crowns of their heads! Maybe this suggests that there could be at least two or more different breeds of the derivative animal as are found in the different continents which led to the existing variations found amongst the primates and men."

Once again I felt a little embarrassed.

"Go on!" Red smiled, "Don't stop now! Tell me - which animal?

I grunted,

"The pig!"

"What! You can't mean that?"

"Don't laugh! Check it out with me. The pig is an important part of nearly all religions. The Jews won't eat it. The Moslems won't touch it. Certain primitive tribes consider it sacred and their women suckle the piglets. Cannibals say the flesh of the pig tastes the same as human flesh. The evil spirits in the bible story asked to be transferred from the mad man into a herd of swine. Bad men are called swine's. So pigs are seen to be sacred or dirty. People say men behave like pigs. Men live and talk like pigs. Some people even look like pigs. Some men are pigs and small men are called pigmies! My spelling! And last but not least, pig organs and parts can be transplanted into man in the same way that human parts are.

So I believe that all the primates and all men do have a common ancestor and I am of the opinion it could be the pig, or maybe I should say, different members of the pig family leading to different members of the human and ape family. Hey!" I smiled "This is only my opinion. I don't like the present theory of evolution because it relies far too much on the 'need' to explain and the 'need' to justify and speculate. I accept that trying to understand does lead one into the arena of chance understanding or misunderstanding. But the commonly accepted perspective of evolution is really a bit of a hairy concept. Evolution basically comes about when there is a need to change to meet changing circumstances like fish living in Lake Malawi of the same family as fish living in the Zambezi River but having differing colours to suit the differing environments. Therefore, although environment or circumstance may bring about certain evolutionary changes, there would appear to be no such situations on earth which would naturally create an evolutionary change leading to the need to be religious or artistic or moral or creative or to a serious variation in IQ.

Of course I am not able to definitely say people and the primates evolved from pigs or one from the other or that they are connected in any special way, but!"

I closed my eyes.

"Well," said Red "It seems you may have hit the nail right on the head."

I stared at Red,

"What?"

"I say again, yes!" continued Red "But do you have any idea how it come about?"

"That's my problem! In evolutionary thinking the hand came before the hooves. The camel still has the remains of five sets of bones in each foot, they, the bones, possibly being originally fingers or toes But then there are people in the Zambezi valley in central Africa with only two toes! And paintings from ancient South America of people with four fingers and four toes! Some people are born with an extra muscle on their chests like the apes have or more than one set of nipples! But in all this I see more and more evidence pointing to pigs being the original source of both mankind and the primates. It seems that there may also be evidence in the bible."

I stared out of the widow then getting up I went into the kitchen to wash the dishes. Red followed me. I said, "I have been to many places where I saw evidence of huge climatic changes. I saw evidence of previous civilisations - many much greater and more scientifically advanced than our own. I saw signs of primitive men being both primitive or being anything but primitive. There is evidence of long ago space travel, of engineering works that make ours look pathetic. Many times has the earth been broken up, closed over, split into sections, drowned, frozen, flooded, burnt, you name it.

What really did happen to the people of Atlantis or the people of ancient Egypt or those of the pre ice age and the Dinosaurs and all the other prehistoric life? Were human beings on earth with the Dinosaurs or the Mammoth Elephants? If so why have no human remains been found in the same strata or eras? Why were there no Dinosaurs on Noah's Ark and if the animals went in two by two what was there for the Carnivores to eat while on the ark for almost a year and when they came off at the end what did they then find alive to eat other than the two of each kind from the Ark itself?

What happened to the ancient South American civilisations and who were the Sumerians who lived a hundred and forty thousand years ago? Who built the pyramids in South America and China and who wrote on the walls in a cave in North India, writings and drawings about flying machines with swept back wings like our modern planes, powered by a special fuel?

Who left the thousands of ceramic disks stored on shelves in a sealed cave in the Himalayas? Disks we have not yet learnt how to read.

Who made the ancient huge landing strips in Alaska and most crazy of all, where did the machined tools come from that were made out of high tensile steel which were found in a bed of coal estimated as being more than six million years old?

Who?

Maybe that's why they say the owl is wise! It can see in the dark!

Why is the same question not asked about God as is asked about creation? If creation needed to be created why does not God also need to be created? If not, what was He busy doing during the mind-boggling infinity of time eternal that existed before creation?

Then comes the big 'bug' questions, who and what is the 'Most High God', who is the 'Father in Heaven', who is 'Jesus the Christ', who is the God of creation or the God of the Israelites. Who are Mahomet, the Buddha and Krishna?

Who and what are all the other Gods?

Most important to me, who and what was this Melchizedek fellow that no one wants to talk about? What were the machines of the Bible that could fly in any direction? What are UFO's? What were the balls of fire that strange looking 'man like creatures' flew into North Africa?"

Closing my eyes I said,

"Ever since the first day I saw my son Peter, I seem to have been living separate from myself - almost as if I am no longer me. So my last question is also my first - WHO AM I?"

Red said,

"Right, I think it may be my turn to talk. You ready to hear my story?"

"Why not? But first, in all this you are still a complete stranger to me. So tell me, who are you?"

"Funny you should say that. You reached out to your kids posing as a stranger. I come to you as a stranger and it was a stranger who started me off on my road of discovery!"

The wind blew a gust of freshness down the valley. The water rippled.

I suggested,

"The sun is low now so let's start on this road of discovery by moving our chairs down to the river."

XXXXXXX

RED'S STORY

Red relaxed in his chair.

"I need to explain something to you before I begin my story. It is to do with curtains. When you draw a curtain across a window it hides both the view from the room out into the garden and the view into the room from the garden. Even if you never open the curtain and so never see inside the room or into the garden, they, the room and the garden are both still there!

So, just as you can draw curtains shut, to hide the inside, or the outside - or both, so can you open a closed curtain and look at whatever may have been hidden inside or outside.

You can apply this to one's self in the way one thinks? I mean with regard to the curtains we all have in our minds!

Well my story starts with a curtain.

One Saturday, many moons ago, I woke up with a sense of impending doom.

Something was seriously wrong.

Thinking back over the previous day I remembered telling a whopping lie to a friend. The story I told was of no real consequence and nobody could in any way be hurt by it, but I felt the need to call him and apologise.

My friend laughed.

Nevertheless I asked myself, why had I who hates lies, told a lie? Did I have a serious problem? I tried to trace back in my memory any other lies I had told! Literally hundreds of small, large, shameful and mindless lies that I had told poured out of my previously blocked memory. Then, in a breathless instant of cognisance, I realised how many lies spoken by other people there were which I had taken into my mind pretending they were the truth.

Did I have a curtain in my mind behind which I hid? Or maybe even two curtains! One curtain preventing me from looking out at the truth outside! The second preventing me from looking in to the truth inside?

Why had I lied? Why so often? And much more serious, why or how had I hidden the fact of my lying from myself for so long?

I looked down the road of my past to my first memory and worked back from there to now. The first trauma I remembered was the day my mother lied to me. The pain I felt is still as vivid to me now as then.

I realised that in order for me to stay with her and keep on loving and accepting her I had to draw a curtain over the fact of her lying to me. The covering of the lie also hid what she had lied about.

So hiding lies in others leads to hiding your own lies. Accepting the unacceptable in the ones you love leads to acceptance of the unacceptable in yourself.

The same curtain covering the problem of my mother's lying also hid the problem of my own lies.

This new understanding led me to remember the times I never spoke the truth when it should have been spoken. Sometimes it wasn't a case of me lying - I just said nothing when I should have spoken out.

The reverse of that was when I heard the truth but refused to accept it.

What a mess!

Without the curtain I had drawn in my mind not only would I have had to separate myself from the wrongs and the lies of the perpetrators but, and far more important! I would have to revert back to being myself!

As I was jolted into this new understanding another even more difficult scenario arose, for when I removed the curtain I had placed over the lies of my loved ones and myself, the things we lied about were suddenly and stunningly revealed.

How could I now live with those, you could say 'unacceptable sins' which I or my loved ones had committed? How could I carry on being with the people whom I had so hurtfully hurt and then denied it? What about when they hurt me and I had accepted by pretending they had not hurt me so allowing me to avoid passing judgement!

I found myself in very deep water!

So I started to think from the beginning again with the questions,

'Who Am I? Where do I come from? Where am I going and why 'AM I?'

I never knew how important those questions were until I asked them. Where you come from could be the start of who you are and point to where you should be going.

So I began with my parents!

My father was, and still is my idea of the perfect gentleman - honest, clean minded, honourable. His desire to go for what is good came from deep inside him - from a place nobody else could ever reach. He was fearless, warm hearted and compassionate. Physically strong and hard working.

My mother was a congenital liar. She never knew she was lying. Not even when she was caught out. She was very beautiful, highly intelligent, gregarious, manipulative and strong willed.

My father was moral! He never even entertained the thought of committing adultery. My mother was manipulative and often deviously immoral.

They divorced. My father never married again. My mother did. She treated her new husband the same way she had treated my father.

I grew up, as I suppose all kids do, having the utmost faith and trust in my parents. As I said, I was devastated the first time I found out my mother lied and also the time I came to realize how cruelly and unashamedly she manipulated my father, my stepfather and myself. It broke my heart!

The day I found out she was having one of many affairs with a friend of my father was the day I subconsciously came to hate her.

I was too young to leave so I had to live with the problem so I drew a curtain over it and carried on with her as if all was well!

When I grew up and married I distanced myself from my mother's manipulations to protect my wife! But! I felt guilty about it. You know, honour your parents!

My wife often said that I hated women because of my mother. But I knew I did not hate women. I hated lies!

I came to understand people falling into deceit, into adultery, into theft, into all sorts of 'sins' because every problem is the result of another underlying problem, which in turn also has a root cause! But I could not tolerate lies spoken to a dearly beloved with regard to serious personal matters.

Slowly but surely I came to do all that I hated in others by hiding behind the same curtain as I hid their wrongs.

Over the years I grew more and more, angry without understanding the source of my anger. My own self-deceit broke down my ability to function properly in all spheres of my life, especially in the sphere of self-discipline and in work.

Then, as I said, one day the curtain tore!

One lie too many spoken by me to a close friend!

I realised I had become all that I never wanted to be!

My disgust with myself wrought havoc with my emotions and my mind. I went into a state of serious stress. But worse than that, when I began to see the light there developed in me an even greater problem - the rending of the curtain put me in the position where I had to choose whether or not to forgive the others who lied and those I called the initiators of the wrongs which resulted in the need to lie!

With my loved ones, forgiveness was easy! With myself it was hard. But there again another new problem arose. What if a forgiven loved one repeated a wrong and then lied again to me about it? Suddenly all the denied but known or hinted at incidents from my past rushed into my mind. My thoughts went into turmoil. I almost lost control.

What must I do when I go back to my friends - to my family - to my wife - to my mother - to myself?

After forgiving, will I be able to tolerate any new lie or the matter lied about? If not - what then?

The curtain was torn! Excruciating pain took over.

Any way my friend, first I had to come to see you, then must I go home to my family and accept that, just like me when I learnt to lie so was there a time, an incident or whatever in their lives which brought them to lie so I have no grounds to not forgive them and I must accept them all as they are.

I do love them!"

Red poured himself a glass of water. Took a deep breath and said,

"To go on with that part of my story which brought me to you - it all started on a windy day late last year when I woke up in a hospital bed.

Brilliant blue light flooded the room.

My body ached all over.

A man at my bedside said,

"Relax. Take it easy. Relax!"

I did as I was told. The warm, bright light seemed to flow into me. The pain died. He smiled. I looked up at him. He was very old, almost ancient!

"Who are you?" I asked, "Where am I?"

"I am here to help you." He said. "You are in hospital."

Suddenly I remembered the man! He had stopped me in town a few days ago and given me a letter.

"That's right." He said, "But you never read the letter!"

Taking an envelope out of the pocket of my jacket hanging on the door, he handed it to me saying,

"Read it now."

I took it from him and read it out aloud.

My very dear friend,

I write to you today having been instructed by the highest authority to tell you of why and what was before! What is now! And what is to come!

I write only that which I am told to write.

Although I may be a part of the story yet must I say, the story is not mine!

Please be patient for I am obliged to use words that you understand in order to explain to you that for which your language has no words!

The story I tell is not new for there is "Nothing new under the sun".

Nevertheless the full implications of it have of necessity from the beginning of time and up to the present been hidden to all but the 'very few.'

I am authorised to invite you to become a member of the 'VERY FEW' and that is a disciple of the 'Redro fo Kedezichlem' and to lead you into performing certain of the 'Redro' functions pertaining specifically to this time, this place, and this generation.

For twenty one years you and a man not known to you named Robert have been led to explore ancient and not so ancient ruins and artefacts in southern and central Africa.

On these expeditions, evidence of the 'Redro' has been brought to your notice and your mind awakened to understandings not otherwise available to the vast majority of people in the world.

You are hereby officially notified to the effect that I have been designated to attend to you in this matter."

Your friend

Eht Regnarts. 01.02.03.

"Well," said Red, "after I read the letter I looked up at the old man for enlightenment. He smiled and started speaking,

"A very long time ago, in the city of Mega, there lived an Astro scientist who predicted an earth shattering near collision with a 'wild card' planet from beyond our universe.

He called a meeting of senior scientists in all relative fields. After serious deliberations they all agreed that there were two possible ways to guarantee the survival of man.

The first was to build a space city large enough to cater for a specific number of selected people in which to escape the earth and fly to a place of safety and remain there until the earth re-stabilised.

The second was to horizontally bore deep into very high solid mountains and establish a safe internal environment where selected people could take shelter and last out the impending disasters.

The anticipated near collision with the wild card planet was cause for concern! Not regarding the planet itself but the fact that it was surrounded by numerous moons and asteroids some of which were dead and cold, others molten and hot!

The combined planet and earth gravitational 'pulls' as they passed each other would wreak havoc on both the earth and on the wild card planet causing climatic change, disruption of water and land masses and the annihilation of a large number of species of life. The possibility on earth of direct or glancing hits by the accompanying asteroids and moons so causing further damage was highly possible.

Accordingly, space ships and a space city were built and fitted out with all the requirements for generating and maintaining a suitable climate for human life and the production of food. A number of explorer craft were built and attached to the space ships. The new technology of gravity generation and anti-generation was urgently explored and developed.

Gravitational propulsion 'machines' were fitted below small exploratory craft, which can be seen as half round revolving 'bulbs' on the thrust sides of space ships. The larger ships used a combination of rocket propulsion, gravity generators and the new technology of cross-reacting light-speed simulators.

The selection of suitable people to take on the mother ships was based on seven perspectives called the seven attributes.

These can be summarised as -

Their inherent mental ability to come to know and then to understand what is known!

Original thought or the ability to conceive of new ideas!

Natural integrity or morality!

Their physical state!

And lastly their DNA!

The general public, those without a high level of all the seven basic requirements, were advised of the imminent disaster and every means was given them to evacuate the predicted worst scenario areas of the world. In order to protect themselves from the impending disaster equipment was designed and supplied which could cut deep into hard rock mountains simultaneously smelting the rock face of tunnels and rooms to produce a protective water proof and shock proof plaster of the inner walls, floors and ceilings. A system was also devised similar to the anti-gravity propulsion machines which would enable them to move gigantic rocks and slabs wherever necessary for the building of protective structures. It was accepted that although in all cases survival was doubtful but possible. The scientists and religious leaders who were to be left behind were given instructions and diagrams on how to keep track of the mother space city and space ships and how to utilise the new 'anti-gravity' equipment to build huge permanent space observatories on earth.

The giant ships left together with many other smaller craft and when I say smaller, I mean relatively smaller. The average size of these smaller ships was one mile long by half a mile square. Their destination was a designated point in space which was to be initially in orbit around the planet Mars. Mars at that time was a 'limited life' supporting planet. The reason for establishing themselves near a limited life planet was to enable them to mine or collect any needed minerals or materials from the planet for use in the space ships with which to build new larger space cities. Mars was the nearest such planet to earth at the time.

Orion's belt was aligned with Mars and the earth with reference to the then position of the North Pole which was situated at that time in what is known today as the Bermuda Triangle. The site known as El Giza was selected as a permanent reference point because of its predicted constant in terms of its position relevant to the old equator and to the predicted new equator at the expected time of regeneration of the space ship people. El Giza is thirty degrees north of the present equator and was also thirty degrees north of the old equator. There are a number of other sites such as one in South America at a point, which was then thirty degrees north of the old equator and is now thirty degrees south of the new equator. The old equator ran from South West in our present perspective to North East through what is now known as Zimbabwe. So El Giza was proposed as a future observation site. Note was taken of the long term oscillating 'after effect' resulting from the later expected close bypass of Venus which set up a sudden and then slow but continual drift of the poles. This would lead to El Giza's longitudinal relationship with the old and new north poles tallying at what was named the 'End Time'. The position of thirty plus degrees was selected for the following reason. If you stand at the North Pole for twenty-four hours you will make one very slow full turn caused by the rotation of the earth. If you stand at the equator for the same period of time you will move at a very fast pace of at least twenty four thousand miles an hour till you come back to your original relative position. The varying speed of the movement of the earth around the poles creates friction between differing sub strata creating what are now known as Ley lines. The most exaggerated Ley Lines are at the thirty to thirty four degree meridians North and South of the equator. The terrific amount of friction between the earth's crust and its innards is concentrated at these meridians as a result of and thereby caused by the differing rotation speeds of the earth at different points.

This energy has enormous effect on both the material structures and the organic organisms in these areas. Proof of this perspective can be seen in that the major world catastrophes such as earthquakes, tsunamis, plate shifts and serious cultural conflicts between humans take place or originate along the thirty to thirty fourth lines of latitude. Naturally there are numerous smaller frictional lines existing north and south mostly parallel to the equator but not as powerful as the thirty to thirty five meridians. The energy generated at many other Ley Lines around the world can and often is felt and used by sensitive humans!

Cults and various orders also take energy from these lines. Certain secret organisations use the energy to manipulate people for their own ends.

Understanding all this would enable the scientists remaining on earth at those times to calculate the position of the mother ships in space relative to the earth, both then and in the future, that is, after the change! Information regarding all matters pertaining to present and future records of human activity in respect of their proposed space trip and hoped for return was passed on to the leaders of the potential survivors left on earth. Details such as Astro maps were urgently drawn up for any earth survivors to study and to use to observe the heavens for signs of 'if and when' the space travellers would return - such return being dependent on the earth itself returning to some degree of normality which although predicted as being possible was in terms of generations to be only temporary! The huge change in atmosphere, water distribution and latent energies would bring about completely new and very different environments on earth. The forests of giant trees and most of the mammals would become extinct. Human types would have to change to fit, in other words human beings would evolve into new and very different genetic perspectives.

The new star maps that were designed and laid out at El Giza and other sites allowed for the expected change in polar points and the shifting of the equator. The maps and information attached showed that on its second return into our universe Venus would draw both Mars and earth into a new orbit and destabilise both planets a second time causing floods and ice age conditions on both planets.

Venus, earth and Mars would then be drawn into a new, stable, orbit around the sun. The three planets would settle into new conjunctions with Venus and earth adopting similar individual revolutions although different to all other bodies in our solar system.

Venus would become more life friendly. Mars would degenerate. The time space involved in the degeneration of Mars would be permanently recorded in similar pyramid type structures on mars. The space cities would then have to move to the Arcturus system.

The Astro maps and information also detailed the anticipated return to our planet, if any, of the space ships and the possible date. This was estimated to be in the generation of the collapse of coherent thought in man and would be subject to the de-stabilising of the earth before the age of heat. Heat rather than cold being the main feature of the end time.

Cognisance was taken of the variables resulting from the predicted catastrophe on earth and the positional changes of Mars and Venus. These would affect both the life style of the occupants of the space cities and the three planets with respect to and regarding space travel at that distance and time. The long term effect on both the approaching planet and the earth regarding such matters as distance from the sun - hours per revolution - cycles - revolution direction in relation to direction of each planet's specific movement around the sun - to time periods in years - conjunctions - and most important, to the inhabitants of the earth and the people locked in space.

The consequential changes in the earth's atmosphere and its geological formations such as continental development, new, old or lost, would direct either the time and manner of operation of resettlement, if any, or the removal of acceptable humans living on earth from time to time to newly stabilized but previously uninhabited planets in the Arcturus system.

The planet Venus passed by the earth as predicted. One of its smaller moons and a number of the asteroids crashed into the earth causing major tidal waves and earthquakes. Some of the molten asteroids were large enough and approached at such an angle as to create new landmasses and islands! Others disintegrated and spread out on contact with the earth creating small craters. One example of new land masses is the island known today as Ireland and another, the section of land connecting North and South America.

The continents remained relatively unchanged but the sea levels rose and flooded such areas as the Mediterranean when the water breached and eroded what is now known as the Gibraltar Straits.

Man survived in very small groups in isolated parts on the side of the earth opposite the major asteroid strikes and in the tunnel sanctuaries in South America. The main force of the strike of the asteroids and the one small moon was in the area now known as the Bermuda Triangle and a large adjoining section of North and Central America. A second strike of asteroids was to the west and south of Ireland. These strikes hammered the earth so hard and at such an angle, as to spin it off its axis. The north-pole was displaced from its old position of approximately thirty degrees north and sixty degrees west through an arc of approximately forty five degrees to its present position. Although the shock of the striking asteroids and the effect of the gravitational attractions of earth and Venus were enormous, the actual movement and slip of the changing axis was slow and other than shock waves and tidal waves there was no collapsing of major structures and so life on the other side of the world tended to survive although it had to mutate to fit the drastically changed new climates.

The new continent of Atlantis was 'squeezed' up out of the ocean. Its life as a continent was limited by the unstable nature of its foundations and it subsided some one and a half million years later when another shower of space debris hit Carolina and the adjoining sea area in North America.

Wildlife in the safer areas on the other side of the world survived and together with the few human survivors adapted and spread out over the earth as time healed the devastated north eastern areas.

But the wildlife and people of the giant forest areas on the old equator and in the now more North Western areas were completely lost. The flood and the humid dust in the air led to a serious drop in temperature freezing over huge areas overnight especially in North Eastern Siberia and adjacent lands. Walls of giant waves caused by the second passing of Venus dramatically changed landscapes.

The climatic changes were for the most part affected as a result firstly of the forming of the new lines of longitude and latitude where in the old times the Antarctic was originally a land of open skies, deserts and greenery, it became a frozen waste.

Secondly the changed oxygen levels and the heavy atmosphere resulting from the excessive dust and moisture from the new volcanoes and boiling seas in the areas of the striking asteroids in and near North America combined to cause new climatic conditions all around the world.

Tidal waves deposited the dead and debris along the western coasts of Europe, Africa and the eastern coasts of the Americas.

Re-colonisation by man and wildlife of the devastated areas of North America and north Eastern Europe took many generations of world life. In human terms half a million years after the second passing.

The land and new peoples of Atlantis developed the first new, though short lived, materialistic and highly sophisticated inventive civilisation.

Unfortunately, the genetically inherent concept of integrity was slowly eroded and the "sins of the world" grew with ferocious intensity. Man became evil and devious without even knowing or caring that this was happening to him.

New religious orders were formed in remembrance of the old world but although memories and records of the past were kept and handed down by the so called learned men, distortion of the truth led eventually to total misunderstanding.

New powerful civilisations developed in far reaches of the world where discipline and morality were considered essential to control human behaviour. They floundered and died when virtue and integrity were replaced with need, greed, corruption, filth and degradation brought about by the demand of the so called elite of the time, be they the aristocrats or the labourers, to take over and enjoy the benefits of power at the cost of and eventual destruction of the productive.

These new ideologies led to the concept of superior groups, sects, castes, political exclusions, unjustified human rights and race superiority. They maintained their positions with cruelty, torture, rape, self-righteousness, sacrifices, lies, wars and religion.

Those men who fought for decency were ostracised or even put to death. The picture of slavery, gladiators, lions killing men in arenas, gang rapes, sodomy, lesbianism, dirty jokes, drunkenness - all became the 'in thing' for each failing civilisation.

When the first reconnaissance space vehicles reached earth from the main space ship the scene that met their eyes was alarming.

On one hand it seemed man had lost his old genetic codes controlling and dictating his physical and mental perspectives and his innate sense of decency! He had lost the ability to determine of his own account the difference between right and wrong or good and evil - on the other hand man had maintained to a large degree his knowledge of the sciences and had developed reasonably well in physical matters.

The result was that the information left on earth (by the people who left in the space ships) for the edification of the survivors of the first major world catastrophe had been misinterpreted and a number of vicious religions were built up on the distortions of the truth. The 'Lie' was a powerful means of maintaining supremacy and power over people. A political balance of human rights and human behaviour was concocted, taught and implemented. It was designed to further undermine ordinary man's initiative, his decency and his essential "I Am!"

Religious based politics claimed supremacy by birth-right or by colour or by creed. This supremacy being in all cases false had to be bolstered by cruel management, by terror tactics and the philosophy of expediency.

Somewhere in the back of people's minds struggled the last glimmer of integrity which hung on to threads of inherent memories of virtue, honour, peace, morality, love and glory.

So they sacrificed virtuous virgins to an imagined God! They made it honourable for young men to die for a temporally ruling regime!

They raised armies to enforce the peace!

They glorified in their own false imaginations.

They rewrote the laws of nature and expected their new laws to overrule nature.

They lied to stay in power!

They misunderstood the meanings of the knowledge of the stars given them by their ancestors and created myths of resurrection and false deities in place of natural regeneration through cloning and controlled mutation.

They worshipped the sun and the stars.

They built more huge pyramids on Earth and Mars using the knowledge left to them, but having no real understanding of the original concepts, they distorted the true purpose. As a result of their misunderstanding of the meaning and purpose of regeneration and cloning for the purpose of bringing long since dead creatures back to life they had their own bodies mummified for later reincarnation.

The first civilisation rose and fell. The second rose and fell.

All civilisations since then and up till now rise and fall for the same reasons.

They rise on integrity and discipline and fall on moral degeneration.

They never learn.

Well! So far I have told you a very sad story but there is light at the end of the tunnel. Literally!

Hope for the world of man arises firstly from the problems facing the space ship people and that is the artificial atmosphere and restricted physical living conditions on the space ships irrevocably led to permanent physical changes in the people, what might be called evolutionary development. This can easily be seen as pictures we have of them show they have large heads, large eyes and ears but very small bodies and limbs. Also, as a result of the restricted living space in the space cities and a new understanding of how to 'live for ever' they, in order to maintain virtue and control population explosion, de-sexed all the members of the space cities. No marriage! No children!

The problem of physical degeneration became so serious that those who relocated to a huge man made space world behind the then stable planet of Venus were hard put to manage despite vigorous fitness programmes. Even those who went on to the habitable worlds being developed in the Arcturus system ran into trouble surviving although a very small minority managed to slowly improve their physical selves. Attempts at genetic engineering resulted in a backlash inhibiting both the immune system and the inherent mental ability which allows for spiritual inspiration which in turn brings about a state of natural morality where the right thing to do is done because you want to do it in your very inmost being and not because you believed in it or were legally obliged to do so, or, because you did it in fear of punishment if you failed.

So it is that the problem on Venus and in the space ship cities was and still is opposite to the problem we have here on earth.

Two task forces were set up to search for an answer, one on earth and the other on Venus.

Their objective – how to bring together the two opposing aspects of morality and physicality as relatively experienced by the people in space and the people in the world without endangering either aspect and always remembering that the ultimate purpose is to recreate a perfect physical, mental, moral, asexual and spiritual human to colonise the seven new liveable planets in the Arcturus system.

The problem of personality came first. As you probably know everything, be it mobile or immobile, has a personality! The physical state of any being enhances or limits the ability of the personality to perform as can be seen in a Scientist or a Politician, a Preacher or a Thief, a Tree or a House, a Flower or a Stone, a Sunset or the Darkest Night. All have a personality. It is the spiritual and physical balance of the joint being that allows and illuminates the personality aspect.

What an individual values is to a great degree dependent on his basic personality in terms of his functional ability to value himself. His self-worth or self-value in turn determines his ability to value anything and everything he finds himself either part of or finds around him.

Simply put, self-worth determines self-perspective and the persons place in creation and then creation itself. The majority of people in to-days world are quite unable to place true values on abstracts such as love, friendship, integrity, honour, loyalty, the other man or woman, righteousness and so on.

In a sense they cannot be blamed for their perspectives therefore they cannot be blamed for their fears, hatreds or lack of understanding.

Any way I am digressing - let me tell you how the task force went about achieving their objective here on earth.

Remember, the objective was to bring physical man back into a morally spiritual state without destroying his self until his personality or 'I am' could be 'Whole'. Then the worldly self must be 'allowed' to die and the new association of flesh and spirit to become perfectly one.

So, by way of illustration, I will call it, the Pigs Parable.

As I tell you this story please remember that it is a parable and as such should not be taken as the truth, the whole truth and nothing but the truth! Yes, the story does run parallel to certain perspectives of the Bible and to certain scientific facts but it is not intended to argue any point or change any truth, rather it is, as I said, a parable designed to illustrate or demonstrate certain perspectives.

Before I start the story may I say that it is worth nothing in relation to how truths are often manipulated, that there have been many occasions where meetings held by various Christian Religious organisations both within and between different denominations and also Christians meeting with politicians and other Religions where they have debated their varying understandings of the Christian Bible resulting in changes in the wording or the belief or perspectives of the biblical writings! One example is the case where the birthday of Christ was changed to fit in with the Sun Worshipper's beliefs and thus agreed to be celebrated on twenty fifth of December - that is the middle of winter in the Northern hemisphere when the sun starts its return from the south to north! In fact His birth was in the summer when shepherds sat out at night with their sheep in the country side! Another example is when they changed the Sabbath from Saturday to Sunday, again to suit the Sun Worshipper's day! A third is when they adopted the fertility celebrations practised by so called pagans over the Easter period to celebrate the death and resurrection of Christ. These changes were made to bring to an end the conflict existing within the Roman Empire at those times between Christians and non-Christians. Also worth noting are the many changes made in the text or wording of the bible as a result of the varying and different interpretations of ancient languages and understandings. Contradictory perspectives have arisen between differing Christian religious groups usually as a result of them genuinely looking for the truth but also sometimes due to ulterior motives or hidden agendas! So please listen to the story I call the 'Pigs Parable' without seeing it as an attempt by me to be contentious!

GOD is the truth! Not the bible!"

XXXXXXX

THE PIG'S PARABLE

"Scientists from the main Venus Space City established a base in a grounded space ship a few hundred miles south west of the present site of El Giza. The force was directed to initiate projects which would lead to the development of an environmentally acceptable humanoid for transfer to an Arcturus system planet. Acceptable in the physical form who would have a natural and permanent moral nature!

In other words a viable, physically modified earthman of integrity! This was deemed necessary as the earth is predicted to burn up at its so-called end time resulting in all life here being exterminated.

The task force based here on earth is recorded as having discussed the problem as follows.

The leader opened the first discussions. He spoke clearly,

"We cannot simply, genetically engineer, a mental change in earth man to create the free and unfettered development of what we call 'the moral perspective' and you may well ask why?

Despite the tremendous knowledge and information available to us in the field of genetics especially in the intelligence and morality fields, we remain with one insurmountable problem.

In our task to bring about the ability to understand and apply the difference between good and evil as a basis for underlying the concept of morality and integrity, we may not force such a concept of morality on man. Simply put, we cannot make a man to be moral because the use of force contradicts the very aspect of the morality which we seek to instil.

At this time man of the earth has a severely muddled physicality and morality!

Also, if we simply teach or enforce morality this learning and discipline can produce reasonable results under controlled conditions but when the controls are removed or lapse, man will tend to revert to his old way of thinking.

The problem is based in the fact that man is both physical and spiritual and, as you know, the two cannot mix unless we use a catalyst. Here, once again, the catalyst must be a 'free agent' or the concept of morality is destroyed.

The inherent or genetic memory and genetic physical inheritance of man on earth resulting from the huge changes wrought by the encounter with Mars prevents us from finding someone who has no 'sin' in him.

With sin in him, the aspect of freedom demands we must allow the sin to find expression. Right!" He looked around the gathering, "Well then this may lead to individuals learning from their own mistakes and the mistakes of others, but alas, as I said before, there is not one man on earth who has no sin in him because the sins of a man's fathers to four generations are in all men at birth.

Man is born in sin!

Although man inherits the mind of his mother he also inherits the attitudes of his father. We cannot change this by genetic engineering because with the change other genetic options will result creating undesirable wild cards."

"Okay" asked someone with huge eyes "If you can't use any man here on earth, what on earth are we doing here?"

"We have to find a physically perfect man with no inherent memory."

"You just said there isn't one!"

"We will make one!"

"How?" Asked a third man with thin legs and arms which were even shorter than the others. His large eyes gleamed with the question. "You said we cannot manipulate him into being what we want! So?"

"Any ideas?" Asked the leader.

"Yes. Take a suitable animal, genetically engineer and mutate it to the physical perspective of a man using the laws and understanding of evolution. The animal will have no human memory bank. It has no morality as it is not spiritual in the same sense as man. It has a limited understanding of the difference between right and wrong. It is reactive and not proactive. It has no sins of the fathers in it in the same way as man has!

Introduce the element of free choice into the new man and fill that free choice with the perspective of morality. You will then have a perfect man both physically and spiritually without any red herring mental distractions to lead him down the path of immorality."

"How do we put a free man's mind into a dumb animal which looks like a man but is not?"

"One way is we graft into the enlarged brain of the new 'animal man' sufficient material from a selected Venus man and bingo, we have a free thinker with an empty mind filled with the concept of morality."

"The problem with your idea is that you cannot guarantee the graft implant will not change into the genetic code of the brain you grafted it into. This is what happens in bone marrow or bone grafts from say calves to humans. The grafted calf bone is gradually overcome and the genetic code of the human takes over. The chance of the grafted calf genes being able to overcome the human bone gene is minuscule."

"Yes it is a chance in a million but it can happen and that sets us free from predestining the man into our version of morality and that is what guarantees perfect freedom which in turn allows for perfect morality to develop."

"Okay, it may be a possibility!"

"Do we have any other choices?"

"Yes. As you say we can genetically engineer a man from a suitable animal and spiritually 'fill' him without programming his mind. Leave him free of any concept and then set him up so as to lead him into a learning curve so developing his own moral attitude based on his learnt understanding of right and wrong. What do you say to that?"

"Both options can work, but as you say, the chances of success are very small - especially when grafting is done in the brain in terms of establishing what may be described as a new thought pattern. There will be many failures and maybe only one success. What will we do with the unsuccessful ones? I suggest that to maintain the essence of freedom and to allow for a balance we will have to let all the resulting 'man creatures' live in amongst and join the existing earth men. The successful ones we will figuratively set aside and protect as we breed from them and help them develop. Then we will remove them either before or after death to the new Arcturian planets which we are now preparing for occupation. Remember that the new Arcturian planets will be in such an environmental and physical state as to be eminently suitable for beings from earth to live on but very difficult for beings from the space cities to migrate to and live on."

"Yes, maybe you are right! We should do both."

"Do you agree that we will have to leave any and all failures to act as a balance so guaranteeing freedom of choice! I mean freedom to choose in the perspective of the real and the abstract."

"You say that when we do achieve success it could be limited to maybe only one new man! To establish others, we may end up having to clone them from him!"

"Exactly! But hopefully we will find a suitable mate from all the other attempts to create an acceptable woman and breed from them! In the event we don't we may be able to clone a number of women from him and select the most suitable one to be brought to the man - one who has the mind we are looking for! That is, she must have the mental and intelligence ability that we need! She must have the faculty of intuition and that is going to be hard to initiate. Probably find only one out of thousands will have it. Meanwhile we could consider the possibility of recreating the ability to breed in selected members of our own community in order to cross breed with selected females from the recreated group on earth and so increase the chance of finding a mate for the first man.

But a problem could and would arise where hybrid vigour distorts the outcome and totally unacceptable offspring could result."

"Ok, so the new man will have no attitude problems to start off with. He will have the ability to think but not the need to think, nor the inclination. He will be like a robot.

The selected cloned woman will feel her way into thinking as she is led by intuition and she will develop the ability to think of more than one subject at a time.

The man, when awakened by the woman into the ability to think, will, as a result, generally only be able to think of one thing at a time.

The woman, because of her nature, will be the first to recognise the difference between right and wrong and will lead the man into testing and understanding. Remember our objective is to bring them into the state of being moral by their nature and not by outside discipline or direction although discipline will help in stabilising their new moral nature. In the final analysis it is important that they must want 'in their hearts' to be moral and be able to recognise the difference at all times."

"So what are we going to use to build up or create the physical man?"

"The pig!"

"What! You don't really mean that?"

"Yes I do! We have studied all the animals available and the pig has almost exactly the same internal organs, skin, bone and flesh type as we do. Their organs and skin are such as can be implanted to replace defective organs in humans. We only have to change its features such as feet and hands and fingers and toes and make it walk upright and so on. You have never been told, but it is known to the leaders and is on record that in the very beginning it was from the pig families that all men and primates originated anyway!"

"We never knew that! Why weren't we told?"

"The leaders were afraid it might lead to degenerative thinking!"

"What else has been hidden from us?"

"Everything you do not need to know at this time!"

"So what place does freedom have in our lives?"

"I leave you free to find that out for yourselves!" They all laughed, "Anyway," he continued, "back to our project! I suggest that those of us who are inclined to genetic manipulation and to manipulative manipulation take over the problem of selecting pigs from all over the world and that you choose where to set up bases for each project. The rest of us can prepare quarantine areas and the necessary facilities for any successful generates from and on each of the seven continents. I shall concentrate on creating the final quarantine area, a sort of Garden of Eden free from worldly influences right here next to this space ship where the final stages of generation by genetic engineering and cloning on selected material may be carried out on the most suitable mutant evolved from out of all the continents."

"This is really exciting!"

"And a lot of meticulous hard work"

xxxxxxx

Seven differing pig types, one from each of the seven continents were selected and a number of isolated mutation engineering stations set up on each continent avoiding areas that had been re-populated with degenerate human beings.

Each station was built on suitable Ley Lines on the western slopes of the highest mountains. Care was taken to distance themselves from the old Orion observatory sites which had been degraded by misunderstanding and immorality into weird religious monuments and sanctuaries.

The projects started.

The pigs being bred in each station were subjected to genetic manipulation and controlled mutation. The young pigs so born were graded into genetic classes and subjected again to the same treatments as their parents.

Selected embryos were likewise genetically engineered and implanted.

As a result pigs were born with longer legs and arms and with their hooves changed in stages into hands and feet. Their brains were enlarged. Long ago reduced or retracted tendons, bone structures and remains of muscles were regenerated. The cartilaginous noses and the head features were reconstituted into acceptable human like faces.

At each station on each of the seven continents a very large variety of mutants resulted. The variation which resulted from allowing freedom in certain spheres to be the control factor led to a range of man-like creatures which were classified and kept alive in order to protect the "free choice" principle.

The new primate types were named, monkey, ape, gorilla, pygmy, primitive man, and so on.

The new humanoid types were named according to both the continent and the deviation they grew from.

The search among the new human equivalents suitable for implants of brain material or line breeding began. The continental groups were subdivided again and again until the common factor of brain constitution was found in sufficient numbers to begin both the sectional brain implant stage and the 'free thinking' stage.

'Free thinking' brain cells with the required genetic codes were implanted in the selected man types on each continent.

The sought after variable, where the implant material was not overridden by the brain it was implanted into but rather the implant over-rode the genetic factors of the recipient brain so causing the brain to develop along the genetic code of the implant, took many years and many failures.

Finally success! One 'man like' pig from the mountains in southern Europe lost his pig nature to the implant material. But most important, the new man had no memory either inherited from the donor or from himself. He was the first free man having the ability to think constructively and without outside interference, able to be naturally and inherently honest and moral.

An urgent search was made among the hundreds of female 'man like' derivatives from pigs for a mate. Unfortunately not one 'free' woman was found to be a match for the first man.

As originally suggested a rib was removed from the successful 'first man' and clones were developed from this rib.

Clones having the problem of losing certain characteristics of the original such as inherent immune systems, blood types and marrow types, led to many failures but eventually one acceptable clone was found.

All the clones had been genetically engineered from concept to be female. Having been cloned from the first male man a few problems could not be completely overcome without infringing on the 'free choice' imperative. As a result the selected woman would bear children in pain and unlike animals she would have the same orgasmic capabilities as man and certain other characteristics related to being a woman made out of a man. But most important, she had the new desired faculty of intuition.

The two new humans were taken to the prepared garden sanctuary for observation and preparation.

To cut a long story short, the day came when the wild card factor of opening up the mind to the difference between good and evil or right and wrong dawned.

The woman was set up by mental telepathy to break the one and only rule in the sanctuary which had been purposefully set up to be backed by discipline and not by morality. She was manipulated into a position where she had to try and see the result of making an intelligent, reasoned choice from within herself without the influence of previous experience either of her own or by teaching or by genetic or inherent memory.

The one law or rule that was laid down in the sanctuary was 'do not think for yourself.' sometimes put as 'Do not choose to know the difference.'

She was delighted with the opening up of her mind and teased the first man into trying to think.

They waited for an opportunity where the controllers were not present and what do you know? It worked!"

The speaker smiled, took a sip of water from a glass and continued,

"A man and a woman, both free from any outside interference were brought into existence where 'morality' was an integral part of them. Morality is not a feature of animals or so called degenerated Earth Man. But it is known and is a part of those who fled the earth before the catastrophe where as a result of their confined physical space in the space cities they advanced spiritually over the millions of years that they lived in an artificial environment where the only way to survive was to be morally right within yourself. There was no room for experimenting in abstract or unreal choices. As a result that which was in them became greater than that which was outside of them.

They were voluntarily people of integrity and self-discipline.

Their old physical selves changed and their internal 'I AM' took over, or as some religions say, they were 'reborn' and so lost the inheritance of the 'sin' of their fathers in them.

Having lost both their worldly selves and most of their worldly physical strength, they no longer needed the law to keep them on the right path. You could say they were a fulfilment of the law.

It was from these 'space men' that the genetically correct implant cells were taken.

The result!

Imagine the first man and first woman on earth ever with the inherent ability and desire to want to know right from wrong so that they could one day make an enlightened and intelligent choice between the two!

Quite something!

Imagine them on the day when the restrictions on their behaviour in the sanctuary were removed.

They were set free.

"Hey said the girl, we're alone!"

"Huh! What do you mean?" Exclaimed the man.

"Alone. The authorities have all left for a meeting in space. We are alone! That means we are experiencing what it means to be free, to be alone! To be yourself! Come on" taking him by the elbow she led him away from their usual resting place. "Let's walk around and see what we can see!"

"Huh! OK, but remember don't think or we are in trouble!"

"Trouble?" She asked "What trouble?"

"Dunno. Something about death, whatever that means."

"Forget that for a while. Enjoy the freedom with me. Let's sit in the shade, it's getting hot. Wait!" she said "Don't just sit down in any old bit of shade. Let's pick a tree and a place under it where the sun won't shine on us until the weather gets cooler towards evening. Then the sun can move into position and warm us up."

"Huh?"

"I mean if we just sit in the shade wherever we find it, we will have to get up again every time the sun moves. Rather let's think about it and work out a place where the sun will only shine on us when we want it to."

"Huh! Clever! OK!"

They selected a spot and lay down to rest. When the weather got cooler the sun peeped around some leaves and warmed them.

"Hey!" said the man, "You were right! It worked."

"Think about it." She said.

"What will happen when the bosses return and find out that we were thinking?"

"You've got a point," she muttered, "Let's cover ourselves with leaves so they see we have changed and we are no longer naked like the animals! Maybe they will be lenient. Think man think! Let's make a plan."

The girl stripped thread out of some weird looking plant.

The man rushed around picking up leaves and then dropping them again. Suddenly he stopped and laughed,

"Hang on." He said, "If I take one big leaf I can carry all these smaller leaves on it and not drop them."

"That's right, now you're thinking!"

And so they took their first steps into imaginative and creative thinking and made skirts to cover their nakedness for they recognised the value of privacy.

The bosses returned with the chief supervisor.

"It worked!" They beamed. "Fantastic. Let's show them how to make more durable clothes out of animal skins and then let them out of the sanctuary. We can take turns to watch over them until they settle after which one of us must remain with them to act as a guardian. We cannot afford to lose all these years of effort now!"

There was great jubilation and celebration in the sanctuary that evening.

The following morning the man and the girl were instructed on how to survive outside the sanctuary. It was explained to them that the purpose of the whole exercise was to enable them, through their own experiences, to learn and understand the difference between good and evil which in turn would lead them into the reality of being set free by the truth. They must also learn to value themselves and the creation they found themselves in and how to enjoy working and develop a purpose in their work and lives. They must learn how to enjoy and support each other without imposing themselves on each other. They would come to understand the meaning and value of peace, of pleasure and being constructive. They would have to develop the ability to be creative and practice the true value of man and woman relationships and of family in the senses of the physical, emotional and individual.

From this they would learn ethical direction and purpose but most important of all, real love.

And so, with the help of attendants called celestials, the first day out of the sanctuary began. The beginning of the future of the new civilised Earth Man rested in the hands of one man and one woman! Their selected descendants would form the bases of a new world order.

Well, that is accepting the fact that at the same time, the other world 'pig derived humans' mixed with existent people and cultures on and in all the continents in the world! Each group not only looked and behaved differently to the next in colour, build, size and intelligence, but they also built up their own perspectives of where they came from, who and what their God is or was and where they are going to when they die. They developed their own religious political and moral perspectives of right and wrong.

There seems to be at least two main purposes behind all this apparent confusion. The first is fairly obvious, it is impossible for any two people or any two nations to be exactly the same or for them to think the same or to react, the same! Having such a huge variation within and between people and groups of people, between incidents and time makes it possible for all of everything pertaining to human life to be experienced within all the variations of natural conditions such as drought, flood, earthquake, animals, war, peace, and so on almost into infinity. At the end, no stone will be left unturned and when at last our eyes are fully opened we will be able to see beyond our own very limited experiences and understandings to the whole of the all of mankind and thereby come to know the whole picture.

The second purpose is to teach us that when a nation creates its own image of its own God and uses that image as a guide on how to live, by that I mean what moral code they must follow and what disciplines they must accept, this will form a culture holding the members together and build them and their nation. When they abandon their God and the principles they developed they and their nation will die.

There are and have been many attempts at defining God and what He is all about. It is the attempt that creates the conditions for growth and it is the abandoning of that attempt which brings about collapse.

Check history.

Not a stone will be left unturned!"

Red and I took a coffee break.

XXXXXXX

"THE STORY OF "WHY NOT?""

I asked,

"And then?"

Red smiled,

"Back to the selected ones known to some of us as Adam and Eve. Everything outside the sanctuary was new to them. They had no preconceived ideas about anything. They knew nothing so they were free to see, hear and understand what was before them as it was and not as they thought it should be. Initially they were placed in a large sheltered area in amongst the mountains, separate from the other original men of the world and the other new 'pig' men!

They had children. The first son was a blessing to them, but he had no imagination, he was incapable of original thought and was given the simple task of herding goats in the mountains.

The second son was highly active and born with both the ability to think constructively and the ability to create. He took over the task of growing crops. He had to imagine how to make a tool to till the ground, how to select seeds and breed up suitable varieties, how to store them as reserves for the off-season. He had to think and come up with original workable ideas. Naturally this led him to believe he was superior to his brother.

The leader of the task force, in terms of his objective, found reason to condemn the superiority attitude of the second son and banished him into the outside world to live with the other humans of the valleys. This annoyed the second son. His nature did not enable him to understand why he, the hardest working one of the pair, was unacceptable. He over reacted and murdered the first son then ran away to live in the real world where he married a woman from the other people.

There was a third son who being acceptable in terms of the objective was allowed to live amongst and within the first family. He was given the most suitable bride available from the other cloned women still in the sanctuary.

From here on the descendants, who were now correctly established in the moral and physical sense were 'line bred' in terms of their father's and their mother's spiritual ability to understand morality and to be moral because in their hearts they wanted to be. These offspring were carefully screened and protected until a sufficient number were born to establish a 'tribe' of totally 'pure' sons and daughters.

Selected members of the family were transported to the space city where the attendants combined the cross culture implant programme with limited and intensely accurate genetic engineering so developing another new family of man, which was resettled on the planets around Arcturus.

Many generations later a number of the offspring in the space cities and in world who were only ninety nine point nine per cent acceptable and had thus failed, were moved into the valleys of the earth where they married local 'world' women. Their children were born with what is known as hybrid vigour resulting from the line breeding in the first man tribe and line breeding in the world tribe. This hybrid vigour grew their children into giants.

Those of the giants who were fertile and had not lost their ability to conceive as happens with mules, inbred and crossbred with each other and other members of the world community until the hybrid vigour dissipated and their descendants regained average world man size and attitude.

Meanwhile the first giants, in their desire to emulate and understand their origins, used the principle of gravity generation to build huge star orientated stone structures at specific points all around the world. These structures were originally intended to keep the memory of the past and an expectation of the future preserved in stone until the end time. Future generations developed distorted religions and tangent faiths around their purpose and built new huge edifices on the old archaeological 'star orientated' sites or mutated the old existent structures to suit new and even more weird religions which they developed with the intent of subduing and manipulating the local people making it easier to rule them.

Although some of the original world civilisations developed advanced scientific projects, they, being subject to the problem of not having the 'morality perspective' naturally in them, developed and put in force a strict disciplinary code to keep the members of those civilisations under control. The code had a serious flaw which led to immorality in specific dimensions and a false need to rule by force using punishment to bring so called law-breakers under control.

Back on the protected mountain the tribe grew into a nation which spread into and amongst the other surrounding world communities. The original purity of the selected people dissipated whenever marriage took place between one of them and the descendants of the valleys. Suitable children selected from such families, having inherited the required basic genetic values through their 'Adam' connection were regenerated into an acceptable moral standard by undergoing what is now called rebirth thereby losing all their attached worldly encumbrances and perspectives.

Once again degeneration within the selected group began to take place as a result of them trying to come to terms with living with and associating with the valley people. Eventually the whole selected tribe, excepting one family made up of a father, his wife and three sons and their wives, sank into the mindlessness of the world around them. Fortunately at this time, Venus was on its way for the second and last bypass. It would create great floods and minor earth upheavals, which promised to drown most but not all of the earths inhabited areas.

The task force leader brought the matter to the notice of the one family and advised them that as their area was to be flooded they should build a suitable floating craft, similar to a space city except that it was earth bound, to house their family and a list of selected animals.

The floods came.

Their world, except for isolated tops of the highest mountains, disappeared beneath the floods.

The problem of carnivore's needing meat both on the floating ark and after moving back to the ground was resolved.

The craft and its family of humans and animals survived.

For the third time the experiment in the world was reduced to one man and his family from which two groups of new 'one nation' people grew up in the Middle East. The first son of the family led the first tribe. He was of pure stock and became the new 'first family' in the new world. The other two sons, of their own accord, rejected their ability to be inherently moral and their descendants developed into the second family or tribe, which spread out over the world joining other survivors in remote places.

The first son's descendant nation grew but the majority of them developed a new sun based religion enforcing discipline by the principles of sacrifice, elitism, honorary death, jail, confinement, sexual degradation and "self" supremacy.

The leaders of the first tribe tried to remould their people into their own perspective of unity. They built an enormous structure reaching out to the star they knew they were linked to without knowing or wanting to understand how or why.

They demanded everyone was equal. They forced all members to speak one language.

It did not work. No one is, nor ever has been, equal in all things to anyone else!

To prevent the total eclipse of the few surviving pure 'first man' people among the new nation, the task leader set the cat among the pigeons. He created division on the meaning of words and a breakdown in communication. Quite literally the language of the nation died.

The groups split up into many small and arrogantly self-righteous antagonistic factions.

Out of this fiasco, once again, one man was found, descended from 'pure parents' who was acceptable. He was led to take his family out of the heart of the most industrious and prosperous of the new small tribes to start a new people.

This principle of re-starting a new family with one acceptable man on the basis of his integrity and encouraging that new family to grow into a tribe and then a nation was enacted time and time again.

But! Always, and every time, the new nation which was built up on morality and industry and recognition of the individual always died as immorality, indolence and the destruction of the perspective of individuality grew to be the new moral code.

In the Bible we see it in Adam, Noah, Babylon, Abraham, Isaac, the Romans, the Greeks, the Persians, the Christians and now it is happening in all the major nations on earth such as the British, the Americans, Eastern and Western Europe, Africa and the islands.

The only maybe in this respect is the new China but the perspective of individualism has as yet not been sufficiently developed there!

Again it was so in every case that the one man selected to start the new nation was a man of integrity and understanding having within him a natural desire to be moral and a code of behaviour such as the Ten Commandments or the American Constitution or the Bill of Rights or the Magna Carter was put in place to control the people who did not understand. Those who were inherently able to understand the concepts of morality, industry, fair play and individuality were always eventually ostracised by the mindless ones who by force of numbers distorted the code of behaviour.

In many cases selected men were transferred by the mentors from earth to the space city and from there, into whatever realm they fitted.

The recurring problem of having to time and again rebuild from one surviving man and his nearest kith and kin after each and every world calamity was acceptable while there was still time for recovery from each worldly disaster. It also allowed a spread of what is known as the God gene through all nations. But when the time came for the last generation of man (in that the next disaster would eradicate all life and all life support in the world) which is due to happen when the world burns up at the so called End Time as happened with the planet Mars, then a new strategy had to be evolved to generate acceptable humanoids in sufficient numbers for the final colonising of the new planets in the Arcturus system.

The taskforce met as it did in the days of Job and decided to initiate a change in their modus operandum. They agreed it was time to abandon the old procedure and reconstruct a new one. After referring to their original objectives and ensuring the new planned programme would meet and justify the intended desired end result they selected one man ahead of his time and programmed his conception and the date of his birth. They drew him out of his family, out of his nationality and out of his religion into isolation from his own and all worldly perspectives including marriage and fatherhood. They led him to understand, accept and apply the principle of regeneration through death of the incompatible old and rebirth of the new and complete. The first man to fulfil this perspective was given the multisided name, 'Melchizedek'.

It was further agreed that despite the continuous degeneration of mankind over the past millennia there were at the time of these 'to be selected and regenerated men' (and would be into the next several thousand years!) sufficient almost pure people available to be led by men such as Melchizedek into dying to the old in order to be born again into the new as acceptable human beings, thereby bringing the whole project to completion before the end time.

The task force reiterated that this would bring to and end the recurring problems resulting from whole families and nations dying off so creating the need to restart the process all over again and again with one new man or family. Selected genetically acceptable, but not totally pure, sons and daughters who despite having been born from the worldly tribes were able to mature and accept the principle of being a fulfilment of the law and therefore not subject to it and could thus be led into willingly accepting the principle of being reborn into the perspective of,

'I AM THE WAY THE TRUTH AND THE LIFE!'

With further reference to these 'one man' men whom we could call the initiators, they were as planned, trained and purified and set free from the world. The last man to be so generated was put through trial and temptation, crucified and resurrected so establishing the new order were members of what you might call his extended family throughout the world could and would learn to accept and thus die to their old ways to be reborn as He was. His return as the final leader is due in terms of the whole procedure - any time now!

As you know there is a saying, 'As you think and act, so shall it be!' For that reason the world today is in its final spiral of decay initiated and drawn by the immoral behaviour of the vast majority of mankind into total destruction. From the beginning of time there has never been such widespread degeneration of morals as is evident right now. Every nation and country is falling. The time of the burning up is very near. The sad part is that those who practice cruelty, rape, fraud, lies, immorality, theft, and so on are not capable of controlling themselves. They cannot see that they are wrong. To make them behave in a right and proper manner they would have to be brought under strict disciplinary control with harsh penalties for misbehaviour. If not, the whole world system will crumble because of their perspective. It bears repeating - this type of discipline has been abandoned and a new order is in place where the filth of the world is made acceptable by law and the good and the decency of man is taught to be 'anti' human rights!

The world could be saved if the principles of individuality, integrity and morality were to be re-introduced and re-enforced so that the mind set of decency could rejuvenate and re-orientate the nature of the world but unfortunately it is not only highly unlikely that such will happen but most surely, it will not!

With the new mindless systems of unfettered democracy where the bottom selects the top and the new elected but unqualified top buys support from the bottom with promises and free gifts stolen from the productive, it is easy to see just where it is all going. The more dependent the masses get the weaker they become and the less chance there is of viable opposition to the governing body. The less powerful the individual is the less chance he has to effectively stand for what is right. The more you steal from the entrepreneur the more you erode his desire to create and the less of his product you will have for trade and redistribution to the poor.

Democracy or Communism or Socialism or Altruism, call it what you will, amounts to the rights of the incompetent becoming greater than the rights of the competent. The incompetent blame the rich and demand their demise forgetting that it is the rich who provide the wealth that holds the whole process together. This wealth will disappear as the rich are taken out of the system and the bottom will end up rotting in mindless poverty.

So it is and will be as predicted and the end result is obvious.

Total anarchy!"

Red closed his eyes.

"Okay," he said, "I listened to all that this strange man called Regnarts had to say, but I had some questions of my own. So I asked him about religion,

'The man called Jesus who is said to be the Son of the living God, is it Him who you are talking about as in the end times? Is He one of those whom you called "initiator"?

More important, in your story and from your perspective, who and what is God?"

Regnarts answered,

"The most important aspect of Jesus is that He is a man and as with all men He is subject to sin except that in His case He does not sin!

He has direct communication with His I Am and His purpose!

He has no sins of his forefathers in Him!

You understand?"

"Yes!"

"He had no curtain drawn over any part of His mind so He could and did see the whole picture!"

"Yes!"

"He did not submit his morality to any religion or law or world order be it that of Moses or the Jews or the Romans nor did He submit to force or manipulation or pain or prejudice or education or circumstance or whatever. He was and He Is 'That Who He Is!'

He did not compromise!

Although He was the same as were many others before Him in that He was one man selected before the dispersal of his nation He had this exception, He was not born into it!"

"What do you mean?"

"There are three ways in which a man can become pure.

First you can be born pure from the selected family.

Second. Being reborn pure.

Third, you can be adopted by God and made pure as in the case of Jesus.

All of these people are no longer subject to the law but are a fulfilment of the law. It is the moral or spiritual nature of Jesus that is the reason for His behaviour and not the result of his behaviour."

"Yes I get it, but wasn't Jesus born of Mary and Joseph?"

"Good question leading to more questions. If his attitude or nature comes from four generations of fathers, we must ask who were the fore-fathers of Jesus?

The gospel of Matthew says the man who married Mary the mother of Jesus, and as such was the father of Jesus, was called Joseph, a just man who was the son of Jacob - the son of Mattahan, the son of Eleazor descended from Abraham! All of them good and just men!

Oh no! Says Luke! That's not right! The father of Jesus was a completely different Joseph! He was the son of Heli, also a 'just' man but descended from Matthat through to the son of Levi descended from Adam!

Then to add confusion, John's gospel says Jesus was the literal Son of God through the Holy Spirit. What does he mean, an implant or a snap miracle, or?

Finally Paul clouds what is left of the understanding when he writes in his letter to the Hebrews that Jesus 'Became' the Son of God in later life when God said to Him,

"Today! I make you My Son."

Does this imply that Jesus was not God's Son before that day?

At about the same time, when Jesus was desperately praying about the problem of death, God made him a member of the order of Melchizedek who is known as a Priest of the Most High God! But take note of this! Melchizedek had no nationality, no genealogy and no religion! He was a man of peace who was both a priest and a King! What? A priest with no religion! A King not by inheritance or by conquest! Then how?

Anyway it would appear that whatever He was, Jesus was set free of the problem of the sins of the many people who were supposed to be or could have been his father and by a combination of adoption and membership he was made pure.

By the way, in passing, it may be worth noting that Melchizedek was the head of the order and that Jesus was made a member of that order!

So, whichever way you take the story of Jesus the Christ, He is usually seen to be the Anointed One of God and therefore without sin! This leads us to your question, who and what is God?

Jesus Christ behaved as he did because he did that which he saw the Father do. So, what is meant by, 'The Father'? Is it 'father' as in a real father or just a way to explain something unknown to man? Is 'The Father' an unknown entity simply described as a father? Jesus being 'The Christ' is not as a result of him belonging to any church, tribe, race, religion or political system. In fact he was rejected and crucified by the local Jewish and Roman religions and political systems. Even his followers abandoned him.

This set him free from the world."

Regnarts paused, Red said,

"It sounds even more complicated than I expected! You say that Jesus belonged to the 'Order of Melchizedek,' which is made up of people who are naturally moral. They are therefore at peace, full of understanding and forgiveness and are fully "I AM.""

"Yes! And I repeat, just as Melchizedek had no nationality or religion so was it with the Christ. It is worth considering the fact that there are reports and records from places like India, America and even England to the effect that Jesus Christ visited there. It might be a good idea to not limit Christ in any way! Nor God for that matter! And never limit people because of their differing nationalities or religions. Maybe it is that anyone anywhere and from any religious or non-religious understanding can be drawn to the Christ no matter what his perspective is if it be that 'The Father' decides he should be drawn!"

"If that is so then it explains why there is such a huge variation in understanding between the thousands of differing Christian churches but it also sets free the people in or part of all other religions and those who are not part of any religion!"

"Yes! And therein lies the answer to the apparent problem of 'What about the people who have never heard of Christ?' Have you ever thought of the answer to the question of what about the people before Christ, those who never heard of him in terms of the Christian understanding, or the people since Christ who have also never heard of him? Suddenly the reason why Christ came so late can be understood! It is to bring the overall plan to fruition in time!"

"Well that raises my main question again, who or what is God?"

"You are certainly persistent! Ok let me explain how I see it. I think the easiest way to describe God is probably that man sees God to be both everything that man does not understand combined with being all that man does understand. Let us assume that a tribe living in limited surroundings resulting in limited understanding comes to believe that the mountain in the centre of their island which erupts with giant force and power is the source of all their land, their water and climate and even themselves. They come to believe that God lives in the mountain and they develop a religion to support that belief. Similarly in a large section of a continent where the people are not limited to an island they might see the sun as bringing them energy, changing the seasons, defining night and day and as a result they come to believe that God is in the sun and they become Sun Worshippers.

Now take a people who know what the mountain and the sun are. They look beyond and see the stars, the universe, infinity and the nature of things but they do not know what causes all of nature to be, so they see God in all and decide that God is the reason for all of creation. They come to worship him as The Creator. Then you get the all sorts!"

"What do you mean?"

"Evolutionists, Spiritualists, New Age Guru's and on and on ad infinitum!"

"So who or what is God to you?"

"Whatever!" He smiles. "What I think is that maybe you should throw away all your conceptions of God, all your understandings and perspectives - they being only a very small part of what God is and wait and see if that which we call God enlightens you as to who He is relative to what He wants you to know. Do not allow self-righteous people be they members of religious orders or atheists or your-self to interfere. Alternatively, if you don't like that idea, you could let God be who you think He is, but remember that the sum total of all of your knowledge and understanding comes nowhere near even a small part of the full understanding of what or who God really is or is not!"

He laughed, "Another perspective is 'Hang on to what you believe making allowances for your limited understanding!' do you remember I once spoke of the advice given by Jesus when he said, 'If you have faith you can say to the mountain, move! And it will move!' Well let's take that a little further, obviously the mountain has to have a personality in order to hear you, to obey you and move! If you relax and learn to listen to that personality you will hear what it has to say! The same applies to God! If you relax and listen to His personality you will hear what He has to say! Listening to the mountain is the starting point. You could say that it is the first stop! In all religions the religious belief is also a 'first step' which when related to what is seen or believed to be God and listened to, will lead one on to hearing, resulting in a fuller understanding of

God. God is said to be both 'in all' and the 'all of all'! Every religion can thus be looked at as a starting point where selected members of that religion who are connected through the ages to Adam can be led by 'listening through their belief to God' which opens them up to being drawn by the Father to the Christ. Remember that Luke writes that Jesus once said 'The Kingdom is in you!' so obviously the King of the Kingdom is also in you!

 Go for it!"

xxxxxxx

"Well!" Red said to me, "That was what he told me and then after that long talk this strange guy just stood up and left!"

XXXXXXX

THE ANSWER TO THE HIDDEN AGENDA

Red made the coffee this time. He brought it steaming and delicious to our table by the river.

"Now my friend," he said, "you are beginning to understand why you have been living your life the way you have! Why your children have lived as they did. Why your 'I AM' which has no beginning and no end has been developing and overriding your 'self' which is of the world and thus severely limited.

It is possible that you and maybe your sons as well, are being led into a Discipleship in the order of Melchizedek. Please note that I said a discipleship and not membership!

If this is so you will be directed to stand for peace regardless of your situation, be it subject to the evil of outright oppression and subjugation or the more subtle evil of being manipulated by the so called, self-styled 'Do Gooders' of this world"

The most important thing you have to know and understand is "Be what and who you are!" And to do this you will obviously first have to come to know what you are! Then recognise the fact that every person on earth is here to fulfil their own part of the overall purpose of creation and that overall purpose is to eventually, clearly and unambiguously, present all of any and every aspect of the so called good and evil for examination and recognition by each and every one of us so that in the end we may all, as a result, jointly and severally, freely, voluntarily and knowingly throw out the evil. In other words, when we come to see the whole picture we will be able to make an, 'enlightened choice!' That will be when our minds are opened to know what it is really all about! Then! And from that! We can come to know who we really are and who other people are, and thus come to understand what the individual task of each one of us in this world is or has been and where it is leading all of us.

A way of explaining this is you cannot decide to remove the rubbish in your yard if there is none! Nor can you move it if you have no idea what part of it is rubbish and what is not, or where to move it to! You can only learn this by experience and as you cannot experience the all of everything that makes up the world and its people, each one of us has to do his own part of the right and the wrong and then we can eventually jointly and severally, by putting everything together and sharing individual understandings, come to see the whole!

Then and only then, can we decide!

Let me repeat it in another way - to be able to throw a rotten apple away you have to see the apple, know of its rottenness and know where to throw it so that it ceases to be a problem! You must also know how to handle the apple without tainting your fingers. Of all of these perspectives, the most important is that if you do not see the evil and recognise it for what it is, you cannot throw it away!

So my friend, someone has to make an apple rotten and show you its rotten-ness. Someone has to make the rubbish and throw it in your yard! Someone has to commit the evil for you to see it as it is. In all cases you have to honour that someone for doing so because you are released by his performance.

Also and equally important! Someone has to show you the good apple for by recognising it you are set free to appreciate it and keep it!

The perspective or personality known as Satan is the prince of the rotten apple to the Glory of God. He, as the highest of God's Angels, was given the hardest task there is, that of running the 'Bad side of the world' so that we can learn from it! He was put in charge of the tree of knowledge of good and evil with the purpose of showing us the evil.

Melchizedek and his order are the Princes of Peace also for a similar purpose, that of coming to know the good.

Everything is made for this purpose and therefore all is to the eventual good when seen in the light of this purpose.

A member or disciple of the order of Melchizedek is one who at a specific place or time or generation is tasked with seeing and knowing the why and what of 'the all' in that which he sees! He knows why the man who commits the evil does so and why the man who commits the good does so! And all this is for the purpose of God in the making of a new world to come where we, all of us, of our own accord through our own and shared experiences can take part in the final judgement so that each one of us having been both good and evil and experienced both through ourselves and other people can expose and prove the difference and can thus knowingly and voluntarily throw out the evil.

Our souls carry the burden of learning to handle the problem inherent in mixing flesh and spirit where the two are incompatible. It is only by experience and involvement that we may be able to arrive at the point where we can say, "I was blind but now I see!"

I said,

"Indeed, I believe you are right, for now do I begin to see!"

"I have a question for you." Said Red "If you accept the concept that we are either descendants or relatives of pigs then you might come to understand why it is that some pigs can be so human! Some religions teach that man should not eat pigs! Some worship them and even raise them as children whilst some refuse to be associated with them in any way!" He paused, looked out over the river. "That is why some men are just plain piggish?"

I laughed,

"I understand what you are saying but I am still not sure it is actually so!"

"Then may I repeat?" Asked Red.

"If you really think you have to!"

"Don't say anything yet, just listen to me. Do not try to make out what it is all about or you will block your mind to hearing."

I sat very quiet and very still!

"Ok so you have heard the story about genetics! Genetic manipulation! Genetic codes! Clones! Mutants! Implants! Hereditary factors!"

I listened. My mind darting in and out of what Red was trying to say.

"Remember, oil in certain areas and not in others. Petrified forests in deserts! Forested mountains and valleys with no oil and only surface evidence of petrified forests. Primates. Prehistoric mammoths. Dinosaurs. Gorillas ninety seven per cent per cent genetically the same as Caucasoid man, that is only three per cent different! But man, in general having a three to four per cent genetic variation within his species. So, for example, there is more genetic variation between men than between Caucasoid man and the gorilla!

And remember, the machined steel mechanical parts found in coal beds millions of years old.

And the missing link!"

A fish eagle called.

"Soar like an eagle" Red said "Ancient civilisations, many religions. The chosen ones! Only a few! The best go forward! Seven nations! Seven continents! Seven deadly sins! Seven virtues! Seven days! Seven heavens! Seven parts of the body!

Three days - three wise men - body soul and spirit – The Trinity?

One God! One Purpose! One all in all!

One flower, one tree, one fruit, one tribe, one nation, one man!

The "Most High God."

The Father is reputed to live in Heaven but Heaven is destined to burn up when the world dies!"

Looking hard at me he said,

"That should be enough for you for now. When you wake up from your dreams tomorrow remember that a very small vision or insight when set free in the mind often opens the door to the most amazing discoveries."

"Thank you Red! May I take a guess at what you are actually trying to tell me?"

"Go for it!"

"I don't know if I ever mentioned the story about the lady from Ireland who said I was too negative?"

"Not that I can remember!"

"She said I must bring myself to realise that everything has a positive and a negative side! I must learn to choose the positive and ignore the negative.

I decided to try it out. I took the dogs for a long walk to the town park. I was exhausted when we got there. I saw a bench at the side of the path and thought, why yes! She was right! Look at the positive side of walking to town! Don't worry about the negative of being tired! There's a bench to sit on and recover. See the positive! Yes and the dogs can lie at my feet!

I walked over to the bench and was about to sit down when I saw that there were three sharp splinters sticking out of the wood.

Again I remembered what the lady had told me, 'see both the positive and the negative. Ignore the negative and go for the positive!' I looked again at the bench. I saw the positive, a place to rest. I saw the negative, splinters in the seat of the bench. Choosing the positive I ignored the negative and sat down.

I had to get a doctor to pull the splinters out of my back side!"

We laughed, I said,

"It seems that since time began people have allowed themselves to come to apparently positive conclusions about creation or about life or God or whatever without bothering to look at the negative or missing aspects of their observations. They then arbitrarily decide that their point of view is right despite the fact that neither they nor for that matter, any one, has ever been able to see the whole picture."

"Come on! You said Jesus could see the whole picture!"

"He could see the whole picture in terms of what was relevant to us and Him at the time. But remember He categorically stated that He did not know and could not see the time when all would be complete! He said that 'Only The Father knows that!'

Anyway, as a result of being limited people throughout the ages have consistently, arrogantly and self-righteously made up their minds that their perspective is right without having the faintest idea about the reality of what they are talking about. If I read the bible from the point of view of a scientist and I look no further, I will be forced to come to the conclusion that God is a celestial! If I listen to a Christian and look no further I will accept that God is the Creator. If I listen to a primitive I will come to believe that God is a Spirit living in a volcano! If you accept my story you will come to believe that men are pigs!"

"So how can one overcome this problem?"

"Simple! Relax and accept everything as it is. Don't put italics around your vision. Be free to see the truth, which is a combination of the positive, the neutral and the negative of everything. Do this and you will develop a better insight into the whole! Then accept that everyone sees differently and it is that difference which makes life so interesting!"

My mind was in turmoil. I slept badly that night.

Dreams.

Nightmares.

Restlessness.

Palpitations.

I was woken by a bright blue light, which flooded my camp. I got up. Outside the countryside was divided into pitch-black darkness surrounding a large area of brilliant blue light. I watched for a while but couldn't make head or tail of it and went back to bed to sleep soundly until I woke a second time.

It was midnight. Remembering the light I got up to have another look! It was gone. A half-moon hung in a bright clear sky above. The round, light side of the moon had a large square patch of black intruding into it. I stared at it.

Confused I went back to bed.

Morning brought the night sounds to an end and the day sounds into being. I got up a third time. I felt very different, young and vibrant!

I realised I was no longer the same. Something had changed. Or had it all been a dream?

Was I feeling the reality of being 'I AM'!

Realising I had spent the last twenty odd years living in the third person as I tried to escape my past, I burst out laughing.

"I am me!" I shouted "Or is it I am that which I AM? Or whatever? From now on it is I that will tell myself, my mind and my body what to think and what to do and not the other way round where my outside self tells my inner I AM what to do! Like right now! 'Body! Go to the kitchen and make tea for Red that old man who is still a stranger to me!' Funny how some of those who you have known all your life are still strangers to you in so many ways while sometimes those whom you never come to know are in many ways not strangers!

Maybe nobody is a total stranger!"

My 'I AM' took two cups of tea out to Red's room.

Red and his bag were no longer there!

"Gone!" I spoke out loud, "Well I suppose it's to be expected! I wonder if that blue light and the shape over the moon had anything to do with it?" I stopped short "Hey!" I shouted, "Of course! For him! That is what it is all about! So very simple! You can come to know someone by what they do, even if they are out of sight, out of hearing, even if you never meet them! So must it be with a perfect stranger! Look at creation and you will see the work. Listen to creation and you will hear the word. Live with creation and you will find the meaning of life. Be as you are created to be, and your 'I AM' will be set free. In your freedom you will see through the whole of creation to 'He' who is a perfect stranger! Him whom we some of us dare to call God and you will come to know the overall purpose! Seeing all in all will lead you to come to know the personality of creation and recognise what that personality is doing and what it has done and what is to come! Oh yes - and don't forget the 'why'?"

xxxxxxx

"At least that is the way I want to go! But of course I must still leave the door open to new insights!"

"Hey!" I thought, "If I study say a flower, or a tree or a stone and I come to see the fullness of that which I study, my first reaction would probably be amazement followed maybe by wonder. Eventually must I come to the most profound respect for the origin or source of that which I study! This respect must surely grow in intensity and perfection as I become conscious of the infinite nature of creation and come to recognise and understand the purpose in it and as a result come to see my own purpose and my place in creation! Another thought, almost like a revelation, look at everything we get from nature, electricity, wireless, tarmac, fuel, radio, plastic, rubber, metals, bricks and mortar and on and on! Why do people not see that and take more care of nature? Even our food and bodies come from nature!"

I stood there outside Red's room with the two cups of tea in my hand,

"I want to go back to being who I was before I changed that night of the sheep in the hail storm. Maybe go back to who I was before the terrorists took me to Zambia. Or better still, go back to 'who' I really am!

A rose by any name is just as sweet!

It makes no difference what my name may be! I am still that which I am!"

The darkness of being separated from Jean, from my children and from my real self, seemed to lift. The camp vibrated with life.

A new calm settled over and in me.

Time to go and find Peter.

XXXXXXX

THE RUINS

I telephoned Fred at his home in Zimbabwe.

The phone rang in a rather broken sort of way.

Someone picked it up.

"Hullo?"

"Hi Fred!"

"Yes! Who's that?"

"Robert!"

"Robert? Really! Where are you?"

"In South Africa! How goes it with you all?"

"Yes well no fine! And what about you Robert? We haven't seen or heard from you for ages!"

"Well you are hearing from me now and you will be seeing me soon!"

"Fantastic! You coming up here?"

"Yes but first a few questions.

What do I need if I want to travel around a bit? Can I hire or borrow a car and if there is a problem with fuel can you help out and last but most important, will you come with me to check out some old ruins?"

"Car, no problem. Fuel? What is that?" He laughed, "Yes, you can buy fuel with American dollars or South African Rands. In fact you can buy anything with Pounds or Dollars or Rands. Sometimes there is trouble in getting the money into the country! And me go with you? What a question!"

"What's the situation regarding security?"

"Absolutely no problem in this part as yet - that is if you stay away from politics and can put up with the bribery and corruption. In fact if you have money this is still a fantastic place to be. Friendly warm-hearted people! When and for how long are you coming?"

"Two more questions and then I can answer that. The first, if I bring in enough pounds can you help me get the things I need and secondly have you got the time next week to spend with me?"

"No problem Robert, just give me an idea of what you want and when you plan to come!"

"Well, firstly, can you get hold of a decent metal detector, one that can read up to twelve feet down and differentiate between different metals."

"I have one that reads down to about three feet! Never heard of one that probes twelve feet but if you give me the specifications I'll look out for one that goes that deep. No problem!"

"And a 'pick up' truck, say a one ton with camping equipment?"

"Again, no problem!"

"Excellent, and picks and shovels? Boxes or cartons and maybe a small motorised digger and a post hole digger, you know what that is?"

"Maybe! Tell me more."

"Some call it an auger?"

"Ok! Still no problem! I've got most of that stuff right here at home. By the way your old Ford truck with the extra fuel tanks and heavy duty springs is still here with me and it is in running order. You can use it, or, you can use my van!"

"Okay then Fred, can you pick me up at the airport Friday evening?"

"Will do, just confirm the time!"

"By the way, I am very grey and old now and I walk with two crutches so if you can bring a wheel chair that would be a great help. Also! Some friends will be coming down by car from Namibia. They're coming through the Plumtree Border Post."

"Hey! Robert my friend! What on earth happened to make you become so old?"

"I'll tell you about it when I get there!"

"Ok! So sorry! Did you ever find Jean and the kids?"

"No not Jean, but I found out where the kids are. They were adopted."

"What ever happened to Jean? You got no idea?"

"Yes well in a way, she couldn't cope with the trauma of my eldest son's loss of memory, she felt guilty about not listening to the beggar - you know the story. Anyway she simply disappeared. No trace of her. Very sad."

"You guys went through hell. But I am looking forward to seeing you again."

"Yes! Me too. See you Friday. I'll confirm the time if your phones are still working."

Fred laughed,

"You're lucky to have got through this time! When the electricity is down, as it is most of the time, we can't charge the phone batteries!"

"Not luck old chap, perseverance! I've been trying for three days! By the way any suggestions on how to bring the money in without it being taken away from me?"

"Not really. You can legally bring in quite a lot if you declare it but sometimes the customs guys try to take it off you by pretending it is illegal especially if you bring in a large amount! You must be aware that the customs guys are alert to just about every conceivable trick! But it's not as difficult as it used to be!"

"Okay old chap, see you soon, bye!"

"Bye Robert."

xxxxxxx

The plane landed at Bulawayo airport.

Some of the lights on the runway and in the terminal were still working! It was raining.

A Matabele man sitting in the seat behind me helped me struggle to the door and down the steps. He held my arms as I awkwardly manipulated my aluminium crutches.

My limp was serious.

On reaching the tarmac I gratefully thanked the man but he just smiled and carried on helping me across to the entry to the airport building. Fred was waiting there with an airport official and a wheel chair. Gratefully I sank into the chair. Handing the crutches to the official I wiped the raindrops off my face, turned to the Matabele man and smiling at him I said,

409

"Thank you kind sir!"

He nodded,

"My pleasure Nkosi!"

We all laughed.

"Hey! By God!" Fred whispered, "You look absolutely buggered!"

The official frowned,

"Is it safe for you to travel on an aeroplane when you are so old?" He asked.

"With all these kind people helping me!" I smiled weakly, "Yes, thank you sir! It is more than safe!"

Fred pushed the wheel chair through customs and immigration. The official carried my crutches and bag. I felt most welcome - even the customs staff were helpful.

The official handed my stuff back to me as we came out of customs, saying,

"Have a pleasant stay in Bulawayo!"

I took a twenty-pound note out of my inner jacket pocket and handing it to him said,

"Thank you kind sir!"

He beamed at me, hid the note inside his shirt muttering,

"You shouldn't bring undeclared foreign money in like that!"

We laughed,

"You want to give it back?"

"No sir! Thank you. Bye."

"Bye!"

Fred wheeled me out to his car.

We drove back to his place in silence. I let the jacaranda trees lining the road and the old colonial houses stir memories hidden deep inside me.

Fred parked near the steps onto his veranda where he got out and walked round to my side to help me out of the car.

Swinging my legs out of the door, I stood up tall and proud. Prodding him gently in the chest I said,

"Wow! It's good to be back!"

"Hey! What happened? Take care! I don't want you falling over and hurting yourself! The hospital is closed!"

I laughed,

"If I fooled you I can fool anyone!"

"You bastard!" He shouted "There's nothing wrong with you!"

"Well I wouldn't say that! But at least I am fit and healthy. You going to help me up the stairs or not?"

"Get lost!" He laughed, "What on earth was that all about?"

"You said I had to think of an innovative way to hide any excessive extra money I wanted to bring in that could not be justifiably declared at customs. So I did!"

"Where did you hide it?"

"Rolled up in the tubing of the crutches and our friend the airport official carried it through for me!"

"You will never change!" Laughed Fred. "But I think you over reacted, whatever you got in the crutches could most likely have been declared without any problem!"

"You told me - "

He laughed,

"No! You over reacted!"

Fred led me to my room. I bathed, washed the make up off my face and hair - put decent clothes on and came back into the living room for dinner.

Fred smiled,

"That's better! You look just as young and fit as when I last saw you! Hey! Please don't tell anyone where you hid the money, if no one else knows then if ever the need arises we can use the idea again "

We ate, talked till late and went to bed with the understanding that we would leave for the ruins early in the morning.

xxxxxxx

Day one!

We were driving head on into the rising sun.

Soft music playing on the CD player!

Fred's van was carrying us, the metal detector, our picnic lunch, some maize meal and preserved meat for any hungry people we might find at the ruins.

A bend in the road and there before us lay the village I had known when I was young. We drove past the old Courthouse and police station, then through town. Everything was closed. The stores, the houses, the post office! No people about. Maybe still too early! Memories flooded back. I felt a desperate sadness creep into my bones. It reached out through my muscles and nerves triggering pain in my mind.

My father. My youth. My hopes and fears all brought to nothing by man's inhumanity to man.

A thin mangy dog stood quivering by the roadside. I beckoned for Fred to stop. I got out, took some food from of the picnic basket and gently offered it to the dog. It cringed. I dropped the food on the ground. The dog stepped away in fear. I climbed back into the car and we drove off.

Fred was looking in the rear view mirror,

"Okay!" He said, "It took the food!"

The road wound through the hillside and across the river down to the lower, open country area. A line of small hills ran alongside the road. I remembered a day on this same road when my father was driving us to the village for a Sunday of tennis. A smell pervaded his car. He glared at me. The smell got worse. My father pulled up. Switching off the engine he turned to me and angrily asked,

"You eat something for breakfast that didn't agree with you?"

"No!" I meekly answered, "I thought maybe it was you letting out air!"

"What?"

The smell got really bad.

My father and I climbed out of the car. He went round to the bonnet and opened it. The stench was ferocious. He laughed,

"See that! The cat left a pile of dung on the exhaust manifold! It must have been sleeping on the engine for warmth and woke with a fright when we started the car this morning."

We scrapped it off with branches and cleaned the manifold with a rag.

Back in the car he smiled as he turned to look at me,

"I thought it was you!"

I said,

"I thought it was you!"

I smiled at Fred as other happy memories came flooding into my mind driving the pain away!

xxxxxxx

"Turn off here!" I said to Fred. "There's not much sign left of the track that used to be here but I know the way!"

We passed the old lookout post built on a high point of a hill and then drove on parallel with another long low hill where the ancient cattle kraals or slave camp was. Cresting a ridge we saw the main ruins stretching out before us.

"How many years ago is it since you were last here?" Asked Fred.

"Too many. We lived on this farm when I was a teenager. I came back again when I was about twenty five - I brought a professor out here to show him something."

Fred drove up to the main ruin. I suggested that he drive around below the ruins and then up past those big trees.

We parked in what would be, when the sun rose higher, a shady spot amongst the trees. Looking at the area between the ruins and the car I said,

"I think this is where I want to start. But first let's walk around a bit - I want to show you what I saw and see if you agree with me!"

The ruins stood as before.

Proud!

Smiling with their hidden meaning!

Proof of a past civilisation! Proof of what else?

I showed Fred the doorways, the air vents, the altars and the lovely stone chevron patterns on the walls. The floor of the ruin was level with the ground at the back but as the ground sloped away towards the front of the ruin so the floor area that was level appeared to rise up two stories higher. Inside the main ruin, near the front and a bit off centre was a round built up section like a house with low surrounding walls and a paved floor area on top. A small stone altar was set on the floor at the far side - opposite the entrance.

The whole of the main ruin area was paved with flat granite stone except where people had dug away at it about a hundred years ago. Early European settlers found gold ingots there which had been left lying in heaps on the ground near the northern perimeter wall. It was supposed that the ingots were abandoned when the original occupants left. Personnel from the Bulawayo museum dug up two air vents to see what lay inside. They found nothing. They made some rather unusual comments as to the nature or purpose of the vents such as maybe they were drainage holes. But who would want to drain loose stone?

I showed Fred where cladding had been removed from two sections of the walls outside the main ruin and a small section of wall inside at the back and that this cladding was made of smaller stones than the other walls in the ruins. Then I showed him where it appeared the cladding had been used to close up two entrances in the inner front walls of the ruins. If you looked from on top of the inner walls, you could see the slightly larger stones in the original walling where they curved in to form doorways and the smaller stones from the broken walls, which had been used to fill the gateways. The altar like structures built on the outside of the perimeter wall appeared to have also been built from the removed cladding. It became obvious when you looked carefully.

We walked back to the van.

"If you like," I said to Fred, "You can wander around, especially to that tower over there," I pointed to the conical tower standing alone some one hundred yards from us, "and also to the grain bins on the other side of the ruins and there's the remains of quite a big village about a hundred and fifty yards to the north.

I am going to use the metal detector to check certain areas where I believe there are underground rooms and see if we get any reaction. The ancients mined both silver and gold so you never know!"

"Okay," said Fred, "when I come back we can celebrate your findings with a cup of tea!"

He took a camera out of the van,

"I will take some photographs so that if you don't find anything we can at least write an illustrated story about it all and maybe make some money that way!"

We laughed.

I took up the detector and started.

First I worked the southern area in front of the ruins and, from there I zigzagged back and forth testing till I got to the western area near the van where I stopped for a rest. As I placed the detector on the ground it reacted!

"Maybe I put it down wrong!" I thought. I picked it up and lent it against a tree. It reacted even more. Surprised, I took it up and scanned around the tree.

Got more reactions!

"Wow!"

I crisscrossed the area and established a site measuring six by four meters by about six feet deep. Surprisingly it was quite a long way from the ruins. I called out to Fred.

He came back asking

"What?"

I showed him.

"Wow!"

We forgot about having a rest!

"I am going to carry on searching around the outside and then inside the ruins. You coming with me?"

He nodded and followed as I took up the detector.

We checked a large area outside and the whole area inside the ruin. Inside and between the wall and one of the air vents we got another reaction. The detector indicated that the area stretched from the air vent towards the main wall where one of the alter like structures had been built outside.

When we had checked out all the places we thought might be relevant we had lunch, packed up and headed on and away from the ruins. But not the way we had come!

About a mile on from the ruins and down by a small stream we came across two huts. An old man, a young mother and three children stood outside the larger hut. They looked worried.

Fred stopped.

He greeted them in Ndebele.

They stood where they were.

I climbed out of the van and dragging a twenty kg bag of maize meal out of the back I offered it to the family.

They looked even more worried. I greeted them again.

"Hullo! We brought you some food and if you want we will give you a job for a few days so that you can earn a little money. What do you say?"

"Thank you too much!" The man said, "What job?"

"We need you to help us with some ground work. Take the maize meal and here," I reached again into the back of the truck, "beans and dried meat!"

The woman burst into tears.

Trembling the old man took the food.

"What is your name? I asked.

"Sithole sir."

"Thank you," I smiled "and my African name is Machaya Nyoka!"

"Hey!" The man looked startled "You the son of Nyama Mbish?"

"Yes!"

"Oh my God!" He shouted "Such a long time ago!" He reached out with both his hands. I took them in mine. The tears ran down his face as he said,

"I worked for your father!"

Fred got out of the car. He stood there with me as the man laughed and joked and told us wild stories about my father.

"Yes, yes!" He cried out, "We will help you. Just call me when you are ready."

We drove back to Fred's home.

The following day Ian, Peter, and their fathers joined us in Bulawayo. They came in from Namibia through Botswana and then via the Northern Zimbabwean border post having decided to avoid the Plumtree route. Ian and Peter's mothers stayed behind at Somewhere Camp while we did our thing in Zimbabwe.

We met up, as arranged, outside the town hall then drove on to stay overnight at Fred's place.

The excitement boiled over. David said,

"I brought my video camera and filming equipment. Even if we don't find any gold we can still make a fantastic story out of it!"

I laughed,

"That's exactly what Fred said! You two will get on for sure!"

After supper I asked,

"Anything to discuss before we go to bed?"

"No, unless you got something to say!"

"I think we should leave late tomorrow afternoon so that we arrive at the ruins just before sunset! Everything is in place now. The helicopter and pilot are on stand-by in South Africa. They can either pick up all of our new found wealth or, if there is a problem, they can pick us up and take us away! Or whatever!"

"You think there will be a problem?"

"No! At least, that is, I hope not! Shouldn't be if we move quickly. The longer we stay out there the more likely will it be for a problem to develop! First of all there is a possibility that Mugabe's men living in the area, the so-called war vets, get to hear of what we are doing and they come to check us out. Could be dangerous! Then there is the simple problem of gangsters or whatever trying to get in on the act!"

"What vehicles do we take?"

"The old Ford truck, it's got a lot of hidden loading space which might come in useful and we can carry food for the locals in case there is a need to reach out and help them. I think we should also take Fred's Zimbabwe registered van."

"Wouldn't it be better to take David's truck, its Namibian and we could then look and behave like tourists with our cameras and stuff?"

"Got a point there! OK! You happy with that David?"

"No problem!"

"OK so then we take all three vehicles! We can load up tomorrow morning, have a late lunch and then go for it. Meanwhile, here's to a good night's sleep!"

XXXXXXX

AT LAST!

My old Ford F.250 truck groaned under its heavy load.

Ian and his father David travelled in their Nissan Safari with some gear in the back. Peter came with me and his dad went with Fred in the van.

We travelled a different way to the ruins than the first time. The only people we saw were struggling locals with hands held out for food. Wherever possible we stopped and passed out a few parcels. The recipients cried their thanks.

About thirty miles on, a few miles after Filabusi, we turned off and made our way along old and hardly ever used tracks to the ruins. Sithole and his family were waiting for us. They climbed into the trucks as the sun was setting.

Half a mile on and the grey stone-walls of the ruins stood out proud amongst the trees and the tangled roots of creepers. A haunting beauty pervaded the place.

History hiding in the silence!

I walked up to the eastern wall and stood there looking at the chevron patterns. Once again memories of my teenage explorations flooded back.

The low full moon flooded the sky driving the last of the warm colours of the fast disappearing sun over the western horizon. The ruins looked surreal in the soft new moonlight. We made camp - cooked our evening meal on a campfire and I reminisced as we ate.

The Sithole family ate every last scrap.

"Ok, let's go!" I said.

Taking up their digging tools Peter with his dad and Fred headed for the ruins to auger into the selected vent hole. Ian, his dad, Sithole and I moved onto the site near the tree where the detector had shown a strong reaction. We started to dig.

Sithole's family climbed to the top of the ruins to keep watch from the highest point, looking out for any unexpected visitors.

Just after the very last sign of sunset was fading from the sky we heard a vehicle.

Sithole's wife ran to me,

"Army!" She shouted.

Everyone hid their tools and ran round to the front of the ruins.

"Oh hell!" muttered Ian's father, "It's an army Unimog!"

"I'll go down and meet them." I said, "You guys sit with the Sithole family where the men in the Unimog can see you." I pointed, "Over there on this side of the ruins near our camp and the vehicles. Oh, and make some tea! We are visiting the ruins and the Sithole's are our guides.

Brief them quickly! Okay!"

I walked out to meet the Unimog.

A sergeant was driving. A lieutenant sat in the passenger seat. Four armed soldiers stood in the back.

The truck stopped near me. The engine was kept running. I saluted the lieutenant and gave him my happiest smile.

"Good evening Sir!" I said, "Nice to meet you, my name is Robert."

He laughed,

"Don't worry my friend!" He said, "We don't get many tourists around here. Is that your camp back there?" He pointed at the fire.

"Yes, would you care to have a cup of tea with us? Or if you are here tomorrow we would like to invite you to lunch. Plenty of food! Yes?"

"Thank you but no thanks! Unfortunately we are in a hurry! Saw your car tracks further back and came to find out what was going on. We won't be here tomorrow for your lunch but many thanks again." He beamed at me, waved at the group sitting under the trees and said,

"Bye! Have a nice holiday!"

"Hamba gahle!" I saluted.

He laughed and pointed his finger indicating to the driver which way to go.

The truck bounced its way back down the old track.

"Wow!" I laughed, "That was interesting. Better hurry up in case they report to headquarters and initiate a follow up exercise tomorrow!"

We dug and shovelled as hard as we could. Peter and his father were the first to hit pay dirt. Their auger finally cleaned out the vent hole and it struck a solid base. Fred put a scissor clamp down the hole and pulled up a gold ingot. Their excited laughter brought me to his side.

We retrieved seventeen gold ingots from the vent hole.

We also struck pay dirt on my side. Maybe? The bottom of our hole was covered with slabs of slate. I used a tyre lever to lift them. Underneath were what looked like the rotten remains of wooden boxes! They were full of ingots of gold and slabs of silver.

I went to my truck. Switched on the radio and called our friend at Messina.

"Pay dirt! Send helicopter urgent! Over and out."

"Roger! Out!"

The helicopter would cross the border after sunset and then it would take, at the most, two hours to get to us.

I went across to Peter, his dad and Fred. Sithole joined us. Looking at Sithole I asked,

"You know what this means?"

"It is gold, yes?"

"It means that you and your family will be very, very rich! Your share will be enough to keep you for the rest of your lives. Do you want it in gold or in money?"

"Gold too dangerous, money better!"

"Okay, some in South African Rands, some in British Pounds and the rest in gold. Does that sound okay to you?"

"What a question!" Laughed Ian.

"Hey!" Laughed Sithole, "I have no idea what that means?"

"Too much!" I laughed, "Now you guys dig up the rest and move it to that flat open area over there where the helicopter will land and

I will get the boxes ready to pack the stuff into. By the way those slate slabs in our hole, did you notice that they have some sort of writing or scribbling on them?"

Peter and I walked over to Ian and his dad. Picking up a slate I held it so that Peter could see properly in the moonlight,

"You're right!" He said, "Looks like a mixture of crazy writing - something like hieroglyphics and pictures mixed together!"

"We must take them too!" Said David.

"Oh yes! We've got plenty boxes! They could be very interesting!"

Mama Sithole brewed another round of tea for us all.

"Hey Sithhole!" I asked, "Will you be able to stay here after we leave? What will happen if the authorities come and demand you tell them what happened? Would they steal your money and beat you up?"

"Yes! Too much trouble!"

"Okay then," I said, "We will give you your money and a share of the gold now and you and your family can have a lift to Bulawayo with these guys. I have a friend there you can trust who has a small workshop in town and a farm in the countryside. He will look after you and arrange for you to change the gold for American dollars - for a small payment!"

"Thank you!" Sithole beamed.

"Hey!" Muttered Fred, "What's this about your friend? What's wrong with me? I can help him!" Turning to Sithole he said, "No my friend, you and your family have been fantastic in helping us so you come home with me - I'll look after you! Ok!"

"Yes!" Smiled sithole, "One hundred percent yes, Sir!"

"By the way, can you drive?" I asked him.

"Yes I was a truck and tractor driver for the last farmer here."

"Okay." I turned to Peter and Ian. You guys go back together in your cars to Bulawayo and if you think it wise you can leave the Nissan there with Sithole and take the other car back to Namibia. But, Sithole, remember that someone might identify the Nissan so you must re-register it."

"Yes Machaya Nyoka!"

We laughed.

I went to my truck with Sithole, took out a brief case and handed him a large envelope. We walked back to the others where he opened the case. Wads of South African Rands inside! There were British Twenty Pound notes in the envelope. He looked up at me, looked around at the rest of us and burst into tears.

"Hey Sithole don't cry! You can collect your important belongings from your home as you all go back to Bulawayo." I hefted up one of the boxes filled with ingots. "This one is also yours! Peter can you put it in the van and give it to Sithole when you get to Bulawayo."

"That's it then. We must leave this area as soon as we can so let's finish moving the stuff."

The Sithole family left to walk to their home and collect whatever. As he passed me he stopped, turned, and looked deep into my eyes. I took his hand in mine.

"Thank you Mr. Sithole. You are a good man!" Turning to his daughter and grand children I said,

"Go well Mamma. Go well kids. Now get your stuff and hurry!" I pointed to the others standing around the loot, "They will pick you up when they leave!"

We finished packing the gold and silver ingots just as the sound of an approaching helicopter beat the air. The moon gave enough light for the pilot to see. I talked him in over the radio. He landed on the level ground where we had stacked the boxes.

The Sithole's did not wait for us to pick them up at their huts. They came back and helped load the helicopter. When all the boxes and the stuff we wanted to send back with the copter was loaded the pilot took off. He circled us once, wagged the copters tail and flew south.

We closed up the holes we had dug and cleared up around the area. Peter and Ian left with their fathers and Fred took the Sithole family.

After Bulawayo the two boys and their fathers planned to travel across to the Botswana border and from there north to the Eastern

Caprivi and then on to Somewhere Camp where they would meet up with their mothers who had stayed together at Somewhere during our expedition. It was planned that from Somewhere Island they would all drive back together to my camp in South Africa on Wednesday.

I watched their tail lights fade with the dust and the dark into the night.

Alone, I finished packing up the camp and the bits and pieces.

I took a last walk around the ruins to say goodbye. One day I will come back and make my home here, maybe at the robbers roost or even up in the hills at the cattle kraals. Maybe? That's what dreams are made of! My heart ached for what might never be.

I left the ruins long before sunrise and travelled through the rest of the night to a point on the Limpopo River where you can drive across to South Africa in a four-wheel drive vehicle. I did this to avoid the border post at Beit Bridge just in case someone had put in a report. You never know!

The sun was rising as I ground my way through the sand and shallow water to the South African side. Resting on the southern bank I sipped tea from a thermos flask as I watched the beauty of the Limpopo River running past me. I remembered canoeing down this river with Jean and some friends many years ago. That was in the rainy season and the river had more water in it then.

That evening I went to sleep without eating supper. Not hungry!

Life certainly has its moments.

The following morning I took the dirt track back to civilisation which led me onto a tarmac road and then on to the small town of Musina with big people living in it. Leaving the old Ford with friends I collected my old Volkswagen and carried on to the Soutspanberg Mountains where I have my camp.

The helicopter and the pilot were waiting there for me. We unpacked the chopper and stacked the boxes in a shed. We shared a late brunch. I paid him the agreed amount plus a large bonus, shook his hand and waved him goodbye.

The chopper rose high in the sky, it crested the mountains to the south and disappeared into the vastness of a hot African sky.

I sat outside on a deck chair.

Alone!

In a few days Peter, Ian and their families would be here. Time now to relax and think about the future. What future?

The moon shone through a window onto the dressing table. The gold pig glowed in the soft light.

I could not sleep. Outside the light got brighter. Must be nearly morning. But it can't be! I looked at my watch. Midnight! Funny! Lying there I watched as the light outside intensified! Finally curiosity got the better of me and I got up, went to the window and looked out in amazement. The valley was full of immensely bright light. I opened the door to the veranda. The light hurt my eyes! I could clearly see tiny leaves on distant trees. They glowed like green diamonds. What on earth was happening? 'Maybe I am dreaming?'

Walking out into the deathly quiet I saw that the light stretched from the top of the southern mountains across my valley to the foot of the northern mountains. Why not up the northern mountains? It was similar to the light I had seen when Red was here, except this was stronger and pure white, not blue!

Looking up I saw it was coming from a brilliant almost square patch at the side of the moon! At least I called it a patch.

Despite the extreme brightness, I could see the patch was actually octagonal.

A jackal howled.

Suddenly the light went out and the soft glow of the round moon took its place.

Another jackal howled.

The night sounds started up again. Owls hooted, crickets sang, mosquitoes hummed, leaves rustled. Everything back to normal!

I sat on the low wall outside wondering what on earth it was all about. A cool wind began to blow. Looking up again I saw to my utter amazement that the shape that had been the light had moved slightly and now showed as a dark shadow covering about a quarter of the moon. Whatever it was, it must have been huge.

I went back into the house and made myself a cup of coffee. Retrieving four letters from the window ledge I opened one which was from a friend at the university at Cape Town with whom I had left some of the tablets we found in Namibia.

I read his letter.

Dear Robert,

With reference to your request concerning the inscriptions on the slates from Namibia which you left with us, three of the slates had identical inscriptions, viz.

It is that which comes to you from the pig which

Causes the blindness in man's understanding.

In order to overcome this inherent problem

You have to go through the curtain within you

into the inner sanctuary of your I am

and see and know the truth that sets you free.

The following was deciphered from another four slates,

I have not been able to get around to working out the remaining the plates. Too busy with exams!

The end of time has now begun. The time of the end is at hand!

It is so sworn by the moving sun as it searches the promised land!

'tis the end of man as he is now - now is the end I say.

For the light shines through the structures

Showing the eternal way.

Six and twenty thousand years it took

For Atlantis to complete the round,

from the time of one to the time of two, far distant, without sound!

Left behind fallen man cried "and to hell with you too!"

As he tortured the guiltless mastermind

Flushing truth down the loo!

He cut down trees and built his story with pyramids and tales of strength,

But it was all to no avail as religion bent their width and length!

So the sun comes up and the sun goes down,

And summer follows spring,

The mystics change all the rules

That could make a sad man sing.

"The end is nigh!" An old fool said

As corruption, greed, deceit and lies fill the young man's empty eyes.

The days grow short! The filth piles high!

The nights grow loud with sin!

The message goes out "It's your right to lie,

Just know when to stop and begin!"

As morality dies and children grow

with nothing to teach them why

no rod, no law! The sightless ones prepare the way for them to die!

The right to freedom denied by the free to the ones whom they wish to harm.

Leading by the way of insanity,

And no one raises the alarm!

xxxxxxxx

Sounds almost Biblical!

We appreciate your gift and look forward to meeting with you in the near future."

Yours truly,   Arther.

The other three letters where all from an old South African friend of mine called Boertjie.

I read the first one dated 12th October.

Hullo Englishman,

How I hate you!

If you were not the most arrogant bastard in South Africa I would not have inherited your title when you left! Yes I hate you for showing me who I am and who I pretend to be! Why on earth did God introduce you to me? I had more hope of finding my way in ignorance but you made me aware that there is more to life than what I and others can perceive!

Why do I need you so when I feel so lost?

I pray to God that I might yet find my way through all this chaos!

You bastard! You are the closest I have ever been to finding in life what is known as Father Love - and then you left me!

Well I guess after all that I do have to thank you! At least you made me aware that I am more than just another ordinary person!

I have been writing a book about us! The problem is that I have to see the places that you visited to give relevance to our story!

My God how I hate you! I was nobody till you showed me more!

I miss you!

I guess that I have loved you more than you will ever know and that is why I can claim hate!

Yours as always,

Boertjie.

The second letter was dated 14 October.

Hullo Englishman,

Sorry for my explosions of emotions in my last letter! It was as a release valve for my own idiotic tantrums! The fact is that most if not all the things I have been asking for are now actually manifesting! It all started many years ago when I met you, you damned Englishman! And you broke me out of a cage of self-doubt that had me trapped for as long as I can remember. The growth was gradual and the experience at times very painful but it turned out that the clay provided for by the potter was as perfect as it was designed in the beginning of time to be! Does this imply that you had no part in the forming of the pot?

What do you say? I say, God is the potter providing the clay of all of his creations but we are given the opportunity to exercise our limited freedom to choose in how we want our lives to be shaped and formed.

In this the potter has made the commandment 'love thy neighbour as you love thyself which is the cornerstone each individual needs to shape and form our-selves as an inspiration to all.

Let that be the end part one of my sermon!

My message to you is actually one of joy and celebration!!!!!!!

For years I have dreamed of doing consulting in the business world and now I am at the very moment of that dream becoming a reality!

Why then was I so upset when I wrote to you two days ago?

Well...........!

Imagine you having always seen yourself as the "odd one out!" Always up stream and questioning everything and then suddenly - you come to realise you are reality in action!

Do I always get what I want? Yes, you know better than me! Or do you?

Remember David Letab? He used to say to me,

"You are the luckiest bastard in the world because you always get what you want!"

We used to joke about this but as time goes by I have found it to be a reality but it does have a down side! When I leave a place where I invested major energy I have seen the deterioration that evolved there after leaving, like a plant dying of thirst!

Well Robert old chap, I have to go now but I will be writing more frequently from now on.

Be brave!

God bless!

Boertjie.

I sat down in the lounge to read the third very long letter. The cup of coffee was almost cold. Raising it to my lips I tilted my head back and in so doing the open door to the bedroom caught my eye. A very soft light seemed to be manifesting inside the bedroom.

"Now what on earth is that?"

Leaning forward I saw the pig on the dressing table. It was emitting a soft glow. Putting the cup and letter down on the floor, I leapt to my feet and ran into the bedroom. The light from the pig faded as I reached out to it and the world went back to normal!

"What on earth was that all about?"

I sat down again and picking up the coffee and the letter which had been written on the sixteenth just two days after his second one, I read,

Once again, hullo Englishman,

I write this as an insight from our joint past.

It is not often that we experience true enlightenment! It is rather less frequent that any of us is so touched by God that we come to understand the fullness of his glory! In the light of recent events in the lives of those around me and my own brief encounter with The Most High God, I bring this light to you to either embrace or discard as your I am guides you!

I always believed that we came alive at birth! It now seems as though birth is merely the start of our journey of creating and recreating ourselves by the choices we make and the ability to change those choices as we progress in wisdom and understanding of ourselves and the true nature of God. Thus I, as a little blond haired boy born in 1965 to some very odd parents who had no idea of where they are or where they belong in the strange world of God-not-God!

During my childhood and my all too brief adolescence I never stopped feeling the urge to find a reason for being! Even while my own children grew up in front of me I did not find the true meaning of life!

"Tut, Tut." I can hear you say. Hog wash and bog tails is closer to the truth! Hey? Well! This is my story and thus my own ideas and so I can lament and philosophise all that I want!

Fact is that we go through life taking direction from our parents, our teachers and so called spiritual leaders and we are discouraged to question or doubt the origins of their teachings! As a result we are alive but yet not living as in that living means we know where we are and where we want to be! A case in point is the whole era of apartheid was forced on us South African whites and non-whites as being a direct order from God! How easy it is to look back and see the error of our ways? To admit that Christianity in the hands of whites was a weapon used to enslave millions of people, both black and white, and force them to believe that wrong is right and right is wrong!

What we need to do now is to concentrate each on his or her own perspective of God and our fellow men while first asking the question who "Am I?" before we can ask "Who are You?" The sad truth is that not many people have the ability to distinguish between what is the truth and what is the lie that they have been taught to embrace. It would seem that over ninety percent of all people are not able to discern whether their leaders are truthful or whether they are leading everyone as sheep to the slaughter.

Lets take the Nazi's! Do you really think each and every German was inherently bad and that all of them wanted what Hitler wanted? The fact is that very few people had the ability to withstand the flow of the majority! Does that mean that the majority was as bad as Hitler? Why? Not by intention but by blind dedication to a leader who was able to gain and hold the trust of the masses!

If we do realize that we are able to discern between the lie and the truth we end up caught like fish out of water with literally no avenue of escape! What remains is for us to express our objections and most important, to live by the truth that is, and in so doing we can protest with the strongest voice of all! The voice and language of example!

From the principle that is universal to all holy scriptures, love thy neighbour, love thyself and only then can you love Thy God!

Not long ago I was introduced to Eastern Religions. It was enlightening to unravel the intricate line of love and fear that undermines all religions! There is always a creator on the one hand and the fear of judgement on the other hand, which together, keep the subjects true to their faith. How these religions evolved alongside each other and how they influenced even the oldest cultures and indeed the whole world is a story all in itself!

Yes it probably comes as a shock to most people but it is true! So looking at the effects of religion on our lives it becomes clear that "We are what we believe!" Or "What we believe leads us into being what we are!"

If you can imagine a Moslem child raised at the knee of its mother within the love and fear of their faith, then will you be able to see how absurd it is to want to convert such a person to another faith! We fear what we don't understand! Yes! It is our nature! But is it right? Far from converting any person to my views or perceptions, my purpose in life is simply to help kick start, wherever possible, the mind of the already seeking person!

If what they say is true, and I have as yet found no reason to doubt it, then God is my Father and I am his child! Obviously if I am his child nothing can change that, not even death! So then I have him in me as the source of my being! So that is where I must look for myself - within me and that is also where I must look for my father! Within me!

Also within my neighbour, my home, my country and indeed in all creation! It follows that if I love me I will automatically love both my neighbour, all of creation and God!

Now I understand what you meant that day so long ago when you explained to me the saying "Greater is he within you than everything outside!" And again, "Without my 'I Am' there is nothing!"

May I add to this my view? I believe we are born free and the Truth in God' is the reason why! To accept this makes each one of us different but belonging. To be different is scary so we tend to choose to remain powerless and poor both materially and spiritually thereby denying ourselves and our children the love, peace, prosperity and harmony that are ours by birthright as children of the MOST HIGH GOD!

God is not entrapped by simple minded humans to dance to their cue but He is a father to all of us be we Moslem, Christian or Atheist and His endless supply of riches and blessings that He longs to pour out over us is subject only to us accepting and acknowledging His Father-ship and King-ship and open our hearts and minds to His love!

You may well ask, Where are we going with all this?' I believe we are heading for the most basic understanding of God and His intentions towards us in contrast to what we have been force fed all our lives! So here is a question. "What can we learn from this biblical quotation regarding us being children - 'assuming you as earthly parents know what is good for your children, then how much more does your Father in Heaven know what is good for you?"

All children are precious in the eyes of God!

This has been a very long letter so enough for now!

Your old friend

Boertjie

The sun rose inciting the morning mist to rise and the mosquitoes to go to bed.

It was time to meet the day.

"Wow! What a night! The lights, the letters and the glowing pig!

Yes I had seen something similar before on the night Red left, but this time it was so very much more than the first time and then followed by the letters from Boettjie!"

XXXXXXX

WHERE ARE THEY?

Three days later and it is now almost time for Ian, Peter and their families to arrive. David had called by radio when they crossed over from Botswana into the Caprivi to say everything was all right with them and that they were on their way to collect the ladies from Somewhere Camp. They would then all drive on down through Namibia to South Africa as planned.

They should be here tomorrow.

I guessed the weight of the gold and silver we had found to be in the region of one ton. Worth many tons of money! The next problem would be converting it into cash. Of course we had worked out various possibilities before we set off to the ruins. I think that a friend of mine in the local mining business has the best answer. I am a little sad at the thought of smelting down all those cross-shaped ingots. Maybe we could keep a few for antiquities sake and donate a couple to some museum.

And the slates? I will ask Arthur to decipher them. Could be very interesting! Wonder if there is any connection between them and the ones we found in Namibia?

Oh well, time will tell.

xxxxxxx

Ian and the others didn't arrive on the expected day so I called them on the radio.

"You guys okay?"

"Yes! Don't worry!" Said Ian, "It's just that something most unusual has come up and we are all trying to come to terms with it. When it is all sorted out Peter and I will come down to your place. Peter's parents have decided to stay on at Somewhere with my parents."

"Is there a problem? Is it serious?"

"No I wouldn't call it a problem, but yes, it is serious! On the other hand we all think it is fantastic! You see, someone from overseas was waiting for us here at Somewhere Camp wanting to share a lot of very interesting information with us and we are all busy coming to terms with it. We believe it could be worth a lot more than all

435

that gold and silver we dug up! It seems to be setting all of us free! Especially me! As I said, we are working on it and with luck we should be finished tonight - so we will most likely be with you in a couple of days!

Over and out!"

He switched off the radio.

Another two days have passed.

I sleep late this morning. I had been thinking and dreaming of Red last night. Just who and what is he? This led me to memories of other occasions when coincidences had led me to meet someone pertinent to what I was doing at the time, like the Sangoma in Zambia.

"Is there a connection between the ruins, the pig, the Sangoma, Red and the nagging feeling growing inside me that there is more than just a 'missing link'? For some reason this thought led me to open the bible and read.

Slowly a new perspective filled my mind. Just what are the stories in the bible that spoke of beings that could be aliens or celestials or angels - and the stories of wheels turning within wheels? As I thought of this I remembered as a young man designing an anti gravity machine. A ball within a ball, each one rotating in an opposite direction! One magnetised and the other electrified, the faster the opposing rotations the greater the power of the generated thrust coming out from them until the balls acted like a giant magnet lunging away from or grabbing at the negativity of matter! When directed in the right way its enormous drive overcame gravity! So much so that if the ball was not tied down it took off at great speed!

Yes, my 'anti gravity machine' and my 'faster than the speed of light mechanism'? Oh yes! I remembered that too! Based on the same principle, if you moved in one direction at just under the speed of light past matter moving in the opposite direction also at just under the speed of light, you created the effect of travelling at nearly twice the speed of light! What happens to the particles involved? And the resultant experience of the effect of moving at nearly twice the speed of light opened my mind to the understanding that it is possible to generate and use this perspective to accelerate to greater and greater speeds until you travel so fast that you could be a multi billion miles away in a second and that explains why and how some people experience being in two places at the same time and how sometimes things seem to disappear, then reappear again!

Why were these memories coming back?

What did they have to do with the light in the valley or the dark shaped object set against the moon? Where did the light come from? Where did it go?

I drifted off to sleep and dreamt I saw the sun reflected towards me off a giant inward curving mirror! Because of the inward curve the light was intensified, that was why the reflection seemed small and very bright! Then, as the sun moved a few degrees, the reflection faded and died - the mirror without light on it became larger and darker especially when seen against a light back ground like the moon. Understanding grew about what might have happened in the sky last night! The object in the sky which could not normally be seen by the human eye because it was designed to bend directed light around it, could be seen either when it reflected light emanating from an angle ninety degrees from the viewer as in sunlight hidden by the earth but shining on the object at night, or when it appeared against the moon as seen by the viewer, with the sun in such a position as to not reflect off it so defining the object as a dark shape set against the moon!

Looked like a huge giant ship or a huge Space City?

Was it Alien or our own?

Next morning saw me serene, calm, and for the first time ever, open to my inner self! My 'I Am' was taking over! I turned the radio on. The news told of sightings in Mexico of UFO's surrounding a passenger plane. The pilot radioed base. The air force sent four jet fighters to check it out. Passengers on the plane took photos and videos of the UFO's. The UFO's flew away at an amazing speed when the fighter planes arrived.

It was mentioned just that one time on the early morning news and never again!

Why never again?

So little sleep last night! I relax and drowse off into a daydream where I imagine a self-righteous man who does not believe in God standing next to a self-righteous man who does! The Atheist prods the believer asking,

"Come on you! The one who claims to know it all! Tell me what does it mean to be religious? Where does your new religious self come from and what happens to your old self? Does it die? Shouldn't you also die to everyone else's perspectives? It seems obvious that no one has an identical understanding to anyone else of what is right or wrong - be it art, war, music, politics, religion, families, education, human rights, cruelty, creation, nationality, what ever! So then, if everyone sees things differently the possibility that no one is totally right seems relevant. This would mean that you and I are probably also wrong!

If this is so, do you think that if I drop my insistence that I am right in all the understandings and beliefs that I now have, it would set me free to be that which I really am? Or! Would I just be changing the name of the game and still be as arrogantly self-righteous in my new wrongness?

The believer answers,

"You're making me think! Wait a minute! I may have an answer! If I abandon the strangleholds of genealogy, family, nationality, religion and political perspectives or positions, I would become a man of peace. That means I would never use any kind of force for any reason whatever! I could become a Prince or King and be free to live on!

I could love because my ability to love would release me from the confines of beliefs and all the worldly perspectives which limit and confuse man's ability to think clearly! I would be able to see the whole picture and this would set me irrevocably and totally free!

If that is the answer then abandoning all of my worldly perspectives would also set me free to be that which I really am!

Come on! Let's both try. Let's do it together and see what happens!"

The two men shook hands and walked off together into the far distances.

They were no longer angry or self-righteous!

They walked the same path, as friends!

I stretched. The daydream faded!

"Maybe that's the answer!" I muttered, "Maybe I should also try! But wait a minute! Isn't that the gist of the story about Melchizedek and Christ? And what about Adam? He was created with no genealogy or sin or whatever in him! So there were three men not two! Adam did not need to use force to be where and what he was. He was not confined by any of the world's perspectives although he was subject to the moral code of integrity!

That makes it possible that there have been more than three!

Ok, stay with the thought. He was the first Adam! The Christ was called the second Adam and there is a promise of a fourth Adam coming at the so-called end time to revitalise man and the world! Here's another thought! Modern man is experimenting with genealogy, DNA and cloning. We are on the threshold of cloning an extinct mammoth from the DNA of the genes of a carcase found preserved in the ice and implanting it into living elephants! It may or may not work, but think of that! An extinct baby mammoth born from an elephant in this age!

Man can also remove certain attachments to selected genes and so eradicate an inherited cause for cancer or Alzheimer's!

Maybe we can add the 'God Gene' to all men? Maybe the God Gene cannot simply be implanted! Ok! After all these generations of interbreeding amongst peoples all over the world the God Gene from the first Adam must have spread into a very large percentage of all races and nationalities from and in every continent so that it is now no longer necessary to keep line breeding. The whole story is beginning to make sense.

The ancient Egyptians had their own understanding of the resurrection, which was to take place in the far distant future, and that is why they had their bodies mummified! It seems that all religions look to resurrection. They say that at the time of the predicted return of Christ some of the dead will rise from their graves and together with some of the living meet with Christ in the air! In the space city? Now it's all falling into place. Could there be an order in to-days world, which I have never heard of? Maybe one that like-minded people belong to, an order like the 'Illuminati' or the 'Masons?'

A crazy new understanding filled me.

The Christ is reported to have said,

"I go to prepare a place for you!" Where will that be? In the heavens, another planet, a space city or a whole galaxy? Why prepare another place? Is this world and universe going to burn up as prophesied in the bible? Maybe triggered by global warming or will some scientist try to manipulate sub atomic particles to create a black hole in order to prove the big bang theory and despite having thought out and implemented what he thinks would be an adequate control factor the black hole will develop its own agenda, heat up, grow, and suck everything in our galaxy into it! Imagine the howling wailing sounds as this happens!

He also said "You have to die to sin if you want to join me!" Or, "You can only come to Christ if God draws you!" So you have to 'be drawn' in order to be born again physically, genetically and spiritually!

He said, "You must choose between life and death!"

Obviously you would have to experience both to be able to choose!

"You must choose between good and evil!"

Again, you have to experience both and share other people's experiences before you can make an enlightened choice. To make the maximum use of your experiences you have to have all the contradictory aspects of your own nature resolved.

"I am the way the truth and the life!" Or, "I am that what I am!" This involves all the perspectives of His 'I am', your 'I am' and my 'I am'!

"Die to yourself!" This will set you free from all your inherited and experienced blindness, which has so far enabled you to live both the good and evil so that you can come to know both.

The life is in the blood? Is that a reference to genetics? Is that why it is recommended that you do not accept a blood transfusion? Could such a transfusion unwittingly introduce unwanted genetic influences?

Hang on! A new leading! A new understanding! The aliens we see or hear about might or might not be from outer space! They could be from this world! Is it us of this world who are colonising space and not aliens from space trying to colonise this world! If there are, aliens with all that technology available it wouldn't take them millions of years to colonise this world! So maybe it is us who built the UFO's we hear about. Maybe it is us who are busy regenerating a race of humans who are having their sins and the sins of their forefathers removed from their genetic make up. Then again it might be that aliens do not want to colonise the earth but are busy breeding acceptable humans here to colonise new planets? Why don't they colonise such planets themselves? Maybe because in their world there is no marrying and so no children! Living forever may take away the need and therefore the ability to procreate! So! Not enough people to go round and as a result they are busy breeding suitable ones here on earth!

Crazy thoughts!

Our history, modern and ancient, tells us that selected individuals from our own people were taken out into space to prepare places for us to go to when this world burns up. All our religions come from deep seated and unrecognised inherited memories of the old world, religions based on how we can achieve immortality and move on into other worlds where there is no marrying, no death, no evil and so on.

I think that it is possible there exists in this world an organisation which you could say, is so secret that despite having operated for thousands of years, it is still not known to the general public. Is this organisation based on the thirty-fourth parallel and in a north/south line aligned with the original site for El Giza, which existed before the great flood? I remember Red talking about the thirty and thirty fifth parallels and how all the predestined earth quakes, tsunamis, wars and political conflicts due to take place in the twentieth century would be caused by the tension existing along and attached to these parallels. At the poles you can stand in one place and do a complete turn-around whereas at the equator you would have to travel thousands of miles to complete a turn around. This causes stress within the faults running around the world at approximately the thirtieth parallel, both north and south, and affects both the land masses and the life living in those areas!

History tells us of major human conflicts being generated in those areas and an interesting observation is the similarity of faces of so called Aliens to the ancient leaders of Egypt and Southern America! That is! Huge eyes, big ears, high foreheads, small noses and chins! It could be that later interbreeding and consorting with the tribes further north or south changed both their features and their understanding.

There are thousands of ancient pyramids sited all over the world, especially adjacent to the thirtieth parallels, all of them pointing to certain aspects of the stars and built or created at about the same time. The builders were probably trying to record for future posterity the understanding of what it was and is all about. As Red told me, the builders of the later pyramids developed their own misconceptions resulting in a change in their perceptions causing them to degenerate, as all nations eventually do! But! A thread of truth does run through their story and their history. Things like mummified burials and burial customs suggesting ancient knowledge of the ability to regenerate living organisms through their DNA and their genetic structures. Religions based on an after life earned by good behaviour and sacrifice, all with a promised resurrection of the dead from the grave.

These beliefs are now being confirmed in a round about way by our newly gained knowledge of the ability to recreate living organisms from the remains of the long ago dead by using their genetic and DNA features - this would obviously include human beings! The ability of modern science to alter genetic structures and remove or add genes opens many doors to understanding the 'then', the 'now' and the 'to be.'

It is possible that the lost and maybe departed people of Atlantis or even people from much earlier civilisations come back from time to time to restructure and reorganise or redirect the work being done in reshaping both human nature and the human material form in order to stimulate the desired rebirth of acceptable colonialists as needed now and eventually en-masse when the end time comes! There has probably always been contact between the earthbound organisation and the people of the space cities.

It is well known that the ancients had fantastic knowledge and intimate understanding of that knowledge! They knew how to build and use anti gravity machines to lift, carry and put in place all those huge rock structures and monoliths. They knew the story of the stars. They knew of rebirth. They knew of batteries and electricity. They understood art. They could see and read the future. They had the equipment to design and lay out, in exact detail, huge alignments of buildings tallying with different aspects of nature. In fact they knew maths, the sciences, geometry, geography, mental telepathy, lei lines, remote viewing and even spiritualism! They had equipment to tunnel into huge hard rock mountains and build sanctuaries in the depths.

Certainly much more than we know! Yes! I begin to see it now! As I said before, maybe it is not that aliens are colonising this world! Maybe it is selected 'our world' humans that are busy colonising other worlds!

Are the UFO's we hear of or see our own? This would account for the fact that so much of the news about UFO's is denied, covered up or hidden!

Ok, so maybe I have been dreaming!

Crazy thoughts do often come from dreams! Although all dreams evolve from within you they usually lock you into your own perspectives, but sometimes on rare occasions! They set you free!

It depends!

Depends on what?

Suddenly another new understanding dawned in me! Everything in our creation is in balance except for where the spiritual is occupying or existing in the physical state. Like Red said, Spirit is subject to morality whereas flesh is not. What the Spiritual entities need is acceptable physical bodies to bring them into balance so that they can make the most out of living in both a material and a spiritual universe. They, the Spiritual beings, have been and still are, working on developing the genetic base of human beings into being in a state where acceptable humans, who are a "fulfilment of the law" and not "subject to the law" can be selected! It is these 'new' or you might say 'morally regenerated' physical beings or humans that are reborn out of their genetic inheritance into freedom, who can be filled with the spirit and move on to colonise the new, at present unoccupied, planets where our physical forms fit! That is why the repetitive mention of 'life is in the blood' is used where genetic knowledge is not understood, as was the case in the days of our forefathers!

And Red? What did all his talk about Melchizedek really mean? Why do religious people avoid talking about Melchizedek? What was Red trying to tell me? What was he leading me into? What was he getting at?

"Hang on!" I thought, "What was common to both Melchizedek and Jesus? How come they were of the same order? What order? Being an order suggests there were or there are many more members! Why not known to us? What could the connection between them and me be? Well! They both had no genealogy! In other words you could say they did not have the sins of the fathers to four generations in them or as you might say in modern times, they were free of the bad genes which we all normally inherit from our parents. Their blood was pure! This again confirms my new understanding of why the book says "the Blood of Christ!"

They both had no religion! Christ and Melchizedek were separate to although alongside of the religion of their time and place - so they were not subject to other peoples limited ideas of God and creation and the purpose of man in this world.

Thirdly, they were both men who, despite being men of peace, were Kings in their own right. So! They never inherited their kingdoms. They were not promoted or elected by men to be princes or kings. They were not there as leaders of a religious organisation. They never fought for their position and they were naturally men of integrity! They both behaved and thought in a certain way not because of their fear of the punishments meted out for breaking the law but because they were a fulfilment of the law and therefore above it and did not need it to keep them on the right path. They were not subject to death as the final answer for all life on earth and they were thus able to fulfil the requirements for regenerated life. Both of them were "full of love and compassion" and the strength to be "I AM!"

Lastly, and most interestingly, they both lived, as did Adam and Eve, between the thirty and thirty-fourth parallels. I ask again, is that where the overall 'order' is now? If so who belongs to it today and by what name is it known?

And us? Does the meaning of having to be born again as in the Christian perspective mean our minds and bodies are thereby literally, physically cleared of our inherited bad genes and the bad acts we may have committed? Does it mean that we are set free to go through life being taught by both good and bad laws and religions - by living alongside worldly politics and customs and human and

444

sectarian rejection where we learn to act seemingly out of context but still subject to worldly discipline.

Yes! Of course! It is the outside discipline that teaches us inner 'self discipline' which in turn results in us growing away from the need for a law to govern us and we are thereby set free to see what it is all about. They say that when we are 'born again' we can see the Kingdom and thus become subject to a new discipline of hardships and separateness specifically designed to teach us and lead us on to total freedom so that we can enter The Kingdom!

Am I being repetitious? Maybe! Any way 'whatever!'

Am I falling into the trap of presumption? Do I who knows relatively nothing, presume to have found the truth?

Am I behaving just like everyone else?

Or maybe - wow! I could start a new religion! After all if one accepts that the new testament bible has evolved over a period of two thousand years and the old testament over four thousand years, and that the original new testament accounts were written by numerous authors over a period of a few hundred years and that the bible has been variably interpreted and reinterpreted by thousands of so called qualified linguists - it is not surprising that there are so many apparent and real contradictions, so many questionable statements and ambiguities.

Much of the truth that was originally given about Christ Jesus has been either, hidden, distorted or lost in the same way as has the truth in all the world's religions dating from distant history! They have all been distorted by time, by prejudice and by varying perspectives! This has led us into an almost endless array of Christian religions all preaching different perspectives and all claiming to know the real truth.

So then, what is the truth hidden behind the veil?

Why and what is it that every religion denies in order to prove its own perspective?

As I said, I remember Red going on and on about Melchizedek, about who or what he was! I think I am now beginning to understand! It appears that despite Melchizedek playing a very strong part in both the Old Testament with Abraham and the New Testament with Christ, He appears to be ignored and treated as if He was and is a perfect stranger to all Christian religions and for that matter to all religions! I believe He is the epitome of the perfect "I AM" - He does not need or depend on any thing other than who He is and by His accepting and being who He is He draws all He needs to Him. As Red pointed out to me, in the letter to the Hebrews in the Bible, it is reported that God said to Jesus "You are my son; Today I have become your Father." And a little further on in the same book God says "You are a Priest for ever in the order of Melchizedek." This implies that before that particular day Jesus was neither God's son nor was He in the order of Melchizedek. So how did He now become a son? How many other people have been led or brought into the order of Melchizedek? Are they all sons and as such strangers to us!

A few sentences after stating that Jesus was now the Son of God it reads, "Son though He was, He learned obedience through His sufferings."

And, "He was perfected through those sufferings to become the source of salvation to all who obey Him as high priest in the order of Melchizedek."

Wasn't He born perfect? He had to learn? This suggests that if you are born again when and if God calls you, you can become a member of the order of Melchizedek and a Son of God and see the Kingdom of Heaven! But! You have to go through many trials and tribulations which prepare you through experience for the next move, and that is to 'Enter the Kingdom'!

And then I read, "Those who were so ordained did not believe!" Does 'so ordained' imply you have no choice? Is everyone programmed to be exactly what and who they are in this world as they occupy their present bodies and their souls and minds and their perspectives? It would appear to be so! In other words you could say that a person is either born with the God Gene or they are not! So then it is not your own decision that leads you to believe in God! Therefore it cannot be your fault if you don't! This answers a lot more questions for it indicates that each person is individually predestined to be that which he or she is designed to be in order to fulfil their special place in the order of things and so contribute to the final answer.

It is obvious that if I did not exist then nothing else could exist because without me fulfilling my part the whole picture would collapse! This seems to suggest that hidden deep inside of me is a 'power' which is more powerful than everything outside of me' a power which is called 'I AM!' It is the anchor on which the whole of creation is dependent!

This concept seems to be confirmed by the man who amongst many other miracles, calmed the sea, stopped the wind, healed people, created material things from nothing and resurrected Himself from the dead.

He is the one, who said,

"Greater is He within you than anything without!" And "If you have faith you can say to the mountain, 'move' and it will move!"

Red explained to me long ago that implicit in this statement is the understanding that the personality inside you can make direct contact with the personality of the mountain and you can speak to it and expect it to hear you and comply with your request! This confirms my earlier perspective that everything, be it physical or spiritual, has a personality and if this personality can hear you, then obviously, if you learn to listen, you will hear it and then you will both hear each other just like Ian and the charging elephant!

I spoke out loud to the whole universe,

"I will strive to be that which 'I AM' and in doing so I accept that just as the whole of everything depends on me, so I in turn depend on the whole." Excitement flooded me and I shouted, "I do here and now discard all the mumbo jumbo heaped on me by the 'know it alls of the world!"

An owl hooted! Grinning I answered,

"Yes wise one I most certainly do! And I hereby both accept and take over control of my own universe and my own environment and my own purpose in it! Aha! At last I seem to be on the right path - the path that leads to trust, to hope, faith, love, and the fulfilment of the plan for life!"

I listened for the owl. It did not call. I spoke out again,

"Thank you once more for now I understand that everyone's 'I AM' is hidden as a perfect stranger deep within them patiently waiting to be recognised so that it can grow and take over! Yes! It is hidden just like the personality of the mountain!"

I sat there grinning and laughing as I realised with unspeakable joy that now, if I worked at keeping myself free from dogma while at the same time accepting that everyone in this world has to start off their lives being subject to some form of dogma or other, I could and would be able to take responsibility for my own life and my own being and eventually come to know and be 'that who I really am! So long as I never insist that my perspective or anyone else's is either right or wrong but rather accept the truth as it is presented to me, I will be able to draw all that I ever want or need of life and creation to me! This concept leads me to another new thought - if every material and spiritual thing, be it animate or inanimate, individual or communal has an energy and a personality of its own as can be seen in a crystal or a mountain, in a tree or a forest, in a person or a community, in a tribe or a nation, the sun or the moon, then it becomes perfectly obvious that the 'sum of the all of everything in creation' adds up to the personality and the power we choose to call God! I listened again for the owl. It did not call. Oh well, maybe I can now come to understand what that Australian friend of mine who was converted from Catholicism to an Indian religion meant when he told me what he believed it was all about.

He said,

'First I had to get rid of my ego!'

I asked him,

'Did you?

'Yes!'

'Fantastic!' I said, 'Please tell me - according to your new religion - who and what is God?'

He answered,

'I am God!'

I laughed,

'Well you certainly couldn't have a bigger ego than that!'

But maybe he was making a point that I missed. Without me the all of everything cannot exist but equally important, without the all of everything, I cannot exist! My body jerked, my muscles tingled, a flow of pure energy rushed through me as I came to understand

and accept that as Jesus is reported to have said 'The Father and I are One!' so then when I come to recognise and be 'That which I am' I will also be able to say 'The Father and I are One!'

The owl hooted! Up till now my "I Am" has been a perfect stranger to me!

At last!

Stretching out I closed my eyes and relaxed.

I drifted into another world and dreamt of my beloved Jean and our lives together in Gokwe!

I dreamt of the camp on the Mtanke River!

The old Land Rover!

The friendly neighbours!

The dogs!

Happy memories!

Ian and Peter!

And love!

xxxxxxx

THE VERY LAST PAGE

The familiar sound of a four cylinder Land Rover with a faulty exhaust wakes me! I stretch! The Golden Pig on the dressing table is drenched in the early morning sun streaming through the window. Streaks of silver light reflect off its Golden body. I stand and looking out the window I see an old bush green Series One Land Rover driving into my camp. There is a woman at the wheel, her silver and gold hair is windblown! Her lovely face, suntanned! She seems very excited! There are two young men with her! Holding up my hand to shield my eyes from the sun I see the men are Peter and Ian! The vehicle stops and the woman scrambles out! She sees me at the window and bursting into wild emotional laughter she cries "Its you! Oh my God! After all this time! It is you! So many years! So many tears! So many hopes! So many fears!"

I run out to her!

The mother of my children!

THE END

Bruce, who has lived a truly amazing and varied life in Central Africa and who is a wildlife artist has written this intriguing book with a subtle desire to answer some of those questions deep down in your soul, leading you into asking new questions which enable you to think "outside the box" and question "Who is the Perfect Stranger or, or, do you already know, or, have you always known, the Perfect Stranger?"

Through wonderful anecdotes and stories based on true events, Bruce manages to open our minds and hearts to new ways of thinking and understanding that which we subliminally know!

He has inspired me to discover what and who "I AM" and so enable me to fulfil my overall purpose!

If you are ready for a provocative, inspiring and fascinating journey, then this is the book for you!

CLAIRE BESTER, PRETORIA, SOUTH AFRICA.

The Perfect Stranger has led me back to "when we!" days in Africa, to the bush, wildlife, comradeship, security call ups and family where we still believed our dedication to a future for Africa would bear fruit.
The essence of walking tall with Bruce as so many of us have done, is built into the stories!
May the book set you free as it has done for me!

ERNIE MOORE, WALES, UK